PRAISE FOR THE CAPTAIN DARAC MYSTERIES

IMPURE BLOOD: U.S. Library Association's Pick of the Month

"*Engrossing…An auspicious début*" – Publishers Weekly

"*Great plot, appealing hero, glorious setting plus taut writing – a real winner*" – Martin Walker, bestselling author of the Bruno Courrèges novels

"*Impressive… will delight fans of international crime*" – Booklist

"*A vibrant, satisfying read*" – The Crime Review

FATAL MUSIC: One of *Strand Magazine's* Top 25 Books of 2017

"*A thoroughly satisfying novel… Morfoot brilliantly captures the sights, smells and attitudes of southern France as well as giving us an engaging hero*" – Mike Ripley, Shots eZine 5 Picks of 2017

"*Pulls you along like an iron bar to a magnet. Crime and mystery readers will consume every last morsel of this book.*" – David Cranmer, Criminal Element Magazine

"*Deftly interwoven plot lines… vividly captured Riviera setting… This strikingly well-written crime novel should appeal strongly to many.*" – Bruce Crowther, Jazz Journal

BOX OF BONES:

"*An accomplished piece of crime fiction. Captain Paul Darac… has become, without doubt, my favourite foreign detective created by a Brit since the late Michael Dibdin gave us Aurelio Zen.*" – Mike Ripley – Shots eZine, 5 Picks of 2018

"*The plot, filled with enough twists and turns for a corkscrew, is intriguing while never losing touch with either reality or humanity.*" – Crime Review

"*Darac leads an engaging and distinctive team of officers, all of whom grow as the reader learns more about them. Not only are the good guys well drawn, but so too are the bad guys and the plot is intriguing and filled with many twists and turns.*" – Bruce Crowther, Jazz Journal

KNOCK 'EM DEAD:

"*Pin sharp…A winner from page one*"
– Dagger-winning author Jim Kelly

Peter Morfoot's policiers featuring jazz-loving
Criminelle comprise one of the best crime seri
fourth instalment, Knock 'Em Dead, is publi.
– Mike Ripley: *Shots Magazine.*

Captain Darac Mysteries

Impure Blood
Fatal Music
Box of Bones
Knock 'Em Dead
Essence of Murder

ESSENCE OF MURDER

A CAPTAIN DARAC MYSTERY
#5

PETER MORFOOT

Galileo Publishers, Cambridge

Galileo Publishers
16 Woodlands Road
Great Shelford Cambridge
CB22 5LW UK

www.galileopublishing.co.uk

Distributed in the USA by:
SCB Distributors
15608 S. New Century Drive
Gardena, CA 90248-2129

ISBN 978-1-912916-51-1
Completed 2021
First published in the UK 2022
© 2022 Peter Morfoot

Printed in the UK

For David and Andy Scott

DARAC MYSTERY SERIES BY PETER MORFOOT
AUTHOR'S NOTE

When I began devising what became the Captain Darac Mystery series, I knew what I *didn't* want for my central character. To be authentic, any character needs flaws but I determined Darac would not be a slave to his. I determined he would not always make the right moves in an investigation; nor would he solve cases over a chat in a bar.

I conceived him as a strong-minded individual but, attesting to the essentially collaborative nature of police work, I needed him to be a whole-hearted team player, also; an interesting dynamic and one that gave me the pleasurable task of creating a permanent cast of supporting players for him. This led to Darac's genesis as a "*poète policier*," a term derived from a resonant assertion by award-winning writer and, to Anglicise his rank, chief superintendent of police, Philippe Pichon: "A poet can be a policeman and a policeman can be a poet." But which art form for Darac? I felt that jazz with its tension between structure and improvisation would give me the most relevant and interesting possibilities.

The setting for the series? With its vibrant light, the spectacular Alpe Maritime mountains at its back and that celebrated azure coastline at its feet, Nice is as beautiful as any Mediterranean resort. But it's also a multi-ethnic city of almost half a million souls. And are there serpents in this particular paradise? Ask Darac, Commissaire Agnès Dantier and the other officers of Nice's Brigade Criminelle.

A senior police officer who also plays jazz in a high-quality group, a significant player therefore in two different sorts of team, was someone I was looking forward to getting to putting through his paces on the page. Unlike some of his fictional counterparts, Darac is a character drawn to living not so much on the edge as on the borderline; a man who chooses to position himself at points of junction or collision with the world. And in the five novels of the Darac Mystery series thus far, he has encountered plenty of both.

February, 2022

LIST OF CHARACTERS

The Brigade Criminelle of Nice

Agnès Dantier: Commissaire
Paul Darac: Captain
Roland Granot: Lieutenant
Alejo 'Bonbon' Busquet: Lieutenant
Yvonne Flaco: Officer
Max Perand: Officer
Francine 'Frankie' Lejeune: Captain, Vice Squad.
Jean-Pierre 'Armani' Tardelli: Captain, Narcotics Squad

Forensics
Raul 'R.O.' Ormans: Senior Forensic Analyst
Erica Lamarthe: Principal Technician

Pathology
Deanna Bianchi: Chief Pathologist
Carl Barrau: Deputy Chief Pathologist
Djibril 'Map' Mpensa: Pathologist
Lami Toto: Technician
Patricia Lebrun: Technician

Other Officers
Astrid Pireque: Sketch Artist
Jean-Jacques 'Lartou' Lartigue: Crime Scene Co-ordinator
Serge Paulin: Beat Officer
Alain Charvet: Duty Officer
Wanda Korneliuk: Patrol Car Driver

Judiciary
Jules Frènes: Public Prosecutor
Albert Reboux: Examining Magistrate

At The Blue Devil Jazz Club

Eldridge 'Ridge' Clay: club owner
Pascal Malata: doorman
Khara Oliveira: waitress
Roger Oliveira: chef

The Didier Musso Quintet*

Didier Musso: piano and bandleader
Maxine Walda: drums
Luc Gabron: bass
Paul Darac: guitar
Dave Blackstock: tenor sax
Trudi 'Charlie' Pachelberg: alto sax
Jacques Quille: trumpet

* It is something of a running gag at the club that Didier Musso's group of high-quality local musicians is always billed as the Didier Musso Quintet irrespective of the number of players on board at any particular time.

STAFF AND STUDENTS AT VILLA DES PINALES

Elie Tiron: Administrative Director
Barbara Artaud: Chief Receptionist
Bruno Gamblé: Night Desk
Jean-Claude Costeaux: Head Chef
Barthélémy Issako: Head Gardener
Lionel Fournier: General Factotum

Courses September 14th – 16th

Depicting The Landscape

Tutor: Astrid Pireque
Students: Ralf Bassette, paper manufacturer
Alan Davies: retired English teacher
Claudine Bonnet: retired HR manager
Babette Bonnet: training officer
et al

Wine Tasting For Connoisseurs

Tutor: Mathieu Croix:
Students: Gérard Urquelle, jewellery firm rep
Laurent Salins: call centre manager
Thea Petrova: luxury goods sales manager
Marcia Calon: retired p.a.
Jérôme Calon: accountant
et al

The Magic of Scent

Tutor: Zoë Hamada
Students: Lydia Félix: critical care nurse
Monique Dufour: boutique owner:
Cinzia Veri: elderly aristocrat
et al

STAFF AT PALAIS MASSÉNA DEPARTMENT STORE

Albert Cassani: Store Manager
Nadine Beaumont: Senior Sales Assistant
Zena Bairault: Trainee Sales Assistant
André Ricolfi: Security Guard
Jade Moreau: Spa Assistant
Madame Triot: Shoe Department Assistant

WEDNESDAY 14th SEPTEMBER

The stone steps curving up to the rear entrance of the Villa des Pinales may have been *faux*-Baroque, but for a slender young woman lugging a pull case, a rucksack and a trio of bulging shoulder bags, mounting them was going to pose an entirely authentic challenge. Balancing awkwardly, Astrid Pireque bent to pick up her case, performed a couple of vigorous shoulder hitches and launched herself onward and upward. The bags unhitched themselves immediately, a move that an increasingly thrust-out elbow did little to correct and, by the time she reached the balustraded parvis at the top, all three were hanging from her wrist. All the more determined not to be beaten, she tottered through the entrance doors and, adopting an increasingly compensating lean, made it all the way into Reception before releasing the load. *Ta-dah!* As if having the last laugh, one of her bags slumped open, disgorging an assortment of paint tubes on to the floor.

'Shit!' she announced, drawing the attention of a distinguished-looking man checking in at the desk.

'May I help, mademoiselle?'

Distinguished *and* gracious. And seemingly not put off by her impromptu impression of a stork with the staggers. 'No, no.' Astrid rounded up the escapees. With any luck, she reflected, Distinguished would turn out be one of her students, the type who, increasingly dazzled by her talent as the course progressed, might commission a work from her at its conclusion. And, judging by the quality of his own luggage, pay handsomely for the privilege.

She straightened, looking past him at an easel-mounted board which showed that alongside her own *Depicting The Landscape*, Zoë Hamada's *The Magic of Scent* and Mathieu Croix's *Wine Tasting For Connoisseurs* were the only alternatives. The latter, she suspected, was a strong contender.

'Pardon, mademoiselle, but I wonder why, with all your things, you didn't simply walk in along the level from the car park?' He indicated the main entrance behind him.

'Oh, a friend dropped me by the south terrace gate. I thought the walk up would do me good.' She smiled. 'I was *so* right.'

He chuckled. '*Chapeau*. You certainly came well prepared but I understood all art materials were provided?'

Result! 'They are, but as I am the tutor, Monsieur..?'

'Bassette – Ralf. Forgive my assumption, Mademoiselle... Pireque, isn't it? But from your bio...' He indicated a spinner stuffed with wads of brochures standing next to her. 'I hadn't expected you to be so young.'

And I'll bet you weren't expecting the blonde razor-cut and the ballet pumps painted as bare feet, either. 'Ralf, you're very kind.'

'Monsieur?'

The receptionist requiring his attention, Bassette excused himself and Astrid began checking her texts. Nothing from her boyfriend. Nothing from a filmmaker with whom she was working on an installation piece. But there was good news. According to a caller ID she didn't recognise, she had been involved in a recent accident and was owed a "consid-eribel" pay-out. Online scammers who couldn't master a simple spell-checker? Reflecting that they shouldn't give up their day jobs, Astrid added the number to her blocked list and returned to her inbox. The final text was from the

Brigade Criminelle's Captain Paul Darac. And it was accompanied by a red flag.

Astrid: Witness J.A. earlier ID'd our blade-wielding friend solely from your sketches.

Granot and Bonbon say: 'She shoots, she scores!' I say: 'superb work.' As always.

Before her role with the Brigade had been created especially for her, Astrid had never dreamt of working for the police or indeed for any organisation. After graduating from the École des Beaux-Arts in Montpellier, she had made her living as a solo artist in a variety of guises and the same was largely true today. But the deep satisfaction she drew from being a player in Darac's investigative team was something she valued tremendously. And that the team valued her made it all the sweeter. She blew a kiss in the general direction of the Brigade's HQ, the Caserne Auvare, and continued reading.

Have a great few days and see you next week. Oh, if you see Zoë, Papa says to tell her: 'We'll always have Paris.' Whether he means the city or the scent, I'm not sure. Kisses, Paul

She grinned. Paul's father, Martin Darac, owner of the small perfume house that bore his name, had apprenticed and later mentored Zoë Hamada. Astrid made a mental note to pass on his greeting, and to get the lowdown on the in-joke for Darac *fils*.

As Ralf Bassette was still discussing his reservation with the receptionist, Astrid decided to check out the reading matter set out on the spinner. It was a good couple of months since she had emailed Villa administrator Elie Tiron with a request to update her bio and, hoping she hadn't found the time so Astrid could rib her about it, she extracted a copy of *Study at the Villa des Pinales* and leafed through it. No luck: the update was in place. Indeed, the entire brochure appeared to have been updated and Astrid spent the next few minutes absorbed in a new version of its opening piece, *The Building and its Gardens*.

Squeezed on to a small, wooded plateau atop one of the higher foothills of the lofty Alpes Maritimes that "stood sentinel over the city to the north," the Villa des Pinales, the writer opined, was both beguiling and deceptive. Grey slate over cream stucco, the steeply pitched roof, corner turrets and pointed conical spires gave the three-storey structure the look of one of the grander French châteaux but in miniature. Its richness lay in its detailing and in the materials used. The Villa's lobby alone was "while not perhaps a symphony, then certainly an *étude* in marble, gilding, porphyry and malachite." Or at least, Astrid read with a grin, "skilfully rendered facsimiles".

The history of the place was surprising and "chequered." Built as a Côte d'Azur hideaway by an ageing American millionaire as recently as the early 1900s, the combination of rich detail and modest scale also characterised the gardens which, by the time the property was acquired by the city of Nice in the 1950s, were so overgrown that the Villa's sole claim to true grandeur – the view it commanded over the entire city and the fabulous Baie des Anges – was almost completely masked.

After a period of refurbishment, the house and gardens reopened as the "Petit Château" but achieved only moderate success as a visitor attraction until a second millionaire, the Franco-German philanthropist Georgina Meier, bought it and, reinstating its original name, repurposed the property as a centre for learning. Depending on student numbers, the

Villa could run up to four day-schools and three residential courses at the same time, each "taught by top experts in their field." And each, Astrid knew, wildly expensive.

At the desk, Bassette was checked-in, ID-d up and, with his one free drink voucher peeping incongruously out of the breast pocket of his designer-label jacket, he was ready to go. He remained. 'The introductory class commences at 8.30, Mademoiselle Pireque?'

'Astrid, please. Yes, 8.30 it is. Salle Fernand Léger.'

'Thank you, But first, I will see you at dinner, I hope?'

A commission. Definitely. Maybe even a portrait. 'And before that, there are drinks on the west lawn.' She gave him an amused look. 'Don't forget your voucher.'

'Astrid, I'm relying on it,' he said, smiling with the easy self-deprecation only the well-heeled can pull off. 'Until later.'

Astrid inclined her head by way of an *adieu* and turned to the receptionist, a tight-faced woman with pinned-back auburn hair. 'Evening, Barbara. How's it going?'

'Mademoiselle Pireque,' she said, riffling through a stack of registration cards. 'I'm well, thank you. And you?'

'Super.'

'Just your signature if you would.' Barbara handed over a card. 'We have your usual room. Top floor overlooking the terraces.'

'Excellent.'

Across the lobby was an open door marked ELIE TIRON, ADMINISTRATIVE DIRECTOR, CLARICE LAVALLE, ASSISTANT DIRECTOR. Slipping a sheaf of A4 documents into the wallet she was carrying, a woman in her mid-thirties emerged from the office and glanced with evident concern towards the entrance. Subtly made-up and wearing a charcoal-grey trouser suit, Elie Tiron's look epitomised confidence, professionalism and sobriety. In her hairstyle, however, sobriety hadn't so much taken the day off as gone on holiday. A reprise of actor Jean Seberg's severely short cut from the classic movie *À Bout de Souffle*, Elie's version was dyed pink.

At the desk, the formalities were almost completed. 'Elie around?'

'In her office, I believe.'

'No, she isn't. Hi, Tridi.'

'Hey, babe,' Astrid said, already smiling as she turned. 'Oh, my Lord, yes! You did it!'

'Rad enough, do you think?' Striking poses, Elie modelled her haircut. 'Suit me? No need to reply. I know it does! Had it done on my birthday. Show you photos later.'

Astrid decided not to mention that, colour included, Elie's new look was a virtual replica of a recent style of her own. 'It's fabulous!'

Barbara busied herself as the two women exchanged kisses, upbeat comments and comic asides.

'I'll give you a hand,' Elie said, picking up a couple of Astrid's bags. 'So, what's new? Apart from my hair.'

They headed towards the lift. 'And the brochure, don't forget.'

'Ah, you've seen it. What do you think?'

'I liked the bit about me.'

Elie laughed.

'And the new piece on the Villa.'

'*I* wrote that.'

Astrid drew down the corners of her mouth. 'You missed your calling.'

Out on the drive, the sound of grinding gravel and a low, throaty roar heralded an arrival of some style. Astrid glanced over her shoulder as a voluptuous carmine red shape skidded to a stop in a thin cloud of dust. 'Now *that's* what you call an entrance,' she said, remembering the low comedy disaster that was her own. If Elie had an opinion, she was keeping it to herself. 'Don't you think?'

The lift was on it way down and Elie pressed for the second floor. 'Never been much into cars.'

'But that's not just a box on wheels, is it?' Astrid said. 'It's like the ones in those vintage motor racing posters you see everywhere.' The driver climbed out. He appeared to be only in his mid-forties but he too had a vintage look. The flat cap and cravat combo, probably. 'Talk about form over function.' Elie gave her a look. 'The car, I mean, not Monsieur Jean Dujardin, there.'

'Better still, *you* talk about it,' Elie said, and then, recovering her smile added: 'And if you do, you'll have eight would-be Picassos hanging on your every word and brushstroke.'

'Eight? Ideal. Any familiar faces?'

'We've got a few repeat students but no artists among them.' Elie opened her document wallet and handed over a list of names. 'Three men, this time. A record.'

'I've already met one of them.' She ran an eye over the sheet. 'Here he is. Bassette, Ralf Adolf. *Adolf*? Jesus.'

The lift arrived. 'Think he would've changed that, wouldn't you?'

'Absolutely.' They clambered into the lift, pirouetting to stand shoulder to shoulder. 'Ralf's such a bad name.'

'Tridi?' Elie said, grinning. 'It's *so* good to see you again.'

Framed through the aspect ratio of the open doors, the scene on the drive took on the quality of a movie. Cravat was unlocking the vehicle's hamper-sized boot as a taxi pulled alongside. On the back seat, a woman who looked as if she was well used to being chauffeured around gave him a discreet smile. Just a few metres away, Cravat appeared not to have noticed. But he had, Astrid felt sure.

'That's a relief,' Elie said, sounding as if she were thinking aloud.

'Relief?'

'Sorry, yes. The newer arrival wasn't entirely sure she could make it, that's all.'

Astrid studied her as the cabbie, scurrying around to the tailgate, unceremoniously threw open her door en route. Clearly put out, the woman stayed put.

'And you were hoping to avoid an argument with her over the Villa's no-show, no-refund policy?'

'Exactly. Thea, her name is. Thea Petrova. Russian. Well, half-Russian. She can be very sweet actually but she has quite a temper on her. As we may see in a second.'

As the cabbie quickly set down a pair of matching suitcases, Thea appeared to decide that the affront to her dignity had been trumped by a greater need. Emerging from the taxi under her own steam, she called out to Cravat, halting him as he set off to reception. Giving the impression that he hadn't been aware of her presence until that moment, he turned and walked back.

'Why is he pretending not to know her, do you think?'

'I'm not aware he does know her.' Elie gave the control panel a nod. 'Give the button another press, will you? Needs a reminder, sometimes.'

Astrid gave it two for luck. Cravat was walking with a slight limp, she noticed. 'Is he one of my other men, do you know?'

'I do and he isn't.' If Astrid had been sketching Elie at that moment, she would have made sure she caught just the tiniest glint of steel in her gaze. 'I took the booking myself. He's wine tasting with Mathieu. As is Thea.'

The lift doors closed out the scene like an old-fashioned wipe cut and the friends found themselves in that moment of sanctuary which encouraged silence or the sharing of secrets.

'So who is this guy?' Astrid said, threading her arm through Elie's as the ascent began. 'And what's your problem with him?'

'Either I'm a poor actor or you're just too observant.'

'Could be both, of course.'

Elie pursed her lips while she thought about it. 'Alright, his name is Gérard Urquelle. That mean anything to you?'

Astrid's blonde brows lowered. 'The surname's familiar. But... it was a woman's, I think.' As always, she saw the image first. 'A brunette. Strong jaw. Sad eyes.' And then the context came to her. 'Yes, of course. I taught her. Here.'

'Vivienne, his wife. The April before last, it was.'

'Vivienne, that's it. Very determined student. Quite hard on herself as I remember. I could never get her to relax and just enjoy the thing. And as invariably happens, it showed in the finished work. But anyway – the husband. Tell me.'

'The wine-tasting course is a birthday present to him from Vivienne.' Elie's mouth managed a smile; her eyes failed the audition. 'A present for being such a good husband. Unquote.'

The irony was easy to catch. 'I see.'

'Actually, I have no real problem with him. That ended...' Her forehead creased as she made the calculation. 'Four and a half years ago. Practically to the day.'

Elie's happy marriage to social worker Adam Tiron, Astrid knew, was no more than a couple of years old. 'An old affair? Is that it?'

'With *Urquelle*? Hardly.'

Accompanied by an incongruously cheerful ping, the doors opened on to the top-floor landing. The pair decamped with Astrid's luggage but car sounds and voices drifting in through the windows encouraged Elie back into the lift.

'Sorry,' she said. 'Seems everyone's arriving at once. I don't get Clarice back until Monday so I'd better go and help Barbara.'

Astrid reached for the call button. 'Not so fast, Madame Tiron.' Her tone was playful but she wasn't about to let Elie go, nevertheless. '*What* happened four and a half years ago?'

'I discovered,' Elie said, taking a breath as if to steady herself, 'I wouldn't have to kill Urquelle, after all.'

Astrid abstractedly released the button.

'See you later, Tridi.'

The doors closed with a thunk, leaving Astrid rooted to the spot, A light, girlish voice called to her and broke the spell.

'*Coucou!*'

The speaker was a delicately featured woman with jet-black shoulder-length hair and a beaming smile. 'I thought you'd given up your living statue act.'

Astrid gave a little bow. 'Come here, you ravishing creature.'

As exuberant as she was, Zoë Hamada was not one of the world's natural huggers and when the two women exchanged kisses, Astrid made a point not to hold on too long.

'So you're going for *Sunshine*, now. Good choice.'

Just as Zoë couldn't resist naming any scent she encountered, Astrid couldn't resist a play fight. 'Hopelessly out. It's Chanel No 5,' she said, eliciting an emphatic rebuttal before the penny dropped and Zoë admonished herself for not catching on immediately.

'*Sunshine* works for you.' She nodded, professorially. 'Believe me.'

'I do.'

They picked up Astrid's stuff and headed off to her room.

'Something on your mind, Tridi?'

'Oh – just then, you mean? No, not really. But there is one thing.'

'Yes?'

'I have a message for you from your old boss.'

'Martin? Great.' Zoë grinned, naughtily. 'But if it's a job offer, I'm too expensive for the *House of Darac* these days.'

'He says, "We'll always have Paris." '

Zoë looked blank, then threw back her head and laughed. As in-jokes went, it seemed a belter, one to which Astrid had intended to pass on an explanation to son, Paul. But as she unlocked her room door, she was already thinking back to Elie and Gérard Urquelle. The expression 'wanting to kill someone' was in common usage, wasn't it? Not meant to be taken literally. Usually. But there had been nothing usual in the way Elie had said it. Elie, Astrid sensed, had meant just that.

★ ★ ★

To avoid a crowd in Reception, Barbara had asked some of the arrivals, Urquelle and Thea Petrova among them, to wait in the lounge.

'Good call, Barbara,' Elie said, joining her at the desk. Making eye contact with the second person in line, she gestured him forward with a raised brow and a smile. A heavily set individual in his mid-fifties, the man had a ruddy gravel-bucket of a face, a blue-ish nose and the whites of his eyes scarcely merited the term. 'Welcome to the Villa des Pinales. Your first time with us, I think, Monsieur..?'

'Salins. Laurent Salins. Yes, first time. I signed up for the wine-tasting.'

Of course you did, Elie thought to herself. 'Just a moment, I have your reservation here. May I ask how you heard about us?'

'I'm a great fan of Marcel Croix's column in *Nice-Matin*.'

So much of a fan, you can't remember his name. 'Tasting Notes.'

'I expect there will be, yes.'

Nor the name of his column. 'O-K... You're in room 7, first floor north-facing. If you would just sign this card for me? And here's a print-out giving instructions and guidance to help you get the most out of both your stay and your course. I'll just go over the main points.'

The man managed to sign his name without mishap but then seemed to listen only intermittently to Elie's spiel. If four years in the job had taught her anything, it was that Monsieur Laurent Salins would lose his print-out immediately and then spend the rest of his stay pestering her or, if she hadn't been on holiday, her assistant Clarice, or receptionist Barbara, gardener Barthélémy, head chef Jean-Claude or any of his kitchen and serving staff, night man Bruno, the tutors and anyone else who happened to be around, for answers on precisely the questions she had just taken the trouble to provide.

'Just to underline that final point, monsieur, check-out is by 9.30 on Saturday morning but that provides ample time for breakfast.'

But Salins and staff management issues, Elie knew, would be the least of her worries for the next few days. If Urquelle had taken the time to look through the brochure, it was probable that her name would have meant nothing to him. At the time of the case, she was known to all as Céline, not its diminutive, Elie, which she had come to prefer latterly.

And she had been single back then, bearing her maiden name of Roux.

But might Urquelle recognise her? As far as Elie knew, he had never seen her in the flesh and no clear photograph had ever appeared in the media. He could well have seen a personal snap but until a few months ago, Elie's hairstyle had been the mop of chestnut-brown curls she had sported all her adult life. And there was another difference. Back then, she favoured contact lenses, not the designer glasses she had been wearing for the past couple of years.

'Next, please?'

★ ★ ★

In the lounge, Urquelle seemed grateful to have lost Thea Petrova to Jérôme and Marcia Calon, serial learners who he'd overheard "so enjoyed teaming up" with Thea the year before. Released, Urquelle went across to a picture window at which a pretty, slightly nervous-looking woman in her early forties was sitting with just a pull-case for company. He stood for a moment before turning to her. 'Beautiful,' he said, underscoring the depth of the reaction with his most sincere smile.

'Pardon?'

'The garden.'

'Oh, yes.' She smiled, prettily. 'Although, I prefer the terraces at the rear. The view over the city and the bay is wonderful.'

'Indeed. You are from the area?'

She nodded. 'Yes, more or less. Roquebrune.'

'No, really? I worked in Monaco for many years. Gérard.' He indicated the chair opposite. 'May I?'

'Please.'

'And might I ask..?'

'Oh, of course.' She coloured, slightly. 'Lydia. Lydia Félix.'

'Gérard Urquelle.' He offered his hand, glancing at her ring finger in the process. It was unadorned but then so was his own. As he sat down, Lydia was frowning slightly.

'Is something..?'

'No, it's just the name. It's familiar somehow but I...'

'Ah.' He smiled, a creation of such archness, it was akin to parody. 'Before we go any further, Lydia, I must warn you that you're in conversation with a hardened criminal.'

'Oh?' Mollified by his manner, Lydia was already on his side. 'You don't look like any sort of criminal.'

'That's not what my next-door neighbour concluded back in June. Happily, the poor Police Municipale officer who was obliged to talk to me about her complaint was rather more of your opinion.'

'What was she complaining about?'

'Oh, the sort of thing dotty old hysterics the world over complain about. *Nice-Matin* enjoyed the story, anyway. If you can call it that. I'm not surprised you'd forgotten it.'

She chuckled but the frown returned. 'You know, I don't think it was this June I came across your name. It feels like much longer ago.'

Urquelle sat back, essaying a look that combined modesty and world-weary charm. It was a winning look and if he knew it, it didn't show. 'Sorry for the misunderstanding, but this half-remembering my name moment hasn't happened in a couple of years now.'

'I still can't place it.'

'Let me help you. I mentioned I used to work just along the corniches from you in Monaco. Do you know *Bertrand et Fils*, the jewellers?'

'Bertrand..?' It took a moment but then it came back

to her. 'Are you the one who foiled the robbery?' She examined him more closely. 'Yes, you are. I can see it now. Gérard Urquelle, the – what did the Press call you? – The "have-a-go hero."'

'Guilty. But I must say I've always hated that term. It's ridiculous. And not least because no one, quite frankly, could be less heroic than me.'

Lydia clearly had other thoughts on the matter and with Thea Petrova looking on intermittently from her imprisonment with the Calons, the two of them fell to discussing the incident which five years before had fed the local newshounds for a good few weeks. Chatting about a notorious case with its star performer acted like a heat pad to Lydia's stiffness and by the end of it she was asking questions with the freedom of a seasoned reporter. Finally, wine-tasting student-to-be Urquelle had a question of his own.

'Which course are you signed-up for, Lydia?'

'*The Magic of Scent.* With Zoë Hamada.'

'Excellent,' Urquelle said. 'So am I.'

'Yes? It's silly but I've always wanted to make my own signature perfume. Used to do it as a child.' She gave a shy little laugh. 'You know, collecting up rose petals and putting them with great ceremony into a jar. Then wondering why they smelled so horrible a week or two later.'

'That's charming.'

'Well, I think I'll do very much better this time.' She glanced away. 'Oh, look - the queue in reception has died down.' She pulled up the handle of her case. 'Shall we?'

A group to their left appeared to have made the same call. Thea, caught in a pincer movement by her jailers, was among them.

'Could we wait just a moment?' Urquelle leaned forward

conspiratorially. 'Don't make it obvious but you see the woman leading the charge? The one with the lank, light-brown hair?'

'The striking-looking woman wearing the suit?'

'And the put-out expression.'

Seemingly swallowing every morsel of bait being offered her, Lydia smiled. 'I see her.'

'Her name is Thea Petrova. *Very* Russian, if you know what I mean. Anyway, for reasons I won't go into, I'm trying to avoid her.'

'Oh?' Lydia's brow furrowed in concern. 'But will that be possible here? She may be on our course. And even if...'

'She isn't,' he said, definitively. 'You're quite right, of course, although it's not as if I'll be dodging out of her way the entire time or anything. I just won't be encouraging...' He looked into Lydia's eyes. 'Intimacy. Are you with me?'

She considered the question. 'I'm with you.'

Urquelle's mobile buzzed in his blazer pocket. 'Do excuse me. It may be business.' The business proved to be a text from Urquelle's wife, Vivienne. As if she might be watching, he glanced around before informing Lydia that, as suspected, he needed to call head office and it may take some time.

'Of course. Listen...' Like a blind person embarking on an untested route, Lydia hesitated before venturing further. 'Why don't I go and check in and perhaps we could meet for drinks later or at dinner?'

'Splendid,' he said.

At the desk, faces familiar and unfamiliar had come and gone but with only the last few to check in, here was a woman Elie knew only too well. 'Thea,' she said. 'How nice to welcome you again. I have the room you requested.'

For a second, Thea performed an impression of a

waxwork figure of herself. And then, eyes wide, her mouth fell open.

'Yes, it *is* me.' Elie handed her a card. 'If you would?'

'What... What have you done with hair? With your hair, I mean.'

Elie didn't know whether to feel irritated or touched that a woman of Thea Petrova's professional standing cared enough to be so obviously appalled. 'Don't you like it?'

'Well, I mean, it's not that I *don't*. It's just...' As if staring might restore its former chestnut luxuriance, Thea's focus was still on the atrocity that had taken its place. 'How long have you had like that?'

Elie had first had it done on her birthday back in April but she had no desire to explain herself further. 'Just a few weeks. Your signature?'

'A passing fancy, possibly. That's good.'

'Signature, if you would?'

'Oh, yes.'

Meanwhile, Barbara was doing her best to attend to the Calons. For the moment though, she had lost husband Jérôme's attention.

'You know, now I'm getting used to it,' he said, talking across her. 'I'd go as far as to say I like it. And it must be cooler in the warm weather than that big old bouffant you used to have. Marcie, what do you think?'

'*Bouffant!*' she said, pushing herself forward. 'That's how much notice to take of him. Now please don't take offence, Elie. From my QA returns over the years, you know I have the highest regard for you. And in her *very* own way, for Clarice. And our dear Barbara here, come to that.'

'But?'

'It's hideous. The style and especially the colour. And I'm sure that's what Thea thinks, too.'

Elie smiled. And you Marcia, are a moon-faced crawler with orange peel skin, mean little eyes and a brain to match. But *I* keep that to myself. She turned to Thea. 'So, first floor, room 9 as before.'

The routine continued in similar vein until there was only one person left to check in. And as yet, he had not emerged from the lounge. Elie felt her pulse quicken. 'Barbara, would you be an angel?'

'In the next life, I doubt it.' She gave Elie a look. 'In *this* one, why should today be any different?'

It was the general factotum's lot to be overworked and underpaid. But one thing Barbara couldn't complain about was being underappreciated. By Elie, at least.

'Barbara, I only ask because I know you'll do it properly and I'm going to be otherwise...' She stopped. Urquelle had finally emerged from the lounge and was heading with that slight limp towards the desk.

'What do you want me to do?' Barbara said, reclaiming Elie's attention. 'I'm due off in fifteen minutes.'

'Uh... nothing. I'll continue here. You may as well go home.'

Barbara needed no second invitation and in less time than it took to say "Wonders will never cease," was gone, leaving the floor to Elie and Urquelle.

'It's Madame Tiron, isn't it?'

That smile. The smile that had started it all.

'It is.' She fished out his registration card and set it on the desk in front of him. 'Monsieur Urquelle.'

Still smiling, he slipped a fountain pen from his pocket and uncapped it. Elie recognised it as the *Lepic* given him by his company as a reward; the one bearing the inscription she knew by heart. But using it to provide his signature, it seemed, would have to wait. Instead, Urquelle appeared to go into a kind of reverie, absently tapping the pen against the corner of his mouth as he kept his eyes on Elie, studying her. And then, as if arriving at some sort of conclusion, he gave a series of nods. He knows who I am, Elie said to herself. He knows who I am, after all. A chill ran down her spine.

'Yes, yes, yes,' he said. 'You know I wasn't quite sure at first, Madame Tiron but it's your hairstyle. Forgive me but I think it is quite wonderful.'

Her stomach turned over. Caring nothing for Urquelle's opinions, she hated being scrutinised by him like this. But it seemed she was still incognito, at least, and that was a situation worth preserving.

'Thank you. If you would just sign the card?'

'Oh, of course. Apologies.'

It seemed to Elie that, perhaps through force of habit, Urquelle made something of a show of handling his oh-so-special pen; a way of drawing attention to it, the prologue to a thousand re-tellings of his oh-so-heroic story. 'And this should prove useful,' she said, taking back the card and reaching for an info sheet.

He took it without looking. 'You know what it puts me in mind of? Your hairstyle? The Patricia character in *À Bout de Souffle*. But with the colour of a Caribbean flamingo. It's fantastic. Really.'

Elie had heard all about Urquelle's gold-plated patter but she hadn't experienced it at first hand until now. He knew what to say and how to say it. And that smile... 'Thank you, again.' Move on. 'You'll see on the sheet that the various wines you will be tasting with Mathieu are available at a 15% discount on the retail price per bottle and 20% by the case.'

'Listen, I have a confession to make.'

Have you? Really? Of course you haven't. You just want to change your room, don't you? Or your parking space. 'Confession? I'm sure not.'

He drew down the corners of his mouth. 'You're going to hate me for this.'

I've hated you for years, you bastard. 'Ah, yes?'

'Yes. You see my wife, Vivienne, whom I know you know and who sends her very best regards, by the way...'

'And mine to her.'

'Thank you.' Centimetre by imperceptible centimetre, he leaned in closer. 'Well, knowing my passion for wine over these many years, Vivienne purchased Mathieu's course for me as a surprise gift. However, I would like to take this opportunity to spring a surprise on *her*.'

Elie remained mute.

'So if it's at all possible, I would love to change the wine into perfume, as it were, and take Mademoiselle Hamada's *The Magic of Scent* instead.' Now oppressively close, he looked into Elie's eyes but, her stomach turning over once more, she took a half-step back. 'Imagine Vivienne's face when I arrive home not with a couple of cases of Burgundy but with a fragrance crafted by me especially for her. She won't have had the faintest intimation it was going to happen.' He lowered his voice. 'But obviously, if it isn't possible to change courses in midstream like this, I would of course, understand.'

Elie explained that it was perfectly possible providing the class numbers worked, which, on this occasion, they would. And Zoë and Matthieu would have to agree to it but she was sure that would prove no problem. And there would be a slight upward adjustment of the fee.

Urquelle produced his credit card. A couple of internal calls were made, the paperwork duly completed and at the end of it, Urquelle had succeeded in setting up the next few days nostril-to-nostril with the pretty and eager-to-please Lydia Félix.

'Don't forget your first session at 8.30 this evening is now in the Salle des Rêves.'

'I won't and I can't thank you enough,' he said, turning to leave. 'Oh, Vivienne mentioned the lift sometimes has its own ideas about one's travel arrangements.'

'It's far less wilful these days.'

'That's good to know. Thanks again.' He smiled, holding the look for a moment. '*Céline*.'

4.31 PM

Captain Paul Darac and his lounge guitar were an easy-going pair. Or so it might have appeared to visitors. A venerable arch-topped acoustic, the instrument required no amplifiers or other equipment to make its rich, resonant voice heard. And spending its off-duty hours leaning against a wall rather than locked away in a case meant it was always at hand, ready, like Darac himself, to be called upon at any time, day or night.

The guitar may have been an everyday presence in Darac's apartment, a rooftop eyrie of a place suspended between the tangle of the old town and the boulevards of the modern city of Nice, but it was only in a figurative sense that it had become part of the furniture. Darac had played some of the most explorative improvised solos of his life on the instrument, some of his most heartfelt blues, and some of the hottest swing. But like the hardworking Darac himself, the instrument needed an occasional break and for the past two weeks, it had been away on R and R. Now fully restored, it was ready to be collected.

The man responsible for the health of all Darac's instruments was a gnarly former rock-and-roller turned guitar tech who still went by his stage name of Elvis Tonnerre. Elvis worked out of his apartment near Gare Thiers, a cluttered warren occupying the floor above one of Darac's favourite couscous joints in the city. He usually timed his trips to drop off or pick up an instrument with lunch or dinner but today, he had contrived to miss both. As Elvis buzzed him into the building, a family party was underway in the restaurant and the spicy tang of tagines and other delights made Darac's mouth water as he headed for the stairs.

A taciturn individual who communicated mainly in grunts and nods, Elvis resticted his comments to clients to four: "I'll do what needs doing." "I'll call when it's ready." "It'll cost x," and, on handing back the guitar in question, "Any problems, bring it back." But there never were any problems and as a bonus, for the first couple of days after returning an instrument to the fold, Darac could smell just the slightest hint of baked meats and fruits rising from its soundboard as he played. On a previous visit, he'd mentioned to Elvis just how much he enjoyed this sensation. The man nodded, said 'Uh-huh,' and Darac loved him for it.

Business concluded with the usual dispatch, Darac laid the rejuvenated instrument into the threadbare velvet cocoon that was its case and, clutching it to his chest – the case had lost its handle years ago – headed back through the spice waft into the vestibule. Something he hadn't noticed on his way in was a full-length mirror newly set into the wall by the street door. Confronting his reflection, he was reminded of a sepia-toned photograph that hung in the hall of his father's villa in nearby Vence. Its subject was a man with a strong, broad-boned face, black wavy hair and soft, expressive eyes. Paul's great-grandfather, after whom he had been named and to whom he bore a marked resemblance, had been the last in a long line of Daracs to farm sheep in their ancestral *département* of Creuse in the heart of the country.

In the photo, he too was clutching something of significance to his chest – not a rescued musical instrument but a rescued lamb. Paul junior had always felt an affinity with this tough but tender-hearted man and he had occasionally wondered what Paul Senior had made of the lives of those who came after him: his son, Jean-Louis, a Jack of all trades until he trained to be a teacher in his mid-thirties and stayed in education for the rest of his life; his granddaughter Sophie, another late bloomer who eventually built up a successful catering business singlehandedly; his grandson Martin, a freelance "nose" in the perfume industry who went on to found the boutique '*House of Darac*' brand of fragrances. And then there was great-grandson Paul junior, a man who enjoyed leading a double life as a so-called *poète-policier*.

What he would make of the lives of his own descendants was something Paul knew he would never have to consider. If, that is, the relationship with the love of his life, fellow officer Frankie Lejeune, stood the test of time as he hoped it would.

Back out on the street, further musings on the themes of ancestry, husbandry and progeny were put on hold when his mobile rang.

'Darac? Armani. When was the last time we went on a stake-out together?'

Except in matters of fashion and sport, drug squad chief Captain Jean-Pierre 'Armani' Tardelli was not given to idle speculation. Unless cash was involved.

'The last time?' The first rays of the late afternoon sun were beginning to find the street and as Darac reached his Peugeot, it seemed to light up in greeting. 'Must be five years ago. Probably more. So do you win it?'

'Bet on a thing of such importance? As if I would. No, the point is, it was years ago, exactly. So it's high time we did it again, right? Picture the scene – the captains of the two most important police squads in the city back in harness. Together again, like...'

'I need both hands, Armani. Wait a second.'

Slipping the mobile into his breast pocket muffled Armani's voice but it was still extolling the value of partnerships after Darac had stowed the guitar case in the boot, got in behind the wheel and docked the phone.

'... Pavarotti and Andrea Bocelli. There!'

Darac turned on the engine, releasing the opening bars of John Coltrane's 'Syeeda's Song Flute' into the air, and pulled away from the kerb. 'Pavarotti, right,' he said, turning down the CD player. 'And Bocelli. But the real reason for shouting out our non-awaited comeback is..?'

'Where are you?'

'At last, we communicate. Just leaving Rue Assalit.'

'Perfect.'

'On my way home, Armani. *Home.*'

'Understood. Completely. But this will only take five minutes...'

* * *

Ten minutes later, Darac was parked outside a car repair place squeezed into Rue Louise Ackermann and Armani, an unopened bento box on his lap, was sitting next to him. Without making it obvious, their eyes were trained intermittently on the low-rise apartment block beyond. Stationed inside were two members of Armani's squad.

'Which apartment are we looking at?'

'Third floor,' Armani said. 'Second one along.'

'The one with the half-open window?'

'That's it. The street door's below and to the right. I've got Luisa and Farid inside. If our man has the stuff and tries to beat it, they'll grab him.'

Darac's brow lowered. 'And so why are we here?'

'In case they lose him.' Armani's "What a dumb question!" face set new standards for the genre. 'What do you think?'

Darac gave Armani a look. 'In other words, we're back-up.'

'I suppose you *could* call it that.'

'We, the captains of – what was it? – "the two most important squads in the city." '

'And proud of it!'

'I see.' Darac enjoyed working out the why and how of things and the challenge presented by Armani's frequent machinations had a fascination all of its own. He decided to have fun with it. 'So your car's in the shop, right?' he said. 'Broke down just around the corner.'

'Sadly.' Armani made a moue and nodded. 'That's why I called you.'

Darac glanced across at the garage. 'In fact, that's it, isn't it? The one in the service bay.'

Roughly following Darac's gaze, Armani considered the question. 'I... think it might be, yes.'

'Look closer... No, no, the white convertible's the one we're interested in. The Audi. The one it seems they're getting ready to valet. Inside and out.'

Armni gave that some thought, too. 'They're very thorough here.'

'Really? I recognise that Audi, Armani. It's yours. Yours and Noëmi's own car.'

'In... a sense.'

'In every sense.' Darac ran an eye over Armani's outfit: 'And what do we have here? Neither the crackhead nor dealer look. But not full preen and primp, either.'

With a dismissive gesture, Armani styled his off-the-peg shirt. 'Semi-preen, at best.'

'The sort of thing you might wear on a day off, in fact.'

The concept clearly appalled him. 'Jean-Pierre Armani Tardelli wear *this* on his day off? Are you kidding?'

'Depends on how you'd planned spending it, doesn't it? For tackling those jobs you've been putting off, such as taking your car to your favourite back-street garage for a spruce-up, it might work.' He cast a glance at the place. 'Looks OK. Tidy. Efficient. But it's a confined space, isn't it? With the best will in the world, there's bound to be the odd spot of grease or oil around. And those piles of old tyres? A brush with any of those things might wreak havoc with your usual off-duty wardrobe. In short, it's a place in which a dressed-down approach would be the call. Such as the one you've gone for.'

Armani essayed an innocent nod. And nailed it. 'Perhaps.'

'I'll talk you through what happened. While you were in there, explaining exactly what you wanted doing and how, you get a call. "Chief? Sorry to trouble you on your day off but that operation we've been working on? We've finally run Monsieur X to ground at an apartment in Rue Louise Ackermann. Yes – right where you are!" "Great work," you reply. "But how do you know where I am?" "We've just seen you going into the garage."'

'I thought you didn't believe in coincidences?'

'I don't.'

'There we have it.' Armani bore the look of a tennis player who had lured his opponent to the net only to lob the ball deep. 'Sorry.'

'Except when they happen,' Darac said, retrieving it for a winner. 'So here you are with a car down on the street and two of your guys are on foot up in the building. Lady Luck has given you the perfect set-up, hasn't it? There's only one problem. Said car is out of action. But even if it wasn't, you probably wouldn't want to risk getting it all grubby or worse if something went down.' Darac grinned. 'So you decide to send for another vehicle. Right so far?'

Armani pressed his lips together. 'It's a theory.'

'But *which* vehicle? Any other senior officer in your position would call the Caserne for a pool car. Or get mobile control on the case. Or Foch. Or, if the case merited it, issue an APB.'

Armani looked hurt, suddenly. 'You're forgetting our brief.'

'*Our* brief!'

Palms upwards now. 'At last, you're on message.'

Darac had one shot left. 'Get your fingers ready, we're going to do some arithmetic. You're down here, as I think we know. You've got two up there – that makes three. What are your other four doing at this precise moment?'

'Razor and Janine are on leave. Not together, you won't be surprised to hear. Mahmoud and Getafix are off sick.'

'Alright, I'll concede that one.' Darac rapped himself on the chest. 'But why drag *me* over here? You could've got *anyone* to—'

'I wanted the best available. And that's you. Alright? Plus you finally closed out the Riquier stabbing case, didn't you?'

'Thanks to Astrid's artistic gifts, yes.'

'So what else have you got to do?'

Darac knew when he was beaten. 'Alright, alright... So how big is this thing?'

'How big would you like it to be?'

'Not very.'

Armani's expression said that there was no need to thank him, but Darac had got his wish. 'My friend, it's even smaller.'

'Uh-huh.' Darac exhaled deeply. 'And when might this underwhelming spectacle get underway?'

'*When*?' Armani shared his incredulity with the invisible sidekicks he invariably had in tow before turning back to his tormentor. 'We're on a surveillance op, not taking our seats at the opera. *When,* he says!'

A half-smile invariably played around Darac's lips. It broadened into something fuller. 'I'm the best, remember?'

'Best *available*,' I said.'

'I'm perfectly happy to leave you to it.' Darac reached for the door catch. 'Afterwards, park it in my usual spot and I'll get the tram home.'

'No, no.' Armani clamped a hand on Darac's nearside thigh. 'You're right. I'm sorry. Farid inside will call as and when. It'll be any minute now, I'm sure.'

*   *   *

Fifteen minutes later, the show curtain had remained resolutely down and Armani still hadn't opened his bento box. In the meantime, Darac had sent emails to their boss, Commissaire Agnès Dantier; to his lieutenants, Roland Granot and Alejo 'Bonbon' Busquet; and to his lover, Frankie Lejeune. In between, he and Armani had visited a range of topics which, sticking to the age-old traditions of the stake-out, had begun at the whimsical end of the spectrum.

'We're in Quartier des Musiciens, right?' Armani

observed. 'Well, edge of. We've got Rue Verdi, Rossini, Paganini...'

'And Berlioz, Gounod...'

Armani shrugged. 'OK, so a few Frenchies got in there as well. But who's this Louise Ackermann?'

'Not a musician. A poet. Nineteenth century.'

'Ah.'

'A Pessimist.'

'She chose the right profession.'

Few people could make Darac laugh as much as Armani. 'You could have a point there but I think it's more a poetic mode than a mind-set.'

'And with that she merits this?' He swept a large, tanned hand over the scene. 'I don't know of a Rue Jean-Pierre Tardelli anywhere, do you?'

After a brief interlude in which Darac's empty stomach turned his thoughts towards the triumph of succulence that was spice-marinated chicken with couscous, prunes, cashews and courgettes, he raised the subject of Armani's bento. 'I take it there's something in that box?'

'It was €12.50 so I hope so.'

'And are you just going to sit there nursing it or what?'

'I'll get to it later.'

'Because we could be in for the long haul? Is that it?'

'Of course not. No, no, no. It'll be—'

'Any minute now?'

Armani's assurance face was a thing of unimpeachable certainty. 'Probably.'

With their eyes never straying far from the prize, the conversation rolled inconsequentially along until, as was the way, the talking points became more personal and, drawing his thumb and fingertips together, Armani asked something Darac suspected he'd wanted to ask all along.

'So, you and Frankie, huh? Your soul-mate. Together at last.' His matinee idol features took on an expression of such hooded-eyed intrigue, Darac almost laughed. But Armani was far from finished. 'Ah, yes. Frankie, the soul-mate. The soul-mate who just happens to be a beauty, a velvet-voiced vixen, a green-eyed goddess, a—'

'Yes, I think we'll stop ticking the boxes there, Armani.'

'You sly...' He gave a lascivious little chuckle. 'So, is it good, or what, being together? Huh? Tell me.'

'Well, for a start, we're not completely together, you know. In a co-habiting sense, at least. Frankie still has her place in La Turbie and I'm very happy up among the pantiles in my spot.'

A worrying possibility appeared to cross Armani's mind. 'But you are..?'

'We are.'

The smile returned. 'Good. So, *together*, like I said. Together with The Gorgeous One. Spill!'

Despite the ridiculousness of his language, Armani's assessment wasn't so far out. Darac and fellow officer Frankie Lejeune had enjoyed the closest of bonds for years and although she had never thought of herself as beautiful, it was a view widely held. But goddess? Darac loved Frankie deeply but he saw her as very much a flesh-and-blood equal, not a divinity to be worshipped. But perhaps he was over-interpreting or just mistranslating from the hyperbolic language that was classical Armanian. The simple truth was that, having finally overcome every obstacle in their path, Frankie and Darac's coming together was proving a supremely joyous experience, a time of profound consummation for them both. The scenario had disappointed some, he knew. There was nothing like a spot of unresolved sexual tension to keep people interested. But sometimes, real life just didn't follow the script.

'It's pretty good,' Darac said. 'On the whole.'

It seemed that Armani's invisible sidekicks were still around. Nodding knowingly, he shared a grin with each in turn. 'Oh, *pretty* good? Not bad? Could be worse, huh?'

'Forget the stake-out for a second,' Darac said. 'Look at me. Quite simply, the past few months have been the happiest and most profoundly satisfying of my adult life. That do?'

Armani's smile lost all its idiotic machismo. 'Yes,' he said, giving Darac's knee a squeeze. 'That will do fine.'

They let the moment breathe a little but Armani could never stay quiet for long.

'And the divorce?' he said. 'Piss Face wants it too, now, I hear.'

'He does, yes, so just a few weeks and it will be final.'

An amusing idea seemed to strike Armani. 'Frankie kept her maiden name with *him*. But will she change it for you? That would make her Captain Darac!' He cracked out laughing. 'Another one! *Fantastico!*'

'That's not going to happen.'

Armani's face dropped. 'You *are* getting married, I hope?'

'In time, we might, I suppose.' He remembered his playful line earlier. 'This time, I'm serious, by the way.'

'But what if you have...' Armani began, and went no further.

It wasn't like him to be lost for words and Darac knew that for all the man's bombast, Armani was a soft-hearted soul. "What if you have children?" he was going to ask, wasn't he? Or even, "What if you have children who have a different surname from their mother?" Was now the moment to remind Armani of a conversation they'd had at their home station, the Caserne Auvare, a few years back? A conversation recounting Darac and Frankie's questioning of an elderly witness about her family in which it emerged that Frankie herself couldn't have children? Perhaps this was the perfect moment to refer to it again. But there were subtler ways of saying it.

'It's a good thing Frankie never had children, isn't it?' Darac said. 'That *really* would have complicated things.'

'Of course.' Armani appeared a little uncomfortable. 'Absolutely.'

A segue to Armani's own home life beckoned and Darac saw no reason to ignore it. 'Noëmi must have – what? – a couple of months to go now?'

The term "proud father" could have been coined for Armani. 'Six weeks today,' he said, beaming. 'Everything is fine. And the baby's a boy!'

'A baby brother for little Emma?'

'Yeah, but she's not so little, now.'

As there was still no call from Farid or any action at the apartment block door, Armani was able to expand on his theme. Tomorrow was *La Rentrée*, the first day back at school for pupils of all ages and the big news *chez* Tardelli was their little Emma was returning as a "*grand*", the oldest of the three classes of children attending *École Maternelle*.

'So she's *six* now?' Darac could scarcely believe it. 'When did that happen?'

'I know!' Armani began scrolling his mobile. 'Check out her birthday party.'

Darac knew what was coming. With each new image or clip, Armani would comment glowingly on Emma's prettiness, her cleverness and her adorable ways, with all of which he would be obliged to concur. Since he valued his life, Darac was prepared to fib if the evidence didn't fit.

'Here we go. Look at that face!'

Circumstances dictated that the screening was more a highlights package than *Emma, The Director's Cut*, but the *après* show began as Darac had suspected. 'Now,' Armani said. 'Tell me honestly.' Holding the phone did little to curb his elaborate hand choreography. '*Che bella* or what?'

Darac didn't need the get-out fib, after all. 'Armani, if such a comment is permissible these days, Emma is a little cutie. Especially in her party costume. Who is she supposed to be – Rapunzel from the nursery rhyme?'

'What nursery rhyme? You mean Rapunzel the *fairy tale* by the Brothers Grimm?'

'That one, yes.'

Armani shook his head. 'How yesterday are you? No, no, no. She's Rapunzel from the movie *Tangled*. Big difference. The Grimms didn't go in for peddling matching duvet sets et cetera.'

'Like that, huh? Well, she still looks cute.'

A motor scooter buzzed past them and slowed to a stop outside the garage. The rider kept the engine running.

'I'll send you this video.' He gave the screen a couple of taps. 'There! No charge. Cutie? She's a cutie, alright. A cutie and cute, if you know what I mean.' He pointed to the screen. 'See her little finger there? No? That's because she's got her Papa wrapped right around it.' Armani finally opened his bento. 'Don't like the look of this *umeboshi*.' He proffered the box. 'You fancy it?'

'Pass.'

The scooter's throttle blipped a couple of times and edged forward.

'The new baby will change things. So they tell me. Got a name for him yet?'

'Fabien.'

Darac rehearsed it. 'Fabien Tardelli.' He nodded. 'It's got

a good ring to it. But it's only half the story. You are, let's see, Jean-Pierre Vincenzo... Luca Tardelli? Or have I missed one?'

'Thomas is in there somewhere,' Armani said, and for a moment it seemed he was going to reveal Fabien's full complement. 'Check out this *teriyaki* chicken. If that doesn't taste good...'

It happened all at once. Armani's phone rang. A duffel bag dropped through the open window. The scooter rider caught it deftly and squirted away up the street.

'What the hell?' Armani took the call. 'Farid? Hold.' He turned to Darac. 'We're going to have to tail him. Nothing rash, now.'

'Nothing is surer.' The scooter still in view, Darac did no more than turn on the engine. 'He had every opportunity to see us. I'll give him plenty of slack.'

Armani nodded. 'Farid? Talk to me.' Armani listened. 'No, we didn't expect it either.'

Ahead, the rider turned left into Rue Rossini. Darac pulled sharply away.

'OK, Farid, we're in pursuit now... What? Oh, I ran into Captain Darac... What? No, a chicken thing... It's tasty, yes. Listen, here's what you do. Call for back-up, then you and Luisa take our friend to the Caserne and get out of him what you can. Relay anything useful soonest. Out.'

'*Now* we need mobile control,' Darac said.

'You read my mind.' Armani quickly set up the link and, critiquing each new mouthful, continued his culinary exploration of Japan as Darac followed the scooter discreetly along Rossini. A red light at the intersection with Gambetta gave the rider time to stow the duffel bag into his pillion box and on green, he turned left. Darac managed to flow through about thirty metres behind. With the Baie des

Anges no more than a tiny azure glint at the far end of the boulevard, several more sets of lights helped to slow things further and by the time the scooter turned right into the Promenade des Anglais, mobile control had two unmarked vehicles closing in on the target from either side.

'OK, you're on the sweep if we lose him,' Armani instructed them. 'So stay back unless you hear different. Out.'

The low September sun was casting long shadows along the Promenade and the pair slipped on their shades as they made the turn.

'Who is he and what's he up to, this guy?' Darac said.

'Two main options. One: he's the man at the head of this little ring – the one we're after. Or two, and this is more likely: he's just a go-between. A guy with a Vespa and hands like Gigi Buffon who's on his way to meeting said head man.' Ahead, a line of motorcycles was parked at right angles to the kerb like horses cinched to a rail outside a western saloon. One space was free and the rider turned smartly into it. 'Pull over and we'll find out.'

'When I can. Who's this Buffon character?'

Armani smiled, fondly. 'You remember what I said about you being the best?'

'Remember? I'm having it stitched into a sampler.'

Thunder face now. 'Well, forget I said it!' As if it were the acknowledged antidote to such ignorance, Armani chomped down on a mouthful of asparagus spears. It seemed to work. 'Hmm, not bad.'

The source of Armani's outrage, the sports-phobic Darac supposed, was that Signor Buffon, totally unknown to him, was no doubt a hero to fans the world over. Or at least in Turin to which Armani's paternal line was attached like an umbilicus. *Tant pis* – Darac wasn't about to change now.

Rolling the Peugeot past the target, both he and Armani

hid their faces by glancing over their left shoulders as if checking for traffic coming up on their outside. Safely past, Armani glanced back the other way.

'Tell me what he's doing,' Darac said.

'He's padlocking the scooter to a parking stanchion... He's taking the duffel bag out of the box... Now he's firing up a cigarette... And it looks as if... Yes, he's going to cross the Promenade.'

'The bag?'

'On his shoulder. It's option two. Almost certainly.'

Darac slowed to a crawl. 'So no jumping out and just grabbing him.'

'Not until he makes the exchange. Then we'll get him and Monsieur Big with one swipe. Well, Monsieur Average.'

Judging they had overshot by a sufficient margin, Darac stopped the car and, squinting across the roadway, tried to follow the rider's progress as he appeared and disappeared between the palms and shrubs lining the central reservation.

'That must be the most densely planted section of the whole Promenade,' Darac said, continuously shifting his point of view. 'Sightlines through are terrible.'

'We can't just sit here.' Armani stuffed in another mouthful. 'We could lose Gigi altogether.'

'No, hang on, I've got him. He's reached the far pavement... He's found an unoccupied bench... He's looking around... And he's sitting down.'

'Facing the bay?'

Darac shook his head. 'The city. People usually look out to sea if there's a choice.'

'He's waiting for his boss, alright. And he's making sure he sees him coming.'

Darac's gaze was still trained on the target. Or at least, he was peering in the man's general direction. 'We could do with Granot. He's got eyes like a hawk.'

Finally finishing his bento, suspect *umeboshi* and all, Armani dropped the empty box into the foot well behind him. 'Tissue?' he said, splaying his fingers like a customer in a nail bar. 'Of course, any proper *flic* would have a proper camera and or a proper pair of binoculars on board.'

Darac took his eyes off the promenade for a moment. 'You've got a nerve.'

'Thanks. Tissue?'

'What's your handkerchief for?'

'Wiping my shades, of course.'

Darac resumed his watching brief. 'Try licking your fingers.'

'I'll try the glove compartment.'

Darac shrugged. 'Or try the glove compartment.'

Shovelling its contents into his lap, Armani began sorting through it with all the finesse of a terrier at a rabbit hole. But he succeeded in unearthing his quarry, sorry specimen though it was. 'Just one. *And* out of its packet.' When its work was done, the tissue followed the bento box into the rear foot well. 'There.'

Suddenly aware of the mess, Darac snatched up a slew of CDs, collated them into a stack and with Steve Swallow's 'Always Pack Your Uniform On Top' aptly uppermost, He handed them over. 'Do you behave like this at home?'

'At home? No, I tend to be a little more... relaxed, shall we say. Slobby chic, I call it.'

Darac had sometimes wondered if Armani's ragazzo-from-central-casting persona was just *that* – a persona it amused him to adopt. His marriage to Noëmi was a particularly happy one, he knew, yet she was a respected archivist who had trained at the Sorbonne.

'Put everything back neatly,' Darac said. 'How the hell

does a classy woman like Noëmi put up with you?'

'With love, gratitude and excitement.' The task accomplished to his own satisfaction, Armani cast a quizzical eye around the scene. 'So what are we going to do? It's the old problem, no? We need to get close enough to see and to act but not be seen ourselves.'

A maverick officer, Darac followed official guidelines only when they made sense to him personally and didn't compromise his sense of justice. Accepting advice from *flics* with years of front-line experience was a different matter – especially if that advice was given by his beloved boss and mentor, Commissaire Agnès Dantier.

'According to Agnès, remember where the best place to hide is?'

Armani nodded but he looked sceptical.' "In plain sight," of course. But in this case, how are we going to do that?'

'I've got an idea,' Darac said, opening his door. 'Trust me. OK?'

This was such a reversal of their usual pattern, it seemed Armani didn't know quite how to respond.

'Remember Pavarotti and Andrea Bocelli?' he went on. 'Together?'

'So?'

It wasn't until Darac opened the boot and took out his guitar case that the penny began to drop. 'Oh, no, no,' Armani said, shaking his head and his finger out of time with one another. 'No, no, *no!*'

'OK,' Darac said. 'We're going back to the classroom. Visual Perception 101: "People see what they expect to see." Right?'

Armani opened his mouth to speak. A vague spluttering sound was all he could muster.

'Visual Perception 102: "Context is everything." Put

this together. Sunny promenade plus passers-by plus two guys setting down a battered old guitar case. What does that add up to in our target's mind?' Darac slammed the boot. 'Buskers. That's what. Particularly when I start playing and you start singing.'

A fusillade of abuse followed, liberally laced with a selection of anatomically impossible suggestions. Darac saw it as an authentic touch and welcomed it. Stand-up rows were *de rigueur* for many a musical partnership. 'Come on, Andrea,' he said, enjoying himself more and more. 'There's a gap in the traffic.'

Aiming for the cover afforded by a low-growing shrub, Darac dragged the *don't-wannabe* Bocelli toward the central reservation and while he waited for the eastbound traffic to clear, he played his next card. 'Listen,' he said, brows high as he eyeballed the animated Monument to Outrage that was Captain Jean-Pierre Tardelli. 'I can *guarantee* you that we will be able to set up right next to this guy without him suspecting a thing. And that means we'll be right there when the exchange is made.'

Armani looked frankly astonished. 'Guarantee, he says!' Another one for the sidekicks.

Darac's brows rose higher. 'A *money-back* guarantee.'

'What money?'

Darac risked a glance around the foliage. The target was still sitting alone on the bench. 'What money? The money that passers-by will heap into my guitar case when they hear your beautiful voice in the flesh. As it were.'

Darac's words affected Armani like a stun gun and it was some moments before he found a reply. 'Beautiful?'

'Yes, beautiful. Ask anyone at the Caserne.'

'Including... Agnès D?'

In truth, Darac had never heard anyone comment on

Armani's singing voice. As for himself, he couldn't remember ever hearing it. He loved Armani but he had been on the end of so many of the man's cons over the years, he couldn't help himself. 'Yes, Agnès is your biggest fan, I would say. She and Erica.'

'Yes. Of course...' Armani gave a little nod. He'd long suspected as much. 'Beautiful, huh?'

On the carriageway, the traffic thinned and cleared.

'So are you still dead against this, Armani?'

'Do you know 'Volare?' he said.

6.16 PM

'Staff discount card?'

The young woman shook her head. 'It'll be a day or two yet, they said.'

'Sorry. Have to put it through at full price.'

Deciding not to argue, she paid in cash and made for the exit where a bag-laden man wearing an orange dashiki was disappearing into the lift. Running an eye over her as he turned, he stuck out a foot and the doors slid back open. Subtle. But she was bound for the staircase anyway and walked past him without a word. After a long day in the store's classroom, tripping down four flights would be good exercise and besides, she wanted to take in the view from the landing windows, her first of the immediate vicinity from such a high vantage point.

Donning her shades against the low September sun, she gazed out over the arcaded lower reaches of the avenue. A tram emerged and she followed it as it crossed Place Masséna and took the curve into the boulevard beyond, the route she would be taking herself in a few minutes. The Place itself fascinated her. As a largely vehicle-free intersection, it seemed to work. But seated figures atop lines of tall poles? Chequer-board pavements? A frisky, over-scale statue of Apollo? Pink walls, pink porticoes, pink everything? As an aesthetic statement, she found it preposterous. Preposterous yet strangely beautiful.

Back on the ground floor, she fell in behind a gaggle of elderly tourists and, fishing out her *Lignes d'Azur* travel pass, edged slowly towards the exit.

'Mademoiselle?' The voice was male and authoritative. 'A moment there, please.'

She told herself to act naturally. Whatever that looked like here. When it came to speech, she knew her accent would sound alien but Nice was a multi-ethnic city and her French itself was impeccable. Trusting her instincts, she added just a touch of irritation to her look of surprise as she turned to face her inquisitor. First, his uniform. Navy-blue. Two-way radio. Shoes, not boots. No visible weapon. She relaxed. The man himself was a match for his voice; the mien impressive, the physique strong. He was, though, some years older than he sounded. And then she spotted the patch on his shoulder: Security.

If he were a cop, as she had feared, he was a retired one. It was a far better option but the encounter, she knew, could still prove tricky. No longer commanding the respect that was once his right, such a man might seek to stamp his authority wherever he could. An ego massage was called for. Losing the look of irritation, she resolved to address him as "Officer" and smile winningly.

But it seemed the smile would not be necessary: he was already smiling at her. Even in her present state of mind, hyper-alert to the point of paranoia, she was in little doubt the smile was genuine. A touch paternalistic perhaps, but well-meaning, nevertheless.

'Yes, officer?' she said, taking no chances.

'Well...' He peered at the ID brooch pinned to her jacket lapel. '... Zena.' He gave a little back-header toward the street. 'Does that look like the staff entrance to you? Entrance *and* exit?'

Was *that* all this was? She almost laughed. 'Sorry, I didn't know there *was* a staff entrance. And exit.' Actually, after "Welcome to our Palais Masséna family" it was the first of the "We don't like to call them rules" the training woman had spelled out in the morning session. Zena berated herself for not having taken it more seriously. 'So I can't go out this way?'

'Not in your uniform,' he said, the kindly smile persisting. 'Staffroom stairs up into Sacha Guitry at the back of the store. That's what you're supposed to do.'

Zena wondered if reciting a few of the stats she'd picked up in her introductory session might encourage the man to take pity on her. Carrying over 600 brands, the store's five vast sales floors boasted a total surface area of 13,000 square metres. Its flagship Paris store excepted, *Pal-Mas,* as everyone called it, was the largest of its kind in the country. Amen. In other words, the place was massive. 'All that way?' she said, annoyed with herself at how lame it sounded.

'All that way.'

'Really? You see, thing is, officer, we were meant to finish by six so I'm already late.'

'This is your first day?'

'Very first,' she said, sensing him weaken.

'So you must have *arrived* for work out of uniform.'

Not so weak after all. She indicated the tote bag at her feet. 'My day clothes are in here.'

'Well if you'd changed back into them, you *could* have gone out this way.'

'Didn't have time. I needed to buy this.' She held the bag open. Alongside a couple of rolled-up garments was a Moka coffee pot, a white porcelain cup and a receipt for both. 'Just moved here, you see.' She felt the moment was right to chance her arm. 'I don't really want to be any later back, officer. If it's at all possible.'

En route to the door, an extravagantly made-up woman Zena recognised from her afternoon session gave the guard a wave.

'Goodnight, André.

'Night, Nadine.'

She gave him a second look. 'You're not giving our Zara here a hard time are you? She's new. We haven't even got her behind a counter yet.'

'Her name's Zena. And I don't make the rules.'

Out in the avenue, a tram, no more than a monochrome blur against the sun, slowed almost noiselessly into the stop.

Nadine wrinkled her nose. 'Let her through. Come on.'

André scanned the sales floor behind them. The coast, it seemed, was clear. 'Alright. But just this once.'

'Thank you,' Zena said, picking up her bag. 'I won't do it again – promise.' She smiled, cheekily. 'André.'

His good humour undented, the guard shook his head. 'You girls. Be the death of me, you will.'

Zena let that pass without comment but she was one of the girls already, was she? The thought pleased her as she walked out into the arcade with her saviour.

'Thank you, too, Madame.'

'Nadine. It was nothing. When you've been in retail as long as I have, you can sell anything to anyone – not just sweeties like André.'

'I don't usually disobey rules. There was such a lot to learn today, I just forgot.'

Nadine had the air of someone who thought she had seen it all and probably had. 'I'll tell you a *good* reason for not wearing your uniform on your way out of the store. Better than simply "It's the rule."'

'Ah, yes?'

'Customers will stop you and say, " Have you got Item Such-And-Such? Where is it? Take me." Telling them to go find it themselves because you're on your way home doesn't go down well. And if reported, will get you the sack.'

'I see.'

Zena was glad of her shades as they stepped out on to the platform where the French public's love affair with boarding an already full tram, bus or train was in full swing.

'You getting this one?'

'I'm over the other side,' Zena said.

'See you tomorrow, then. And well done, today.'

As Nadine disappeared into the press of bodies, Zena crossed the avenue and checked out the passengers lined up on the platform. Back home, she knew the best spot to board at any tram stop in the city. Here? A group gathered at the tail end of the platform had the look of locals so she invited herself to the party and when the tram rolled in no more than a minute later, the doors of the rearmost car duly opened directly in front of her. Paying attention to every face, she boarded, validated her pass in the machine and stood by the doors. Out of habit, she reached for her iPod but, reminding herself that she needed all her wits about her, she abandoned the idea. Debussy or MC Solaar or Richard Galliano could wait. A couple of men squeezed into the car at the last minute and the tram pulled away.

Zena was a bright, slender and, by her mother's account,

"pretty enough" young woman. Perhaps that was a view shared by one of the latecomers, a middle-aged man wearing a *Lacoste* T-shirt who appeared to have his eye on her as the tram crossed the Place and slinked around the curve into Boulevard Jean Jaurès. Or perhaps his interest had nothing to do with her looks. Breaking her journey was the easiest way to find out.

Zena let the first stop come and go but at Cathédrale Vieille-Ville, she got out and, keeping her eyes on the tram's rear doors, walked the few paces to the end of the platform. Emerging at the top of a flight of steps between a sandwich shop and an appointments—only medical lab, she watched as a steady trickle of passengers followed in her wake: a woman, a second woman, a couple of kids, a man. But there was no sign of T-shirt and Zena began to breathe a little more easily. But just as the doors were due to close, there he was, once again leaving things until the last second.

She needed an escape route. Exposed in either direction, the boulevard was a non-starter so she began dancing down the steps toward the labyrinth of narrow streets and alleys that made up the old town of Nice, a quarter some locals called the Babazouk and which thus far, she had explored only on a map. Gauging that she had descended far enough, she turned and, standing on tip-toe, peeked back over the top step. As the tram whirred away from the stop, T-shirt was all-action, smartly crossing the tracks to the opposite platform, continuing across the adjoining roadway and, on reaching the far pavement, disappearing through a door set into hoardings screening off the building site beyond. Relieved and exasperated in equal measure, Zena walked back up the steps and returned to the platform.

The departure board promised a Pont Michel-bound service in nine minutes. Adding another sixteen or so for the ride and then the four-minute walk, it meant she should be back in her apartment in just under half-an-hour. Or forty minutes if she took fright at the first face she saw on the tram and let it go. She told herself not to overreact like that again and settled in to the wait.

She spent it taking in the street life of the boulevard and contemplating the building site opposite. Extending from Place Masséna to the Théâtre National de Nice, which was still some distance off, the site was huge. The hoardings, unlike any she had seen before, were themselves interesting, a combination of photographs and *trompe l'oeil* representations of the development they were concealing: extensive gardens, a children's playground, a water jet *miroir d'eau*. There was no Place Masséna-style preposterousness here. Assuming the completed reality lived up to the images, the new "Promenade du Paillon" promised to be stunning. But it was the concept outlined in the accompanying blurb that exercised Zena most. Due to open next year, the space would serve as "a 12-hectare green lung in the heart of the city." What? With the mountain air of the lofty Alpes Maritimes at its back and its feet washed by the glittering waters of the eponymous Côte d'Azur, did the city of Nice have any need of a green lung? Zena wondered what the planners could have dreamed up to ventilate some of the places she knew. Places that could *definitely* use a lung. Of any colour.

She heard a muffled ringtone, one of the two prepaids, and following best practice, checked the space around her. No one was within earshot but as she fished the mobile out of her bag, she believed the point was academic, anyway. What were the chances of a bystander understanding a single word of what she was about to say?

Apparently, no one had briefed her that Nice's connections to Russia and its citizens dated back over a century and a half.

Exchanging the usual preliminaries in her native dialect, she listened to what she knew would be just the first of a string of questions.

'I had a couple of moments,' she replied. 'But they were nothing. I'm on it, don't worry.'

Another question.

'Blue suit. Cream blouse. Lapel badge.' She gave a dry little laugh. 'Yes, blue – the colour of a field of Provençal lavender.'

As the call progressed, the scope for wry observations diminished and by the time her tram was on the approach, Zena had only one more point to clarify.

'The day after tomorrow,' she said. 'If all goes to plan.'

6.32 PM

Standing apart from the others, Thea Petrova ended the call and would have made a second but for the sudden attentions of a florid-looking man clutching a near-empty wine glass. Quickly slipping the mobile into her handbag, she took out a Spanish fan and opened it with a snap. 'Yes?'

'Laurent Salins,' he said. 'Could do with a fan, myself. It's like an oven out here. Too hot for this white. I've had to go on to red.' He brandished the glass as proof. 'They haven't thought it through.'

Salins may have had a point. With the shadows cast by one of its celebrated stands of pines falling unhelpfully on the box hedge that enclosed it on three sides, the Villa's west lawn was a trap for the late afternoon sun. The younger ones appeared to be revelling in it. Gathered in clumps, the older types had the look of flowerbeds that had gone over in the heat. And that was despite the efforts of the fan-fluttering ladies among them.

'Not thought it through at all,' Salins said. 'And you are?'

'Unavailable,' Thea replied, a verdict that sounded particularly final in her Russian-accented French. 'Excuse me.'

Wearing the sort of expression unlikely to encourage further conversation, Thea strode purposefully away. Salins followed. 'I just wanted to ask if you knew when the admin woman goes home? Madame Tiron?'

Thea pursed her lips and kept going. One of the clumps parted and without missing a fan beat, the climber that was Marcia Calon threw out a tendril and snagged Thea's arm. 'Oh, do join us. Jérôme? Bring drinks. What would you like, Thea?'

If Laurent Salins knew when he wasn't wanted, it was clear he didn't care. 'Do any of you know when Madame Tiron goes home? I've something to take up with her.'

As Jérôme scurried off to the bar, Thea granted Marcia an audience, thus leaving the others to deal with Salins's question.

'Sorry, monsieur. This is my first time here.'

'She goes at different times. And sometimes, she stays overnight.'

'Look round the side. If there's a grey Renault 5 parked there, she's around.'

'It's beige, isn't it?'

'No, grey.'

'Look, if she's in her office, she usually keeps the door open. Worth a knock, though, if it isn't. Right?'

At last, Salins had something to work with. 'Where *is* her office?'

'Opposite Reception. Where you registered. Didn't you get a sheet?'

'If Elie's gone home, her assistant might still be in the office –

Clarice. She'll be able to help you with anything.'

Marcia excused herself from Thea, momentarily. 'Clarice is on holiday,' she announced. 'So there you have it, monsieur. A *full* picture.' Implying, "Now skedaddle, you annoying little nonentity," she concluded with a brows-high stare.

'Right, I'll go and see.' Salins trundled away, muttering, 'For what we're paying, you'd think they'd tell you this stuff, wouldn't you?'

When Marcia turned back, Thea, too, had taken her leave, but for an altogether different reason. Carrying two brimming champagne flutes, Gérard Urquelle had arrived on the scene and was clearly looking for company.

'Well!' Marcia said, her eyes locked on Thea's trajectory like a coastguard tracking a suspect vessel. 'What does she want with *that* disgrace of a human being?'

'Why do you say that?' someone asked.

'He has a gun and he... he shoots...' Marcia looked ill, suddenly. Ill and spitting angry. 'He shoots cats!'

'Who shoots cats?'

Spilling some of the contents, she gestured toward Urquelle with her wine glass. 'That man. *Monsieur* Gérard Urquelle. They call evil men animals, don't they? Let me tell you that it's not animals who are evil.' She slopped a second libation on to the lawn. 'I would put a bullet in *his* brain without a second thought!' Her face crumpled and it was with some difficulty that she managed to say again, 'He shoots *cats!*'

Looking almost amused at the assertion, a tall, pleasant-looking man in his sixties shook his grey head. 'With respect, Madame Calon,' he said with just a hint of a foreign accent. 'He does not shoot cats.'

'Yes, he does! Just a few months ago, it was. I read it in *Nice-Matin*. What is your name again?'

'Alan Davies. Retired teacher of English. *Depicting The Landscape* with Astrid Pireque.' He recited his CV as if he'd supplied it at least once already. 'I read that story, too. Monsieur Urquelle shot at just *one* cat with an air rifle, merely to scare it away from a garden, his own, which the animal, unimpressed by a succession of less-explosive disincentives, had been using as a toilet for the previous two years.'

'You are English. You do not understand how we live here in France.'

'Madame, I have been living in this area for almost forty years. You may have forgotten how Monsieur Urquelle acquired that limp of his but I have not. He can shoot at defecating cats all day long as far as I'm concerned.'

'Well!'

Davies raised his glass. 'Enjoy your wine-tasting.'

★　★　★

'Mademoiselle Hamada?'

'Zoë, please.' She beamed and making just the hint of a bow, extended her hand. 'Are you one of mine?' She laughed. 'So to speak.'

'Lydia. Lydia Félix, yes, I am and I can't tell you how much I'm looking forward to the course.' She let go of Zoë's hand. 'I just wish it lasted three weeks, not three days.'

Urquelle slipped in next to Lydia. 'I am also yours; I also wish the course lasted longer; and I, too, would love to be able to call you Zoë. Champagne?' The women indicated their pleasure at the offer and he handed them over. 'I'll get one for myself in a moment. I'm Gérard, by the way.'

Zoë performed her greeting ritual once more. 'Gérard? Ah, you're the one who swapped courses.'

'Uh...' His eyes slid to Lydia. She was frowning. Uncertain. A fix was needed. But first, he needed to attend to Zoë. 'Yes, sorry you got saddled with me at the last minute.'

Born in Grasse of Japanese-American parents, Zoë was something of a linguaphile and she couldn't resist a grin at Urquelle's use of the compound verb "to get saddled". It suggested that matters had been out of his direct control. Other forces had been responsible.

'Hey, no problem,' Zoë said. 'Mathieu's loss is my gain.'

Urquelle's eyes were still on Lydia and, seeking to work the duplicity to his advantage, he produced a series of variations on his default smile that, without uttering a word, nevertheless conveyed a complex message: yes, alright, he had fibbed to her about which course he'd actually signed up for − and it had been far from easy to change it so late on - but having met Lydia for just a few short minutes, all his interest in wine had evaporated. He hoped she would understand. He hoped she would forgive him. And, if she didn't mind helping him a little in class because he was sure to be absolutely hopeless, he knew that they would have great fun together. And perhaps, even... Who knew where it might lead?

At that moment, a woman wearing a little black dress some might have considered wrong for her strutted behind the trio on to the lawn. Neither Lydia nor Zoë caught the discreet nods that were exchanged between Urquelle and the woman, Monique Dufour, with whom he'd struck up a conversation just twenty minutes before. She too had signed up for the perfume course. As had her friend, yet to appear. In subtly expressing his interest in Monique earlier, Urquelle kept to himself that although she may have made his squad for the next couple of days, she would be remaining on the bench if all went well with Lydia. *Firmly* so, he added, amusing himself further.

Meanwhile, Lydia broke into a smile that conveyed a message of her own. No, she hadn't been put off by Urquelle's naughtiness. If anything, she was charmed by it. She was flattered. She was, in short, his for the taking.

The sun continued to bake the lawn and all around them, the hum of conversation had been increasing in volume like slowly rising dough.

'There's quite a few of us out here now,' Zoë said. 'I must go and say hello to some of my other students.'

'Of course,' they said in unison and laughed about it.

'But first, is there anything you'd like to ask me?'

'Will we be making a start on our own perfumes after dinner?'

Zoë beamed, a signature look. 'You're keen – perfect! No, that's for tomorrow. This evening is very much an introduction and our first exercise will be to smell – and yes, I do use that word as both a verb and a noun – we'll begin by smelling replicas of some of the most celebrated fragrances from the *Conservatoire International des Parfums* in Versailles.'

'The *Osmothèque*?'

Zoë nodded. 'Ah, you know it? Excellent.'

'Oh, that's marvellous!' Sharing the good news, Lydia smiled at Urquelle. 'I don't remember reading about that in the course notes.'

Zoë performed her other signature look: serious business. 'I always like to surprise my students. And then we will go on to sample some modern classics, prime exemplars of the different basic types of scents.' The beam once more. 'Fragrances such as the *Aurore d'Argent* you're wearing, Lydia. See you later.' She gave Urquelle a less fulsome smile and took her leave.

'Wow,' Lydia said. 'Did you hear that? She identified my

scent. Just like that! Didn't even get close to me.'

'Well,' Urquelle said. 'Isn't she the silly one. More champagne?'

★   ★   ★

Astrid still hadn't put in an appearance at the drinks party and it was looking as if she might not make it at all. As tutors were expected rather than obliged to attend, it was of no real concern. Attending the dinner that followed was a different matter. But in any event, however pressed for time she was, Astrid never refused a free meal – the privations of her life as a struggling artist were too recent in her memory. And meals prepared by the geniuses in the Château's kitchen were something else. On more than one occasion, she had contemplated proposing to head chef Jean-Claude. Or chef Omar. Or chef *Lisa*, come to that. If a person were capable of transforming stuff like tofu, parsnips or sea urchins into glorious masterpieces of culinary art, what did accidents of gender matter?

Astrid had almost finished researching the man Elie had once harboured a desire to kill. A package of clips from the local news programme, *Télé-Sud*, had proved interesting. Chief reporter Annie Provin had twice interviewed Gérard Urquelle. The first was shortly after the incident in which the have-a-go hero had played such a key role. Too shortly afterwards, perhaps: the man appeared still to be in shock. Way to go, Annie, Astrid said to herself, recalling some of the many run-ins the Brigade had had with the reporter. The second interview had been recorded many weeks later. Urquelle was clearly no longer in shock but his mood seemed to Astrid very, even worryingly, low. Now five years on, vintage sports car and all, the man appeared, at least on the surface, to be fully recovered.

The pages of *Nice-Matin* online had also contained some useful material. But when it came to understanding what had actually happened in a criminal case, there was nothing to compare with the police databases to which, thanks to an intervention by Commissaire Agnès Dantier, Astrid had been granted limited access. Since the incident had occurred in Monaco and was therefore outside French jurisdiction, Astrid had had to route her search request via Europol. It had all worked well and now, she had just one document left to read.

Considering the ostensible state of Urquelle's mind days after the shooting, his account of it to the police immediately afterwards was remarkably clear. Tuesday April 8th five years ago was a cool and damp day in the principality. As manager of *Bertrand et Fils*, a jewellery store on the Boulevard Rainier III, Urquelle was going through the process of closing up the shop with the only other employee still on the premises, an assistant in her late twenties named Karen Bicoud, when at 18.11, a gunman forced his way in, smashed the CCTV camera by the door, threw an open kitbag on to the floor and began shouting incoherent instructions at the petrified Bicoud. Confused, she hesitated. The gunman raised his weapon. Urquelle threw himself at the assailant and in the ensuing struggle, four shots were fired. One bullet winged Urquelle's right foot. One caught Bicoud square in the forehead. One buried itself harmlessly in the ceiling. The other entered the gunman's torso above the left lung, wrecking several vital organs before it exited through the man's right hip. In less than a minute after the gunman had entered, Urquelle lay injured, Karen Bicoud and the gunman, subsequently identified as a certain Eddy Lopes, were dead.

After a thoroughgoing forensic and pathological examination of the evidence, officers of the criminal investigation division of Monaco's Police Judiciaire corroborated Urquelle's story in its entirety, a conclusion in which the eyewitness testimony of a passer-by named Denis Marut had played a significant part.

Astrid closed her laptop and gazed out of the window but for all she took in of the terrace and the panorama beyond, she might as well have been back in her flat overlooking the old port. It was clear that while Elie had come to change her mind about killing Urquelle, she still felt a degree of antipathy toward him. It was also clear, vis-à-vis her reference to the timeframe, that these shootings were the cause of her hostility. Looking at the bare bones of the case, it seemed Elie must have had a personal connection with either of those Urquelle had accidentally killed. Although Astrid had worked with the Brigade long enough to know that no possibility could ever be ruled out, the gunman Lopes was not the percentage play. It was far more likely that Elie knew, or knew of, the unfortunate Karen Bicoud and had originally believed she would be alive today but for Urquelle's reckless intervention. Perhaps believed it until the eyewitness came forward with his testimony.

Astrid glanced at her watch. Maybe there was time for a pre-dinner drink after all and if Elie stuck to her usual practice – seeing the party through to the end before going home for dinner – perhaps there would be a moment to talk.

7.01 PM

For more years than she cared to remember, Commissaire Agnès Dantier had been moving mountains at the Caserne Auvare: mountains of files from one side of her desk to the other. After a good seven hours of it today, she had arrived at the enticingly thin little thing that was the final item. Nonetheless, she refrained from feeling for her sling-backs under the desk with her bare feet. Despite its lean and hungry look, she knew from experience that such files often proved to be the most time-consuming. Heading home may still be some way off. 'Let me have about me files that are fat,' she said aloud, and then chuckled. *I really must retire. I've turned into Julius goddamn Caesar.'*

She began reading but a figure striding in through her open door made her look up. Saying nothing, he approached the desk and stood quite still in front of her.

'Armani?' she said, parking her reading glasses in her ash-blonde bob. Immediately, she knew he had something on his mind. Something portentous. 'To what do I owe this pleasure on your day off?'

Clasping his hands loosely together, he closed his eyes. Transfixed more in incredulity than wonderment, Agnès looked on deadpan. And then Armani began to sing.

> *Vide 'o mare quant'è bello,*
> *spira tantu sentimento,*
> *Comme tu...*
> He held the note.
> *a chi tieni mente,*
> *Ca scetato 'o fai sunnà.*

Palms together now, as if in prayer.

> *Guarda gua' chistu ciardino;*
> *Siente, sie' sti ciur' arance:*
> *Nu prufumo accussì fino*
> *Dinto 'o core se ne va…*
> *E tu dice: "I' parto, addio!"*
> *T'alluntane da stu core…*
> *Da sta ter..!* Impassioned now. He held the
note. And held it some more.
> *… ra! del l'ammore…*
> *Tieni 'o core 'e nun turnà?*

Arms spread wide. Pleading.

> *Ma nun me lassà,*
> *Nun darme stu turmiento!*
> New heights of ardour here. *Torna a Surriento,*
> *Famme cam…* He held the note. Tightly. Then,
in a paroxysm of emotion, roller-coastered up and
down the scale as he threw it away. *Pààààààà!!!!!*

Armani finally opened his eyes.

Silence.

'Thank you,' Agnès said, at length.

Armani blew her a kiss, turned on his heel and made his
exit as quickly as he had come.

When moments later, Darac peered tentatively around
the door, Agnès was sitting back in her chair, brows lowered,
the tip of an arm of her reading glasses resting contempla-
tively between her lips. 'Paul. Come in.'

Darac wasn't sure how to play it here from here. His
double-act with Armani on the Promenade des Anglais had

worked even more perfectly than he had hoped. They had indeed been able to set up their pitch within a few paces of Gigi the Vespa man without alerting him and when the capo of the outfit turned up, he too, had been completely fooled by the busking shtick. As the duffel bag was handed over, Darac and Armani grabbed both men and held them without difficulty until Mobile arrived moments later to take them into custody. Problem solved. Job done. Time to decamp to the Caserne to report.

In its way, Darac's impromptu solution to the situation, based as it was on proven principles, had ultimately been as audacious as the kind of improvisations he loved playing with his jazz group, the Didier Musso Quintet. There had, though, been one enormous difference.

'You look puzzled about something, Agnès?'

'Hmm.' Her feline features set into a grin. 'And you look sheepish.'

Darac related his late afternoon encounter with Armani, climaxing the performance with a blow-by-blow account of the scenario on the promenade. At the end of it, Agnès was wiping tears of laughter from her cheeks.

'And he wanted to *carry on* busking? Even after... even after Mobile had gone?'

'No stopping him.'

More laughter. 'Only Armani...' Agnès took a deep breath. 'Only Armani could go from wallflower to superstar at the drop of a hat.'

'You should have heard his 'Funiculì, Funiculà!' "

'Stop it, Paul!' Agnès binned her tissue and took out another. 'What on earth did you come up with to make him change his mind?'

Ah. The tricky moment Darac was hoping to avoid had arrived. What he had come up with was shamelessly using the love, worship and adoration they all felt for Agnès to con him into it. 'We-ell...'

The black desk phone rang. An internal call. Not for the first time, it seemed Darac may have been saved by the bell.

'It's Forensics,' Agnès said, glancing at the number. 'Do you think they could hear Armani all the way across there?' She picked up. 'Hello?' Mouthing "Erica," Agnès gestured Darac to stay put. It soon became obvious that Erica had also been the victim of a walk-by singing.

Interpreting Agnès's wheezing responses, it seemed that having subjected her to 'Torna a Surriento,' the spree had continued with 'O Sole Mio.' So Armani was touring the compound, serenading people at random? But then Darac remembered he'd told him that Erica, too, was greatly enamoured of his way with a song. Thank God, I didn't add Granot and Bonbon to the list, he said to himself. Over the years, the tolerance of Darac's two trusted lieutenants had been stretched to breaking point by his persistent promotion of jazz. But Armani relentlessly pelting them with song? Of *that,* Darac knew, he would never hear the end.

Agnès finished the call, took another tissue from the box and said: 'Short of swirling a silk-lined cape, Armani's exit could hardly have been more dramatic. Oh Lord!' A final dab of the eyes. 'But where were we? Ah, yes. What *did* you say to change Armani's mind about singing?'

The truth was always best. Especially with Agnès. Darac ran a hand into the black, wavy thicket that was his hair and kept it there. 'Can't remember now,' he said.

Unable to spot Elie on a quick tour of her beat, Astrid did
what she should have done in the first place: approach the
formidable Bruno on the night desk. 'Gone home already,'
he said. So, deciding to leave out any reference to the
elephant in the room, Astrid sent Elie a text:

> *Babe, we'll sizzle on the griddle – sorry, take drinks on the
> lawn – some other time. See you tomorrow, Sloppy kisses, Tridi*

With most having repaired to their rooms for a
pre-dinner freshen-up, Astrid found only a few stragglers
left on the lawn. Her eye was immediately taken by Gérard
Urquelle, standing over in the far corner with... who was
the Russian woman he'd seemed anxious to avoid earlier?
Thea, yes. Thea Petrova. Astrid watched them and the way
they were together. The nods and moues. The occasional
asides. The companionable silences. It all seemed so easy. So
familiar.

'I didn't forget the drinks voucher.'

Astrid's portrait-subject-in-waiting, Ralf Bassette had
arrived and he was holding two glasses of champagne. 'So I
see,' she said, smiling as she took one.

'*Santé.*'

'*Santé.*' Astrid took a sip. 'Hmm. I think our Mathieu
Croix might say, "Baking baguette; ripe Williams pear;
urgent mousse.'

'What would *you* say?'

'Yum yum, probably.'

Bassette laughed. 'So would I.' He took a sip and,

checking his mobile was on mute, slipped off his jacket. 'Gosh, it's hot out here.'

'Hate to tell you this but we'll be spending a good three hours *en plein air* tomorrow morning. Alongside the Canal de la Vésubie just over the way there. Do you know it?'

'I'm not familiar with this part of the city, I'm afraid. Canal? I hope the towpath will be in the shade.'

'Oh, it's not navigable – just a narrow water course. And it's sinuous, not straight, so you can always find shade. Plus, you won't have to carry your own stuff up there. Lionel, the Villa's maintenance man, doubles as a sherpa.'

'Impressive.'

'The greatest hazard we'll face are the local joggers.'

Urquelle and Thea were still on Astrid's mind and she glanced across. There had been a change. Thea hadn't moved from the spot and was talking animatedly into her mobile but Urquelle was heading back into the building. Catching Astrid's eye, he waved, made a couple of jaunty remarks concerning the dinner to come and the introductory class to follow, and was gone. Still turning over questions about the man in her mind, Astrid managed no more than a bland comment in response. Bassette, she noticed, didn't manage even that.

'Do you know Monsieur Urquelle?' she asked.

'Not at all.' He appeared to go to a different thought and it was a pleasant one. 'Since we met in reception, I've been looking at some of your work on the internet. Astrid, I thought it wonderful.'

Ker-ching! 'Thank you. That's kind.'

'I very much enjoyed the Pop-Arty things. But I *loved* your drawings on paper. Mind you, I am a little biased in that regard, I suppose.'

Pecuniary considerations aside, Astrid was beginning

to feel a certain kinship with Monsieur Ralf Bassette. In a range of media, the basis of much of her best work was her École-honed drawing technique, an approach she knew was on the endangered list in many quarters. 'So your thing is drawing? That's refreshing.'

'My thing is paper.'

'Paper?'

'Don't get me wrong, I do love drawing as I say, but I'm very much into paper.' He smiled his patrician smile. 'In the sense that I make it.'

One of Astrid's fellow students at the Académie had made paper. Hours of drudgery with recycled scraps normally yielded at least enough new material for a couple of thumbnail sketches. She sensed that Bassette's operation was on a somewhat larger scale. 'Oh?' she said.

'Yes. Writing and printing paper, mainly. Are you familiar with *Plume d'Oie?*'

Ker-ching suddenly seemed inadequate. Perhaps only the ubiquitous Clairefontaine company offered a wider range of high-quality stationery. 'I think I may have come across it.'

'Ah, yes? Well, I own it. At this point, I used to add "for my sins" but I've been told it's passé, meaningless and predictable.'

'By whom, if you don't mind me asking?'

'My wife, Anna.' He smiled, proud of her, by the look of it and Astrid expected to be shown a photo at any moment. The mobile, though, remained in Bassette's pocket. Maybe Anna had told him that that, too, was a no-no.

Astrid glanced at her watch. 'Listen, I hate to tear myself away but I really must say hello to my other students.'

'Of course.'

Bassette's buoyant mood appeared to sink a little. 'Will we have the pleasure of Monsieur Urquelle's company on the course?'

'I thought you said you didn't know him.'

'I don't. But I do recognize him as a man Anna once found far from passé, meaningless and predictable.'

Astrid's brows rose. It seemed Elie might not be the only one with a reason for hating Urquelle. But whether Bassette did or not, he had just added 'forgiving' to the qualities she had identified in him earlier. Or maybe he was a spineless fool. 'Ah,' she said, and left it there. 'It's quicker if we go through the bar.'

'Right you are.'

They moved off and by an idiosyncrasy of the flow of sound waves in an enclosed outdoor space, Astrid caught a few words of Thea's phone conversation still going on in the corner. A phrase Astrid heard clearly was "not a chance." Another was "change things" or perhaps "changes things." And finally, something that might have been "it's better." Speaking in Russian, Thea had sounded slightly tense, Astrid felt. But of one thing, she was sure. Thea was a native of the St Petersburg area. It was an accent Astrid knew quite well.

Looking on from the open doorway, a red-faced heavily set man wearing a sweat-stained shirt gave the pair a nod. 'Looking forward to getting down into that cellar at some stage, I can tell you.' He drained the glass of red he was nursing. 'Laurent Salins.'

'Charmed,' Astrid said, keeping moving while her companion stopped and offered his hand. '8.30, Monsieur Bassette,' she called out. 'Salle Fernand Léger.'

'Indeed!'

As Astrid continued on her way, she could have sworn she heard Bassette introduce himself to Salins with just one word: 'Anything.'

Except that there was no social media device, the contents of young Emma Tardelli's bedroom were typical of many a six year-old French girl's of the time: single bed with themed linen and a family of soft toys in residence; desk for homework and chair; dressing table with hairbrush, slides and other grooming ephemera; wardrobe with mirror on the inside of the door; boxes in primary colours full of toys, some recently acquired, some "from when I was little;" wall shelf laden with books, pictures and her own collection of DVDs.

And finally, Emma's pride and joy. Presiding over her bed was her poster from the movie *Tangled,* slightly dog-eared and festooned with real, if miniature, lipstick kisses, its twin stars peeping out into the room through a wall of entwined tresses.

Noëmi kissed Emma on both cheeks and since baby Fabien had chosen that moment to start kicking his way out of her belly, she stayed sitting on the bed.

'Will Papa come in and give me a kiss tonight?'

'When Papa's late home, he always comes in to give you a kiss.'

Scrunching her shoulders, Emma clasped her hands against her cheek and giggled. 'Can I capture him and make him take me all round the world?'

'Can't I come too?'

'No, I'm Rapunzel and Papa's Flynn. You've got to stay here.'

'That's alright. I like it here.' She took Emma's hand. 'Feel. He's kicking.'

In one seamless movement, Emma sprang on to her knees and with almost heart-breaking concentration, felt her way around the miracle that was her *maman*'s tummy.

'Think, sweetie, when you go to *Maternelle* tomorrow, you're going to be a *grand*, aren't you? Won't Fabi be proud of his big sister?'

Emma nodded, her expression balancing gravitas and hauteur in a way that was her Papa to a T. 'Yes,' she said. 'Fabi will be very proud of me. Can I wear make-up now?'

'No.'

'Can I play with yours when I come home from school?'

'If you're good.'

'Thank you, thank you, thank you!'

Noëmi gave Emma three final, *final* bedtime kisses and settled her down for the night.

★   ★   ★

It was half an hour or so later that Armani returned home and, true to Noëmi's word, almost the first thing he did was to kiss his sleeping princess goodnight. The very first was to kiss her almost sleeping mother.

'Tired?'

'No-o.' She grinned. 'Just pretending.'

'Is this what I get for being the perfect husband?' he said, chucking her under the chin. 'I'll get us some refreshment.'

Noëmi was already stretched out on the lounger by the time Armani took a couple of cold drinks out on to the balcony. He drew up a chair and to the staccato *click-clack* from the *terrain de pétanque* down to their left, the pair, as they did almost every evening, watched the light gradually fade on Place Wilson.

'You and Fabi have a good time together today?'

'Wonderful. Except when I was putting Emma down.'

'What happened?'

'He decided to replay *La Coppa Italia*.'

'*La Coppa*? Tell me *Juve* scored this time.' Remembering his team's 2-0 loss to Napoli in the final still hurt. 'Preferably three.'

She raised her brows. 'I think they did.'

'*Sforza!*' Armani toasted the triumph with a mouthful of *Peroni* and then took her hand. 'Six weeks today, sweetheart. That's all it is.'

'Yes. It was lovely, really. Emma felt him.'

Armani kissed Noëmi's hand. 'Her last day of the holiday... You know from *Mat* onwards, I hated *La Rentrée*. Emma takes after you.'

'In some things.'

'She's still excited about tomorrow?'

'Excited? Mama told me she'd re-packed her backpack half a dozen times before I picked her up.' Noëmi frowned as she shifted her weight on the lounger. 'And she's done it twice since we got home.'

Armani felt a sense of such deep contentment at that moment, he could have laughed or cried or both. Instead, letting go of Noëmi's hand, he reached forward and adjusted the cushion under her feet. 'That better?'

'Hmm.'

Down on the street, lights were going on in the restaurants and the evening bustle was getting underway. In the Place itself, the *pétanque* game appeared to be coming to the last shot of the last end and Armani stood resting his elbows on the balcony rail to watch it. The appearance of the player charged with taking the shot made him smile. A matchstick glued implacably to his lower lip, the player conveyed an air of unassailable confidence. Above the Plimsoll line of his tiny, shiny shorts rose a bulky mass of flesh covered in a holed basketball-style singlet at least two sizes too small. The same could not have been said for the football socks slumped in slack resignation half-way down his skinny calves. What looked suspiciously like brand new trainers completed the ensemble.

Judging that the man's outfit was not redeemed but made worse by his gleaming footwear, Armani couldn't help feeling for him, too. The game situation looked hopeless. The tiny target, the *cochonnet,* was surrounded by a ring of enemy shots, with one of them virtually touching. To win the game, that boule would have to be fired out. But where would that leave its confrères? Any shot in *pétanque* was a hostage to fortune – that was one of the beauties of the game – but no amount of helpful ricochets would save the day here, surely. There was only one way to win this one: the last shot would have to expel the almost-touching boule without moving the *cochonnet* more than a centimetre or two. Each of the player's teammates seemed to have an opinion on the best way to achieve the dead shot this required and a lively debate sprang up which soon turned into a flaming row.

'This is getting good,' Armani said, but then quite suddenly, the fracas subsided and the player was ready. He stood stock still. His legs flexed. In one quick flick of the wrist, he let fly. The players hushed. The silver orb arced into the failing light and fell. There was a *clack* but no *click*. A chorus of cheers and jeers went up simultaneously: the shot had cannoned away the enemy toucher and finished right up against the target.

A grinning Armani tapped his mobile a couple of times and on the *terrain,* the hero of the hour bent to extract something from his sock. 'Was that shot for the game, Granot? And you're on speaker so mind your mouth.'

'Of course it was for the game.'

'Bravo! So your lucky old outfit came through for you again, huh?'

'Listen, three months ago, all I could get on were the socks.'

Armani let that one lie. 'So what's with the new trainers?'

'My old ones were getting a little past their best.'

Stifling a laugh, Armani turned his back on the scene.

'Noëmi with you?'

'Evening, Granot!' she called out, covering for her husband who was still hiding his amusement at Granot's sartorial idiosyncrasies.

'Did you see my winning shot?'

She hadn't. 'It was brilliant!'

'Then, I dedicate the match to you.'

'You darling!'

Armani went to sit down and Noëmi gave his knee a pat. 'Invite him up for a beer.'

Armani relayed the message but Granot had made plans with his team-mates and the call ended with the promise to do it another time.

'Pity he couldn't make it. And en route, he could've popped into *U* and got some of those prune yoghurts we like.'

'I'll nip down and get them later.' Armani sat back in his chair. 'So how was MAMAC today?'

'Routine. Boring, even.'

Armani couldn't resist a grin. '*Bella*, you're archiving a collection of artist's letters and papers, no? Not working as a trapeze artist.'

'Listen, I really enjoy it when the guy writes *about* art. Or love. Or life. What I've been ploughing through for the past three months is a dispute over a plumbing bill. And the positioning of a boundary fence.'

'You should get Granot on the case. He *loves* that kind of thing.'

'Yes?' Noëmi shrugged. 'Anyway, I don't think I'm going to miss work much when I go on leave. And I certainly won't miss seeing all my lovely work colleagues. Unlike you, I haven't got any. Colleagues, I mean.'

'Working solo's satisfying. But teamwork *is* more fun.' Noëmi's glass was empty, he noticed. 'More carrot juice? You've probably only drunk about four litres of the stuff today.'

She contemplated the glass. 'Nnnnn...Yes.' She handed it over. 'You're sweet, you know. I don't care what they say.'

'All I know is that if our baby comes out orange,' he called out as he went inside, 'we'll know why. A child of mine clashing with the paintwork? *Que disastro!*'

The apartment building ran the entire south-facing side of Place Wilson. With its primrose yellow-washed walls and duck-egg blue shutters, it presented a sunny, harmonious face to the world and the Tardellis had loved it at first sight. Their six-roomed place occupied a prime spot on the top, fifth floor and directly below was something else they loved: a modestly equipped little children's playground they soon came to regard as an outdoor extension in which Emma could run free – as long as at least one of them was on hand to supervise.

For six years, Emma had been the sole focus of their parental love and both had wondered how she would take to her role as Fabien's big sister. For a moment, Noëmi pictured Emma coaxing the little one on to the slide, helping him climb the stairs to the cute little house at the top, then encouraging him to wave at *maman* and *papa* before whooshing down. It was a joyous thought. But *is* that would it would be like?

'Thank you.' Taking the refilled glass, she turned her thoughts to the here and now. 'How about you? Not much of a day off, getting caught up in a work thing.'

'Ah, that's where you're wrong.' He took down another mouthful of beer. 'Where to begin?' A natural storyteller, Armani loved teasing things out. 'If anyone asked, how would you describe my voice?'

'Deep. Manly. Gorgeous accent.' Allowing her head to fall to the side, she grinned at him. 'How am I doing?'

'Great. And my singing voice?'

'Uh, let's see...' She scrunched her brow while she looked for the *mot juste*. 'Terrible just about covers it. Still doing great?'

Armani laughed, then laughed louder still before recounting the scenario on the Promenade des Anglais.

'Well, Paul's plan worked anyway,' she said, giggling. 'He's amazing, isn't he? To have thought that up on the spur of the moment?'

Armani drew down the corners of his mouth. 'He's got his points.'

'And only you, my big, idiotic *carissimo*, would have had the...'

'Balls?'

Noëmi's turn to laugh. 'Yes, *balls!* Great big ones, to carry it off!'

Armani brought the fingertips of both hands together and shook them. 'You haven't heard the cream of the jest. To get me to go along with the plan, Darac tried to fool me that Agnès and Erica *lurve* my beautiful singing voice, right? *Super* fans. He'd forgotten I'm Armani, King of the Kidders.' He grinned devilishly. 'They will be cursing him for ever because they don't know where it's going or when it will end!'

'Who will be cursing him?'

'Agnès D and Erica.'

'And what's the *it*?'

Armani's account of his appalling but impassioned recitals at the Caserne had Noëmi in stitches and it was with some urgency that she told him not to go any further. When the laughter had finally subsided, she gave a start and took his hand. 'Feel.'

Armani's face was aglow with wonder.

'*Juve* just got a fourth,' Noëmi said, softly. 'Don't you think?'

9.47 PM

A fully fledged *poète-policier*, Darac was in his element leading a double life. Having a stake in two worlds offered the best of both, didn't it? Potentially. Determining where the doubling ended and the halving might begin was a question he had often turned over in his mind and it had formed the basis of many a debate. He was a Frenchman, after all. "A quintessential Frenchman" according to Dave Blackstock, the one English member of his group, the Didier Musso Quintet. "What's *quintessentially* French about me?" Darac had once asked him. "Or any French person, come to that?" "Let's just stick to you,' Dave had replied, without hesitation. If the observations he was about to make had been a pint of his beloved Kentish ale, it seemed he'd been waiting to serve it for some time. 'You're a jazz-playing homicide detective – that sort of sets the tone, doesn't it? And let's look at your taste *in* jazz. Plenty of people love Louis Armstrong. Plenty of people love Ornette Coleman. You love both *equally*. Hint of a contradiction there? Check out your attitudes in general. You're a single-minded individualist, right? But you're a down-with-the-guys team player, too. You're an atheist but a devout one. You're also a passionate rationalist, a reverent iconoclast, a... I could go on and on but in short, *Captain* Paul Darac, guitarist extraordinaire, you are a walking collection of contradictions and paradoxes. And if that isn't quintessentially French, I don't know what is."

Given more time, Dave might have illustrated his argument with something that was familiar to everyone in the DMQ. Many fellow players and fans might have regarded an evening at their holy of holies, the Blue Devil Jazz Club, as a sort of pilgrimage – if a hip one. But few would have felt obliged as Darac did to follow a set pattern of moves on arrival which, however casually performed, had the feel of sacraments. For a player whose greatest love was to improvise, such a rigid approach might have come as a surprise to those who didn't know him. Unless, of course, they were quintessentially French, too.

Tonight's performance was proving no exception. As required, Darac's first port of call had been to exchange a word or two with club doorman Pascal. Too fly to be reliable but too reliable to be authentically fly, the lanky French-Canadian had been a fixture at the Blue Devil as long as Darac could remember. A man whose wardrobe appeared to consist mainly of colourful *djellabas* and pork-pie hats, joyously, he sometimes wore both together.

Then, with photographs of some of the world's most revered players looking on from their niches, and with the sounds of the music they made great becoming ever more distinct, Darac next descended the steep stone steps towards the club's much-photographed portal. The draw wasn't its shabby red-painted doors but the 50 year-old poster attached to the wall above them. Later entitled *Blown Away By The Brass Section*, it derived from a photo taken at the club in the 1960s. It was an object of great significance to Darac and he never crossed the threshold without reaching up and touching it for luck.

Next came his exchange with club owner Eldridge Clay, a venerable New Yorker with a way of speaking French all his own. He also favoured using his pet name for Darac, 'Garfield,' for the resemblance he saw in him to the old Hollywood star, John. In the fifteen years Darac had been frequenting the club, virtually every visit had begun with Ridge asking if police detective 'Garfield' had kicked anybody's ass that day. On the couple of occasions this had failed to materialise, something strange had happened later. It had been a complete coincidence, of course. And yet...

Before the revels could properly begin, there was just one further sacrament to perform and it was a far from onerous one: sharing kisses of greeting with Khara, the club's Senegalese barmaid, waitress, first-aider — the list was endless. Before she had eventually fallen for and then married the club's livewire chef, Roger, it was thanks to Darac's relentless string-pulling that Khara had been granted the indefinite right to live and work in France. He had great affection and respect for her and the feeling was mutual.

Just as Darac had contrived to bisect lunch and dinner when picking up his lounge guitar earlier, he had arrived at the club during the featured band's set break. The Alma Warner Sextet from the U.S. were a happening outfit and the place was packed. While Alma herself was spending the break signing CDs in the lobby, the remaining members of her band were holed up in the Blue Devil's famously dilapidated green room upstairs. Over the PA, Biréli Lagrène was sprinting through 'Move' and at the bar, Khara and co-worker Carole were multitasking at a similar tempo.

'Learned a new English word from the band,' Khara said, raising her voice over the buzz. ' "Grungy." ' Her smile could have lit up the whole of the Avenue des Diables Bleus outside. 'Is that how you say it, Carole?' Her fellow barmaid nodded. '*Grun-gee*,' Khara repeated, savouring it. 'Good word, no?'

Darac grinned as he squeezed a *Chimay Red Top* on to the last remaining space on his tray. 'I bet I know what they were referring to.'

'It's one of those words that sounds like the thing it is.' She started off a second tray with a double brandy and soda. 'Even though the thing itself makes no sound.'

'Deep one.' Darac enjoyed chewing the philosophical fat but this wasn't the moment. 'Here's another English one. Have you come across: "Let's take a rain check," Khara?'

' "Some other time" in other words?'

'Exactly.' He picked up the tray, half-turning towards the crowd. 'Listen, you two have got your work cut out here. I'll come back for the other one in a minute.'

'*Begg naa la*,' she said, pouring another *Red Top*. 'That's *my* language.'

'What does it mean?'

'Look it up.' Eyes wide, Khara's mouth fell open. 'Just don't do it in front of Frankie!'

'She's not the jealous type!' he called out, catching what he hoped was the correct inference and, as Biréli Lagrène gave way to Tony Kofi, he began his way cutting through the crowd. 'Gangway, people!'

Managing to remember each of their orders, he served seven members of the quintet – the term was nominal – on his first foray around the floor. The four band mates at his own table had to wait until he arrived back with the second tray. Not that bassist Luc Gabron, young drummer Maxine Walda, alto sax player Trudi 'Charlie' Pachelberg, or pianist Didier Musso appeared to mind or even notice. The four of them were in heavy and heated debate. The band's first set had divided opinion.

'It's true what they say,' Darac said, handing out an assortment of beers. 'There's no easy job in catering and hospitality. How the hell Khara and co keep this up all night, I'll never know.'

Maxine cast him the quickest of glances. 'Waiting tables is shit,' she said, and pitched back into the fray. 'And the drummer's pocket? Loose is one thing. Full of holes is another, man.'

Poised to take the first mouthful of his *Leffe Tripel*, Darac smiled at Maxine's verdict – it could have been her teacher, the DMQ's founding drummer Marco talking.

'So we're agreed that just playing a fretless doesn't make you Jaco Pastorius, right?' Luc said, decorating his moustache with a second one made of froth. 'But, me excluded,' Who's got the best *acoustic* bass sound around?'

'Clovis Nicolas,' Didier said, earning a nod from Trudi and a "Who he?"' look from Maxine.

'No, no,' Luc countered, and took another gulp. 'Not best *around here*. Best in the *world*.'

'Clovis Nicolas,' Didier said.

Luc was a big man with big hands, two moustaches and an arsenal of withering looks at his disposal. 'You think a guy from Digne–les–Bains, a place where the biggest excitement of the day is when the Train des Pignes from Nice pulls in, you think that guy has a better sound than Ron Carter? Or Dave Holland? Or George Mraz?'

'Yes.' Didier raised his glass. 'Santé.' He took a long,

draining pull. 'Everybody's got to come from somewhere and anyway, Clovis works out of New York these days.'

Luc turned to Darac. 'Captain Brainbox? Tell them.'

'Nicolas does have a beautiful sound. And more besides.'

Luc seemed to regret having placed his trust in a mere guitarist. 'Of course he does but that's *not* what I asked...' He looked distracted, suddenly. Something at the back of the room had caught his eye. 'Darac? Over by the entrance.'

He saw the large figure of Ridge Clay and as their eyes met, the big man beckoned him discreetly to join him. It was difficult to assess the degree of urgency or seriousness of any issue that was on Ridge's mind; his dignified and grave bearing tended to lend weight to even the most inconsequential of things. But whenever he appeared like this, it usually signified that one or more of the good citizens of Nice had got themselves killed and Darac was needed.

As being called away on cases went with the territory, Darac was used to having his evenings at the Blue Devil cut short. On more than one occasion, he had been in the middle of playing a number with the DMQ at the time. Tonight, though, was something of a first. All he had done was buy a round of drinks, hand them out and sit down. So much for the efficacy of observing the sacraments.

'Guys, it looks as if...' It was only then that Darac noticed the woman standing in Ridge's shadow. Frankie's appearances at the club were rare occurrences in themselves. Frankie wearing an expression to match Ridge's was rarer still. 'Excuse me.'

The conversation at the table went on hold as Darac picked his way through the crowd towards her. Two minutes later, as Pascal kept a weather eye out for the "parking Nazis," the pair got into the back seat of her car and, her head on his shoulder, began talking through a slow-burning situation that had come to a head in the past hour.

'Why didn't you tell me this before?' he whispered, her hair tickling his chin. 'Sorry, sweetie. Go on.'

'I didn't want...' She took a deep breath. 'I didn't want to mention something that might have just resolved itself in time.'

'I can see that. Completely.' He felt her shudder, slightly. 'Hey, hey, come on.'

Pascal rapped on the nearside wing.

'We should move on.' Frankie sat up. 'Drive away now, I mean.'

'Listen, we established some time ago that you're a better driver than me, right? But this evening? No, no, no. I'm driving.'

'To the airport?' She put on her seatbelt. 'It's less than 10 kilometres.'

'Doesn't matter how far it is.'

'Five months ago, I drove there with my eyes practically shut after I'd been on duty for 36 straight hours.'

Arguing with Frankie, Darac knew, was only stiffening her resolve to drive but he felt he'd earned another play. 'Frankie, five months ago you hadn't just learned that your father is in hospital fighting for his life.'

Another rap. Darac opened his door a crack.

'I know you two could tell those lovely people you're working on a case,' Pascal said. 'But I don't want you to have to say nothing to nobody, you know?'

'Thanks, man. We're just leaving.'

★   ★   ★

Frankie did drive to the airport but Darac stayed with her and much was said as they waited for her flight to Geneva to be called. Just before she headed off, an update from her mother, Calista, had provided more detail on the heart attack that had propelled husband Benjamin into the I.C.U. Major surgery was on the cards. But there were concerns. Grave ones.

As they parted, Darac could feel a world of emotion in Frankie's kisses, her eyes, her whole body. She did love her father, he knew. But there was something else here, he sensed. Another problem, quite different.

He watched her walk away.

Was there another problem? I've been a flic too long, he thought to himself – *that's* the problem. This isn't a criminal case, for God's sake. So yes, Frankie speaks more warmly about her paternal grandfather than she does of Benjamin. She absolutely adored that old man. And her grandmother, too – something of a role model to her. But what of it? It looks as if her father may be on his death bed and the guy is only in his early seventies. How do you expect her to react? And apart from its own payload of meaning, perhaps the situation with Benjamin has brought the loss of her beloved grandparents back to her. Or perhaps it's the ones you love less that you might miss most – the relationships that could no longer be healed. And what if... Ai, ai, ai... Enough!

Driving Frankie's car back into the city, Darac's thoughts turned to his own encounters with Mama and Papa Lejeune. He hadn't been sure what to make of the pair from the first. Their Jewishness was something that exercised him. Perhaps it was a conscious reaction to the stereotype, but Ben and 'Lisie' Lejeune seemed so completely its opposite, Darac had momentarily entertained the idea that they weren't Jewish at all. Before she had moved to Vice, Frankie had worked virtually every shift side by side with Darac and on a stake-out one long, winter night, the notion had come back to him.

'Frankie, have you heard the one about the Jewish mother and the boa constrictor?'

'As in, "What's the difference between them?" At a guess.'

They chorused the punch line together: "A boa constrictor will let go eventually."

'Uh-huh,' Frankie had said, nodding. 'And what kind of thinking would you say lies behind that gag, Paul?'

'Clichéd, racist, pig-ignorant thinking?' he replied. 'At a guess.'

'Ah, Paul...' As if charmed by his contrition, she smiled but it quickly disappeared. 'No! It's the thinking that comes from long and bitter experience. *But...*'

'You have to be Jewish to voice it?'

'It helps.'

If there had been any lingering doubt in Darac's mind, Frankie expunged it the following day by bringing in the Lejeune family tree to show him. With branches of the clan in virtually every country on the planet, French-born Benjamin and Calista's immediate heritage was traceable just three generations back to Jewish communities in Greece and Egypt. Darac's first observation had been a banal one.

'I can see where you get your colouring from.'

'That and my love of moussaka. And pyramids.'

'Point taken.'

Frankie's parents had been happily resident in the city of Geneva for the past twenty years. While the demands they made on Frankie were few, a point he had at first found refreshing, when balanced against other factors, he became less sure. How proud were the pair of Frankie's achievements in her chosen métier? How proud were they of her as a person? What value did they place on her thoughts and opinions? Now that he knew them better, he still didn't fully know the answers to these questions.

What they had made of the break-up of her marriage with Christophe was, fortunately, less of a mystery. It transpired that they hadn't liked the man from the start and were pleased to see the back of him. The jury, it seemed, was still out on his own union with Frankie but as long as she didn't mind that, then of course neither did he.

If circumstances had been different, Darac would have enjoyed his drive along the Promenade des Anglais. With darkness having fallen, the Baie des Anges's sparkling azure had morphed through ever-deepening shades of purple into an infinite, Mark Rothko-like blur and it was a progression he loved.

Stopping at a red light by the *Centre Universitaire Méditerranéen*, he took a mental snapshot of life on the promenade itself. Night-blooming girls; boys on the make; couples of all ages, some arm in arm, some arguing the toss; joggers, cyclists, rollerbladers, Segway riders. And there was another category of promenader, a group whose appearance at this hour frequently surprised visitors of an Anglo-Saxon persuasion: young children. Darac's eye fell on a little boy who appeared to be out with his grandparents. Every so often, the youngster would totter away from them only to return and set off once more, each time venturing further until grand-mère had had enough and called him sharply back to her side. After no more than a few paces, the boy's penchant for exploration was already overcoming his instincts for survival and the cycle began all over again.

Reflecting that the kid might make a great jazz musician one day, Darac pulled away and with the turn to Gambetta approaching, he was soon passing the scene of his busking triumph with Armani – a bitter-sweet triumph as it had turned out. But who could have predicted that the thing would have gone to the man's head? And that Darac's name would have become mud with everyone at the Caserne as a result? With the threat of further off-key performances hanging over the place, Agnès had instructed him to have a quiet word with the atonal assassin.

'And shatter the man's illusions?'

'Yes,' Agnès had replied.

It was a daunting task and not just because few words with Armani were ever quiet. By Jean Jaurès, Darac was still wondering how to approach the problem when he felt a throb against his chest. He reached into his breast pocket and angled the phone.

Paul, looks as if they're going to operate tomorrow. All love, F

10.41 PM

Following a drinks party and a three-course dinner with wine, introductory classes at the Villa des Pinales tended to be a tricky call for students and tutors alike – even for those who hadn't travelled far on the day. But contrary to Fault Finder General Laurent Salins's much-stated observation, the "powers that be" had indeed thought things through. The drinks party was designed as an ice breaker pure and simple, not a means of rendering the clients legless before dinner. If it had been, twice the amount of time would have been allocated and a more convivial spot chosen. And dinner itself, always of gourmet quality but light enough to give students a fighting chance of staying awake afterwards, was another well-conceived option.

Astrid's introductory class had gone well. There were

signs that one of a pair of middle-aged sisters, Claudine Bonnet, might prove to be hard work but the students were a keen bunch and that was all Astrid needed to give them a rewarding time. Now the final gig of the day beckoned – a mingle in purdah with her fellow smokers. Astrid was in need of her wind-down fag.

*   *   *

'Lovely evening,' Jérôme Calon said, hovering in front of the bench. 'May I join you?'

Englishman Alan Davies blew smoke away to the side and gestured the man to sit. 'Of course.'

'Couldn't trouble you for a light?'

The pair went into an illuminated huddle as Davies produced a match.

'Thank you.' Calon sat back and, looking especially contented with life, took an almost childishly shallow pull on his *Marlboro Gold*. 'That's better.'

'Your wife not joining you?' Davies smiled, if not unkindly, then at least knowingly.

'Uh, no.' Another shallow puff. 'Marcie doesn't smoke.' His eyes began to water. 'What are you on?'

'On? Oh, *Camels*. It was the packet design that attracted me when I was a youngster. Stuck with them ever since.'

'I'm a Marlboro man.'

'Hmm.' Davies pursed his lips. 'Listen, Jérôme, isn't it? I'm afraid I was rude to your wife earlier. At the drinks party. Over the issue of Monsieur Gérard Urquelle and the cat. The cat who shat. In his garden. Monsieur Urquelle's – not the cat's.'

Calon waved the thought away. 'Oh, don't worry, don't worry..?'

'Alan.'

'Alan, yes. Marcie, bless her, rubs a lot of people up the wrong way. She's a very passionate woman, you see.' He took a deeper drag and coughed. 'Well, you saw.'

'Oh yes, indeed.'

'And cruelty to animals, it just... drives her wild. I worry, sometimes.'

'Uh-huh?'

'Cruelty to people, though?' He stared into space. 'That doesn't seem to worry her quite so much.'

As if it conferred a degree of protection against such a person, Davies took in a deep lungful of smoke. 'Enjoyable class?'

'What? Oh, yes. Croix certainly knows his stuff. We'll be tasting some interesting things tomorrow. You?'

'I think it's going to be wonderful. And not just because I'm madly in love with Mademoiselle Astrid Pireque. Did you notice her shoes? Very funny. And *brilliantly* painted.'

Calon's ears pricked up. 'Are you?'

'Am I what?'

'In love with her?'

Davies found Calon's concern difficult to take seriously. 'No, no, I was just...' Calon's expression hadn't changed. 'I do think she's lovely but no, I'm not in love with her. It's just my English exaggeration humour thing coming through. Even after all these years.'

'Ah.'

*   *   *

'Not much of a view, Laurent, if I may?' Urquelle said, indicating the scene with an insouciant waft of his cigarette hand. 'Still, I suppose that's the point.'

Laurent Salins took a deep pull on his *Gauloise*.

'The point?' he gave a disdainful snort. 'So it's alright for non-smokers to be given the terrace?' He gave a back-header in its general direction. 'With light flooding cheerfully over the gardens, and beyond, a view over the city with what that bloke Davies would call the "Bay of Angels" as a backdrop. And our backdrop? The dubious charms of the Bay of Compost, a shed, couple of outhouses, and a line of recycling bins.'

Urquelle raised a brow. 'A poetic description.'

'I've done the odd creative writing course.'

'I can tell.'

'So what did you make of that so-called Sauvignon Blanc at dinner?'

'The Veil Creek?' Urquelle blew a little smoke. 'The Australian?'

Salins nodded.

'Wonderful, I thought. And did you spot its ABV?'

'Uh...' Salins clearly hadn't. Or perhaps he had no idea what "ABV" meant. 'What did *you* think of it?'

Urquelle's forehead creased as he took a pull. 'I thought it was very clever of them to be able to deliver that degree of fruit, acidity and weight at only 9.5 %'

'*That's* why it didn't taste of anything.'

'It was a success, I thought. Typical Malcolm McDevitt approach to winemaking. Have you tried his Shiraz-Cala-trava blend? There were bottles in the bar, I noticed.'

'Think I might have done. Yes, I have. Good. Very good,'

'Ripe. Gorgeous.' He contemplated the lit end of his cigarette. 'Rather like Lydia Félix, don't you think?'

Salins took refuge in his *Gauloise* while he thought about it. 'Who?'

'Lydia Félix. The woman with whom I sat at dinner. The

woman you could hardly keep your eyes off. The woman you watched walk with me all the way over to the Salle des Rêves for our session with Mademoiselle Hamada when your classroom for Mathieu Croix is literally on the opposite side of the building.'

'I got lost. There's no one to tell you anything here.'

Urquelle leaned into him. 'Tell you what, Laurent. Why don't I go and get a bottle of the Shiraz-Calatrava and we'll split it? Here and now. A few glasses of wine, a few smokes. And proper, unfiltered smokes, too. A *Gauloise* man and a *Gitanes* man getting to know each other better.'

Salins seemed to revive at the idea. 'Why not?'

'One reason why not would be that there's no wine maker named Malcolm Whatever-it-was I said, no blend featuring Shiraz and *Calatrava* who's an architect, by the way, not a variety of grape.'

Even in the half-light, Salins's ruddy complexion took on a ruddier hue. 'So I don't know much about wine!' He stood. 'That's why I came on the course, you patronising... Piss off!'

Urquelle's eyes stayed on Salins as he stomped away and Astrid noticed this as she arrived on the scene. It was a look she associated with birds of prey. Alert. Dispassionate. Calculating. If the odious Monsieur Salins had been a mouse, she judged he might have had about three more seconds to live.

Checking the congregation for a familiar face, she caught Alan Davies's eye and the two exchanged smiles. But it was Urquelle who spoke up.

'Good evening, Mademoiselle Pireque.'

I'm not going to be anybody's bloody mouse. 'Evening, Monsieur Urquelle. How is your wife, these days?'

He glanced around quickly before answering. 'Vivienne is on excellent form, thank you, and she asked me to make sure I gave you her very best regards.'

'And mine to her.' Go for it. It could be interesting. Damned if she was going to cosy up alongside him, Astrid drew up a chair, produced a tobacco tin and began rolling a cigarette. 'Is she still painting?'

'A little,' he said, stubbing out his own in the ashtray provided. 'She mainly throws pots these days.' He gave it his most winning smile. 'Not one has hit me yet!'

Astrid fought a powerful impulse to say "Pity." 'Does she sell many?'

'Uh... Yes, I believe so. I'm afraid I'm away on business so often, I sometimes lose track of what's going on at home. Shamefully.'

'What do you do?' Astrid already knew this but she was intrigued to hear what Urquelle would say. 'If you don't mind me asking?'

'Not at all. I'm in the jewellery business. Spend most of my life representing the company at trade shows. Europe and the Middle East, mainly. But beyond, sometimes.'

Should I press him? Let him think I remembered his name? Tackle the thing head on? No. Wait for Elie, tomorrow. You don't know anything. 'Do you get to spend time in the places you visit?' She lit up. 'Or is it all work?'

'Usually it's just fly in, set up, *yadda yadda yadda,* take down, fly out. Not as glamorous as you would think, I'm afraid.'

Flogging stuff seldom is glamorous, she thought. 'Shame.'

'Indeed.' Lowering his gaze, Urquelle produced his pen and began absently tapping it against the corner of his mouth. The inscription on its barrel would have been legible to Astrid had she looked closely at it. But it was where Urquelle was looking that exercised her. He was staring at her feet. 'That's it,' he said, using the pen as an aerial exclamation mark. 'Or I think it is.' Second thoughts induced more tapping. 'No, I'm right. Salvador Dali. Didn't he paint a pair of shoes like that?'

'All my ideas are derived from other people,' Astrid said, relieved that Urquelle had finally raised his eyes.

'I'm sure not.'

'She took a long toke on her roll-up. 'Very nice car you drive, by the way.'

'You think so? Then I must take you for a ride in it.' Mugging shame, he slapped his wrist. 'Do excuse me. Or *you* can take the wheel, of course.'

'Thanks but I have no desire to do either. It just took my eye as an object when I saw you arrive earlier. What make is it?'

He looked nonplussed for a moment. 'Oh, it's a 1957 Jaguar. XK 120. You saw me arrive?'

He doesn't like that. 'Oh, yes. You kindly offered to carry your Russian lady friend's bags in. One of Mathieu's students, I think.'

'She's not my... Yes, she is taking the wine course, I believe.'

But why doesn't he like it? It couldn't be that Urquelle was trying to keep the connection between him and Thea secret. At the drinks party, the pair had stood together in plain sight. But not everyone, Astrid realised, was as sharp-eyed as she was. Not everyone would have had read their body language so clearly.

'Listen, mademoiselle, I'm going to be awfully forward here and if the suggestion I'm going to make is of no interest to you, please just say.'

Nothing could be surer, you slimy arsehole. 'Yes?'

'My car, as you'll probably have guessed, is quite my pride and joy.' He frowned. 'Next to Vivienne, of course.'

You slimy lying arsehole. 'Of course.'

'I won the *Concours d'Élégance* at *Provence Retro d'Auto* in 2004 and 2005 with her. It was a particular pleasure because she was little more than a rusted heap when I began restoring her. I did everything myself and my collection of photographs illustrating each stage of the process is, I think, second to none – certainly in France. What I do *not* have, though, is a painting of her as she is now. A portrait, if you like.'

Astrid stared at him.

'I know from Vivienne just how highly you are rated. I would consider it—'

'Sorry. I don't take commissions.'

'Uh-huh,' he said, taken aback, and not a little put out. 'Right.'

He's *so* not used to rejection. 'It's against the rules.'

'But, between us, quite honestly... who would know?'

Telling. 'Me, for one.'

'I see... Well, this has been a most pleasant tête-à-tête but if you'll excuse me?' He stood. 'I have some messages to send before I turn in.'

'Of course. Good night.'

Happy to have put a flea in the man's ear, Astrid toked away contentedly on her roll-up until she, too, judged it time to turn in. She walked back into the building with Alan Davies.

'*I* used to teach, Astrid,' he said.

'You taught Astrid and you lived to tell the tale? *Chapeau*!'

He laughed. 'I meant that I, too, used to teach. English, in my case. And when introducing a new grammar rule, I would often tell my students: "There are absolutely no exceptions to this" to help them get the thing into their heads. Only later on would I give them the bad news.'

Astrid essayed an English-accented French accent: 'You remember what I said about never sounding the letter *e* at the ends of words? Well, actually...'

Davies grinned as he completed the thought. ' "... guess what? *Sometimes*, you do." Exactly. I wondered if I'd detected the same principle at work when you told us earlier that if we learned to draw accurately a sphere, a cone and a cylinder, we would be able to render every single entity in nature.'

'Ah, no,' she said, straight-faced. 'That's one rule to which there really are no exceptions.'

He summoned the lift and the doors opened immediately. 'None, eh? Interesting.'

'And if I can't fit into this thing, it will be because my nose has grown too long.'

'Excellent!' He pressed for the first floor. 'And you're on the..?'

'Top. Servants' quarters.'

Nothing happened.

'It's thinking about it,' Astrid said. 'Does that sometimes. Give it a reminder.'

'A lift with a mind of its own?' Davies glanced at the manufacturer's nameplate as he pressed again. 'French, wouldn't you just know? Sorry if that offends.'

'Only half-French, actually. Just enough to *sooo* take offence.'

'Ha! And what's the other half?'

'Finnish. My mother's from Helsinki.'

The pair continued in the same light vein as the lift decided to put in a shift after all. Astrid could sense that she was quite a hit with retired teacher Mister Alan Davies. She also sensed that he was a true gentleman.

'You chatted with Gérard Urquelle, I noticed.'

What's coming now? 'Yes, I did.'

'Do you know who he is?'

Someone who completely creeps me out. 'Someone with a vintage sports car. A lovely thing. Do you know him, then?'

'Not yet,' Davies said, as he stepped out on to his floor. 'But I hope to.'

'Ah.'

'Enjoyed this evening very much, Astrid. Looking forward to tomorrow.'

'No exceptions on that one.'

The door closed. "Not yet," Alan had said. " But I hope to." Hope to *what*? Chat to Urquelle about the car, as she had? Or kill him, as Elie had once contemplated? On balance, she favoured the former but who knew? 'All will become clear,' she said aloud, reprising one of Darac's often-used lines.

All was quiet on the top floor but as Astrid went to close her room door, she heard the sound of a creaking floorboard out in the hall. Zoë had been known to enjoy a late-night chat *tous-les-deux*, and Matthieu Croix was fond of sharing choice nightcaps with his fellow tutors, another gig Astrid was usually up for. But feeling bushed, she hesitated and when her mobile throbbed in her bag, it made her mind up for her. She may be urgently needed on a case. Or perhaps her boyfriend was sending her something he'd just finished. Or the filmmaker had finally got his act...

Tridi, just picked up your message. Will tell you everything about G.U. tomorrow.

I'll see your sloppy kisses and raise you a hug, Elie

Had the text come in even a second later, Astrid would

have craned her neck around the doorframe to see who was there. Realising that person might still be in view, she took a look anyway and saw a broad back disappearing around the corner towards the service stairs. She had never seen Bruno or the night security man moving that quickly. It was most likely one of the students but which? Someone scared of lifts, perhaps. She made a mental note to check out who was occupying the few rooms allocated to non-staff on the floor.

She locked her door, quickly committed the image of the retreating back to a page in her sketchbook and, kicking off her bare-feet shoes to reveal the real thing, padded into the bathroom.

★   ★   ★

In a room on the floor below, Laurent Salins unlaced his shoes and slipped a mobile out of his trouser pocket.

'Hello?' He listened. 'I have, yes but I think I've signed up for the wrong course.' As the caller continued, Salins unbuttoned his trousers, let them fall and adjusted the hang of his balls. 'Indeed, but you know what the man said who jumped off the Eiffel Tower? So far, so good.'

11.49 PM

As bedtime reading went, Palais Masséna's guide for trainee sales staff, the *Induction Course Handbook,* may have left a lot to be desired but for the past half-hour, Zena had hung on its every word. Her motivation was tomorrow's induction course exam in which she would have to "demonstrate a working knowledge of the store's protocols and practices." The exam had been variously described to her as "a formality," "a gimme," and "piss simple." One instructor had told her that she had already done the hard part in being accepted as a trainee in the first place. "The initial interview," she had said, "That's where the real weeding-out goes on."

Zena wondered if *any* candidates had failed the course over the years. The handbook, replete with stats on a number of topics, was mute on that point. But the odds were stacked in Zena's favour, anyway. The 70% pass mark was arrived at by combining scores from a written paper and a practical test. She was confident that even if she forgot most of what she'd learned and thus performed poorly in the written part, her bright, savvy personality would more than compensate for it in the practical. Nailing a role play in which she would have to serve "a difficult customer" held no fears for Zena. Difficult customer? As she turned off her bedside light, she laughed at the thought.

THURSDAY 15th September

It was 24 years almost to the day since Noëmi had attended *École Maternelle* as a *grand*. She remembered little about it, but she knew she had been super excited. Half-walking, half-skipping, six year-old Emma was clearly cut from the same cloth. 'We're here, *maman!*' she said, tugging at Noëmi's hand. 'I go in by myself, now.'

'First, we have to see Albert.'

Greeting mother and daughter as if they were both children, an approach to which many of Noëmi's friends objected but which she judged harmless, the security man checked them through into the scene of contrasting emotions that was *Maternelle Niel's* outdoor play area. 'My dears,' Albert had declared. '*La Rentrée* is always like this.'

Waving to a group of girls, Emma tried once again to extricate herself from her mother. Noëmi held on tight. 'We grown-ups kiss each other goodbye, remember?'

Emma's cred momentarily in shreds, she gave a little jump and declared, 'I wasn't ready!'

Kisses of parting were exchanged.

'Shall I call you Noëmi, now, *maman?*'

'No.'

'Alright!'

'Go and join your friends, darling.'

No second invitation was needed. Noëmi watched Emma's *Tangled* backpack shrink into the distance as Emma ran to her friends.

'Hey, Noëmi!'

She spent the next few minutes with a group of her own friends. At the end of it, she set off to work feeling quite nauseous but buoyed by the consensus view that she looked "blooming."

When she arrived at work, the consensus was that she looked awful.

8.58 AM

The HR person in charge had become something of a favourite of Zena's. A sweet-natured woman with a relaxed manner and a disarming propensity to stress random words in her sentences, she had smiled at each trainee in turn as they had entered the classroom. Nevertheless, the atmosphere had become surprisingly tense by the time her introductory talk neared its conclusion.

'So just *to* sum up, you've all done very well to reach this stage and as long as the overall pass mark *is* achieved, you will be joining us as full-time members of staff *in* the positions you applied for.' Big smile. 'Here at Palais Masséna, *our* standards are very high, but the purpose of this written paper is to demonstrate *to* us what you have learned, not to *catch* you out. Everyone will make a make a mistake *at* some stage. From time *to* time, I myself do. What is important *from* managers, office staff, sales assistants, goods-in and cleaning crews, for all *of* our family in fact, is knowing how to react to, and how *to* rectify those mistakes. And that will be a focus of our practical test this afternoon.' She looked around the room. 'What a lot of worried faces!' Another big smile. 'There's no need, honestly. You may turn over your papers.'

Zena may never have worked in retail – not that the HR department were aware of that fact – but she had passed a good many exams in her young life. The first rule she had learned was to follow any instructions given in the rubric to the letter, then to ensure that she gave answers to the questions posed, not to those that could have been.

She turned over the paper and noted that all questions were to be answered. No ranking issues. Good. She began reading through the first one.

Describe the process by which credit and debit card transactions...

9.31 PM

Eight kilometres to the north, the day's classes were getting under way at the Villa des Pinales: Astrid was leading her troupe of artists along the joggers' paradise that was the Canal de la Vésubie; Mathieu Croix was en route to the Salle de Bacchus where his trainee wine experts were waiting for him; and characteristically, Zoë Hamada was already ahead of the game in the Salle des Rêves. Seated in pairs, her students, equally characteristically, were in an upbeat mood.

'First,' Zoë said, 'I hope everyone remembered to forgo putting on perfume this morning?' She made a show of scanning the room for culprits. 'Come on, at least one person always forgets.' Zoë's surprise turned into astonishment. 'No one? You are the first group *ever* to do that!' She treated the class to a full-on beam. 'Gold star!'

Grins. One or two handshakes. Asides. The class was as pleased with itself as they were with Zoë.

'So with my guidance, today each one of you is going to devise *and* produce her own,' she indicated Gérard Urquelle, 'or *his* own, unique, signature scent. Are you all up for that?' If the class had responded with a collective "Yeah!"

111

it wouldn't have seemed out of place but many made their feelings known anyway. A solitary hand went up.

'Yes, Gérard?'

'Just to clarify – unless I go *very* much off-course, the perfume I make won't be for me. It will be a gift. For a lady.'

Parfumier Zoë Hamada certainly knew her audiences, but so did seasoned jewellery salesman Gérard Urquelle. Working like a charm, his "clarification" extracted a collective "Aah" from most of his fellow students. Zoë greeted the sentiment less enthusiastically.

'I hope you know the lady in question well?'

Urquelle smiled. 'I think so.'

Sitting next to him, Lydia Félix tried not to blush.

'Then tailoring a scent to her particular personality should at least be possible.' Zoë turned to the whole group. 'OK, let's begin but first, here's what my former boss used to refer to as an "interesting point to ponder." Every single day of the year, somewhere in the world, a commercial perfume house launches a new product. These scents, each of which has been developed in a sophisticated lab, may have gone through ten, a hundred or even several hundred versions before being judged ready to hit the market place. But does that mean that each of you, even after just one introductory class, could not produce something unique and wonderful today?' Heads shook. 'Exactly, no, it doesn't. And who knows? By the end of our sessions, one of you may have crafted a product with genuine commercial potential. You may even have on your hands what we in the industry call...' She picked out every face. 'A killer scent!'

The class members had little time to ponder that or any other point as Zoë instructed them to open the paper packets she had handed out earlier. A ripple of amused anticipation was soon running around the room.

'Yes, everyone, blindfolds! Put them on.' She indicated the door behind her. 'And when you have, I'm going to pop into my little kitchen there, briefly.' She watched as the class members put them on. 'Is that everyone? Good. Back in just a moment.' She returned carrying a tray of plastic food containers and, explaining that she had made them all a little additional breakfast, set one down in front of each student. 'Now until I ask you to take them off, keep your blindfolds on, alright? No cheating.'

As if auditioning for the role of class clown, Monique, the woman Urquelle regarded as a likely substitute should things not work out with Lydia, stretched herself into an awkward position at her desk.

'I can se-ee you, Monique,' Zoë trilled, lifting the mood in the room a further notch or two.

'Crick in my neck. Sorry.'

Zoë clicked her tongue. 'You fibber! She's trying to peep under her blindfold, everyone!'

Chuckles. Calls for Monique to be sent to the naughty step. And worse.

'I'll let you off with a warning, this time.' Having got off to such a good start, Zoë couldn't help beaming at the class even though no one could see her. 'OK. When I say "now" and keeping your blindfolds *on,* I'd like you to click the lids off the boxes I set down in front of you. And then, I want you to take a good deep smell of the lovely treat I prepared. Ready?'

They were ready.

'Now.'

Following a fusillade of clicks, the sound of ten pairs of sniffing nostrils made no more than a gentle susurrating sound in the room. But there was nothing gentle about the reaction that followed.

Once again, Zoë scanned every face. 'Come on, that wasn't so bad, was it? In fact, many of you rather liked it, I can see. Yes, why not, Anne-Marie, go in for a second hit... OK, let's start on the back row and work our way forward. Carolina – what did I prepare for you?'

'Hard-boiled eggs?'

'Interesting. Kelly?'

'*Rotten* eggs. Disgusting!'

A few chorused their agreement.

'Would I do that to you? No, no. Lydia?'

'Hard-boiled eggs, yes. With perhaps just a dash of *moutarde de Meaux*?'

'*Very* precise. I'm going to have look to my laurels. Gérard?'

He grinned. 'Actually, although I'm loath to say this in front of all you ladies, I think it smells like something Monsieur Le Pétomane might have offered up in his time.'

The room hushed a little. The man may have misjudged his ladies.

'I've lowered the tone. I'm awfully sorry.'

'No, no,' Zoë said, 'It's an absolutely valid observation. There's nothing prissy about the perfumer's art, as you'll see when we sample some of the chemical compounds known as aldehydes used in our industry – including one rather celebrated example that smells strongly of...' She gave it a tension-building beat. 'Bitter almonds.'

A frisson ran around the room like a collective shiver. 'Next we have... Cinzia. Verdict?'

'Boiled eggs, definitely. Not chicken eggs, perhaps. Duck?'

Zoë completed the round-up and then instructed the class to remove their blindfolds. Sitting under each nose was a bowl of pink slush.

Gasps of astonishment... Double takes... More sniffing...

'Not what you were expecting? I can assure you that no chicken, goose, or other fowl was involved in creating that pronounced ovine smell you all so correctly detected.' On the bench behind her were two large bowls covered by a cloth. 'So what ingredients do you think I combined to create your eggy cocktails?' She grasped the cloths in the manner of a conjurer poised to make a reveal. 'Anyone?'

'Something and food colouring?' Monique said, amused at her wit.

Zoë nodded. 'You're half right. It's actually something. And something else.'

Laughter.

Zoë ripped away the cloths and once again, the reaction was exactly as she had hoped. 'You can see that one bowl contains lovely, sweet, fruity strawberries; the other, crushed ice. So how did I turn them into eggs?' She gave it a beat. 'I shooshed them together.' She produced a hand blender to back up her story. 'But what did that do in detail? The answer, as always, can be found in chemistry. Initially, the fruit released its sweeter-smelling compounds but as the mixture cooled, that reaction slowed down until ultimately, only one group of compounds, normally undetectable in strawberries, remained active: those compounds containing...?' She looked expectantly around the class. 'What? Anyone? Yes, Lydia?'

'Sulphur?'

Zoë beamed. 'Go to the top of the class. Yes, sulphur, is right.'

Lydia smiled modestly at Urquelle who returned it with what appeared to be genuine appreciation. Monique looked less impressed.

Zoë continued with the explanation as she began taking

trays of vials from under the bench and setting them out on top. 'And what does this, I hope, fun demonstration suggest? That while the chemical properties of natural substances may be fixed, their olfactory performance in any given situation depends on a range of other factors, in this case – temperature. And this is one reason scents behave differently on our skins as they warm up.'

The point of the exercise suddenly clear to all, a range of nods, smiles and approving asides accompanied Zoë as she buzzed busily around the room collecting up the slush bowls. At their paired desk, Urquelle leaned in close to Lydia and whispered, 'I would love to warm up on *your* skin.'

Lydia seemed both excited at the prospect and perplexed. 'Géri, after you came in from the garden last night, I thought you said that Monsieur—'

'I'm working on it.'

★ ★ ★

In the Salle de Bacchus, the celebrated bon viveur Mathieu Croix had lined up his students as if they were soldiers on parade and he, their somewhat eccentric commanding officer. Each was sitting at a poseur table bearing a quart-ca-rafe containing a couple of mouthfuls of almost purple liquid, a demi-carafe of clear liquid, an empty glass, a box of tissues, and a bowl for spat-out samplings.

'By the close of our final session tomorrow evening, you are going to know the wines we shall be tasting as well as you know your most intimate friends. Better, indeed, because every quality, every nuance, however surprising or hidden, will have been revealed to you.'

Marcie Calon smiled at those around her as if her pleasure in the moment somehow validated it for them, as well.

'*Mesdames et Messieurs,* please pick up your wine glasses.'

Slightly out of step with the others, Laurent Salins did as he was instructed.

'Last evening, using flavoured water, we learned how to pour liquid into a glass intended for sampling. We learned how to assess its colour, its perfume, and most importantly, we learned how to assess its taste. So now, we are going to turn, *at last,* I hear you say...' He treated the troops to a knowing grin. Most responded accordingly. '... to the real thing and put what we learned into action.'

Around the room, mouthfuls of the purple nectar were poured, glasses were tilted against the light, twirled from the stem, noses inserted, and the slurp, gulp and spit of actually tasting the stuff undertaken.

'Excellent. Truly excellent. And now I want to hear your verdicts and I'm going to make a list of them. Starting with...' Mathieu glanced at his class plan. 'Jérôme. What do you detect?'

A guilty man under cross-examination had scarcely looked so rattled. 'Uh...' A glance at wife Marcie failed to deliver the hoped-for coaching. 'I detect... well, fruit.' Mathieu nodded emphatically as he jotted down the comment. Encouraged, Jérôme ventured further. '*Berry* fruits, in fact. Berry fruits and...'

'Yes?'

'Vanilla.'

'Excellent work! Uh... Marcia?'

'Well, hedgerow fruits, obviously. And vanilla. But there's something more savoury here, isn't there?'

Mathieu looked at her over his glasses. 'And what might that be?'

She took another sniff. 'Is it... tobacco?'

'Ah! Very, *very* interesting.'

Marcia sat back, as proud as Punch with a new slapstick. 'Laurent, now.'

'The same as the others, really. But for a red wine, it doesn't have much body, does it? It's light. Sweet tasting, almost. Low-ish ABV, I would say. Despite the colour.'

'Hmm. Another interesting observation. And... you, Thea?'

Whether it was being put on the spot, or being made to listen to the opinions of people for whom she clearly had little regard, or some other, unknowable attack on her wellbeing, it seemed Thea had little interest in playing Mathieu's game.

'All or none of the above,' she said. 'Maybe Italian? I don't know.'

'Ri–ight. Let's hear from... Damien.'

Unimpressed by Thea's contribution, the man added his own without hesitation and when all the verdicts were in, Mathieu read out the jury's findings. 'So, as a group, you detected: hedgerow fruits...'

At her poseur table, Marcia smiled at Mathieu's use of the term she had used.

Mathieu continued: 'Hedgerow fruits times two, and vanilla... ditto tobacco; more hedgerow fruits; chocolate; *stone* fruits; coffee; more tobacco; vanilla again; violets; more chocolate; more stone fruits; and last but not least, a second call for violets.'

Mathieu set down the list and, with a distinctly theatrical flourish, went into his tasting ritual. All eyes were upon him and behind those stares, was there a single student who didn't long to have their own assessment corroborated by a man whose syndicated columns were read all over the country?

'I tell you what *I* detect,' Mathieu said, producing a supermarket Tetra Pak from under his bench. 'I detect *this*. Rather tasty, you all thought. It's a cocktail of cranberry, grape and blackberry juice. Very low sugar. I get it in Monop'.'

Thea clapped her hands in glee but she was all alone in her merriment.

'Let me get this straight,' Salins said, already looking as if he was going to ask Elie Tiron for a refund. 'You mean what we tasted wasn't wine at all? You told us it was the real thing.'

A wave of discontent breaking in the room looked set to carry the majority away but if Mathieu felt any shame over his deception, it didn't show. Instead, he went on the offensive. 'Because I told you all to raise your wineglasses? That didn't mean they contained wine. And neither did I say that the thing in them was real *wine*, did I? And although you, Laurent, didn't go as far as to make *quite* that point in your assessment, you were the only one with the sensitivity *and* honesty to note the non-winelike lightness of the liquid in your mouth.'

Salins gave Marcia a look but he would have to wait to flaunt his newly won status. Her lips set in an angry pucker, she was staring at the ceiling, counting, by the look of it, to somewhere well beyond ten.

The mood in the room continued to be hostile.

'Now you may all be wondering why I, Mathieu Croix, so celebrated for what some perceive to be the fanciful exactitude of my descriptions of wine – so much so indeed that I am frequently lampooned for it on TV and in the pages of *Le Canard Enchaîné* and *Charlie Hebdo* – why am *I* of all people stressing the value of straight-talking and honesty? Because, my good friends, without it, you will get absolutely nothing from this course and you will have wasted your money and my time in signing up for it.'

The class, which only moments before had been on the

verge of mutiny, seemed somehow reassured, even strangely galvanised, by these few words. Judging the moment to be right, the great man nodded towards the doorway and a posse of kitchen staff entered carrying trays laden with wine bottles.

'Now the storm is happily behind us, and our ship of discovery is set fair for the voyage ahead, should anyone have decided that they no longer wish to come aboard with the rest of us...' He looked directly at Marcia, her gaze now returned from the ceiling. 'I would deeply regret it though I would of course understand.'

As the waiters went about their well-grooved routine, class members exchanged questioning looks with one another and, as had happened on all previous occasions, every one of them stayed put.

'Thank you,' Mathieu said, essaying humility. 'Now, we shall begin.'

* * *

As promised, "Sherpa" Lionel had transported the art class's equipment and materials to the canal side, set it all down in a pleasantly shaded corner, and then stood guard while he waited for Astrid and the party to appear along the path.

'Alright, mademoiselle? I'll be back at 12.30 to pick up the stuff.'

'Thanks, Lio. See you then.'

Checking everything was in place, Astrid felt good to be back in a location whose sights, sounds and scents were not quite like anywhere else she knew. Not blessed with an especially acute sense of smell, she could nevertheless have identified the place with one sniff. Over the pervasive resinous tang of sun-warmed pines floated occasional top notes of sour, slow-moving water, decaying green waste, and musky garden shrubs.

Inevitably, it was the sights that excited her most. A gap in the trees served as a viewpoint over a panorama that would have captivated artists of any school at any time – a response shared by her students who had lined up at the spot immediately on arrival. For Astrid, the site's graphic potential didn't end there. Providing human interest, the first of what was sure to be a steady stream of joggers trickled past behind the group; and behind the path, the clotted conduit known as Le Canal de la Vésubie slid torpidly along like a conveyor belt made of sodden vegetation.

'Worth the stroll, huh?' Astrid said, finding a blank page in her sketchbook as she gathered the class together.

'Absolutely!' Babette Bonnet, said, leading the chorus. Fanning herself with a straw hat, her sister Claudine appeared to have other ideas on the matter. For the moment at least, she was keeping them to herself.

'So what do we see in front of us?' Astrid went on, selecting a sanguine Conté crayon from one of the many battered tins in her shoulder bag. 'We see landscape.' With the group gathered behind her, she began depicting the scene with such speed and control, it brought gasps. 'We see cityscape.' A few strokes and blurs of the crayon and Nice, quite unmistakably, began to appear on the page. 'And seascape.' There was the Baie des Anges, the Corsica ferry sailing off into the distance. 'In short, we have a view. And *what* a view.'

'We would have practically the same view from the Villa's terrace,' Claudine announced, earning a stare from her sister. 'Without having to traipse up here.'

Astrid worked on without a pause. 'You're right, Claudine – in the sense that there *is* slightly more elevation here. Another plus is the unique atmosphere this location has. But don't worry, after lunch, the terrace it shall be.'

'Bit late, then.'

'OK,' Astrid said, sailing on. 'We have a view. But what is that view made of? Revisiting what we were discussing last evening, we have volumes...' In Astrid's hand, the crayon worked its magic once more. 'We have straight and curved lines...' It did so again. Tones...' Ditto. 'And we have many different hues, too....' She opened another tin and set a palette of blues, reds and greens to work. 'Now, organising the complex interplays of these things into a coherent state- ment can seem daunting and that's why it's useful to simplify. Remember that everything we see in nature is a variation on just three essential forms.' Her eyes met Alan Davies's and they shared a smile. 'We have the sphere... the cone... and... the cylinder.' Once more, she executed her illustrations with effortless precision. 'Learn to master these three basic forms, and the whole world will be yours.'

Closing her notebook to an impromptu round of applause, Astrid smiled as she turned to face her audience. 'You have very good taste,' she said, earning a few laughs into the bargain but she had some serious points to make, too, and changed her expression to fit. 'What I just put down on paper was the quickest of impressions, a lightning sketch. But if my goal had been to render the scene before us as accurately as I could, what would I have done first?'

'*Looked* accurately at the scene?' Ralf Bassette said.

'Exactly, Ralf. "Look, look again, and look some more," an old tutor of mine used to say. Look *and* measure using the techniques we discussed last night. A final word before you get going. There's so much of visual interest along here, some of you may prefer not to tackle the panorama at all and I would be completely happy with that. It's up to you.

Set up where you feel most inspired. Use whatever medium you feel like using and, like an irritating little wasp, I'll keep buzzing around to see how you're getting on. Let's have a good one!'

As the group began to disperse, Alan Davies took another look at the view and, turning his back on it, set up his easel facing a far less spectacular subject: a modest little footbridge spanning the watercourse. Intrigued by his choice, Astrid decided to begin her rounds with him.

'That was super, Astrid.'

'Yes, it was, wasn't it?' She shrugged. 'One of these days I must learn to accept a compliment gracefully. Like you English.'

'We are by far the greatest exponents of self-deprecation on the planet – that's true,' he deadpanned. 'But seriously, don't change a thing, Astrid. It would spoil the fun.'

'Thank you.' She gave it a beat. 'There. Easier than I thought.' She gave a nod to the bridge. 'So – interesting choice of subject. I've drawn it several times, myself. And painted it. What's the attraction for you?'

'I like that repeating curlicue pattern on the wrought iron railings. I like the light and shade effects of the September sun on the foliage masses behind it, though capturing that looks challenging. But most of all, I love the ragged, clumpy surface of the water itself. Wouldn't think it had much of a connection to the lovely Vésubie, would you?'

'If you say so.'

'Still, I'm sure it's all realisable using nothing but our three old building block friends.'

Astrid grinned but, remembering another aspect of their conversation the previous evening, her thoughts turned to Elie and their planned get-together. A further text exchange had established a place and time: Elie's office before dinner.

She cast an eye around the location. With a couple of exceptions, everyone was setting up facing the panorama. No one was in earshot.

'You mentioned one of Zoë Hamada's students yesterday. Gérard Urquelle.'

'Did I?' Alan opened his haversack and took a box bearing a scene depicting the English Lakes on its lid. 'Oh, yes. I did.'

'You hoped to meet him, you said.'

He opened the box and took out a clutch of Conté pencils. 'Uh-huh.'

'Would you mind telling me why?'

'Not at all. It must be... yes, five years ago now that he played the starring role, as it were, in foiling the armed robbery of a shop over in Monaco.'

Pretend you've never heard this. 'Ah, yes?'

Alan's light, urbane countenance took on a whole other look. 'He managed the place, a jewellers'. To prevent his assistant being shot, he made a grab for the gunman's weapon but it went off in the struggle. Urquelle was injured, the assistant tragically killed, but so, happily, was the gunman – a walking piece of human garbage named Eddy Lopes.'

Pretend you're not used to hearing things like this. 'Oh, Lord. Did you... did you know this man, Lopes, then?'

'No, but the granddaughter of a friend of mine got to know him all too well. She was a dear girl but she'd always had problems.'

Astrid recalled the material she had dipped into in her room. Lopes, frequently homeless and a drug addict with a long history of mental illness, had had numerous problems of his own. 'I'm so sorry,' Astrid said, meaning it.

'After falling in with Lopes, the girl's problems got dramatically worse. Among other things, he prostituted her to keep them both in the drugs he'd introduced her to in the first place. After about a year of it, she died suddenly. An OD. My friend has been dying slowly ever since.'

'That's... Ah, there are no words for things like that.'

'I've got some. Lopes deserved to die, didn't he? So you'll see why I believe Monsieur Urquelle did the world a favour in killing him, albeit accidentally. And at some point, probably over a smoke this evening, I intend to shake his hand and tell him so.'

Astrid was wondering what to say next when what passed for a tragedy in the world of Claudine Bonnet – she'd forgotten to pack her elderflower pressé – brought the conversation with Alan to a premature close. As Astrid took her leave with the woman, she had a parting thought. 'Alan, when you come to tackle those tricky foliage masses?'

'Yes?'

'Give me a shout.'

'In this heat,' Claudine began. 'I never go anywhere without my pressé. I know I packed it. I *know* I did...'

11.03 AM

Armani's face was a mask of pain. 'But..?' Unable to go on, he turned and gazed out into the compound.

'Oh, don't get me wrong,' Darac said, shaking his head in warning as a brace of lieutenants appeared in his doorway. They held their ground. 'Your *busking* voice is... is very fine.' As if judging the moment appropriate, the air-con unit began to perform its impression of a faltering helicopter. 'But I may have...' In the doorway, Granot and Bonbon Busquet shared a baffled look and, withdrawing no more than a pace, ignored Darac's repeated backhand flicks to shoo them away further. 'I may have *slightly* overestimated Agnès's and Erica's reaction.'

'You mean they *don't* find my singing...' The helicopter buzzed the floor a couple of times, then cut out completely. Armani turned. '... *Beautiful*?'

The poor guy was taking it harder than Darac had hoped. 'Uh...'

Making a noise like a burst balloon, Bonbon was the first to let the cat out of the bag and Granot, collapsing against the door, wasn't far behind. But it wasn't until Darac noticed Armani's triumphant smirk that he realised he'd been had. 'When?' he said, simply.

'When did I see through your ruse? The second you suggested I could sing, *pazzo*!'

'Right away?'

'Of course!' Although working for years under cover had sharpened Armani's innate talent as a character actor, his impression of Darac's speaking voice was sketchy at best. That didn't matter to Bonbon and Granot as he relived the scene on the Promenade. "Oh, how Agnès and Erica *love* your voice!"'

Twinkle-eyed mirth tended to be Bonbon's reaction to most things in life. When something truly hilarious was going down, he could barely breathe. 'I would have given anything...' He exploded once more. '*Anything*, to have witnessed you croaking away to the boss. *And* to Erica. Genius!'

Darac himself was chuckling now and as Granot peeled himself off the door and staggered in, the office resembled the scene of a nitrous oxide attack.

Darac's desk phone rang. He composed himself, and picked up.

Out on the south terrace, Astrid's students had been rising to the challenge of depicting a tricky subject – a menagerie of topiary animals basking in dappled shade – when the daily test of the Villa's now seldom used water feature drew a temporary halt to proceedings. As tutor, Astrid was supposed to issue due warning about it to her students but it was much more fun for everyone if she let it come as a surprise. As long as she ensured all of them were out of harm's way.

'I thought I heard the midday mortar going off,' Ralf Bassette said, pausing in mid brushstroke. 'But it's the middle of the afternoon and we're nowhere near Château Park.'

Babette Bonnet turned away from her canvas. 'I thought I heard it, as well.'

'Me too.' Alan Davies, this time. He cocked his head. 'Listen... It's coming from behind us.' All the students turned. 'An orchestra? It sounds a bit like...'

Ralf Bassette smiled. 'Tchaikovsky!'

'The 1812 Overture!' Babette couldn't have looked more delighted.

The piece was emanating from speakers hidden in the shrubbery surrounding the terrace's monumental fountain. At first, the modest plume of water bubbling away at its centre did no more than rise a metre or so but then, in time with the cannons' blatant blasts, it began throwing spouts high into the air. As surreal spectacles went, projectile vomiting set to music was up there with the best and there were moans of disappointment when it sputtered to a stop after no more than a couple of minutes. Donning her tour guide's hat, Astrid enjoyed informing the class that in the

Villa's days as Le Petit Château, performances of *Les Eaux Dansantes*, "this exultant marriage of music and hydraulic engineering," could go on all evening. Exquisite, preposterous, sublime, vulgar – the Villa, it seemed, had everything.

'OK, show's over. Let's get back to it, everyone.' Astrid stayed her ground while the class members wandered back to their set-ups. 'I'm really encouraged by *all* your work this afternoon, by the way.'

It was only then that Astrid realised the class had gained an extra member.

'I'm sorry to have gate-crashed the party, Mademoiselle Pireque,' the interloper said, checking in with her as she headed back towards the building. 'Thea Petrova.'

'Astrid.'

She felt the penetration of Thea's gaze as they shook hands.

'I'm on a mid-class break and I couldn't resist coming out to see this. I do each time I visit. I'm such child.' She clicked her tongue. 'Such *a* child, I mean.'

A very impressive-looking child, Astrid thought to herself. Impressive, sexy and determined. Get her talking. 'You're a returning student?' She knew full well she was.

'This is my fourth time here. I'm tasting wine with Mathieu and I thought it was going to bore me, but he's wonderful and I'm *really* enjoying it.'

Astrid indicated her own students. 'I hope there might be a fifth time for you.'

'Actually, I'm tempted? The last time, I did Garden Design with Fred Lucasse – *brilliant* – and it was *really* the artistic side of it I loved.'

That accent. The St. Petersburg area. Definitely. 'I can see just by the way you're dressed that line, colour and form matter to you. That's all I need to work with.'

Accepting the compliment with a slight, almost regal tilt of her head, the woman felt no compulsion to return it, Astrid noticed. T-shirt and cargo cut-offs didn't hack it in Thea World, it seemed.

'Is horticulture your line of work, then?'

'No, no, no. Furs and fur accessories. Fakes, so don't kill me. Expensive fakes. But fakes all the same.'

Luxury goods. This is how you know Urquelle, isn't it? You met him at a trade show somewhere. And you're here together now. But how does he feel about that? 'Interesting.' Flatter her further. 'You design pieces, or..?'

'I just sell them.'

Thea glanced at her watch. Astrid glanced at it, too. A *Cartier*. A gift from Urquelle, perhaps? 'You have a shop?'

'No, no I travel. Here, there, everywhere.'

A way forward. 'I saw you chatting with Monsieur Urquelle. He too travels for business, I believe.'

Thea's expression didn't change. Or at least, to someone less visually acute than Astrid, it would have appeared so. 'Gérard and I are always bumping into one another.'

'Quite a coincidence.'

'I *love* coincidences, don't you?'

What would Darac ask now? Astrid's mind was a blank. Just wing it. 'This is not a coincidence as such but we do have something in common, Thea.'

'We do?'

'You're half-Russian, I believe.'

No acuity needed now. Thea clearly didn't like this turn.

'But you are not, I think. And how do you know this?'

'I happened to be in reception when you arrived. Elie Tiron pointed you out and commented on the connection. Well, half-connection. My father was born in Paris and still lives there. My mother's from Helsinki. Yours?'

'Do you go there much?' she replied, ignoring the question. 'Helsinki?'

'*Ainakin khadesti vuodessa.*'

Thea nodded almost imperceptibly, a tell that she had understood Astrid's reply. 'And that means?'

'At least twice a year,' Astrid said.

'Ah.'

Go for it. 'And do you go back to St Petersburg much?'

She thought about it. 'It's no brainer. I live there.' Another glance at the watch. 'Now I must go.' She grinned, archly. 'You know how these tutors are.'

'Good to talk to you.' Astrid smiled and was just about to rattle off something relevant in Russian but she thought better of it. 'I'll be back here next May. Think about it.'

'*Actually*, I will.'

Wondering if she had learned anything of true value in quizzing Thea, Astrid watched her head back up to the Villa and was once again struck by the almost proprietary confidence with which the woman from St. Petersburg desported herself in this grand setting. It was an impression that was only sharpened when Thea paused to exchange a few words with head gardener, Barthélémy. Had there been such a person, the châtelaine of the whole Villa des Pinales estate could not have looked more the part at that moment.

'In English, we have a phrase,' Alan Davies said as Astrid resumed her rounds. 'A penny for them?'

'What's the "them"?'

'Thoughts. Yours.'

'Ah.' She examined his work. 'Getting there. Very much so. I think you learned a lot from tackling those masses of greenery this morning.'

He produced a truly disarming smile. Or just perhaps, he was as skilled in the art as con artist Gérard Urquelle.

'Thanks so much but I didn't mean my work.'

'No?'

'It's none of my business but I couldn't help noticing the way you watched that rather forbidding woman from the wine-tasting class sashay back into the Villa.'

'I'm not sure my thoughts on her are worth a penny, Alan.'

His smile persisted. 'If you say so.'

6.16 PM

'I'm early. Is it alright?'

'No,' Elie said, rising to greet her. 'It's better than alright.'

They held the hug.

'You look bushed, babe.'

'If I had a euro for every client that's come through that door today... It's been like Châtelet – Les Halles in here. In the rush hour.'

'I think you should review your open door policy. Review as in stop it. Especially when Clarice isn't around.'

'No, no. It's all part of the personal touch the clients love. *And* pay through the nose for.' She brightened. 'Anyway, I can now put *this* on the door.' The sign read: OFFICE REOPENS AT 9 O'CLOCK TOMORROW MORNING. 'Just need to check something briefly but I'll be back in a moment.'

Astrid set down her bag and glanced around. There was half-an-hour's good reading on Elie's office walls: health and safety regulations; fire drill protocols; a handwritten mission statement from the Villa's owner Georgina Meier; certificates of culinary excellence; planners headed accommodation, courses, and holidays. But Astrid was interested in only one thing: the collection of postcards pinned to the cork board behind Elie's desk. Astrid had sent a good few of them herself and unpinned a couple to revisit the holiday memories they conveyed. And then her eye was taken by a card she hadn't seen before: an uncaptioned shot of a green circular building topped by a flat, wedge-shaped roof.

Elie came back in and locked the door behind her.

'This is extraordinary, Elie. Where is it?'

'Copenhagen – from my holiday this May. It's the student services building for the Faculty of Science.' She indicated the empty desk. 'Clarice is *very* into architecture. Didn't you know?'

'So am I but the one you sent me was a composite of The Little Mermaid, The Tivoli Gardens, the Nyhavn wharf and... some other cliché with "Welcome To Copenhagen" written in letters made up of rosebuds.'

'That's because you're also *very* into kitsch.'

Astrid grinned. 'Point.'

Smiles faded and with them, the lightness of mood both knew was no more than an overture for the heavier stuff to come. 'Elie, trying to make sense of what you said, and I believe meant literally, yesterday, I've looked in some detail into the Urquelle case. And not just the media reports.'

'I thought you might. In fact, I knew you would if you had access to them.'

Quite unconsciously, Astrid began to reproduce the rhythm and tone Darac adopted when interviewing a sympathetic witness. 'Would you share with me just why you felt as you did about Urquelle at the time of the preliminary hearing?'

'You didn't find *that* out, then?'

'No.'

'You would have done if the hearing had taken place a

few weeks before. I was all set to make quite a stink.' Elie produced an attaché case from her desk. 'This contains only a fraction of the stuff I had back then but it's more than sufficient to explain. Probably all by itself.'

'Talk me through it anyway?'

Elie laid out the material on Clarice's empty desk: a clutch of photos; handwritten letters, some several pages long; newspaper clippings of the incident and of the hearing; a couple of personal items, one of which was a silk scarf.

'It's Hermès.' Elie handed it to Astrid. 'I can't bring myself to wear it.'

'It's beautiful,' she said, turning it over in her hands and holding it up to the light. 'Why don't you wear it?'

'Guilt, I suppose.' She picked up one of the letters. 'Look – three, four... five double-sided pages. My reply?' She drew down the corners of her mouth. '*One* page, probably. Just enough to comment politely on each topic Karen had shared at length with me.'

For Astrid, life was just too short to maintain one-sided friendships. If that's what this was. 'You *kept* her letter, though.'

She handed over a photo of two young girls grinning at the camera. 'We're 12 in this one.'

Astrid smiled. 'Arm-in-arm.'

'Yes, we were close as kids. Quite literally, as you can see.'

Astrid could also see that, if the shot were representative, it was Elie who appeared to have been doing the holding on back then. 'Karen seems a little... hesitant?'

'She was shy, that's all. Unconfident. And she had no reason to be.' Elie scrolled screens on her mobile. 'This is us 16 years later, around the time of my birthday. We're in the English Tea Room at Villa Rose on Cap Ferrat. A waiter took it, naturally.'

At the table, Karen was leaning into a slightly uncomfortable-looking Elie. 'You're wearing the scarf.'

'She had just given it to me. It's the last photo of us taken together. Three weeks after this...' Elie's face crumpled but she fought the feeling and won. 'She was dead.' Saying the words aloud achieved what the thought alone could not.

'Come on, Elie. Let it all out.'

The two women hugged and when all tears were gone, Elie recounted the story of how the innocent Karen had fallen for her boss, the charming but married Gérard Urquelle; how he had favoured her first with his attentions, then with his sexual prowess; how Karen had never felt so fulfilled, so deliciously transgressive, so alive, so... in love. At the start, there had been talk of divorcing Vivienne, a life together.

'It was all shit, I imagine,' Astrid said. 'A serial adulterer's patter.'

'Absolutely. When someone new came along, Urquelle tired of Karen very quickly.' Elie lowered her gaze. 'What I'll never forgive myself for...'

'Hey, hey!'

'No, no. Let me say this. When Karen told me what Urquelle had said when he tried to end the affair the first time – that he'd got a kick out of her devotion to him at the beginning but devotion was one thing, clinging neediness another, and that now he felt completely suffocated by her – I'm afraid I felt a certain sympathy with him.'

'I can understand that completely. Anyone would.'

Elie exhaled deeply. 'Perhaps.'

'They *would*, Elie.'

'Anyway, what happened next changed everything. Karen told Urquelle that if he left her, she would meet up with Vivienne and tell her all about their affair in graphic and exhaustive detail.' She shook her head. 'Timid Karen, of all people, saying that!'

'How did Urquelle react?'

'Surprisingly, it made him see sense, she told me. And so the affair was back on. Big time.' Elie's forehead creased in exasperation. 'Tridi, I tried my level best to get her to see sense and drop him. But she wouldn't hear of it. There was no one to compare with him and never would be, she said.'

'Did Urquelle know Karen had a confidante who was counselling her to drop him? If he did, he might well have told her to listen.'

'He may have done. And since Karen's flat was the venue for most of their assignations, he may well have seen a photo of me. There was one of the two of us as 15 year-olds in her bedroom.'

'You said it was surprising that, as Karen put it, he "saw sense" about the situation?'

'In part, it was. Yes, Urquelle daren't risk Karen telling his wife anything about their affair. Why? Because Vivienne is the one with the money in their marriage and if she had grounds for divorce, he would certainly have suffered financially. *But,* do you think a man as predatory and self-serving as Urquelle would have just accepted Karen's threat? Without, apparently, any argument?'

Gravity was an unfamiliar look for Astrid but she was certainly conveying it as she turned to the nub of the matter. 'Elie, looking at the events of April 8th, five years ago...'

'I'll help you, Tridi. Until the hearing, I blamed Urquelle directly for Karen's death.'

'You believed if he hadn't chosen to play the hero, she would still be alive?'

'No. I believed that having convinced the so-called gunman Lopes to appear in the shop as if to hold it up,

Urquelle took the gun and deliberately shot and killed Karen, thereby removing any possibility of her causing trouble with Vivienne. He then turned the gun on the hapless Lopes, so removing, as I initially believed, the sole eyewitness to the killing.'

The change in tempo was so abrupt, it made Astrid's heart skip a beat. 'Shit, Elie.'

'I sent an anonymous letter to *Nice-Matin* outlining my theory. They didn't print it, fortunately. And I also...'

'Yes?'

Elie steadied herself. 'I also sent a copy to Urquelle himself.'

Astrid winced. Despite the anonymity of the letters, now it *wasn't* so good that Urquelle might have known who Karen's confidante was. 'Shit, shit, *shit!*'

'Quite.'

'Elie, when he checked in...'

'Did he recognise me? For a number of reasons, I didn't think he had.'

Astrid didn't like the way this was going. 'But?'

'His parting words to me were: "Thanks again, *Céline*." And he made sure I'd registered what he said.'

'His way of saying, "Despite the hair and the surname change, I know who you are" ?'

'I'm not sure. Possibly.'

Elie looked anxious about this, Astrid could see. Wondering if Vivienne might have unwittingly played a part here, Astrid thought back to her early days on the Villa's teaching panel. 'It's just over two years since I first taught here and I've never called you anything but Elie. But I'm trying to remember how your name appeared on the written correspondence.'

'When I got this job four years ago, I was Céline Roux

and I signed myself as that. I started calling myself Elie not long before I got married.'

'So when I taught Vivienne, she knew you only as Elie Tiron, too?'

'Yes, and so if it ever came up, she no doubt referred to me as that to her husband.'

Another possibility occurred to Astrid. 'You know, whatever else Urquelle is, he is certainly a slimy sod. I can imagine him making a show of using the full form of your forename in an attempt to appear gallant.'

'A gentleman doesn't take the liberty of using the diminutive of someone he doesn't personally know?' Elie pursed her lips, considering the point. 'I hadn't thought of that. It *is* the sort of crap he would pull.'

'Exactly,' Astrid said, smiling. Feeling that she had allayed Elie's anxieties at least a little, she pressed on. 'I can so see why you initially felt the need to punish Urquelle. What made you change your mind?'

Elie riffled through her newspaper clippings. 'The evidence given late in the piece by this man. One Denis Marut.'

'The eyewitness.'

'Yes.'

'Uh-huh,' Astrid said, wondering whether to share something a little added research had thrown up just minutes before the meeting.

'But for Monsieur Marut, I might be serving a life sentence now for killing, yes, a rat, but not one guilty of a double murder.'

'Let's go for a drink,' Astrid said.

The last play of the match hadn't set the *terrain de boules* on fire like Granot and his cronies had done the previous evening. But it didn't matter to the Tardellis: Emma's return to *Maternelle* had provided quite enough drama of its own. And following an evening meal in which the little girl had oscillated between woebegone silence and teary outbursts on the unfairness of life, school and everything, the drama had only ended when Armani had put Emma down for the night. Or so he and Noëmi hoped.

'Children, huh? They bring magic to our world, alright.' He took down a long mouthful of his *Peroni*. 'They also bring misery!'

'Shhh, you'll wake her.'

'And I tell you what else children bring. Chaos!'

At the bus shelter on the far side of the Place, a trio of single-deckers swung in perfect formation to a stop. Armani found the manoeuvre strangely reassuring.

'Chaos!'

As if muting the volume for her baby's benefit, Noëmi laid both hands onto her bump. 'Shhh, you'll wake Fabien!'

The strategy worked.

'Good job I'm only half-Italian,' Armani said, grinning. 'I'd be twice as loud.' As he gulped down another mouthful, his thoughts strayed on to a less urgent issue than Emma's nasty *Rentrée* experience. Less urgent, but just as perplexing. 'You know I had a lot of fun with Darac yesterday?'

'Yes, but don't you think we should continue discussing – quietly – what we're doing about Emma?'

'Yes, yes, but this won't take a second.'

Noëmi could see he was troubled. 'OK, sure.'

'It wasn't laughs all the way.'

'Oh?'

'Darac let me know that he and Frankie won't be having children.'

'Really?' She pursed her lips while she thought about it. 'Well, it's not written into the constitution that couples have to, you know.'

'Of course, of course, but the question is *why* won't they? The impression he gave was that Frankie can't have children.'

Noëmi looked blank. 'But she can. I remember telling you.' Her brow lowered. 'You didn't tell *him* that, did you?'

Armani's invisible friends seldom showed up at the apartment. But they did so now. '*Bah!* Of course not.'

'Good. Yes, it came up when I shared my concerns about I.V. treatment with her.' Noëmi absently massaged her bump. 'It was *Christophe* who couldn't have children, not Frankie.'

'That's what I thought.' At the shelter, the lead bus pulled away, breaking the formation. 'But it seems that Darac doesn't.'

'Are you sure?'

Armani took a last sip of beer. 'Pretty sure.'

Noëmi shook her head. 'Well... there's a miscommunication here somewhere.'

'And how.' He crushed the can. 'Some more carrot juice, *bella*?'

'Yyyyy... no.'

'Well, I'm going for another *Peroni*.' But first, he lowered his face to Noëmi's bump. 'You didn't hear any of that, OK?' he said, and gently laid his ear against it. 'What was that? Right. OK.' He straightened and shook his head. 'Fabien didn't hear a thing, he says.'

A dedicated officer who was also a handsome, roguish, and supremely narcissistic individual, Armani was regarded with both respect and fond amusement by friends and colleagues alike. But his capacity to love those who mattered to him knew no limit and naturally, Noëmi experienced this more than anyone. Perhaps it was the state of her hormones, or the day she had had, or her husband's foolishness with their unborn child, or the confusion over Frankie's fertility, or all of these things and more but at that moment, her awareness of just how much she loved him was so heightened, it felt almost too much to bear. She grasped his hand and a look of great intensity passed between them. It was some moments before she let go.

'Perhaps I will have some more juice,' she said. 'Just a drop.'

Armani kissed the top of her head and while he went to do the needful, she began to think again about Emma's first day back at school. How petty her four so-called best friends had been. How cruel. "Look, Emma's still got a *Tangled* backpack!" "*We* have *Sacs* ones now!" "Rapunzel, Rapunzel, *you're* a pee pants!" "*I've* got a mobile phone. *So* has Danielle. *So* has Sara. So has Marine." "*We* send texts!" "Emma sleeps with dollies!" "*My maman* lets *me* wear make-up all the time!"

On and on it had gone until one of the teachers got wind of it and had given the bullies a stiff dressing down. Noëmi had been glad to hear that but she suspected an unintended consequence would have been to strengthen the clique, thus further isolating Emma. On returning home, Noëmi had sought to explain what she didn't really understand herself. And then, balancing a firm hand with the need for granting some concessions, she had included Emma in formulating a plan to tackle the problem. It had not been an unqualified success.

'Thanks, darling.' Noëmi took a sip and set down the glass. 'Emma?'

'Sound asleep.'

Noëmi let out a long breath. 'Thank goodness. The poster?'

'Still on the wall and I think I detected an extra kiss. The backpack, though – tossed into the basket. *Finito*. Toast. "You've got to look like all the rest?" I said to her. "Did *maman* and I get where we are by doing that?"'

'At six, *I* did. To an extent, at least. You probably skipped off to *Mat* wearing *Gucci* and *Scarosso*.'

'I wish!' He caught Noëmi's look. 'What I meant was: that would have been ridiculous.'

'En route to school tomorrow, I'll get her a new backpack. *Chic-Y* on Pastorelli stocks *Sacs*. So does *Étoile*.' She gave a little shrug. 'I need a couple of new bras anyway. But *that* is all our little princess is getting. They've got *mobiles*, for heaven's sake some of those six year-olds! What's wrong with the parents?'

'Are they American, these people? English? They've got funny ideas about kids, some of them.' He drew his finger-tips together. 'But whatever the parents are, what I'd like to know is how this... *coup* happened? Emma's spent half the summer playing with those kitty cats.'

'I know and happily too, it seemed. It's little Clara. She's the ringleader. Pleasing her is all that matters at the moment, it seems.'

'Why? What does Clara have?'

'She's very bright and precocious. *And* she's very pretty.'

'Whoa, whoa. Emma is not bright and pretty?'

Noëmi smiled. 'Oh, baby. Yes, of course she is but by the time Clara's out of her teens, she'll have the world by the tail –just you watch. Is *that* what Emma and the others recognise, do you think? Clara, a star in the making? As tiny as they are?'

'I'm not sure.' He thought about it. 'Maybe.'

Noëmi raised the glass to her lips and for the first time in months, the smell of carrot juice appeared to have lost its allure. 'I don't want this after all. Sorry.'

'I bet it's too much of that stuff that's been making you feel sick all this time.'

'You could be right. It's not usual to still feel nauseous this far into a pregnancy. When I got to work this morning, I actually thought I was going to be sick.' Armani gave her foot a squeeze. 'Things brightened up, though. Until I picked up Emma.'

'Hey!' Armani called out, exchanging a grin and a wave with a passer-by below. He turned back to Noëmi. 'Jean-Paul off to the *boulangerie*.'

'Our morning baguettes are in safe hands, anyway. But what happens afterwards?'

As if prompted by the mention of hands, Armani took Noëmi's in his. 'Let's just recap our battle plan for Emma.'

'Absolutely,' she said, looking into his eyes. 'But I just want you to know...'

'Yes?'

She squeezed his hand. 'If you start singing *Che Gelida Manina*, I'm going back inside.'

Enjoying an after-dinner smoke with Ralf Bassette, Astrid watched as Laurent Salins emerged into the courtyard and for the moment, held his ground. Her mind went back to their first encounter.

'Do you know that man, Ralf?'

'We've had the odd chat. Strange mixture, isn't he? Exhibits a sort of... belligerent helplessness.'

Astrid nodded as she blew smoke. 'That's it exactly. But I meant, did you know him before?'

'Know him? No, what makes you think that?'

Don't push it, Tridi. Remember you're just a tutor. 'When he came sidling up as we went in to dinner that first evening, it was the way you spoke to him, I suppose.'

'As if I knew him? That's the relaxed familiarity with strangers routine one learns in business circles.'

'That explains why it's a skill *I* don't have.'

He smiled. 'You do alright,' he said, reaching for another *Marlboro*. The packet, he discovered, was empty.

Astrid proffered her tobacco tin. 'I've got a couple ready to go if you fancy one.'

'Can you spare it?'

'Ralf,' she said, betraying the merest hint of frustration. 'If you would like one, take it.'

'Yes, madame.' Opening the tin appeared to be a deeply nostalgic moment for him. 'Hmm, haven't smoked a rolly in years.' He took one and fired it up. 'Excellent. Thanks.'

Astrid wasn't sure she believed Ralf's story about Salins and her gaze fell on the man once more. He hadn't moved.

'Well, there's the helplessness,' she said, indicating him. 'Maybe the belligerence will show itself in a minute.'

Having agreed to meet Urquelle for a smoke, Salins hadn't expected him to have company. Male company, especially. He watched as Alan Davies stubbed out his cigarette, shook the man's hand and rose. Like a moth to the flame of Urquelle's own cigarette, Salins set off across the courtyard towards it as the man slipped what looked like a diary out of his pocket and continued to smoke as he began making a note.

'Monsieur Salins,' Davies said, in passing. 'Nice evening.'

'Hope it's cooler later. Can't sleep when it's hot. Especially in these beds. Can you?'

'Like a baby. But I've got a tip for you.'

'Tip?'

'Are you familiar with Alfred Hitchcock's movie, *Rear Window*?'

'The one with what's-his-name in it?'

'That's the one. Do you remember the scene in which a couple with precisely your sleeping problem take bedding out on to the fire escape to sleep? Think on.'

Omitting to mention that in the movie, a heavy downpour eventually sent the sodden couple scurrying back inside, Davies smiled, gave Astrid and Ralf a wave and went on his way.

At the bench, Urquelle seemed to be pondering something but then he completed the note and slipped the diary back into his jacket.

'Monsieur?'

'Ah, Laurent.' Urquelle gestured him into the adjacent seat. 'And how are we?'

Salins gave a nod in the direction of the retreating Alan

Davies. 'Funny, some people. He wants me to sleep on the fire escape.'

'English eccentricity at its finest. Or strangest. But enough of that – how did you enjoy your wine today?'

A wary look rearranged the beads of sweat pocking Salins's forehead. 'Some of it was alright.' With a practised flip of the wrist, he slid a single Gauloise from its packet and, patting his pockets, sat down.

Urquelle produced his lighter. 'Here.'

His brows still lowered, Salins accepted the light and it was then he noticed the dressing strip on the back of Urquelle's left hand 'What have you done to yourself?'

'What?'

'Your hand.'

'Oh, spilled quite a lot of some cucumber-smelling stuff on it.' He grinned. 'As one does. Had some sort of reaction.'

'Don't know why you want to make perfume in the first place. Anyway, you wanted a word?'

'Yes, and keep your voice down. The walls may not have ears but Mademoiselle Astrid Pireque most certainly does, and probably that puffed-up puppy Bassette, as well.

Salins cast the pair an anxious look as if he hadn't been aware of their presence until then. 'Alright. A word, you said?'

'Yes, you know full well what made me opt for Mademoiselle Hamada's class so let's cut to the chase. How much?'

'What?'

'Drop the dumb act, Lolo. How much do you know?'

'I think you've been sniffing more than just cucumbers or whatever it was.' Salins took a deep drag on his cigarette and shifting his weight forward, levered himself upright. 'Goodnight.'

'Let me put it a different way. How much do you want?'

Salins may have been about to walk away, but he went no further than the thought.

'That's better. Sit down.'

11.17 PM

Perfectly matching Darac's mood, 'Four On Six' was a restless tune and he was turning it inside out on his lounge guitar when his mobile rang. The caller's ID made him slam on the brakes in mid bar.

'Sweetie,' he said, taking the phone out on to his roof terrace. If it was one of those almost ridiculously beautiful Babazouk nights, Darac didn't notice. 'So glad you called. How did Benjamin's op go?'

'It didn't. They wanted certain functions to have stabilised further and the good news is they're achieving that. They're monitoring the situation constantly, of course, but the hope is that by tomorrow afternoon, Papa should be able to cope with the procedure. Certainly better than he would have done today.'

Darac felt a weight lift from his shoulders. 'And that procedure is?'

'It's a quadruple bypass, as we suspected.'

'Ai.... And you, Frankie? How are you coping?"

He could hear her take a breath in, then exhale, then taking another breath.

'Ohhhh... There's so much to say but I just...'

Darac knew the feeling well. 'No, no. Wait until you're home.'

'Yes, let's wait. What's it like with you?'

'If I were Armani, I would say that only you being here

146

could make it more beautiful.'

'And can't *you* say that?' Frankie said, sounding more like herself. 'Or do you need Armani to do your sweet-talking for you?'

'No, no, no. But telling you in person is another thing that can wait until you're home. Deal?'

'Deal. *Maman* sends her love, by the way.'

'Lisie used the L word?'

'Oh, yes. She thinks you're marvellous. As does Papa. Apparently.'

Darac wondered if the life-and-death situation they found themselves in had perhaps prompted her parents to tell Frankie just how much they valued *her*. But that question, too, could wait. 'And she's holding up under the strain?'

'If there is anyone on this planet more resilient in a crisis than my mother, I'm not sure I would care to meet them.'

That, Darac conjectured, may have already answered his question.

11.52 PM

After chewing the fat and sinking nightcaps with Mathieu and Zoë up in her room, Astrid kissed them goodnight and prepared to turn in. She had had a fulfilling day. All three sessions with her students had gone well and at the end of them, even professional nitpicker Claudine Bonnet had acknowledged that she had opened up a whole new world of creative possibilities for her.

But it was Elie's situation with Urquelle that exercised her most. At first, Elie's take on what had happened in the jewellery store seemed improbable in the extreme. Urquelle was clearly a predatory creature but there were easier ways of discarding an unwanted lover than killing her. And even if Urquelle had such scant regard for human life, was it likely that he would have staged an armed robbery to achieve his objective? So many things could have gone wrong – including being shot and killed himself – which he almost was. As an exercise in risk and reward, Elie's theory just didn't seem convincing. But then Astrid remembered the far more daring and outlandish murder at which she herself had had a front-row seat. And no financial assets had been on the line in that one.

She glanced at her watch. Night owl Darac was certain to be still awake. She reached for her mobile. Of course, there was his now full-on relationship with the gorgeous Frankie to consider. She tapped the phone against her chin. And decided it could wait.

11.53 PM

A critical care nurse with some twenty years experience, Lydia Félix was always ready to come forward in an emergency. And for handling more minor mishaps, she never went anywhere without her well-stocked first-aid kit. You just never knew when someone might fall over, faint or cut themselves. But it was an item from her make-up bag that she slipped into her pocket before venturing out of her room.

She peered along the length of the corridor in both directions before knocking twice on Urquelle's door, leaving it a couple of seconds and then knocking twice more. It opened.

'Your hand,' she said, reaching into her pocket for a small glass jar. 'I thought this might be of use.'

'Well, come in and we'll find out.'

FRIDAY, 16th SEPTEMBER

8.39 AM

Zena hadn't been a Niçoise long enough to deem it a "typical" mid-September morning but for the third day in a row, it was bright, warm and still in the city and the signs were set fair for it to continue. If, that is, she made it through her first day in her new job. Before that, she had to survive the approach of a motorcycle accelerating hard toward the junction with Rue Gioffredo, just a few metres away. Shouting "Shithead!" as she dodged back on to the pavement, she continued on her way without missing a word of her call.

'Nothing,' she said. 'Just behaving like a local.' She listened. 'Passed with flying colours? Yes, but don't get excited. Everyone does.' She listened again. Questions. Advice. Orders. 'Yes, yes, yes. I'll be on the shop floor right away.'

The staff entrance was directly opposite now and Zena brought the call to a close. Although Rue Sacha Guitry was no more than an alley-wide one-way street, she looked in both directions before crossing. After all she had been through, it would be idiotic, she told herself, to fail now.

8.54 AM

The last thing Alan Davies expected to see as he arrived back at the Villa, was the figure of Gérard Urquelle tripping down the steps toward a waiting taxi. A whole day of classes lay ahead.

'Giving it up as a bad job, Gérard?'

'No, no. I... ' It was then that he spotted the severely distressed camera case hanging from Davies's shoulder. 'You wouldn't happen to have a vintage Leica in there, would you? An M4, perhaps?'

Davies smiled. 'Yes. Well, M4-2. The old 'Plain Jane' as they're rather unkindly dubbed.'

'Indeed. It's still a beautiful camera. And far easier on the pocket. I had an M3 at one time...'

Getting into character for his role as 'Sour-faced Man' in the city cab company's production of 'I Hate The World And Everything In It,' the taxi driver rolled his window. 'Monsieur?' He tapped his watch. 'If you please!'

'Coming!' He lowered his voice. 'Better go. Having to nip into the city to pick up something and there won't be time after classes.' He leaned in conspiratorially. 'If I'm not back before Mademoiselle Hamada cracks her whip, there may be trouble.'

Davies remembered that Urquelle had a vintage item of his own in tow. 'Why didn't you shoot down in your Jag?' He nodded toward the taxi. 'You could avoid Monsieur Swinging Good Times there, for one thing.'

Urquelle laughed. 'You English are funny. My Jag? I'd street park it in *Monaco*. In fact, I *have* done several times.' He essayed an almost comically dubious look. 'In Nice, Alan? Risky.'

'I see. Well, don't let me keep you.'

Urquelle continued the cabbie's agony by making a further point to Davies but he finally climbed into the back of the taxi and was away.

Two women had watched the exchange with interest and Davies ran into one of them at the top of the steps. She appeared strangely ill at ease, he felt.

'Madame Petrova.'

'Monsieur.' She smiled, awkwardly, as she slipped her mobile into the hip pocket of her jacket. 'Was it something *I* said?'

Davies looked blank.

Her eyebrows assumed their familiar arch. 'I thought English persons were renowned for their sense of irony.' She jetted a glance at the drive. 'Monsieur Urquelle in the taxi.'

'Ah.' Davies smiled. 'After forty years living here, I think I may be in need of an irony supplement.'

Seeing the joke, Thea laughed fully and freely and Davies seemed rather charmed by it, Astrid felt as she looked on from the lobby. But where was Urquelle was scooting off to? And why? Alan, she felt sure, would tell her, if he knew.

'Morning, Astrid.'

It was Bassette.

'Ralf. Excellent work, yesterday.' She was still hoping for a commission from him but she never flannelled a student. 'Particularly in your handling of the topiary.'

'You are a very good teacher.'

'Hey! So all set for today?'

'Oh yes,' he said. 'Very much so.'

8.58 AM

Darac had been on a major high ever since his band's appearance at the Nice Jazz Festival back in the summer. But the DMQ's triumphant performance was only part of the story. On that same evening, he and Frankie had been able to clear the way at last to securing a future life together.

An unrepentant romantic, Darac had nevertheless been

struck by the speed and extent to which his newfound happiness had welled up and flowed out into every corner of his existence. He normally drove to work, taking the same route from his space in the Promenade des Arts car park to the Brigade Criminelle's HQ at the Caserne Auvare. On his first morning back following that doubly momentous day, he was stopped at the lights beside Nice's Museum of Modern and Contemporary Art, MAMAC – just as he was at this moment – when he suddenly became aware of the absence of something so usually present, he had ceased over time to notice it: a feeling of anguish that rose in his guts like a tide, then washed around the outer reaches of his consciousness all day before falling back in the evening. The circadian rhythm of a homicide detective.

As he pulled away on green, he was aware that disturbing feelings, absent for the past three months, were stirring once more. Or, at least, a variation on them. As if he needed a clue to its source, the next intersection brought him face to face with it. Rising from the Esplanade John F. Kennedy opposite was the city's principal conference, performance and exhibition complex, the Palais des Congrès et des Expositions. Housed in an ensemble of structures built to mimic the upthrust profile of the most famous rocky outcrop on the planet, the complex was named in honour of it, Acropolis. Just in case Darac had forgotten the Palais's connection to its ancient Greek progenitor, letters three metres high spelled it out for him. It may as well have spelled FRANKIE LEJEUNE, because Frankie, her parents, their Greek ancestry, and all that they were and had been, were uppermost in his mind this morning. By the end of the afternoon, would Frankie still have her father?

And Darac had another, more familiar, feeling to contend with. A sense that something wasn't quite as it should be. It was a feeling he often had when working on an investigation but in this case, it had proved to be something troubling Frankie; something he suspected had nothing to do with the crisis involving her father. Whatever it was, she didn't feel able to share it at the moment. "Let's wait until I get home," she had said. Deciding to allow Django to take his mind off things, he hit play on the CD player.

★ ★ ★

At the Caserne, the barrier man admitted Darac with a high-voltage example from his repertoire of livewire quips. Although it was the manner of its delivery rather than the gag itself that made him chortle, Darac headed off to his space reflecting on the efficacy of humour at providing what chief pathologist Professor Deanna Bianchi called "insulation." As the youngest member of Darac's team, Max Perand, had succinctly put it, "Laugh or cry – it's up to you."

The compound was the usual bustling scene: officers from various units coming on shift, others going off; cars threading their way between them. But then something happened that Darac couldn't recall happening before. As if it had been choreographed, Darac and Bonbon pulled into adjoining spaces and cut their engines at precisely the same moment. The only difference was that in doing so, Darac lost the last few bars of 'Nuages.'

Locking their doors to simultaneous chirruping a tone apart, the pair shared Côte d'Azur-style kisses of greeting – one peck on either cheek – and headed off to Building D pleasingly out of step.

Unlike his second-in-command, Granot, Darac's other trusted lieutenant was usually game for a spot of philosophical speculation.

'Do you know what turning your engine off just now appeared to achieve, Bonbon?'

His foxy eyes were already twinkling. 'The car refusing to... Correction, the car just not going any further?'

Darac pointed an emphatic index finger at him. 'You got in one. What it *also* appeared to do was turn off Django's 1953 version of 'Nuages' in my car.'

'Turning off *your* engine brought that about.'

'Ah, but how can you be sure? Are you familiar with Leibniz's Analogy of the Two Clocks, Bonbon?'

'Those rumours are greatly exaggerated. One date a long time ago – that's all we had.' He produced a flat round tin from his jacket pocket. 'Anis de Flavigny?'

'Pass. *Do* you know that analogy?'

'No, but thanks to your steer, it must be a causality thing, right?' He popped a small white orb into his mouth. 'Say that... on each occasion the hands of a clock which doesn't have a bell reach the hour point, the other one, which does have a bell, chimes. Since both clocks are set to the same time, it would have done that anyway but that's not how it looks. It *looks* as if the behaviour of the first clock influenced the second one into doing something it wouldn't have done otherwise.'

'Brilliant. And you know, in a way, what you just did is what I do when I'm playing jazz.'

It was nicely finessed but Darac's latest attempt to turn his colleagues on to the music he loved was destined to go the way of all the others.

'When you're playing, you suck aniseed balls?' Bonbon said.

'I was going to say that I pick up on a new idea and take it on. But let's just forget it.'

'Good idea.' Bonbon's foxy features set into an even

naughtier grin. 'But I've got an even better one. How would you like to hear *me* sing, huh?'

'Sure. Try 'Long Ago and Far Away.' '

Bonbon looked disappointed in his boss. 'Chief, Chief, Chief.'

'Yes, that was poor. Feel a bit uninspired this morning.'

'Frankie's father's travails?'

And whatever they were, Frankie's own problems, Darac sensed. 'He is facing one hell of a challenge.'

'He's a tough old bird, you know.'

'Is he? I don't really know.'

They were nearing Building D when a tall young woman with straight blonde hair and fine, delicate features hove into view. Her characteristic gait, a sort of light-footed prance, seemed heavier than usual.

'The doom-laden trudge,' Bonbon said. 'Classic symptom of one of Armani's victims.'

'Gentlemen.'

'Erica.'

More kisses.

'Did I hear the word "victims?" Discussing a case? Didn't know we had one. At the moment, it's as slack around here as a... whatever's really slack.'

'Don't worry.' Darac gave her shoulder a pat. 'As my bandmate Didier is always saying, "It'll pick up." ' He and Bonbon headed up the steps into Building D. 'See you later, Erica.'

At this stage, no one could have known just how prophetic Darac's sentiment would prove to be, nor how quickly it would happen.

'You said they...' Emma's words bubbled up through tears. 'You said they had them!'

Marching the little girl towards the exit on the end of a straight arm, Noëmi released her hand and turned to face her. 'Do you know something, young lady? If Papa and I had behaved like this when we were your age, *our mamans* would have smacked our bottoms. Now *that* is enough of your nonsense!'

'You said they *had* them!'

'That's *enough*, I said. You're a *grand*, remember? You're behaving more like a *petit*. Hold my hand.'

With *Chic-Y* and now *Etoile* having sold out of the golden fleece that was a *Sacs* backpack, Noëmi had time to try only one more store before depositing Emma at school and heading off to work. But which? They emerged on to the avenue and Noëmi glanced across at *H & M* which didn't look heaving. Service would be relatively speedy. But trams approaching from both directions meant waiting at the kerb and with time so tight, and with Emma so fractious, keeping moving seemed the better option.

'Just one more shop, Emma. *One*! Right?'

'Nooooo! It's not fair!'

The long march resumed.

9.25 AM

To Zena's eyes, one or two of her colleagues were made-up more like the sort of girls a former boss had referred to as "high-class pay-and-lay." She herself had gone for a more subtle look. Indeed, she scarcely appeared to be wearing make-up at all.

'Nervous?' the departmental manager said, indicating the sales floor as if it were the stage of the Bolshoi Ballet. 'Don't be.' He directed her gaze to an impressive-looking woman wearing the uniform of a senior sales assistant. Zena recognised her as Nadine, her saviour from the encounter with security man André on her first day. 'When we have finished our little chat, report to Madame Beaumont there. She is your section head.'

A break. 'Yes, I know her.'

The manager continued as if Zena hadn't commented. 'And she has forgotten more about selling cosmetics than I will ever know.' He held out a slightly clammy hand and Zena shook it. 'Good luck. Not that you'll need it.'

That's what you think. 'Thank you.'

The *Éspace Beauté* was vast, well-lit, and sweet-smelling. And in Madame Nadine Beaumont, Zena knew, she had a champion.

'I'm so glad I've got *you.*' Nadine said, drawing stares from some of the others and noticing it, dropping her voice. 'I shouldn't tell you but you achieved a perfect score in your course exam.' She smiled. 'Only one person has ever done that before.'

'Was it you, madame?' Zena said, remembering that formality was the order of the day on the shop floor.

'No, no. I was hopeless at the start. Wouldn't say boo to a goose, for one thing. You, Zena, are a natural and you look just perfect.'

Nadine set about introducing her to the other assistants, to her counter, and to the backstage cupboard containing fill-up stock and demo samples.

'Got your key for this?'

Zena brandished it.

'Of course you have.' She opened the cupboard. 'Now, as you know, we believe our promotion this week, *Chanson de Minuit,* has the potential to become our biggest selling unisex fragrance ever. But it has got off to a slow start.' She ran an eye over supplies. 'Looks as if...'

'Nadine?'

It was a member of the Wellness Team.

'Sorry to interrupt but I've got a lady who says she paid for six Body Tone and Tingles, *and* she's got a receipt, but only four are showing on the system. Could you just..?'

'I'll be right there.'

'You're a star.' With her white mules slapping against her heels, the Wellness woman headed back to the floor.

'Another fire to put out,' Nadine said, resuming her impromptu stock-take. 'May need a few more spray cards by tomorrow but the scent itself will hold out.' She turned to Zena and smiled. 'So! Get your weapons ready and I'll breeze by later.'

'Thank you, Nadine.' Zena said, squeezing her hand. 'Thank you for everything.'

Nadine seemed strangely moved. 'Oh, it's... You'll be great. See you anon.'

Zena watched her go and, her heart beginning to beat faster, she turned back to the cupboard.

★　★　★

Busying herself with a task that enabled her to keep a discreet eye on Zena's progress, Nadine was beginning to wonder if she had done the right thing in asking her to cruise the floor. The girl would certainly have found life

162

less challenging behind a counter – everyone did - but she had been so perfect in role play, it had seemed a waste of her talent. It took a particular type of character to walk up to a complete stranger, especially if she or he were merely passing through the department, and "sass" them; that is, persuade them to stand and sniff scents. It just went to show, Nadine reflected, that even a girl as confident as Zena found that strutting your stuff in the classroom was an entirely different call from working the floor. So far, she had let at least a dozen very approachable women escape her attentions without so much as a smile. It was perhaps time to intervene.

But as Nadine came out from her cover, Zena at last stepped forward. Nadine hovered. The target was a male in his forties. Well-dressed. Quite good looking. I *knew* I was right, Nadine said to herself. Having taught her that it was much more difficult to sass the male of the species, Zena *was* rising to the challenge after all. It was almost as if she had been waiting for this man. She smiled as she kept talking, something only an accomplished actor could make look natural. She was interesting him, Nadine could tell. Better still, she was charming him. Show him the atomiser, Zena. Now before he decides... Good girl! Cards, come on. Where are your cards? Don't say you've forgotten them...

Nadine kept watching as Zena appeared to apologise about it but in remarking further, seemed to beguile the man all the more. He was asking a question. Yes, it is for *Madame*, but it is also for *Monsieur*. That's right, it's unisex. And it's Now. It's Bold. Would you like to try it? She was making a game of it. And he was playing along, proffering his wrists like someone volunteering to be handcuffed. She said something. He turned his wrists, exposing the pulse

163

points. Brilliant! She levelled the atomizer at them as if it were a gun. She hit the trigger and stepped back. The man sniffed the scent and smiled. *He* liked it. He loved it, in fact. But would his wife/mistress/girlfriend/boyfriend like it? Zena was talking again, reassuring him, enveloping him in an atmosphere so pleasant that he...Yes, he nodded. He was sold on the idea. She had done it. Her first sass and it was a sale! Now point him...Yes, she indicated a free counter assistant. The man smiled, said something in parting that even at a distance Nadine could tell was gracious, and headed away to make his purchase.

'Sorry to disturb you, Nadine.'

'Ah, Jean-Louis,' she said, smiling as she turned. In one way or another, the young man from Martinique disturbed most of the store's female employees. 'To what do I owe this pleasure?'

'Goods-in phoned us to say the room divider you ordered had come in. But looking at the packaging, I wasn't sure it's what you had in mind. So, long story short, we've put it together up in the furniture department. Want to come and check it out?'

'You sweethearts.' Nadine cast an eye over her domain. Everything appeared to be ticking over nicely. 'I'd love to.'

As the pair left the floor, Nadine tried to attract Zena's attention but the girl's eyes were on her customer at the counter, her first ever sale and one she would forget in time but for the moment was the centre of her entire world. The man was having his purchase gift-wrapped, Nadine noticed. A present, therefore, for someone special.

'See my new girl, over there, Jean-Louis? The one on sass with the light-brown bob?'

'Ye-es?'

'Zena Bairault is her name. Remember it. That young

164

lady is going to go far. Very far, indeed.'

Zena watched as the man who had gratuitously introduced himself, and even more gratuitously addressed her by
name, was now engaging with the girl at the counter.

'Zena, is it?' A voice said to her in passing. 'Don't forget
our female customers.'

It seemed Nadine's second-in-command was not quite
so enamoured.

'I won't,' Zena called after him.

But when, en route to the exit two minutes later, her
sole customer's face had deformed into a mask of agony
and, grabbing at his shirt collar, staggered and crashed to the
floor, Zena still hadn't approached a female customer. No
one screamed but as members of the store staff and public
alike closed around the fallen figure, Zena was hurrying
towards the staffroom.

9.34 AM

'All the kids want these, this year.' The assistant said, scanning
the barcode. 'Next time round, they'll be "sad *Sacs*," won't
they? You can just hear them saying it.'

'All too clearly.' Noëmi paid in cash. 'Thanks so much.
Oh, would you not wrap it, please?' Making an apologetic
moue, she plonked last year's must-have on to the counter.
'Need to transfer things.'

The assistant smiled. 'Of course, madame.'

Emma clapped her hands in glee. 'Thank you, *maman*.
Thank you, thank you.'

'*What* a polite girl,' the assistant said, engaging with her
as she turned to the next customer. 'And you're going to be

a big sister.'

'Yes. Fabi will look up to me.'

Emma was going down a storm with anyone in earshot but her mother had repacked and was ready to go. En route to the stairs, the little girl had another thought.

'May I have my very own blush stuff and lipstick, *maman*? I'll be good. Promise!'

★   ★   ★

As Tardelli *mère et fille* headed for the shoe department exit into Rue Gioffredo, the collective mood had improved considerably. Noëmi had lost the feelings of nausea that had troubled her earlier; she was no longer having to drag a seriously disgruntled Emma about the place; and she was in time to walk her to *Maternelle Niel* en route to MAMAC. For her part, Emma was skipping around like a spring lamb in an old-style Disney cartoon.

No one saw the collision coming. At one moment, the street door was a just few metres away and Emma was obeying the call to return to her mother's side; the next, a young woman in a tearing hurry attempted to slip through the narrowing gap, misjudged it and in tripping herself up, sent Noëmi sprawling across one of the displays.

The young woman scrambled quickly to her feet, blurted out something in a foreign tongue that could have been an insult or an apology and dashed out through the door. Immediately, Noëmi was the focus of everyone's concern.

'She's pregnant, look – the mother.'

'Let me help you, madame. I'll put everything back – don't worry. That's the way.'

'What was that stupid girl doing?'

'Are you alright, madame?'

'Yes, yes. I just lost my balance. Where's Emma?'

'*Maman?*'

They were reunited.

'*Maman!*'

Noëmi rubbed her hip. 'I'm alright, darling.'

'That girl. Running, for God's sake! Somebody ought to report her.'

'Are you absolutely sure you're not hurt? One can't be too careful when one...'

'Is in my condition? Let me tell you that what just happened was the least of my problems this morning.' Noëmi held out her hand. 'Come on, Rapunzel.' Old habits died hard. 'Come on, *Emma,* I mean. Or we'll be late.'

Emma straightened her *Sac* and, very carefully putting her hand in her mother's, kept pace with her as they headed for the door.

'Don't worry, *maman,*' she said, '*I'll* look after you.'

9.41 AM

With no time for the luxury of clarifying anyone's intentions toward her, Zena boarded the first homeward-bound tram to appear and stood with her face to the window. It wasn't until the particoloured streetscape of downtown gave way to the beige tower blocks of Pont Michel that she risked a look at her fellow passengers. No one was standing within a dozen strides of her so as the tram snaked up and over the Nice to Tende railway line, she crossed the car and as if checking to see they were still there, scanned the tracks. No, no one had ripped them up in the past hour and a half. The tram slowed into the stop and remembering her training one incident too late, Zena hastened but did not dash away.

She hadn't meant to barge into that woman back in the store. Pregnant, too. Good thing her little kid took it well. She could easily have screamed the place down and that wouldn't have helped. Wrong people, wrong place, wrong time – that's all there was to it. Still, it shouldn't have happened. Had any real harm been done to them? Zena hoped not.

In the apartment, everything she needed to take with her was packed but, fighting a losing battle with the need to be sick, Zena put any thoughts of making an instant getaway on hold. Nothing would draw attention to her more than throwing up in public.

9.44 AM

Kisses of parting had been exchanged but Noëmi had one last point to make.

'Bye, darling. And remember, if those girls try to bully you again today...'

Emma was bobbing up and down with excitement. 'They won't, *maman*.'

'Listen to me.' She held the look. '*If* they try, go and tell Madame Poidatz immediately.'

'Yes, yes. But they won't!'

'Off you go.'

She misted over as she watched Emma make a beeline for her tormentors of the day before. It would break Noëmi's heart if... But no, it looked as if she was *persona grata* once more. And she was saying something that appeared to be going down well.

'Morning, Noëmi. Everything fine?'

'Childhood, Anne-Sophie,' she said, her eyes still on the group. 'How does anyone ever survive it?'

'I'd like to do it all again, but knowing what I know now.'

'That's cheating,' Noëmi said.

The two women walked away.

It was just a short walk to MAMAC and before she began cataloguing today's thrill-packed instalments of artist Karl Fritjof's plumbing problems, she punched in a number on her desk phone. There was no reply so she left a message.

'Hi, darling. Just got in from dropping Emma at *Mat* and her magic new backpack seems to have done the trick with the inner circle. Is this going to be the way of things from now on? Hope not.' For a moment, she considered telling Armani about her performance as a *cochonnet* to that foreign girl's *boule* in *Pal-Mas*. But she felt absolutely none the worse for the experience and, knowing he would only worry, she decided it could keep for their evening round-up on the terrace. She continued, 'Anyway, Herr Fritjof and his suspect toilets are calling me which after the past couple of days, is an inviting prospect, believe it or not. Take the greatest of care. And no singing! See you this evening. Kiss kiss.'

9.57 AM

Gérard Urquelle had concluded virtually every presentation he had given with the lines: "Of all man's creations from the mineral world, the most precious and beautiful has to be a cut and polished ruby. Or sapphire. Or diamond. The choice, ladies and gentlemen, is of course yours. Our greatest privilege here at *Bertrand et Fils*, is to help you make that choice."

Vivienne Urquelle required no such help. For her, the most precious and beautiful creation of "the mineral world" was something far less shiny: the dull, inchoate and quite literally lumpish substance that was a ball of clay. With no more than her wheel, a little water and her coaxing hands, she could make that inert grey blob rise and grow, the starting point for an infinite variety of forms.

It was as the glistening tower between her hands was at its most vulnerable that the phone on her studio wall rang – she must have forgotten to mute it – causing a momentary loss of concentration and the collapse of her pot-to-be. But since the miracle of resurrection was an everyday occurrence at the wheel, she knew all was not lost as she wiped her hands and walked between the spatters to the phone.

'Madame Vivienne Urquelle?'

'Yes.'

She listened to what followed in near-silence. At the end of it, she was leaning against the wall, staring back at the lifeless ruin lying slumped on her wheel. For some moments, she considered returning to it – there would be time before the car came. But with a smile playing on her lips, she strode towards the studio door instead. The resurrection could wait.

10.12 AM

Frequently sombre, always interesting and above all, valuable, Commissaire Agnès Dantier's weekly team briefings had been known to go on all morning. They had also been known to generate the occasional laugh. This morning's show had failed to deliver on any of these fronts.

'So that's the Riquier case done and dusted. And finally...' Agnès closed the file and turning to the one remaining item of business, began running an eye over a single sheet of A4. 'An update on our long-promised live feed camera set-up... Blah, blah, blah...' Agnès added the note to the stack. 'Still promised, but we've been upgraded from "soon" to "any day."'

' "Any day?" Armani said. 'Hope so – Erica's demo already feels like ancient history.'

Young officer Yvonne Flaco shook her tightly cornrowed head. 'Six buttons at one end; four at the other? It's easy, Captain. Easier than learning how to use a new mobile.'

'I'm reassured.'

'Ditto,' Agnès said, equally flip. 'Any other business?' She slipped her slingbacks on – a sign she expected there to be none. 'No?'

Sitting in his familiar contorted posture in his familiar position in the room, Bonbon set his mouth into a most unfamiliar sneer. 'Got something here, boss.' He brandished his mobile. 'Murder. And it's one of ours who's responsible.'

Among gasps of dismay and disbelief, Darac wasn't alone in smelling a rat. It was a slow morning, and when it came to deadpan comedy, only the great Ambroise Paillaud could better Lieutenant Alejo "Bonbon" Busquet.

'I'll read out the charge. On the afternoon of Wednesday, 14th September, Captain Jean-Pierre "Armani" Tardelli did wilfully and knowingly murder a selection of popular Italian songs...'

Laughter; calls for Armani to be sent down which he vehemently opposed; calls for Darac to be sent down with him which Armani opposed even more. The meeting may have been short and dull but it was ending on an upbeat note.

One of the desk phones rang and Agnès picked up.

'Go ahead, Charvet.' Darac and the team chatted quietly among themselves as she listened to what appeared to be a routine call from the Duty Officer. Routine but lengthy.

'A second, everyone,' Agnès called out, hanging up. 'Semi-suspicious death of one Gérard Urquelle, a 45 year-old male who was shopping for perfume in *Pal-Mas* when he suddenly collapsed. Volunteers?' Youngsters Yvonne Flaco and Max Perand, who had joined the squad within a week of each other three years before, were treated to one of Agnès's most feline smiles. 'Yvonne, Max? Thank you, chicks.'

'It was nothing, boss,' Perand said, curling a lopsided lip. The cause wasn't the punch he'd taken in the mouth at the conclusion to the Riquier stabbing case; many things about Perand had an off-balance, out-of-kilter quality.

'At least the corpse should smell sweet.' Flaco said, rising. 'For once.'

Agnès's smile had faded only slightly. 'The corpse is residing in the morgue at l'Hôpital St. Roch.'

Granot was capable of a class-leading look of astonishment. He produced a choice example. 'The body was removed from the scene? Who authorised that?'

'No one. I did say it was a *semi*-suspicious death.'

'What is that, anyway?' Perand was still in full moan mode. 'One where the bullet or the knife or whatever kills only half the victim?'

'Technically,' Bonbon said, twinkling away, 'that would be a suspicious semi-death.'

'All we know is that that the male shopper collapsed apparently under his own steam and despite the efforts of a couple of first aiders at the scene and then an ambulance crew, he died en route to A and E.'

'So what's even *semi*-suspicious about this, Agnès?' Darac said.

'One of the first aiders was a Monsieur André Ricolfi. Ring any bells?'

'Beat officer,' Granot said. 'Works or rather worked out of Foch. Good bloke.'

Bonbon nodded. 'Retired from the force must be... five or six years ago.'

'These days, he works as a security guard at *Pal-Mas*. He didn't like the look of the stricken Monsieur Urquelle. That is, it didn't seem to him that the man had succumbed to a heart attack or stroke or any of the usual suspects. Next, one of the morgue technicians at St. Roch didn't like the look of the corpse, either.'

'It gets better,' Perand said, producing another lopsided moue. 'Question, boss?'

'A quick one.'

'There aren't another 200 equally weird looking stiffs piled up in the store behind this Urquelle, are there? Waiting for the excellent Monsieur Ricolfi to send them off to the morgue for a second opinion?'

'No, Perand,' she said, as if to a child. 'There aren't.'

'So it's not a Tokyo subway type thing, then.'

Flaco gave him a look that would have flayed a more sensitive soul. 'Why? Would you like it to be?'

'No but it would keep us busy, wouldn't it?'

Granot had lost a lot of weight recently. But he was still a massive presence in the room. 'Perand, your mouth?'

'Still sore, Lieutenant.'

'Keeping it shut might help.'

The young man shrugged assent or dissent; it was difficult to tell them apart.

Agnès gave him a look. 'If I may continue? Said morgue technician then summoned the duty pathologist who also didn't like the look of things and she called the Palais de

Justice where our beloved Public Prosecutor Jules Frènes...'
The usual groans went up. 'Quiet please... Frènes interrupted
a crucial call to his tailor to instruct his secretary to contact
the Forensic Path Lab about the death. Denouement: Map
has agreed to take a look at the corpse immediately.'

Darac's close friend and neighbour Suzanne was a senior
nurse at St. Roch. Not just a source of info on all matters
pertaining to the hospital which was valuable in itself,
Suzanne had come to the rescue of the Brigade in a literal
sense on more than one occasion. Darac wondered if she
might have more on the Urquelle situation and if she hadn't,
he knew she would find out. He resolved to give her a call
after the briefing.

'Shall we begin by liaising with this Monsieur Ricolfi,
Commissaire?' Flaco said, as ever, eager to get down to brass
tacks.

'By the time you get there, he'll be expecting you.'

As the meeting finally broke up, Armani cruised in
alongside Darac and put his arm around his shoulder. So
far, so normal. His expression, though, was anything but.
'Granot just mentioned Frankie's father to me. They're
operating today, he says.'

'That's the plan. Three o'clock.'

'Courage!' He gave Darac's shoulder a squeeze. 'Listen,
Noëmi was saying that if Frankie wanted to talk about
things, she would be more than happy to. We both love her,
you know that.'

'Thanks, man.' He patted Armani's cheek. 'We do know.'

'You'll pass it on?'

'Of course.'

It was only when Darac was almost back in his office that
he wondered what had prompted Noëmi to suggest what
she had – Armani had heard nothing of Benjamin's travails

until the team meeting that had just taken place. Maybe it had just been his way of saying that he hoped Frankie realised she had an open invitation to Noëmi's shoulder. Another mistranslation from the Armanian, possibly.

Bonbon was also making a beeline for Darac's office. 'Despite what a certain doctor advised, chief?' he called out from behind. 'Is there an espresso going?'

'Already had three today. Better make it just one.'

Bonbon lowered his tawny brows and nodded.

'One, of course.'

'One double?'

'Now you're talking.'

'I'll just make a couple of quick calls and you're on.'

10.15 AM

An alpine chalet. Rocks. Waterfall. Depicting a scene from *Heidi* might not have been a challenge Astrid's students were expecting to have been given for their penultimate class, but as she observed as they climbed out of the Villa's minibus, 'This is the Côte d'Azur, right? A lot of things aren't what they seem.'

'What *is* this place?' Babbette Bonnet, said, wide-eyed.

'It's called *La Cascade de Gairaut*. Built to commemorate the completion of the Canal de la Vésubie where we were working yesterday morning.' Astrid turned to the driver. 'We'll set up over there, Lio. I'll help.'

'Much appreciated.'

Ralf Bassette was shaking his head in wonderment. 'Who would have thought *this* was here? As the crow flies, we must be no more than... a kilometre from the Villa?'

'Something like that,' Astrid said. 'Couple of extra pairs of hands would be useful here.'

'It may have been a kilometre as the crow flies,' Claudine Bonnet said. 'It felt like *five* crammed into that damned van.' But then she remembered that in spite of everything, she was enjoying herself. 'However, it was worth it.'

'*Attagirl!*' Alan said to her, en route to Astrid. 'Do you know that English expression?'

'No,' she said, warily.

'It means that underneath, Claudine, you are quite the trouper.'

'Oh.' Smiling as if it were a novel experience, she found her sister with a look. 'Hear that, Babette?'

'The man has lost his reason.'

As Alan joined Lionel and Astrid, Ralf was still conducting his site recce. 'The iconography of the thing is clear enough. The Vésubie rises way up in the Alpes Maritimes, right? But why is it so *kitsch,* this thing?'

'There you've got me,' Astrid said, grabbing armfuls of bags. 'But isn't it wonderful?'

'Particularly like the cave. Concrete stalactites and all.'

'The water's real enough,' Alan said. 'I think, anyway. When you're ready, Ralf?'

'Oh, sorry.'

Alan turned to Astrid. 'I've been up here before, Astrid. If you go through that gap in the hedge behind us, you emerge above a cemetery laid out on terraces on the hillside. Very stark and stony to my English eyes, even now. Would it be alright—?'

'If you went for that subject instead?' She gave him a reproving look. 'Of course it would. Providing you set up here and not in the cemetery itself.' She smiled, cheekily. 'The locals who are still upright don't like that sort of thing.

Even though as resting places go, it lacks that... solemnly sylvan quality you prefer.'

Alan laughed. 'Astrid, you have a great turn of phrase as well as a fabulous way with a brush. To say nothing of pencils.'

'And don't leave out my faves – crayons.' She turned. 'So you'll set up just through there?'

'Yes, it's just a few paces so I'll be well in reach of the teacher for a ticking-off. However, I'll help with the others' stuff first so maybe she'll be kind.'

'Doubt it. She has a heart of stone, that one.' Her mobile rang. 'Elie?'

'Are any of your students in earshot?'

She sounded anxious. 'Wait a second.' Astrid moved away from the minibus and, slipping through Alan's gap in the hedge, the cemetery duly appeared below. Her eye was such that, even as she prepared to take what was clearly a significant call, Astrid saw what Alan's English eye had seen. With its one solitary tree and sarcophagi spaced in a strict rectilinear grid, the cemetery was indeed a stark and stony place. A parking lot for the dead. To complete the image, a crow was circling overhead like a security guard making rounds.

'We're fine now,' Astrid said. 'What is it?'

'Urquelle went into the city before his class with Zoë and didn't come back.'

'He had something to pick up, Alan Davies told me. It's still early, he probably—'

'He's dead, Tridi. Vivienne Urquelle just called me.'

'Gérard Urquelle *dead*?' Away from her work with the Brigade, Astrid's first reaction to news of any sudden death was to picture a mass of mangled vehicles: she had lost an uncle and two close friends to road traffic accidents. Had the taxi Urquelle taken gone off the road somewhere? Easy.

Easy. 'How, Elie?'

'He was on his way out of *Pal-Mas* when he just... collapsed.'

'Heart attack or something?'

'All Vivienne would say was that apart from his limp, he had no health issues that she knew of. Just the opposite. She's gone off to ID the body.'

Astrid's gaze locked on the circling crow. The effortless grace of its flight; the graceless screech of its call; she found it captivating, suddenly. A group of them was called a murder, she remembered. 'All will be revealed at the autopsy, Elie.'

'Indeed.'

'Have you let Zoë know?'

'I didn't want to nuke her morning, Tridi, so I told her only that Urquelle had been called away and wouldn't be joining them. I'm going to say the same to Mathieu. Just before 5 o'clock, I'll put something more definitive up in Reception so people will see it only after the concluding classes.'

Astrid felt this was a mistake on Elie's part, but a much bigger one was in not levelling with Zoë now. She would have been more than capable of keeping such a secret under her hat while running the show. Mathieu, too, probably.

'And how do you feel about it, Elie? Urquelle's death?'

'How do I feel?' There was a pause in which Astrid thought she heard a sigh. 'I am absolutely thrilled. That's why I don't want to announce it, myself. I'd probably grin or even laugh. But Tridi?'

'Yes?'

'I never said that. Alright?'

Below, the crow tilted its wings against the breeze and peeled away.

Having worshipped at the altar of the goddess Gaggia once already, Darac and Bonbon were contemplating a transgressive second communion when Suzanne called back from Hôpital St. Roch and saved them. She had news but she began by making an encouraging observation on the type of operation Frankie's father was shortly to undergo.

'Thanks for that, Suzanne. On the unfortunate Monsieur Gérard Urquelle, has anyone informed his next of kin, do you know?'

'Yes, she's due here shortly to formally ID him, the poor woman. And an HR person at the company he worked for has been informed, also. Urquelle was on a few days' holiday, it seems.'

'Some holiday, eh? Any developments on the death itself?'

'Your wonderful Doctor Mpensa has finished liaising with our Duty Path and he went in to look at the body himself just a couple of minutes ago.'

'Anything filtering through?'

Noises off.

'Lord, he's returning already. Hang on, I'll have a word.'

Darac heard murmurings and then Suzanne came back on.

'I have Doctor Mpensa for you, Captain.'

'See you soon, and thanks again for what you said earlier. I'll let Frankie know.' He heard the vague but unmistakable sounds of a landline phone being handed over. 'Map?'

'I'm glad there are some sharp eyes around, Darac.'

Darac gave Bonbon a look and flicked the phone on to speaker. 'There are grounds for people's uneasiness, then?'

'In a word, yes. I think Monsieur Gérard Robert Urquelle may well have been poisoned.'

On hearing this, nine out of ten senior officers would have repeated the word "poisoned", adding an interrogative upward inflection. 'Poisoned?' Darac said, proving that his reactions were not always an exception to the rule.

'Don't ask me *which* poison yet but Urquelle's body and his effects are going back to our crime lab as soon as the next of kin has completed the formal ID. She's due here within the next few minutes, apparently.'

'So you think that however Urquelle engaged with this possible poison, it wasn't accidental?'

'Statistically, accidental exposure is the most likely scenario but there's certainly a doubt and in any case, ours is the best equipped facility to find out more.'

'Sure.'

'If it *is* poison, one thing I am sure of is that he didn't take it consciously. A suicide doesn't take, for instance, hydrogen cyanide and then go shopping. And I would also say that an orderly, well-lit space like Palais Masséna, especially on a none-too busy Friday morning, is no one's idea of a toxic environment, is it? So, I'm putting Patricia and the Red Zone team on standby. And can you do the same with Raul Ormans's forensic people?'

'No problem but I'll have to ask Agnès to OK it – I'm not Acting Commissaire at the moment. To be clear, Map, no one else at the store appears to have been affected?'

'No and no other corpses in a similar condition have shown up elsewhere but one can't be too careful where poison is concerned. *If* that's what this is. When we have something more concrete, I'll let you know immediately.'

'Excellent. Whatever you find, it looks like we'll be needing a breakdown of Urquelle's movements prior to the collapse. I believe you've got the next of kin's details there?'

'Are you familiar with something called the National Police Database?'

'Not sure. Bonbon, are you? No? Sorry Map, we've never heard of it.'

'What's with the cheeky mischievousness, Darac? Have you been spending time with Armani?'

Darac grinned. 'As I matter of fact, I have.'

'It shows. Just a second.'

Darac heard a muffled exchange with Suzanne and then Mpensa came back with a Menton address and phone number. Since it was a round trip of about an hour-and-a-half by road from Nice, it would have been convenient to have asked Madame Vivienne Urquelle for details of her husband's movements at the formal ID but in such circumstances, Darac's preferred practice was to allow next of kin as much recovery time as possible. In most murder cases, resources were stretched and time short so it was a principle he couldn't always follow. As yet, though, there was nothing to suggest that all hell was about to break loose over the dead body of Monsieur Gérard Urquelle.

'Thanks, Map.' As ever, Darac's head was teeming with possibilities. 'Is Deanna around at the moment?'

'Around as in working in our home lab, you mean?'

'Yes.'

'Thankfully she is and I'll be able to assist her all the way. We're so used to being overworked, it will feel strange to be able to take the proper time over things. What's happened to all the local crims? You arrested them all or is their turn to go on holiday, or what?'

Scared of the consequences if he didn't, Bonbon rapped three times on the side of Darac's desk.

'Bonbon's got things under control, don't worry.'

'That's good. We'll report back soonest.'

'Thanks, Map.' Darac ended the call and tapped key #1 on the phone.

'Poisoned?' Bonbon said, his wiry red hair appearing to bristle at the thought. 'I'd hate to go that way.'

'Depends on the speed, I think. Do you remember our old friend Rocuronium? In the right dose, it can dispatch you in one second flat.'

Bonbon drew down the corners of his mouth and nodded. 'Hmm. Might keep a stock in. Be handy if cousin Guim comes to stay again.'

Darac was chuckling as Agnès picked up.

'Paul. What's funny?'

'Oh, Bonbon's just talking about killing himself.'

The man gave the desk another three raps.

'Yes, that is funny,' she deadpanned. 'So?'

'Map's just reported in from St Roch on the Urquelle death. For semi, read *fully* suspicious.'

'Because?'

'It seems the man was poisoned. Only *seems*, note. Map will have more on that later. Nevertheless, he's suggesting we put R.O.'s team on standby.'

'Duly authorised. I'll ring him immediately after our call.'

'I'd like to draft Lartou in right away, though.'

'Ditto.'

'He can begin looking at any CCTV footage the store may have of Urquelle's collapse. Which he'll be doing behind the scenes, of course, and that should please the management. Before we get to the "screw 'em!" stage, it's better to have them on board.'

'I taught you well,' she said, the smile audible in her voice. 'I've already been on to the store manager, one Albert Cassani, and told him about Flaco and Perand's imminent arrival.'

'And how did he take that?'

'He was accommodating. Charming, even, particularly when I told them they were wearing civvies and it was just a form-filling exercise.'

'Excellent.'

'I've met Cassani at a couple of parties. Civic things. He's dull as mud but he was very pleasant to me – pleasant, shading into hopeless infatuation, actually. My suggestion that if the store had any issues whatsoever with this thing, he should discuss them with me seemed to go down *very* well. So should the heat come on at some stage, I should be able to absorb any that radiates from that particular quarter.'

'Agnès, if I didn't know you better, I'd accuse you of using feminine wiles to produce an entirely different sort of heat in the man.'

'Guilty! Anyway, the kindling was already smouldering. I merely blew a little air over it so it would catch. Subtly, of course.'

'You are incorrigible! Either that, or yet again you're taking one for the team – whichever you prefer.'

'Admit to being either savvy or a martyr? No contest!'

Over the years, Darac had enjoyed hundreds of similar exchanges with Agnès but they were becoming increasingly bittersweet for him. It was some time ago now that she had first mentioned her intention to retire in the not too distant future. That future was coming closer all the time.

'Quite right,' he said, and left it there.

'Map's concerns mean I'd like you to check things out at the store. If it proves to be nothing, no harm will have been done; if it *is* a poisoning, it would be good to have you on the ground.'

'Sure. I'll update Flak and Perand.' Bonbon raised a hand. 'Oh, and now Bonbon has a reason to live, he's signed up as well.'

'Perfect. I'll inform Cassani. And on a different note, Paul...'

For a moment, that note failed to sound.

'I'm listening.'

'Just let Frankie know I'll be thinking of her later, will you?'

10.27 AM

As they walked through the colonnade into the lower Jean Médecin entrance of *Palais Masséna*, Darac found himself saying, 'Imagine having to evacuate a place this size, Bonbon.'

'Five huge floors? I'd rather not.'

'Don't worry. If this comes to a full Evac job, I'll eat my lounge guitar.'

'It would almost be worth it.'

Darac didn't need the help of a sign indicating that *L'Éspace Beauté* was away to their left.

'If ever there were a case for just following your nose, Bonbon.'

Bonbon sniffed. And sniffed again. 'What is it with you Daracs? I can't detect even a hint of it.'

'If things get any slacker, I'll recount some of the olfactory feats of our ancestral sheepdogs. Now *they* had noses.'

'Oh, mate.' Bonbon grinned wickedly. 'I literally can't wait for that.'

'Better still, I could teach Armani a couple of *Creusois* folk songs on the subject. Think *Volare* promised more than it delivered? Wait until you hear the man grinding through the inspiring tale of *Coco And The Vole*.'

Bonbon muttered something comprehensible only to the earthier members of his Catalan brethren and the topic was dropped.

Once in the department, the pair joined a clientele browsing in an atmosphere that conveyed not the slightest hint of the shocking death that had taken place within the past hour. But then they spotted a coned-off section of floor about the area of a family car.

'Where's our man?' Darac said. 'And where have Flaco and Perand got to?'

'Hello, Lieutenant.'

Bonbon's twinkly eyes twinkled more brightly as he turned and extended his hand. 'André. Good to see you again. This is Captain Paul Darac.'

'Captain.' They shook hands. 'André Ricolfi. I've just said to your junior officers that I knew there was something queer about our little excitement earlier.' He nodded toward the cones. 'But a possible poisoning?' He shook his head. 'Wasn't expecting that.'

'I believe you were close to the man when he collapsed.'

'Pretty close, Captain. I heard a kerfuffle behind me, turned, and saw him stagger, then hit the floor. In real distress, he was.'

'And you didn't have it down as a heart attack or something equally routine, I understand. Why?'

'No, it was more as if...' He couldn't seem to find the *mots justes*.

'Just describe how he looked.'

'It's bizarre this, but with one important difference, the only time I saw anyone in a state like that was on the forecourt at Foch thirty years ago – a gangster named Louis Brac. I was right there when a member of a rival outfit set him on fire.'

The pair involuntarily expressed the connection between sex and eternal damnation. 'What was that difference?' Bonbon asked.

'Brac screamed his head off. Monsieur Urquelle hardly made a sound.'

'Did you clock Urquelle at any point before he collapsed?'

'I see what you're getting at, Captain. No, I'm afraid I didn't. But there should be CCTV footage of it. And of him arriving, and so on. The cameras are recording all the time.'

'Is it contracted out, the surveillance?'

'Company called A1 did it until recently but we were told they kept upping their charges.'

Darac shared a look with Bonbon.

'A1, eh?'

'You know them, gentlemen?'

'We know them,' Darac said, simply. 'So what happens now on that score?'

'Surveillance? We do it ourselves.'

Darac had mixed feelings about this. At times, surveillance companies could be very clingy with their product. But Agnès's charm bracelet hold over store manager Albert Cassani notwithstanding, the *Pal-Mas* brass might be even clingier if it emerged that Urquelle had come into the store to complain about the decommissioned nuclear reactor he'd bought there on spesh.

'What does that mean in practice, André?'

'I'll give you the theory first. Overnight, a couple of guys patrol the floors and monitor the screens.' He gave a wry little laugh. 'In practice...'

Bonbon beat him to it. 'The guys play dominoes or chess all night, taking occasional breaks to stretch their legs?'

André nodded. 'But you didn't hear it here.'

'And when the store's open?' Darac asked.

'We could do with more people, to be honest, so we generally have our hands full out on the floors. Nevertheless, we try to ensure that *someone's* keeping an eye on the screens. But there are inevitably gaps.'

'And at the time of the incident?'

'That was a gap. And then with the *brouhaha,* all hands were needed here. But as I say, the cameras are always on so the footage *will* be there.'

'Has anyone viewed it since?'

'I doubt it.'

'Do you know Jean-Jacques Lartigue – "Lartou" we call him?'

'Your crime scene co-ordination guy? Heard of him.'

'He'll be here any minute. If someone could just show him where set-up is, he'll do the rest.'

'It's down in the basement. I'll get Marcel to show him – Marcel Fraille – he probably knows most about it.'

'Good, thanks.'

Feeling the familiar throb, Darac fished his mobile from his jacket pocket and glanced at the screen. A flagged message from Flaco. He read it, then angled the phone for Bonbon. It began:

I've got someone who wants to talk to you.

'How do I get to the senior staffroom, André?'

'That's also in the basement, Captain, but at the opposite end. Take the stairs down at the back of this floor.' He indicated the direction. 'And then it's the door on the right. I could take you, if you like, but I'd need to get someone to watch the coned area.'

'No, you continue with Bonbon.' He turned to him.

'Stay tuned, mate.'

As he walked away, he heard Bonbon ask if any of André's colleagues in security may have seen more. He was out of earshot by the time the reply came.

* * *

With its glass entrance door, wipe-clean surfaces and matching high-backed chairs, the senior staffroom put Darac in mind of a dayroom in a *maison de retraite*. Perhaps it was because his investigative juices were beginning to flow but he couldn't help wondering if the décor was a ploy by the management: a subtle hint to the seniors that life after *Pal-Mas* would be a much emptier business. Association; intimation; persuasion – it was all in the retail game, wasn't it? Not for the first time, he felt glad that his father's successful perfumery was very much a boutique operation.

The room was deserted except for Flaco and her charge, a woman Darac *Père* would have described as "just a little too beautifully made-up." She was also holding a red-flecked tissue to her left nostril. Its predecessors, Darac noticed, lay in a gaudier crumple in the bin at her feet. The bleed, therefore, appeared to be slowing, but concerned about its possible connection to the poisoning, he felt a frisson of unease as he sat next to Flaco.

'Madame Nadine Beaumont here is prone to nosebleeds, Captain,' she said, allaying the obvious implication. 'She is in charge of the floor where the incident took place.'

'I'm Paul Darac, madame. It's clear that you are indisposed but it would be a great help to us if we could go ahead.'

'It's fine.' She lowered the tissue momentarily. 'Darac, did you say?'

'Yes.' He saw what was coming but there was no time for it. 'No connection with the perfume house, I'm afraid.'

Flaco, fortunately, appeared to see the reason behind the lie.

'Shame,' Nadine said, cryptically and gave her right nostril a tentative dab. 'I think it's stopped. Excuse me.' She examined the tissue. 'Yes, it has, and once it stops, it's stopped.' She consigned the tissue to the bin. 'It's a nuisance but it happens sometimes when I'm upset. Silly.'

'It's understandable, madame. Witnessing a customer stagger and fall to the floor in distress would upset anyone. And as to reactions, trained police officers have been known to faint at the sight of blood.'

'You're very kind but I need to say that...'

She went no further as Darac's mobile rang.

'Excuse me. Perand?'

'Lartou's arrived, chief. André's detailed a Marcel Fraille to look after him.'

'Good. Listen, I may need a gatekeeper here. Get down to the senior staffroom as soon as you can, will you?'

'Alright.'

'That's it.' He returned his attention to Nadine. 'So, madame, Officer Flaco here reports you have something important to tell me.'

'Yes.' She exhaled deeply, anxious, it was obvious, at the prospect of telling her story. 'First, I was going to say that I didn't actually see the dead man collapse. I was involved in something on the top floor when it happened. The top floor rear annexe, in fact. One may as well be in Outer Mongolia up there. We didn't know anything about it.'

'So it was hearing about the death later that upset you?'

'No. Well, yes, in a way.' As if maintaining eye contact might derail the process, Nadine's gaze fell on the row of empty chairs opposite. 'It was what happened before then. A new girl started with us today. She was from somewhere in Eastern Europe originally, I think. Zena. Zena Bairault.'

'Spell her surname, madame?' Flaco said, and wrote down the name in her notebook.

'She mentioned where she was from?' Darac said.

'No, it was her accent. Her French itself is exceptional. In fact, she's an exceptional girl in general. Very bright. Not conventionally attractive, I suppose you would say, but blessed with the most winning personality.' Nadine seemed far away, suddenly. 'Different from my other girls, somehow. She was tasked with promoting this week's featured fragrance, *Chanson de Minuit*. We call what she was doing "sassing"– getting the customer to stand and sniff the fragrance while giving them three good reasons to buy it. *Chanson* is unisex. Between us, it's rather a difficult sell at the moment. In time, I believe it will catch on but we have sold very little to date.'

From Stop and Search, to Stand and Sniff, Darac knew a great deal about sassing but he didn't want to slow Nadine's narrative.

'Interesting. Please continue, madame.'

Nadine went on to describe Zena's engagement with Gérard Urquelle exactly as she had witnessed it. At its conclusion, she said, 'I realise it looks bad. But Zena isn't some terrible criminal, Captain. She's a wonderful young woman. Really, she is.'

Darac shared a look with Flaco that suggested a different interpretation. 'We need to speed things up now, Madame Beaumont. Considerably. Where is this Zena Bairault at this moment?'

Nadine was clearly disconcerted by the change of pace and tone in Darac's mien. 'Uh... She went home. Terribly upset at what had happened, I suppose.'

'Where is home, do you know?'

At last, she looked Darac in the eyes. 'I have no idea.'

'But your HR department will have her address and phone number?'

'Of course.'

And they would also have a current photograph. There wasn't time to go through the process of obtaining the court order strictly necessary to acquire this information. But thanks to Agnès, there was a way forward. Darac opened his bag and handed Flaco his laptop. 'Check our database for Zena, would you, Flak? I'm just going outside. Be right back, madame.'

Gatekeeper Perand had either abandoned his post temporarily or hadn't arrived yet. Either way, Darac had no time to go looking for him so with his eyes trained on the stairs, he called Bonbon with the update and instructed him to contact the store's HR department without delay. Citing store manager Albert Cassani's imprimatur if anyone got sticky about it, Bonbon was to obtain from them Zena Bairault's address and photograph. They both suspected, even expected, the address to be a phoney; the photo, however, would necessarily be genuine. Bonbon was then to email these details to Agnès. She would do the rest.

'Finally, get hold of Perand, will you, Bonbon? He's needed here *now*. He knows why.'

'Will do.'

'Anything, Flak?' Darac said, resuming his seat next to her.

'Not yet, Captain.'

'Madame Beaumont, you said that when Zena approached Monsieur Urquelle, it was almost as if she were waiting for "this one customer" to appear?'

'Well, yes.' Her forehead crumpled in exasperation. 'But

only because she let so many other customers go without approaching them. They were nearly all women, though, and as I said, I think she was waiting for a man because I had told her that it was a much greater challenge.'

'Uh-huh. Because you were monitoring her performance from the beginning, you are certain that the man later identified as Monsieur Gérard Urquelle was the first customer of either sex Zena approached?'

'Yes.'

'Do you know if she approached anyone after him?'

'As far as I know, she didn't.'

'Were any of your other staff sassing *Chanson de Minuit*?'

'No. Just Zena. I had three other girls working the floor but they were promoting different products.'

'One or more of them must have witnessed Zena's encounter with the man who died, surely?'

'No. We don't have our girls hunting in packs like wolves. We space them well apart. It's far more comfortable for our clients that way and therefore far more effective.'

'After Zena went home, was anyone else given the task of sassing *Chanson de Minuit*?'

'No one.'

From the point of view of public health and safety, Darac had been reassured by Nadine's responses thus far. But there was a way to go yet.

'*Chanson* is made by the *Arcelle* company, I believe.'

'Ye-es, it is.'

'You say this promotion has been going on for several days?

'Since Monday.'

Five days and no other incidents reported until today? Darac's picture of what had happened was becoming clearer all the time. 'Are the sales people who sassed customers with

Chanson de Minuit earlier this week working today?'

'No, neither Jeanne nor Muriel is here today or I would have had at least one of them on sass with Zena.'

'We may well have to talk to them.'

'I dare say.' She set her jaw. 'But I have to tell you that I count *both* of these women as friends. *Both* have worked here for many years and *both* have spotless records. It's absolutely absurd to think that either of them could have been involved in anything *underhanded* let alone something as appalling as murder.'

Statistically, Madame was of course entirely correct. But over the years, he'd encountered many a lovely, reliable person who had planned or executed a murder. 'However unpromising they may seem, we have to pursue all avenues, madame. Perhaps you would let us have their full names later?'

She shook her head but said, 'Alright.'

'Your stock of the product – was it all just one consignment?'

'One, yes. It hasn't been popular, as I say.'

'That notwithstanding, I think it wise to have all Arcelle products removed from the shelves.'

Nadine sighed at the thought but then brightened, suddenly.

'Oh, I see. You mean someone, perhaps in the perfumery, might have adulterated the scent and Zena *inadvertently* sprayed it on the victim?'

There were other possibilities but Nadine's eagerness to help Zena looked certain to ensure her co-operation and that was a useful line to take. While he still could.

'It's possible that's what happened,' he said, quite truthfully. But then he got to the real nitty-gritty. 'And the scent itself, Zena sprayed. It was an eau-de-toilette, I imagine?'

Whoops. 'Or something else?'

Nadine raised her perfectly sculpted eyebrows. 'You imagine correctly. Are you sure you're not Martin Darac's son? You resemble him, actually...'

'Madame, please.'

'Yes, sorry. For sassing a customer, initial impact in a fragrance is key and anything less concentrated than a toilette doesn't have it; anything more concentrated is too expensive.'

'And was the scent she used regular stock, a tester – what?'

'Tester. In the form of a glass vial, 25 mil capacity.'

'An atomiser?'

'Yes, she took it from a small box in the supply cupboard.'

'Containing how many originally and how many now?'

'Twenty-four, originally. If there was still some left in it, she would have put it back in there at the end of her shift. Each girl does that. How many now? I'm not sure. Over twenty. Possibly, twenty-two.'

'And was the one she used, new and unopened at the start of the day, or was it half-full? Did you notice?'

Nadine hesitated. It was clear to Darac that she realised there was an opportunity to give Zena a helping hand here. 'Yes, madame?'

'No,' she said, her gaze lowered like a flag at half-mast. 'I'm afraid I can't say I did notice.'

Darac had already formed a largely favourable opinion of Madame Nadine Beaumont. It had just become more favourable still. 'But could you see that the atomiser she used during the encounter with Monsieur Urquelle appeared to be the same as all the others?'

'Oh yes, it had the black concentric circle design all their products have. That I *did* see.'

Darac ran a hand through his hair. 'We need to impound that box of testers which, thanks to its diminutive size, one of my team can carry out quite discreetly. May I have your key?'

'Uh... Certainly.'

As if on cue, the door opened and Perand appeared in the crack. 'Here, chief. Got caught up. Sorry.'

'Come in, I've got a job for you.'

Darac told him what he wanted. 'And don't, repeat *don't* spray any of the stuff. *Or* sniff any empty vials. Got that?'

'Got it.'

'Here's Madame's key. Bring it back immediately afterwards. En route, call André and get him to detail someone to stop people coming down here.'

'Check.'

'Don't lose my key!' Madame called after him as he took his leave.

'As for clearing the shelves of stock, madame, what would be the quickest and most unobtrusive way of achieving that?'

'If you would permit me to call the stockroom, Hamad and his crew would have the shelves cleared and the stock stacked neatly away in ten minutes at the outside.'

'OK.' Darac looked into her eyes. 'Madame, I am relying on you—'

'I won't say anything out of turn, I swear. And in fact, it will seem far more natural if the order comes from me. There'll be no fuss at all about it.'

Darac was sure she was right. 'Go ahead, please.'

While Nadine fished her mobile out of her handbag, Darac gave Flaco a look. She shook her head. That there was still nothing on Zena Bairault meant it was almost certainly an alias.

'Hamad? It's Nadine. Sorry to be a pain, but we've had

a bit of a stinger from head office.' She listened. 'Yes, *again*. I was going to mention it before but with that poor man collapsing...' She listened, indicating by a look that it would have seemed odd not to have referred to the incident. 'Yes, people should look after themselves better.'

Darac gave her an approving nod and she continued.

'Anyway, would you be a darling and get a couple of your people to remove all the Arcelle stuff from *L'Éspace*?' She listened. 'Yes, straight away, please. Everything with *de Minuit* after it, that's right.' More listening. 'Just in the stock-room and put a please leave on it. Thanks, Hamad. I must get on.' She ended the call. 'There.'

'A very convincing performance, madame.' Worryingly so, perhaps. 'I may need you to reprise something similar.'

'Ah, yes?'

'It would be useful to know if anyone other than Monsieur Urquelle purchased an Arcelle product this morning. We may need to trace them. *Could* someone check that?'

'It *could* be checked, and if the customer paid by card, it would be easy to trace them eventually. We French still prefer cash to cards but our clientele is truly international and so there would be many such purchases recorded. You have to bear in mind, though, that this is a huge, open store, Captain. Customers go from one department to another. A list of Arcelle sales could be put together but it would have to be done overnight, not before.'

'Understood.' Once again, Darac gave Flaco an enquiring look. Once again, she shook her head. Once again, he returned to Nadine.

'Madame, you mentioned that Zena sprayed Urquelle's pulse points. The usual practice is to spray a card, isn't it?'

'It is but she had forgotten to take them out on to the floor. It shows just how talented she was to be able to persuade a man to offer his person in the way she did.'

'She was bright as well as talented, you say?'

'Very.'

'And yet she left behind an essential tool of the trade? Along with the sample of *Chanson de Minuit* and the cupboard key, a supply of cards was one of only three things she needed?'

Nadine looked away, considering the point. 'Yes.' She gave a sad little shake of the head. 'That's not what I would have expected.'

'Madame, before his encounter with Zena Bairault, Monsieur Urquelle seemed to you to be well and functioning normally?'

'Apart from a slight limp, yes. But he didn't pay any attention to that – it was obviously something he was used to. I was called away a minute or so after he had parted from Zena and he seemed as perfectly well and happy then as he had before. As did Zena herself.'

'So she didn't dash away immediately after the encounter?'

'No.'

'The store's CCTV – does it cover the spot where Zena approached Urquelle?'

Nadine stiffened. 'Don't you believe my account?'

He gave her a mildly rebuking look. 'Please just answer my question.'

'Yes, alright.' She took a breath. 'No. There are cameras all around the store but they cover the tills areas and most of the entrances and exits. Including the lifts. Nowhere else.'

'Flak, anything?'

'Still trying.'

'How long were you absent from the department, madame?'

'About 25 minutes all told. You see I was—'

'And how long did it take you to discover that a man you learned had collapsed and been removed to hospital in your absence was the *same* man Zena had sassed earlier?'

'Not for about another... twenty-something minutes.'

'What led to that discovery?'

'It was when I...' She hesitated but, perhaps sensing that she was going to be given the hurry-up once more, she pressed on. 'It was when I realised Zena was not on the shop floor. She didn't answer a staff call and so I went to check the junior staffroom. Her locker door was ajar. She had gone.'

'Earlier, madame, you said she had gone home, upset.'

'That's what I supposed.'

Darac stared at the floor for a moment while he put the thing together in his head. In not rushing off immediately after approaching Urquelle, the salesperson-cum-possible assassin Zena Bairault had potentially achieved four objectives. One: she hadn't drawn attention to herself. Two: she hadn't planted in the minds of onlookers that her flight was connected with her contact with Urquelle. Three: in waiting until the man had collapsed, drawing all eyes to *him*, she had been able to melt discreetly away, apparently unnoticed. And, finally, she had had ample proof that her handiwork had paid off. Or to put it another way, her mission had been carried out successfully.

'You said earlier that, culminating in her flight from the store, the sequence of events involving Zena which led to the sudden death of her customer looked "bad" for her. In other words, it suggested her guilt. Madame, did you share that assessment with anyone else?'

'For the very reason that it did look bad, I kept it to myself. But there wasn't time to share it, anyway.'

'It was at that very moment you began to feel ill?'

'Oh, I didn't feel *ill* at all. It was just my nose starting up. It's a strange reaction to stress, I know, but there it is. I've always had it.'

She *didn't* feel ill, Darac noted. And no other members of staff had reported sick, either.

Nadine continued: 'And then within a minute or two, this young lady and the other officer arrived, and then you.' She shrugged. 'There we have it.'

Flaco's eyes finally left the screen. 'Captain?'

Darac got to his feet. 'Just remain there, madame. Officer Flaco and I are going outside for a moment. We can see you through the door so you'll be quite safe.'

'Of course I'll be safe!'

It also meant that they would see if she tried to phone anyone. As soon as the door closed behind them, the sound of feet lurching down the stairs suppressed Flaco's news for the moment. The feet proved to be Perand's and the bottom-up reveal disclosed he was carrying a small cardboard box in one hand and a paper bag in the other. 'Twenty-one unopened testers in the box,' he announced, still descending. 'Two empty ones in the bag. I got those out of a bin in the supply cupboard. Before you ask, I didn't sniff the empties and André will be here any second.'

'So that's just one missing. *One,* note. Good work, Perand. The bag and the box will have to go over to the lab.' He indicated the laptop. 'But we've got something. Flak?'

'I've discovered the existence of five Zena Bairaults living in France. None is our suspect. Whoever she was, she was using an alias.'

Three crucial calls now needed to be made and as speed was of the essence, Darac opted to share the load.

'Perand, you haven't heard this yet but Urquelle's death is looking more and more like a targeted hit.'

'What?' he said, carefully setting down his treasure trove. 'Jesus.'

In three succinct sentences, Darac summarised the evidence.

'Now we need to get busy.'

It was a mark of the complete trust he had in Flaco that he had no qualms in giving the young woman from Guadeloupe the most crucial task.

'Flak, call Agnès and outline the Zena Bairault development. That will ensure all relevant wheels are set in motion here in the store *and* beyond. Tell Agnès I'll call her a.s.a.p. Then start checking out Gérard Urquelle. We'll get more eyes on this later but see if you can find a motive for his poisoning. It could be something quite clear and obvious – like he was an ex-KGB officer who had defected. It seems Zena has an East European accent, remember.'

'A Litvinenko-style assassination?' Perand said. 'Jesus Christ.'

'Considering the setting and so on,' Darac said, 'I think it most unlikely but nothing can be ruled out.'

'Urquelle's never been inside' Flaco said. '*That* we do know. Managed to run a quick eye over the convictions database.'

One of these days, Darac knew he would lose Flaco to a promotion. It would be a great day for her; a sad one for the team. 'Well done. Keep looking, if you can.'

She nodded.

'Perand, call Deanna or Map at the Path Lab and update them on what you've just heard. Don't forget to point out that they have come by a useful control: Urquelle's effects contain an unopened bottle of the same perfume brand, fragrance and concentration that Zena is supposed to have had in her vial tester – an atomised sample of which wound up on Urquelle's wrists and may have killed him. Also, the other testers you've got there will be with them shortly. Clear?'

'Clear.'

'Right, whoever finishes their call first, that person calls Granot and updates him. The sooner we get him here, the better – especially if we end up having to triage witnesses.' He looked up and down the corridor. 'I'm going to swap updates with Bonbon but we can't have three voices echoing around.' It was only then he noticed the brace of pay phones attached to the end wall. 'You two go there – the cowls should muffle things sufficiently. I'll call from here and keep an eye on Madame through the door. When I've finished my call, I'll resume with her. OK, that's it.'

With Perand loping along after her, Flaco hastened away and Darac put in his call. He gave his own update first and then Bonbon reported that, without the sanction of a court order, HR had indeed been averse to divulging information on the woman calling herself Zena Bairault. Nor did they take Bonbon's word that store manager Cassani would okay the request. Valuable time was wasted arguing the toss but a call to Cassani was eventually made and the information – address, phone number, photograph and all – duly provided. With no further delay, Bonbon emailed it to Agnès at the Caserne.

As Flaco and Perand continued their calls, Darac signed off with Bonbon and picked up where he had left off with Nadine Beaumont.

'Sorry to have kept you waiting, madame. You mentioned that when Zena sprayed Urquelle's wrists, she took a step back.'

'So you are continuing, then?' Nadine said, acknowledging that Flaco's search hadn't come up with a result that quashed Darac's suspicions. 'Even more urgently.'

'Forgive me, but the step back?'

'It's part of the routine.'

'At that moment, did Zena look away also? Or close her eyes? Or did it look as if she might be holding her breath?'

'You're asking if she tried to avoid inhaling some of the scent, aren't you?'

'Yes.'

'If she did, it wasn't obvious. Not obvious at all.'

The questioning continued along similar lines until the door opened and Flaco reappeared with Perand and Bonbon. There had been further developments, clearly.

'Is André out there?' Darac said, rising.

'Policing the top of the stairs, yes. He's diverting senior members to the general staffroom on the other side. They don't like it but they're doing what they're told.'

Nadine made a harrumphing sound but said nothing.

'Apologies, madame. We require another moment alone.'

'That's fine.'

Darac shepherded the trio out into the corridor and, with sounds of sporadically raised voices reverberating down the stairs, the impromptu summit got under way on an upbeat note.

'OK, Flak,' he said, glancing back through the door. 'Take it.'

'Commissaire Dantier said, "All wheels are turning," unquote.'

That Agnès was in every sense on the case gave Darac the sort of charge he felt when working with his band on their best nights; a feeling of complete trust and confidence in their talents and his own. 'Spin those wheels, Flak.'

She reported that Agnès had already prepared a note advising the augmentation of surveillance at critical air, sea, rail and road hubs and routes. On receiving Bonbon's email containing the fugitive's details, she made five moves in quick succession. First, attaching her note, she forwarded the email to Eric Novotny, chief of RAID, an élite tactical unit based at the Caserne; to Commandant Pietrangeli at Commissariat Foch; and to the heads of the local and regional gendarmerie. Next, she dispatched a quartet of officers standing by with Haz-Mat suits at the ready to Zena's declared address, *Les Appartements Raymond Kopa, 14,* in Pont-Michel. Thirdly, she gave the address to Duty Officer Charvet and instructed him to approach Estates Finance at the *Mairie* to check the registry of property owners – *le cadastre* – to determine who rented the apartment to the fugitive. Then she passed on Zena's specified mobile number to the Brigade's technology wizard Erica Lamarthe and asked her to work whatever magic she could to trace the young woman. And finally, she called Monsieur Cassani, thanking him for his assistance thus far, and making further arrangements for the store.

'Brava, Agnès!'

'Just one more thing on this, Captain. When *all* the wheels were turning, the Commissaire said, then and only then, was she going to call Public Prosecutor Frènes to obtain what she called his "posthumous green light." '

Grins of admiration all round.

'You didn't say *what* arrangements for the store,' Perand said.

'Not difficult to guess,' Darac said. 'Agnès will have informed Cassani that the cosmetics floor will have to be cleared of customers and staff; that it will be forensically examined; that any personnel who were present during the incident will have to be questioned; and that an appeal will have to go out for any customers who witnessed it to come forward. For openers.'

Flaco nodded. 'Almost word for word, Captain.'

'Have you had time to look into Urquelle?'

'Just criminal records. He's clean. But he did receive a caution a few months back for discharging an air rifle in his garden. It was only to scare a cat, though.'

'Maybe Bairault's a member of the Feline Defence League,' Perand said. 'Seriously. Animal lovers are fucking mad, some of them.'

'Be that as it may, keep delving, Flak. Bonbon?'

'I have just one point. It was Serge Paulin that Agnès dispatched to Pont-Michel. Serge with a team of three and Wanda Korneliuk at the wheel – they'll be there by now for sure.'

Darac almost called out "Yeah!" but he said "Perfect" instead.

'Anything on the *cadastre* request?'

'The apartment is owned by a Madame Gourdon who lives in Lyon. She's not supposed to have sublet the place but it's not unknown. Since Wednesday, she's been holidaying in London. Due back next Wednesday. A call has been made to the hotel in question.'

'Probably out for the day. Perand, who did you speak to at Path?'

'Map, chief,' he said, scrolling notes on his mobile. 'Urquelle's body had only just turned up from St. Roch so they hadn't got started yet. By "they," I mean Map and Professor B, by the way.'

Map and Deanna Bianchi made another dream team, Darac reflected. The pathology department's answer to Lester Young and Billie Holiday.

'I told them about the spraying incident and mentioned that Urquelle's effects include a bottle of the same stuff Zena Bairault is meant to have used, and that the remaining testers, including two empties used by other employees earlier in the week, were being sent over soonest.'

'Good summary. Map's reaction?'

'It's big but I'll kick off with the little. The red zone team is *Go* and they should be here any minute. Anyone who assisted Urquelle *physically* – and from the store, that means André, basically – will need to be checked for contamination. Hôpital Pasteur are sending an ambulance car.'

'*Two* first aiders gave Urquelle CPR, remember.'

'The other was a customer, though. Foch are putting out feelers for her.'

'Does *André* know he's to be checked out?'

Bonbon grinned. 'I told him just now but he says he feels fine. In fact, he hasn't enjoyed a day at work as much as this in years. More practically, he's got a colleague standing by to keep the hordes at bay if we're still down here when they come for him.'

Darac could understand André's relish at being back in harness but such things had been known to skew judgment. 'He may *feel* fine but does he look it?'

'Absolutely, he does.'

Darac thought about that for a moment. 'Good enough. Next, Perand?'

'Map stressed that priority *numero uno* was to find the atomiser Zena actually used. It might have a lot of lethal shit still in it.'

'R.O's team will look for the bottle, of course, but she'll still have it with her, I'll bet. Next?'

'Samples from any section of the floor where droplets of the stuff may have landed are to be removed to the lab immediately for analysis. That's it.'

'Good.' Darac took a couple of paces and shouted up the stairs. 'Are you alright up there, André?'

'Never better, Captain. Ambulance car? Don't know what all the fuss is about!'

'Better safe than sorry, buddy.'

'Pah!'

Reflecting that Foch had lost a doughty officer when André had retired, Darac was about to lead the trio back into the staffroom when their mobiles throbbed and chimed and pinged simultaneously. It was a curious anomaly that the indolent Perand was always quickest on the draw in such situations.

'Email from Lartou,' he said. 'Headed "Urquelle, Gérard: Fatality Footage." '

A moment or two to download and then with Perand's device once again a little ahead of the others, they each watched as, clutching the string handle of a small paper carrier bag, Urquelle began to cross the frame right-to-left. André, looking away from the camera, was standing chatting to someone he seemed to know in the background. The time tag read 09.32. Urquelle looked completely at ease as he continued toward the exit but then he paused, knotting his brow as if something incomprehensible had suddenly appeared in front of him. In the next second, the reaction extended to everything around him. But then he appeared to find meaning and it was the meaning of pain.

His face contorted, he tried to walk on but it was as if his body had sprouted strings and a puppet master was pulling them at random. A female customer gasped. André's acquaintance exclaimed something and André turned. The puppet tore at the cravat at his neck and, his mouth agape, he crashed to the floor as if the strings had been cut all at once. The speed at which the crowd gathered was such that André, already calling an ambulance, had to push his way through bodies to attend the stricken man. A professional-looking woman came forward also. They conferred for a brief moment and as the victim's condition worsened,

André went into full CPR action.

Reflecting that André had painted an entirely accurate picture of Urquelle's collapse, Darac broke off watching the video to call the sender. 'Thanks for the footage, Lartou. You emailed it to Path also?'

'Absolutely, chief.'

'Good. I'm three minutes in and I see it lasts a few seconds over ten minutes altogether. What's happening at the end?'

'The removal of the stretcher-borne Urquelle towards an ambulance. Lignes d'Azur held tramway traffic between Jean Médecin and Opéra Vieille-Ville for a few minutes to allow the closest access.'

'Right. Anything strike you overall?'

'Just the suddenness and the degree of suffering the man endured. Interestingly, there's no one looking on in triumph or anything like a perp might do. That said, at 7.52 in, one of the crowd does take a photo or photos with her phone.'

'7.52? We'll look out for it.'

'It's when the ambulance crew rush in to the store.'

'Is Marcel... Fraille still with you?'

'Yes, he is.'

'Ask him to show you footage of any of the locations one Zena Bairault might have crossed in leaving L'Éspace de Beauté at 09.32 and subsequently fleeing the store, would you? HR have a photo of her if he doesn't know who he's looking for.'

'Spelled B-É–R–O?'

'B-A-I-R-A-U-L-T.'

'Will do, Captain.'

'And that was quick work, Lartou.'

Darac returned to the video and at the end of it, he called for the others' thoughts. There was little or no divergence from Lartigue's reaction.

'You're quite the photographer, Bonbon. What did you make of the woman from 7.52? What was she up to?'

'Judging by the angles and where she was standing, et cetera, I'd say she was shooting the arrival of the ambulance crew. Bit odd but it *was* quite a spectacle, I suppose. And not once did she point her phone at Monsieur Urquelle himself.'

'My feelings, too. Any counter theories?'

There was none.

'Let's get back in there. I think we can wrap things up with Madame Beaumont for the time being. Flak, I'd like you to stay with her for a little while. Engage her in small talk.'

'Good luck with that,' Perand said, with a smirk.

Darac pressed on. 'Off guard, she may just let something slip.'

She was cutting an increasingly forlorn figure, Darac felt, as they entered. And the investigation had barely got going. 'Madame,' he said, with a most *sympa* smile, 'Sorry to have kept you waiting once more. Here's some information for you. We've learned that *L'Éspace de Beauté* is to be cleared of customers; that each member of your staff is to be questioned; that an intensive forensic and pathological search for the atomiser used in the attack and for any attendant droplets of its contents is soon to get underway.'

'Oh, no. That poor girl.'

'What about her poor victim?' Perand said, unable to help himself.

'Perand!'

He shrugged.

'I want to thank you, Madame Beaumont. We may well need to talk some more but that will be all for now. For reasons I hope are self-evident, I'm assigning an officer to keep you company for the time being.'

'I may as well be under house arrest.'

'Sorry, I wasn't clear – you don't have to remain in this room. Officer Flaco will accompany you initially and then another female officer will take over.'

'Very well.'

'Later, Flak.'

'Right, Captain.'

As the trio left them to it, Darac was already swiping his mobile.

'What were you saying about eating your guitar?' Bonbon said, as Darac tapped key #1. 'Evacuating the whole store's not such an impossibility after all.'

'No one else but Urquelle is down, Bonbon. No one else seems to be sick in any way.'

'It does have *pro hit* written all over it, this thing.'

'Paul?'

'Agnès. We've got a free hand here thanks to you so that's fantastic.'

'Depending on how things go, it may not last but it should ensure a good start.'

'It already has. What's the bigger picture looking like?'

'What Frankie once memorably referred to as The Acronyms from Paris are showing an interest. The DCRI especially.'

The unexpected reference to Frankie gave Darac another positive charge but the prospect of interference from the State's many special forces units mitigated its effect somewhat. The Brigade had been shunted down that road before. With far from perfect results.

'They're not about to descend on us, are they?'

'Events may overtake us but so far, Eric Novotny's RAID

group at the Caserne is the only one on active standby and that's fair enough – in fact, I asked for them. But GIGN, UCLAT, etc – let's hope no one thinks we need those outfits. R.O. and his forensics team will be with you shortly, and along with Deanna and Map over in the lab, *that's* the combination I hope will ultimately provide the key to this thing.'

'Let's hope they provide it quickly. And let's hope we apprehend the woman calling herself Zena Bairault quicker still. She must be approached with extreme caution, though. In the attack, it appears she used only a minute quantity of the 25 millilitres of material those atomisers hold. If that doesn't put a tick in the Armed and Dangerous box, I don't know what does.'

11.03 AM

With her new backpack hanging proudly from her peg, Emma's fortunes appeared to have changed completely since yesterday. She hadn't made a single mistake reading aloud from *Polly La Futée et Cet Imbécile de Loup*, and everyone, including Clara, the prettiest and most powerful six year-old in school, had laughed at Emma's characterisations and voices.

After reading, music was next on the timetable and as teaching assistant Mata good-humouredly handed out the classroom instruments, the redoubtable Madame Poidatz released her nylon-strung guitar from its bag and tuned up. Not one of the world's great undiscovered talents on the instrument, Madame's genius was to get every child singing and playing along with gusto, regardless.

'Let's sing our song about clever young Polly and the silly old wolf, shall we?'

'Ye-es!'

As the song progressed, Emma's discovery that her maracas contained only one bean between them did little to dampen her spirits. Her four best friends, Clara, Danielle, Jamilla, and Sara liked her new backpack. But nobody in the whole world knew what was hiding *in* it, did they? No one except Emma. She gave the bean a particularly joyful shake to celebrate.

Yes, she knew she would have to wait until playtime to show them. And she mustn't let Madame or Mata see. But she knew how to do it. Clara had smuggled in some eye shadow once, and all five of them had had a go! Emma couldn't wait to see their faces when she got out what *she* had brought.

'Emma?'

'Yes, madame?'

'The song has finished.'

'Oh!' She set down the maracas. 'I liked it.'

'Thank you, Emma. That's nice. Now everyone get out your workbooks. We're going to write down what we've just been singing about.'

Desk lids rose and using hers as cover, Emma whispered something to Jamilla who passed it on and the message continued on its way right up to the top: Clara. The rendezvous had been set by the time the lids had been lowered. And Emma's stock had never been higher.

Relayed through speakers from the carriage in front, the guide's commentary was doing a good job of keeping the eyes of Zena's fellow passengers off her and on the ever-changing views outside. That, and the fugitive's subtle but effective wig and spectacles disguise was giving her at least some confidence that she would make it back.

'When the train swings to the left in a moment, if you look up to your right in our direction of travel, you will be rewarded with a glimpse of Peillon, one of the most beautiful *villages perchés* in France and the first true marvel on our journey in this, *Le Train des Merveilles*. A cluster of medieval buildings and narrow vaulted passageways clinging to a cone of rock, Peillon, according to a stone map table in the village, is some 376 metres above sea level. *All* reference books put the village's altitude at 372 metres. I think when you see it, you'll forgive the *Peillonnais* their little exaggeration. Ah, we're turning now... Almost there... And... There it is!'

The sight was greeted with general approbation and not a few cries of *Aaaah!*

Except for a suit tapping away at his laptop, Zena's was the only head of the dozen other passengers in the carriage that didn't turn. Seemingly lost in her battered English language version of John Kennedy Toole's *A Confederacy of Dunces*, she was playing the "I come this way often so don't bother me" card. But if someone couldn't resist striking up a conversation with her, she was ready with her cover story: Me? No, not on holiday. I work in the library at Sophia Antipolis's Parc Valrose campus in Nice. So secluded and tranquil. Yes, I am lucky to work in such a beautiful place. Where? Oh, just a studio flat in Rue de Bruges. No, not so lucky with that one. Travelling today? Family lives in Turin and I go home one weekend in every four. And you? *Preferably not Tende. And definitely not Fontan-Saorge. If it is, I'm travelling beyond and coming back later. And there's no fucking time for that.* No, no, I change in Tende. Why the train? Hate flying. Yes, this train does take hours but I like that. Pass the time? Reading, as you can see. Love to unwind with a good book. The commentary? No, I don't hear it any more. Besides, only one train a day has it. Must get back to my book. Lovely to meet you, too.

For those on the run, there were contrasting views on the value of such exchanges. Some maintained that it was a good idea to chat to people because it looked less suspicious to the police than keeping yourself very much to yourself. But there were obvious downsides. Among them was that the people to whom you had been chatting were much more likely to remember you afterwards. If you were long gone, it probably wouldn't matter. If you weren't, it might.

Zena checked her last remaining prepaid. Nothing. She was tempted to call her contact, herself. But no. Best to wait to be called. She was pretty sure the police would have got to Pont-Michel by now. It had been a risk providing the store's HR department with her actual address but it would have been even riskier to have given them a fake one. Providing an up-to-date photo, though, was unavoidable. It was no doubt already being circulated.

Sneaking a glance at her unfamiliar reflection in the window – a good omen – Zena's thoughts returned to her cover story. She had had misgivings about it from the start. Her true destination was the village of Saorge which offered the safest covert crossing into Italy and through which she had entered France just seven days before. Sited well below the village, the station of Fontan-Saorge came three stops before the terminus of the line at Tende where, the story had it, Zena was to change trains en route to her home city of Turin. Then why, she had asked her contact, didn't she simply swap Saorge for Turin in the story? The woman had replied that there was very little chance of Zena encountering a fellow homeward-bound *Torinese* on the slow first leg of a journey that had begun back in Nice and involved changing trains at both Tende and Cuneo. The "Train des Merveilles" was mainly for tourists or locals going just one or two stops. Indeed, that was the great advantage to the fugitive of using this train in the first place – the watching authorities were sure to be be concentrating their efforts on faster, more direct forms of flight. And, her contact had continued, even if Zena *did* have to chat to someone with intimate knowledge of Turin, the city covered a vast area and its population wasn't far short of two million – she would be able to say almost anything about her fake life there with impunity. The population of Saorge, however, was less than five hundred. It was a no brainer, the woman had said.

But that was then. Zena now realised that one of the strengths of the Train des Merveilles as a means of escape was also its weakness. By rail, it was just 38 short kilometres from Zena's boarding station in the northern *banlieues* of Nice to the wild, gorge-riven valley of the Roya over which the village of Saorge lay like a collection of pale plaster ornaments arranged on a shelf. But it was a 38-kilometre journey the train took 82 minutes to cover. Worse, there were all of nine station stops en route to her destination. Nine stops for new passengers to board. Nine sets of fresh eyes and ears – people who may have just seen or heard a news bulletin about the sensational incident at Palais Masséna. Nine stops also for passengers leaving the train to report their suspicions about one of their fellow travellers. But far, far, worse was the nine opportunities it afforded police officers of every stripe to board the train; fully informed *gardiens, gendarmes* or *flics* who knew what and who they were looking for and would walk slowly through the carriages scrutinising every face. At each new station stop, Zena knew her anxiety levels would rise higher.

She glanced at her pocket timetable. Four stations had been safely negotiated so far. Five to go. It was that fifth, the stop immediately before her destination, she feared most. Breil-sur-Roya was the most important station en route to Fontan-Saorge and it served the largest community. Worse still, by that point in the journey, many minutes would have ticked by since the police were first called, more details would be known, and the likelihood of capture, therefore, would have increased exponentially into the bargain.

She glanced at her watch. It was about 40 minutes to Breil where, to add to her problems, the train would wait for five whole minutes before continuing to Saorge, arriving 15 minutes later. But if all went well, by just after noon, she would be almost safe. All that would remain would be the two-hour trek through the wild Vallon de la Madonina where she had not encountered a single soul the week before.

While maintaining the appearance of being absorbed in her book, Zena resolved to pay attention to the commentary for a while. It just might help her relax. Although the village itself was no longer in sight, it seemed the guide's paean to Peillon was continuing.

'Was that not wonderful, everyone? And unlike so many

other *villages perchés*, the once marvellous Saint-Paul-de-Vence comes perhaps first to mind, there is not *one* tourist-trap trinket shop to mar the beauty of Peillon.

'Apart from the simple pleasure of wandering the medieval ruelles, a visit to La Chapelle des Pénitents Blancs near the very top of the village always proves an edifying experience. Built in the middle of the fifteenth century, La Chapelle became something of a film star in the twentieth. Or rather a supporting player in an important film. Are any of you familiar with the true World War II story of the kidnapping of Nazi General Heinrich Kreipe? It happened on the island of Crete and the escapade was filmed by British director Michael Powell in 1957 as *Ill Met By Moonlight*. Has anyone seen the film. No one? Do try to see it if you can. It's a fact known to few but many of the rugged Cretan landscapes shown in the movie were actually filmed in *this* very area. La Chapelle itself, features in one sequence. Over on the left shortly, the cement works at Blausac...'

Kidnap? That could work in a crisis. Especially with the atomiser right here in her jacket. She could hear herself: 'Back off or he gets it!' She rummaged through the objects in her pocket. The atomiser was not among them. Must be the other one. It was empty. *What the hell...*

'Excuse me interrupting your reading. Are you here on holiday, mademoiselle?'

It was the suit.

Zena's heart thumped, missed a beat and thumped again.

'Me? No, I work at Parc... Parc Valrose. The Faculty of Science library. In Nice.'

'Really? My son works at Sophia Antipolis.'

Shit. '*Does* he?' she said.

Darac was on the point of giving Frankie a quick call when his mobile rang. When it came on, Djibril Mpensa's voice was unusually urgent.

'Darac? Urquelle's c.o.d. is definitely poisoning. Some sort of organophosphate, possibly. No more details as yet but rest assured I'll let you know when we have anything significant.'

'Wait, wait. Just one question. Could the poison have been sprayed?'

'Could? Yes. Later.'

He rang off. And Darac's call to Frankie went on the back burner.

11.29 AM

Word had got around. Whenever *Tele-Sud* newshound Annie Provin got the scent of a crime in her nostrils, particularly if it turned out to be as juicy as it seemed at first sniff, there could be no other outcome. At least the various police, forensic and pathology teams were able to work without her pack breathing down their necks. Agnès was co-ordinating the operation and not for the first time, she had instructed the crowd control team to brook no argument in keeping all-comers well back from the action.

Although policing the store's many entrances was a tough call when four out of its five floors were operating more or less normally, it seemed no covertly taken still or video images of *L'Éspace de Beauté* had as yet appeared; no comments from store personnel had been finessed out of them; and any media type discovered approaching the red zone or anyone involved in the investigation in any way had been cautioned not to do so or else. As things stood, Agnès was happy with the security side of the operation.

The only public statement on the incident made so far had come in the past few minutes. Briefed by Agnès herself, Public Prosecutor Jules Frènes had still almost managed to let slip the name of the victim but he had recovered in time to deliver the key message that, despite the arrival of forensic teams wearing Haz-Mat suits, no Tokyo Metro-style attack had taken place here; and that the deployment of personnel so equipped was precautionary. Yes, he announced, the suspected murder of a 45 year-old man had occurred, and he went on to cite the person of interest sought in connection with it as a woman going by the name of Zena Bairault, 26, latterly of *Les Appartements Raymond Kopa*, Pont-Michel. He concluded by confirming that a combined police effort was well underway to apprehend Mademoiselle Bairault; that all forces were in possession of an up-to-date photograph of the suspected assailant; that said photo was now being made available to all media; that no member of the public should approach Bairault who was believed to be armed with a lethal close-range poison contained in a small perfume atomiser, and finally that neither Frènes himself, nor any other law enforcement officers, or members of the store management team would be answering questions at this time.

For once true to his word, a chorus of questions went unanswered as Frènes left the microphone.

'Monsieur! Was it a terrorist killing? Was Zena working alone?'

'What's the victim's name? Was it a man?'

'Zena sounds foreign! Is she an immigrant?'

'Over here, Monsieur Frènes! How did Zena do it?'

'Is there CC of the killing?'

'Where is she now?'

* * *

Corralled on the opposite side of the Place, Annie Provin was already summarising Frènes's statement for her TV audience and even as she spoke, the ticker running at the foot of screens all around the region changed from *Pal-Mas Shopper Slain By Sales Girl?* to *Pal-Mas Shopper Poisoned By Scent-Spraying Sales Girl?* with the addition of *Suspected Immigrant Zena Bairault Sought.*

But not everything was depressing. On his arrival at the store, Granot had realised immediately that the best way of providing a controllable space in which to question staff and potential customer witnesses was to evacuate the remainder of the ground floor. He had then done his usual stellar job of triaging what was a fair-sized crowd into prioritised, segregated groups. Combining officers from Foch as well as the Caserne, a large number of statements had already been logged.

As yet, no one other than Nadine Beaumont had reported witnessing new employee Zena Bairault's encounter with Gérard Urquelle and although rumours and theories about what had happened were naturally circulating around the floors, none had originated from Nadine herself. In solitary confinement nursing her nosebleed at first, and in the charge of police officers ever since, she had effectively been in quarantine from the moment she had discovered Zena had disappeared and realised to her utter dismay what it implied.

Apart from a courtesy visit from concerned store manager Albert Cassani – a meeting witnessed in full by Flaco – Nadine had not had the opportunity to be in contact with any of her colleagues.

Another blank being drawn was that, the matronly Nadine Beaumont excepted, no one appeared to have had a meaningful exchange with Zena or vice-versa in the few days she had been a presence in the store. The question would continue to be put, however. If just one employee passed on something useful, the time it took would have been worth it.

* * *

Relieved to be divested of the Haz-Mat suit in which he'd unproductively cast an eye around the red zone, Darac joined Granot and Bonbon under a hanging ad card bearing the words *mais pourquoi pas?*

'R.O's teams find any sign of the atomiser?' Bonbon asked.

'None – as we suspected. And he's had a lot of people looking. They also drew a blank with Zena's staffroom locker. She's got it with her. *Has* to have.'

'Agreed. Agnès rang while you were over there. In fifteen minutes, I'll be off for a *sympa* little chat with Madame Vivienne Urquelle. Agnès arranged for a room to be set aside at Foch.'

Darac's brow lowered. 'That's excellent but is she in any fit state? It's only an hour or so since she ID-d the ravaged corpse of her husband. The guy had looked full of the joys of life only moments before he collapsed.'

Bonbon nodded, shaking the shock of coppery wires that was his hair. 'Map reports she was remarkably calm at the ID, too.'

'*Was* she?' Darac said. 'Of course, she hadn't been told at that point that he had been poisoned by a hit woman posing as a shop assistant.'

'Or that the affair would soon be headline news.' Granot added.

Darac glanced at his watch. 'Any more from the search?'

More in hope than anticipation, Granot checked his mobile and after a few moments made a guttural sound in his throat. 'I know they haven't been at it long and I know we have nothing like the coverage the English and Americans do – and rightly so in my view – but we've got Lartou on camera duty here, yes? Foch, the Gendarmerie and other forces have got people scrutinising footage from streets, from trams, the airport – you name it. And what have they come up with? Nothing. No sign of how Typhoid Marie alias Zena Bairault alias Who-bloody-ever slipped away from *L'Éspace de Beauté* and just disappeared.'

Bonbon shrugged. 'The beat officers haven't fared any better pounding pavements and asking good old-fashioned questions.'

'It is early,' Darac said. 'And therefore we know very little. With every passing minute, we know more but Zena gets further away. Or so logic would dictate. She *could* be lying low locally.'

Bonbon nodded. 'Serge Paulin and the team that shot off to Pont-Michel are by no means sure she headed there after leaving here. The apartment looks spotless and it's empty. We know her ID is false – the address probably is, too, as we suspected at the beginning. Anyway, R.O. has sent a guy over to dust for prints and Serge and co are asking neighbours if anyone recognises Zena's photo. None has as yet.'

In need of a lift, Darac scanned the busy but orderly

scene in front of them. 'Well done on this, Granot,' he said. 'I take it no one has as yet corroborated or contradicted Madame Nadine Beaumont's account of things?'

A recently imposed health regime had seen the monumental Granot trim down to a comparatively svelte 103 kilos. But grizzled and blubbery, his chops still had the look of an affronted walrus when he shook them. 'No, not so far,' he said. 'And in the end, no one may have, you know. The busier the venue, the less time people have to check out what others are doing.'

'Remember that stabbing at Le Stade du Ray years ago?' Bonbon chipped in. 'There were nearly twenty thousand people there.' His tawny brows rose. 'One person saw it.' A stage direction for his look would have stipulated "With astonished certainty." *One.*'

At that moment, Flaco appeared with a young woman wearing a white tunic and navy-blue slacks. 'Gentlemen, this is Mademoiselle Jade Moreau. She works in the spa on the top floor. Mademoiselle – this is Captain Paul Darac who is in charge of the operation on the ground, and Lieutenants Granot and Busquet.' Flaco brandished a signed statement. 'Tell the Captain here what you have just told me.'

'I do facials and that,' she began, without hesitation. 'But I needed to check something out with one of the *Clarins* girls so I trotted down the stairs to the ground floor.' She raised both hands palms-out. 'Don't talk to me about lifts! Anyway, I found out what I needed to and I was on my way back when I saw this girl on the sass – sorry that's what we call—'

'We know, mademoiselle,' Darac said, pleasantly.

'Oh, you know? You want to try doing it.'

Flaco grinned. 'I'm needed back there, Captain. I'll check in later.'

'Thanks, Flak.'

'*Love* your cornrows,' Jade said, in parting.

Well-meaning or not, the compliment was the only one about her appearance Flaco ever seemed to receive and she failed to acknowledge it as she took her leave.

'Moving on,' Jade said, registering the slight, 'I saw this girl and I thought who are *you*, darling? Never seen her before. I know she's called Zena now but I didn't at the time. So anyway, she comes up to this guy, right, the one who dropped dead later? And—'

'Hold you there a second,' Darac said, feeling the need to pull in the reins of the runaway horse that was Jade's story-telling style. 'Did Zena appear nervous to you?'

'Of course, everyone *is* to begin with. It takes panache and not everybody has that. Do you know what I mean?'

'To be absolutely clear, the very first you saw of Zena was the moment just before she approached the man who later died?'

'Yeah.'

'Did she recognise him, do you think?'

'How could I know if... Oh, I see what you mean. No, she didn't look excited suddenly or pissed off – excuse my English – or anything like that.' Jade looked around as if what she was about to say was for police ears only. 'I'll tell you what I thought *she* was thinking.'

Darac could almost hear Granot and Bonbon's cry of *Objection!* But as inadmissible as it was, Jade's observation, Darac sensed, was worth hearing. 'Go on.'

' "It's now or never." That's what I thought. Ever done a bungee jump?'

Nonplussed, the men shook their heads simultaneously.

'I have. Never again! You say to yourself: If I don't go now, I never *will* go. It was like that with Zena.'

Darac could picture the scene Jade described, perfectly. But it was difficult to put an exact interpretation on it.

'But I tell you what, guys, once she had taken the plunge, she did great. Had the fella eating out of her hand. You can't teach that.' She nodded, sagely. 'You just can't.'

Occasionally prompted to take her gallop down to a canter and stick tighter to the rail, Jade went on to give an account of Zena's encounter with Urquelle which corroborated Nadine Beaumont's in every respect.

'Thank you, Mademoiselle Moreau,' Darac said. 'Granot, have you anything?'

'Do you know Madame Beaumont well, mademoiselle?' Granot asked.

'Not that well. A real pro, she is. Loves her girls. But she wouldn't do *anything* for them, if that's what you're thinking. No way, Jo-*sé*.'

'Have you spoken to her since the incident? Or texted each other? To express solidarity or whatever?'

Jade gave a knowing grin. 'Or to get our stories straight? So she's said the same, has she?'

Granot the Affronted Walrus was back in the house. 'Just answer the question, please.'

'Of course I haven't spoken to her. No one has, have they? And texted? Me and Nadine? Not much lifestyle overlap there, darling. Haven't even got each other's numbers.'

'Thank you. That's all.'

Bonbon answered Darac's enquiring glance with a shake of the head.

'We greatly appreciate your contribution, mademoiselle,' Darac said. 'Is there anything you would like to add from your own perspective?'

The suggestion appeared to twist Granot's whiskers further; ever curious, Bonbon seemed intrigued at the prospect.

'I'll have to be quick,' she said. 'Been down here ages already. Anyway, we all realise you lot think this Zena girl is bang in the frame for murder or we wouldn't be doing all this, would we?'

'I'll correct you straight away. By the sound of it, you've seen *Engrenages* or other cop shows on TV, right?'

'Yeah?'

'Then you'll understand that until we get hard and fast evidence from our pathology and forensic people, we won't know for certain *what* happened.'

'You took the words right out of my mouth. If it turns out Zena is a complete nut job, you *might* convince me she smuggled some poison in to take out some poor sod at random – *and* managed to do it without killing herself or anyone else while she was at it. And I *could* just about believe she had planned it if it turns out she knew the victim had murdered her mother or something. But what are the chances of stuff like that?' Brows high, lips pursed, Jade challenged them to disagree. 'I'll tell you what happened. Either, the guy had an allergy to something in the fragrance. *Or*, he was already ill with something weird and he died. We've all got to go sometime, haven't we? In other words, it was a big fat coincidence. And now I really must go.'

'Thanks, mademoiselle. You really have been a great help.'

As she disappeared towards the stairs, the trio shared a look.

'Good to have corroboration of Madame Beaumont's account from young Jade,' Granot said. 'But had she been in possession of all the facts, I doubt she would have arrived at the conclusion that Zena is innocent.'

Bonbon nodded. 'True enough.' He glanced at his watch. 'Right I'm going to talk to Madame Urquelle. At the very least, I'll try and get a breakdown of Monsieur's prior movements.'

Darac's mobile rang.

'Erica,' he announced, halting Bonbon. Checking the coast was clear, he put the phone on speaker. 'What have you got for us?'

'A list of all calls on Mademoiselle Zena Bairault's declared mobile number over the past five days – which is when her *Bouygues Télé* account began. For what it's worth.'

'Nothing of interest, huh?'

'Sharp as a tack as always, Darac.'

'It's given to few, I know. Just for the record?'

'Four out: the first of which was timed at 11.10 last Monday morning to Bouygues; the next, five minutes later, duration four minutes ten, to apartment owner Madame Gourdon in Lyon; the following two to *Pal-Mas's* HR department, at 14.02 and 15.37 on Monday afternoon. Duration: six minutes forty, and one minute fifty-six, respectively. No calls in. *None*, note.'

'Noted. Adding such a small number of calls to the facts that she was new to the city and using a fake ID suggests she's got a burner or two up her sleeve, doesn't it?'

'Definitely.'

'Do you have the locations those outgoing calls were made from?'

'I do. Just need to scroll a couple of screens.'

'At this very moment, your Serge is leading a team up at Zena's stated address in Pont-Michel. Say that's where it was and you'll be entitled to a prize.'

'He's all Haz-Matted up, I hope?'

'He is, don't worry.'

'And the prize, as if I didn't know?'

'Tickets for the DMQ, naturally. The Blue Devil, tomorrow night.'

'Of course. Hang on – Saturday? You lot play Thursdays.'

'Usually, we do. Surprised you remembered – I'm touched.'

'I'm touched you are. Right, I have those locations... Sadly, no prize for me. All were made from the Rue de L'Angleterre area, near the Basilique. One of the cafés, probably.'

'Ah. OK. Thanks, Erica.'

Darac ended the call.

'Fitted the picture we're forming, didn't it?' Bonbon said, finally taking his leave. 'Later, guys.'

Granot took a deep breath. 'And I'm going to join forces with Perand in the mix zone. That's how bad things are.'

Darac's mobile rang again and with the caller's voice crackling in his ear, he confided his valediction to a good luck wave.

'Papa?'

'Just been watching Annie Provin reporting from outside *Pal-Mas*. Are you down there, Paul?'

'We are.'

'Is it safe?'

'For *L'Éspace de Beauté*, read *L'Éspace de Surréalisme* but apart from that, it's fine. The main thing is that there's no *public* health aspect to this as far as we can see.'

'That's a relief. I realise you can't say much, and there's no time, and someone else is bound to call you any second, but the message seems to be that one of those awful migrant women infiltrated one of our true red, white and blue institutions and to show her gratitude, sprayed something noxious over an unsuspecting customer.'

'Take out the racism et cetera and it's not far off what we understand so far.'

'If Annie Provin had any class, she would have referred to the young woman you're seeking as the Sass Assassin, wouldn't she?'

'Far too clever for the likes of her.'

'Listen, if you need any help with the perfume side of things...'

'If we do, you're on-board, *papa*.'

'It would be a pleasure. So to speak.'

Darac *fils* was about to mention Nadine Beaumont's approving allusion to the *House of Darac* earlier but as his father had predicted, another call came in and as he brought the conversation to a close, the thought joined the others jostling for space on the back burner. His eyebrows rose slightly. 'Astrid? Wasn't expecting to hear from you.'

'You're at *Pal-Mas*?'

'Oh yes.'

'Have to be quick – I'm still teaching my morning class *en plein-air*.'

'Go for it.'

'About an hour and a half ago, a former student of mine rang the administrative director here at the Villa – Elie Tiron. I don't believe you've ever met but you've heard me talk about Elie, and your *papa* knows of her through Zoë Hamada.'

'OK?'

'My ex-student's call was to report that her husband died unexpectedly this morning and without giving any details, Elie passed that news on to me. She's just rung me again with your thing which is all over *Télé Sud*. Question: Is the unnamed man who seems to have got himself murdered in *Pal-Mas*, a certain Gérard Urquelle?'

Darac ran a hand through his hair. 'It is indeed. Your ex-student is Vivienne Urquelle?'

'Yes. They're saying Monsieur was shopping for perfume at the time he was attacked by this Mademoiselle... Bairault.'

'Bairault is the suspect, yes. Go on.'

'That's weird *enough*, right? Cop this: afterwards, Urquelle was due back here at the Villa to continue the perfume-making course he was taking with Zoë.'

'Wha–at?'

'I know.'

'Got any theories on why he came into the store?'

'No, but if he was thinking of substituting a proper scent for the stuff he was concocting here, Zoë wouldn't have been fooled for a second, believe me.'

'Not a gifted amateur parfumier, then?'

'For students and tutors alike, non-academic courses such as ours work best in an engaged but light-hearted atmosphere. Treating the thing as a bit of a joke though, which was Urquelle's approach apparently, pissed Zoë off immediately, and some of his classmates, eventually.'

'Urquelle had the perfume he bought this morning gift wrapped, incidentally. Any thoughts on that?'

'Elie told me Urquelle had changed courses at the last minute so he could surprise Vivienne with a bespoke gift.'

'You don't believe that was his true intention?'

'No, but I haven't got time to go into that just now. We'll talk again later – OK?'

'Time for just a few quick ones now?'

'If they *are* quick ones.'

'When did Urquelle check in, do you know?'

'With the rest of us at about 4.30 on Wednesday.'

'Know anything about his movements prior to coming into the city this morning?'

'Not in detail, but others here will. I do know he had breakfast because I saw him, and I do know he took a cab giving every appearance he intended to return. A City Cab, it was.'

'Excellent – they'll have a record if we need it. Did you speak to Urquelle at all?'

'Not this morning, happily. Don't like speaking ill of the dead as a rule, Darac, but in his case I'll make an exception. Fifty years ago, his type would have been called a ladies man. Or to suggest a more industrial approach, a womaniser. Some might still find that kind of thing acceptable, even charming. Me and my circle? Not so much.'

'With you all the way. Was it just Elie who was keeping you in the loop about what happened here in *Pal-Mas*?'

'Yes, she's called me twice: first, when it looked as if Urquelle had simply died, she told me she was going to tell the wine tutor Mathieu Croix and Zoë only that Urquelle had been called away. Which I thought a mistake.'

'Called away is one way of putting it.'

'Alright, but it was with the best of intentions, Darac.'

'Even if it was, I can see why you thought it a mistake. When word filters through that Urquelle was not merely absent but dead, then not just dead but murdered – and that word *will* filter through – I hope the others will be as forgiving as you.'

'I'm very fond of Elie, Darac. And so is Zoë. Most people are who know her. Anyone can make mistakes at times of stress. Can't they?'

'Sure.' The earnestness of Astrid's defence surprised Darac. Elie's error was one of administrative misjudgement not criminal negligence, after all. 'Back to Urquelle himself, if he *had* returned to the Villa, what would the rest of his day have looked like?'

'He would have had this morning's class, then lunch and finally, a two-hour session with Zoë breaking for coffee half-way through, after which he and the other sniffers would have been given lovely presentation bottles of the

perfumes they had made. That timetable and the celebra-
tory feel goes for the other classes, too, incidentally. In mine,
students vote for their favourite work and the winner cops
a pretty decent voucher for art materials; Mathieu awards a
bottle of Krug to his Taster of the Week – that sort of thing.
Then there's a couple of hours break before the celebration
dinner. Check-out time is 9.30 Saturday morning which is
the same for all of us. Oh, just hold a second – one of my
students is talking to me. Yes, Claudine..?'

So many possibilities and ideas began to collide and
connect in Darac's mind, he didn't know what to go with
first. But then one "what if?" situation began to insinuate
itself louder than the others.

'We're alone again, Darac. Listen, I have to go but I've
got a lot more of interest to pass on to you about Urquelle.
Lunchtime – OK?'

'OK, but one very last quick one?'

'Shoot.'

'What kind of a person is Vivienne Urquelle?'

11.31 PM

For six year-old Clara, playtime show-and-tell was so much
more exciting than Madame Poidatz's classroom version.
In class, *grands* could bring in any non-electronic possession and talk about it. Especially favoured were books, the
products of hobby crafts and, as long as they weren't living,
"things from nature." Just under eight weeks ago, in the
final class of their time as *moyens,* Emma and Jamilla had
loved seeing and handling the seashells Enzo had foraged
from beaches all along the coast with his *grand-père.* And

when Leila had showed her little gruff-faced wooden doll and asked how many even smaller ones were hiding inside, no one had guessed, not even Madame, that there were six more. *Seven* little dolls altogether!

In Clara's playtime show-and-tell, there was no place for such childishness. Thanks to the numerous zipped compartments and pockets of their *Sacs*, Clara's set could smuggle a phone or an item of make-up or jewellery into school without difficulty. And once let loose in the playground, *telling* each other about these forbidden treasures was easy. But how could you *show* them without being spotted by Madame or Mata? Forming a glimpse-proof huddle around the object, a sort of shield made of girls' backs, would seem to be the answer but, streetwise beyond her years, Clara knew that this would be the surest way of attracting the prying eyes of teachers. So how, she asked herself, could she and her group shield the shield itself? The answer, she intuited, was to shift the contextual meaning of the shield in the minds of onlookers.

And so, adapting a warm-up drill she had seen her actor father performing with his theatre company, Clara devised *main-à-main*, a quick-fire point and match hand gesture game in which players stood shoulder to shoulder in a closed circle. Playing a few rounds was all it usually took to ensure that Clara's set would be left, sometimes literally, to their own devices.

This morning however, they were having a problem and its name was Nathan. Improvising a conversation between two construction workers, the eight year-old was hovering over the group like a crane over a building site.

'Go away, Nathan,' Clara said. 'Or I'll tell Mata.'

'Stand by to pick up ballast? Lower bucket!'

Nathan's arm tilted toward the backpacks gathered in the

centre of the circle.

'No!' chorused the girls.

'Crashing!' Nathan shouted, accompanying the cry with a loud screeching sound. 'Crashing!'

'Mata! Nathan's spoiling our game!'

An insightful child psychologist, Mata was also one of life's great conciliators and after calming everyone down, she suggested that if the girls taught Nathan to play *main-à-main,* he wouldn't feel the need to wreck their game. The negotiation went on for some time but ultimately, Mata's proposal was rejected. Softening the blow with the promise of including the boy another time, they waited until he had skipped off to drop cargoes elsewhere before resuming the action.

With the need to play extra rounds, the first reveal was going to come later in the proceedings than usual and Emma began to worry she wouldn't get her turn until the next break which was at lunchtime. She thought that unfair. Her treasure was bound to be best and she was bursting to show it. How long did they have before they had to go back into class? Emma wasn't allowed a watch at school but all was not lost. Beyond the playground fence, the street ran down to the boulevards flanking the site of something every child in Nice couldn't wait to be finished – a new promenade complete with the spurting water spouts of a *miroir d'eau.* Through the gap at the end of the street, Emma could make out the face of a clock tower rising above the site hoardings. She had learned to tell the time a few months back but having neglected the skill during the summer holiday, just when she needed it most, it deserted her. But there couldn't be much of playtime left. Of that she was sure.

As befitted her status, Clara was first to delve into her backpack. As the others continued with the game, she bent down and produced a small white box which Emma recognised from adverts as an iPad. Or was it an iPod? Anyway, you could hear music on it and they all had a go. Emma cut her turn short on purpose.

Next, it was Danielle's chance to impress. She had a silver ankle bracelet which they all thought pretty but the catch wouldn't fasten and Danielle wasted time insisting everyone tried harder. Jamilla was the only one who managed it but Clara said "That's enough" and Sara was up next. At that moment, Emma knew she was going to be last in line because she had been last to get a *Sac*. It didn't occur to her that Clara could be challenged and that her word wasn't law. She just knew that pleasing her was the most important thing in the world.

As Sara produced her treasure, which she admitted having "pinched" from her big sister's handbag, Emma peered at the clock tower once more. The long hand looked to her worryingly close to what her *papa* had told her was a "Roman numeral."

Fortunately for Emma, the significance of Sara's offering, a small cotton wool plug wrapped tightly in cellophane, was lost on the group and not even Clara knew what it was or found it interesting. Casting Sara into lip-trembling gloom, she declared the object "boring" and went on to Jamilla.

Emma's heartbeat quickened. Jamilla sometimes chose things that would have earned the approval of Madame Poidatz and that meant they didn't last more than a couple of seconds in playtime show-and-tell. Perhaps that would happen again? Perhaps Emma wouldn't have to wait until lunchtime to show what she had to offer, after all?

She began to lose herself in her own thoughts, picturing what had happened in the store after *maman* had bought the backpack. She did feel a *little* bad about it. But neither *maman* nor that lady had hurt themselves when they fell over. And the treasure *had* jumped out of the lady's pocket and landed right at Emma's feet like a present. *Chanson de Minuit*, it was called. That lady didn't look after it and what does *maman* say? "If you don't look after your things, perhaps you don't deserve to have them."

Emma hadn't even noticed what Jamilla had offered up to the gods, but whatever it was, it hadn't survived scrutiny long enough to reach her spot in the circle.

'Your turn,' Clara said to her.

Emma clapped her hands, picked up her backpack and rummaged in what she already thought of as its secret compartment.

Behind her, Madame Poidatz appeared at the entrance doors to the building itself, gave Mata a smile and went back inside. The young woman raised a whistle to her lips and in three sharp beeps, Emma's hopes were dashed. But as the group got its things together and went to line up, her desolation began to dissipate. It wasn't long to the lunchtime break and she knew she would be first on. And then, nothing would stop her spraying her perfume on herself just like *maman* does – on her wrists and on her neck. And she was going to spray the others, too. See what Clara thinks of that!

11.45 AM

'Goodbye, mademoiselle.'
   'Bye.'
   'Hope to see you again on this route.'
   Not going to happen, pal. 'Indeed.'

'Have a good journey.'

The guide had described Breil-sur-Roya as a "glittering river-and-lakeside gem" and as the train slowly skirted the scene on its approach to the station, Zena did not demur. Neither did she care. All that mattered was that her new best friend the suit was alighting, none the wiser about her true identity. Or that was her distinct impression. Having to contribute to potentially tricky exchanges on the connection between the Faculty of Science's Valrose campus back in Nice – where Zena was supposed to be working part-time – and its partner institutions at the Sophia Antipolis complex in nearby Valbonne – where the suit's son apparently worked very much *full*-time – had failed to materialise. This was not due to Zena's skilful handling of the situation, but to the self-absorbed monologue suit senior had kept up for their whole time together. It had been a unique experience for her to feed an impoverished but already over-nourished male ego by confining her input to "Ah, yes?" "Agreed," and "Hmm." But now the man had gone, she already felt more exposed, vulnerable and nervous – a reaction to which the train's five-minute wait in this small town's vast station – what was the story there? Come on, guide, *now* you can distract me! – was unlikely to relieve.

For reasons Zena didn't understand, the train jolted to a halt well beyond the shade of the station buildings and the wait began. At least there was no other stop between Breil and her destination and that meant this was the last time Zena would have to scrutinise every departing and arriving face. She glanced at her watch. In 20 minutes, she would arrive at Fontan-Saorge. 20 short or long minutes – Einstein was on to something, wasn't he? – to safety. So far, she had detected no sign of the manhunt – no, *woman*hunt for fuck's sake! – she knew would now be in full swing.

Calm down, Zena! Calm down! Calm... down. Reminding herself that she had got this far not by panicking but by being vigilant, she began to take deeper breaths and it quickly had the desired effect. Checking her watch again, Zena focussed on the positive that one minute of the wait had already elapsed, not the negative that four minutes still remained. Shielding her face, she rested her chin on the heel of her hand and watched as a mercifully thin trickle of humanity began to pass by her window. Prospecting for space, most peered in but as yet, no local or tourist had appeared in her carriage.

Three minutes remained. Then, two, and there still had been no invasion and now the trickle passing along the platform was drying up. Zena began to feel more confident. For Zena, *Le Train des Merveilles* was living up to its billing in a way SNCF had never envisaged. Her contact had been right all along, hadn't she? There had there been no hint of a uniform other than the railway variety at any of the station stops so far. And when the train had taken on a substantial number of passengers at Sospel, Zena hadn't heard a single mention of her name, or of *Pal-Mas*, or of poison, or perfume, or...

What was this? *Two* uniforms marching along the platform to the head of the train. Male. Armed. Not heavily. But armed. Shit! Why did I have to go and drop the vial? What were they, these *flics*? Police Nationale? Municipale? Gendarmerie? But they sweep in fours, don't they? Zena turned and, pressing her face against the window, looked back toward the rearmost carriage. She couldn't see far enough so for the first time since she had boarded, she stood and pulled down the window – Thank Christ for regional trains! – and craned her head out. Bodies. Virtually all retreating. Only a few advancing. Uniforms? No. No more uniforms. Good sign? Yes.

She looked toward the head of the train. The armed officers were approaching the front carriage. What now? Keep going, men! You're not getting on the train. You're after some other poor sod. The driver's window pulled down. A three-way conversation struck up, the uniforms talking into a void. Nods from the uniforms. Back headers. Were they telling the driver about something that had happened in town? In the station building? Not on the train, alright? There's no reason to board! None at all! Smiles. Joshing? Smiles, anyway. Laughter now. This was all just routine, wasn't it? Another day at work. Another chat with the driver of *Le Train des Merveilles* – Alain or Beatrice or Charles. A good laugh, they are. One of the uniforms kicked out a foot. The other shook his head and he kicked out, too, but differently. Football? Yes, they're talking football. Thank Christ.

As the uniforms waved the driver farewell, Zena took another calming breath and looked at her watch. It took a second or two for her eyes to focus but when they did, she saw the five-minute wait was up. A whistle blew. A door slammed. She looked back to the head of the train. The uniforms were nowhere to be seen. Shit!

They must have boarded the train.

11.51 AM

On the previous occasion Bonbon had interviewed a woman at the Police Nationale's city centre headquarters, Commissariat Foch, she had lifted him off his feet and pinned him against the wall. It had taken a series of ungentlemanly headbutts to dislodge her.

Although looks were so often deceptive, it didn't seem likely that the slight, soft-featured woman of about fifty sitting opposite him would launch a similar attack this morning; especially as the intimidating physical presence of Yvonne Flaco had been added to the equation, and she was capable of giving a charging bull second thoughts.

Bonbon's interview with Vivienne Urquelle had been set up in the hope of discovering her husband's movements immediately prior to his death. Following Astrid's necessarily brief but instructive call to Darac from the Villa des Pinales, that question had become largely redundant. When Darac passed on what he had learned to Bonbon, the pair almost certainly knew more about husband Gérard's movements than Vivienne herself.

The addition of a female officer to the interview of a murder victim's widow may have looked like an orthodox protocol but Flaco's gender was coincidental to the decision. In her call, Astrid had suggested that there had been problems in the Urquelle marriage and that once her teaching obligations were over for the day, she had "a lot more of interest" to pass on. Darac had decided to upgrade Bonbon's interview to a full two-up operation on the spot. Quite different from the original brief, the focus was now to explore the question of Madame Vivienne Urquelle's possible part in the murder of her womanising husband.

To reach the point of asking, "Madame, did you hire a hit woman to poison your no-good louse of a husband?" Bonbon knew would be the proverbial thousand-kilometre journey that began with a single step. And so, comfortingly combining warmth with gravity, he began by expressing the Brigade's condolences for her loss, and its gratitude for her most kind co-operation. Although it was not without risk under the circumstances, he also gave her his assurance that if at any time she wished to take a break or postpone the interview for another day, the car that had brought her from Menton was still at her disposal and would return her home whenever she wished.

'So, may we begin?'

'We may but I have to report this is a little surreal for me.'

'I'm sure.'

'Oh, no – not because of what happened to Gérard. It's your voice and that accent. You sound virtually identical to a customer of mine. My best, actually.'

'Customer?'

'I'm a potter.'

'Ah, yes?'

'Yes, he runs a ceramics gallery in Collioure. Born and bred there.'

'I know it well.'

'I thought so.'

Small talk? Perhaps it was a coping mechanism. 'We really must...'

'Of course.'

'For the record,' he said, and rolled his eyes apologetically. 'You know how these things are, madame, I have to ask when you last saw your husband?'

'He worked away a great deal but he had been home since Monday. Holiday. Yesterday lunchtime was the last time I saw him. He left the house for Nice at about 2 o'clock. He was booked on a short residential course in wine tasting at the Villa des Pinales.'

Bonbon smiled. 'I see.'

'The driver you mentioned?' she said, evidently keen to move the conversation on. 'After we have finished here, I'd like him to run me up to the Villa. Gérard's suitcase is in his room. I rang Madame Tiron, the director, to break the news earlier and she mentioned his car is parked there, too. I can put the case in the car and drive it home so there's no need for your man to wait for me.'

Coolly impressive? Bonbon wondered. Or coldly matter-of-fact? Whichever it was, Vivienne's wish could not be granted.

'On that last point, madame,' he said, turning up the warmth of his smile a couple of notches, 'I mentioned that our car was still at your disposal and indeed it is; your original driver, however, isn't. He went off shift. It will be a woman, now – Wanda. She's an excellent *chauffeuse*.'

She was also an excellent snoop and were she to suspect Madame was not behaving as might be expected in the situation, she would subsequently report it.

Madame shrugged.

'Lieutenant... Busquet, isn't it?'

'It is.'

'I really don't care who drives me there. Alright?'

'Fine. However, this tragic situation being as it is, I'm afraid Monsieur Urquelle's suitcase and his car will have to remain in quarantine, as it were, for the time being. Within the past few minutes, a local officer has taken the suitcase into custody and has cordoned off the vehicle in question. Said officer is standing by until further officers arrive to protect the arrangements.'

Bonbon studied Vivienne's reaction: the irritated pout; the opaque, dry-eyed stare; the slowly exhaled breath.

'We will return everything to you just as quickly as we can. I'm sure you understand.'

'As inconvenient as it was, I understood why I couldn't take his things from the hospital – the things he had on him when he died. But what could you possibly want with his case and his car?'

It was obvious, wasn't it? 'We have procedures to follow, madame.'

'Well he had his wallet and his... lighter et cetera on him. So don't forget to get them from the hospital, will you?'

They had been taken over to the Forensic Path Lab but Bonbon decided to keep that to himself.

'Each item of the Monsieur's effects has been logged, madame.' Bonbon's smile was working overtime. 'You really need have no concerns.'

She seemed reassured. 'Alright, Lieutenant, but I still need to go to the Villa. Don't worry, I'll leave his precious car alone. From courses I have taken there, I know Madame Tiron well and I want to speak to her in person. *That*, surely, doesn't contravene any rules?'

'Not in itself.'

Vivienne's pout was gone but the stare was still on full-beam. 'I believe the purpose of this meeting was to help you put a picture together of what my husband was doing immediately before he was killed? Other than what we have already discussed, I can tell you in four words. *I have no idea.* Now may I go?'

By stressing that the exit door was going to be open throughout, Bonbon had hoped Vivienne wouldn't have felt the need to walk through it quite so soon. With the road ahead still looking every one of its thousand kilometres, he replied, 'Of course but if you *could* just bear with us for a moment?'

Back at Palais Masséna, Darac still had had no word of a sighting, or even a potential sighting of Zena Bairault at Nice airport, Gare Thiers, the port and ferry terminal, the border crossing point at Vintimille, or any of the major transport hubs. Added to this, Lartigue hadn't come up with any footage of Zena's exit from the store. Perhaps she had simply kept her head down in the crowd and/or had donned a disguise. Or, more probably, she had slipped out of one of the exits not covered by cameras. Or both things combined. Only one thing appeared to be certain. She *had* left the building: a comprehensive search of the premises had drawn a blank.

Darac's mobile rang. The caller was trusted uniform Serge Paulin, a young man who, like Darac himself, had a passion for an art form from which he could have earned his living had he so chosen – if you could call playing rugby for money an art form, and playing jazz for money, a living. For his sporting talent and for having the distinction of being forensic tech specialist Erica Lamarthe's steady boyfriend, Serge was the envy of many of his peers at the Caserne. But today, things were not going his way.

'I'm still at Pont-Michel, Captain, and Zena's apartment is clean. Far *too* clean to have been vacated by a legit renter.'

'No prints anywhere?'

'None and R.O's forensic guy dusted in all the spots that tend get overlooked by amateurs.'

'That's certainly suggestive.'

'A couple of my lot went through the recycling outside and found nothing of interest. *But,* one neighbour confirms a young woman did move in to number 14 a few days ago. He didn't speak to her and got only a back view but I showed him a photo, nevertheless. "I prefer her arse" was all he could come up with, unfortunately. But one of the other neighbours might have something more – most of them are out at work at the moment. The trouble is by the time they come home...'

'It will be too late.'

'Exactly. Anyway, that's the score at the moment, Captain. Whoever the girl with the appealing derrière was, it looks certain she was up to no good and she probably is our suspect. But we don't know for sure. Not yet.'

Darac thanked him and ended the call. Two considerations struck Darac with some force at that moment and as he stared at the floor, he connected them to make a third. The first was that a close watch on the fast principal routes out of Nice was yielding absolutely nothing. The second was that the probability of Zena's declared address being the true one was now looking high. Although he hadn't taken it in years, he knew that the touristy *Train des Merveilles* was readily accessible from Pont-Michel, and from its end station, Tende, there were connections to Italy. The journey may be painfully slow, but to a fugitive, perhaps that was its attraction. There was certainly no more unobtrusive way of fleeing the country. Checking his mobile for the route timetable, he discovered that trains were very few and far between but that one had departed at 10.42. Possible. *Entirely* possible. He tapped the phone icon and then #1.

'Agnès?'

Of Professor Deanna Bianchi's many seminal papers, articles and books on the subject of forensic pathology, the one Darac himself found most useful was her introduction to a work on core principles intended for first-year students. Particularly illuminating, he found, was the section on toxicological analysis in which she explained the challenge all pathologists faced when attempting to find and identify a poison in a bodily tissue or fluid: namely, that it was essential to have a clear idea of what it *might* be at the outset. She held that, given sufficient time and materials, any pathologist with access to a gas chromatograph and a bank of mass spectrometers would come up with a result eventually. From his own experience, Darac knew that pathologists were not equally skilled in interpreting such results but happily for the Brigade, it was a talent which Deanna and Mpensa possessed in abundance. However, born of her vast knowledge and experience, Deanna's true genius lay in knowing which poisons to test for *first* in any given situation, thus saving their own technicians and the Brigade valuable time.

This was the situation Deanna and her team found itself in at the moment. While business had been on the slow side, assistant chief pathologist Djibril Mpensa had looked forward to taking his time over the next case that came his way, especially as he would be spending it in the most rewarding way possible: at Deanna's elbow. But when it came, the next case proved to be such a flat-out sprint that Deanna had split the tasks involved and scarcely a word had passed between the pair since it began. That was about to change. She leaned in to the intercom.

'Map?' she announced in her *Gitanes*-rasped tones. 'In here. Pow-wow time.'

On the slab in front of her, the corpse of the person that had once been Gérard Urquelle lay like a partially excavated archaeological site, its yield of finds still being recorded, removed item by item and analysed by the team. Slipping between them as they came and went, Mpensa appeared and took up station at Deanna's side.

'Talk to me,' she said, her sharp, brown eyes shrinking as she flipped up the lenses of her exam glasses.

'So far, the contents of all the perfume bottles from stock match each other and they're free of any contaminants.'

'Good. The vial atomisers?'

'Ditto. And we've analysed all of them including the empties.'

'How long to finish?'

'Twenty minutes at the outside.'

'When you have, R.O. needs to know immediately. He'll inform Darac and the others.'

'Check.'

Deanna directed his attention to a tray containing Urquelle's left hand. 'What do you see?'

Mpensa bent forward. 'Well, the corneum is quite reddened in the area of the radiocarpal ligament. Peeling, you might say.'

'You might indeed. Now examine the mouth.'

He moved across to the main site. 'Hmm. The labial fissure has similar reddening.'

He straightened and the pair stood facing one another.

'It does,' she said. 'Doesn't it?'

Darac was taking a call from Armani. En route to the Caserne following a drugs bust in the Rue de France, the man was in an upbeat mood.

'It was a tip-off from one of the guys we nailed yesterday, Darac – at the free concert we gave on the Promenade.'

'Knock-ons, too? Told you the busking shtick was a good idea.'

'Credit where it's due. Listen, I'd like to call in at *Pal-Mas*, if that's alright? This poisoning's big news and I love watching a well-oiled machine in action. Think Maserati.'

'Is that why your own car's an Audi?'

'Harsh. Very harsh.'

'Listen, you won't have to limit yourself to watching – you can be part of the machine. We need all the help we can get.'

'See you in ten minutes or so. If Farid here gets his foot down, that is.'

Darac heard the police car give a whoop by way of a response and he rang off.

'Chief? This is Madame Triot.'

The voice was Granot's and Madame proved to be a middle-aged black woman wearing the uniform of a senior sales assistant. She was also wearing the expression of someone being presented to the officer in command as a key witness. 'She works in one of the shoe concessions here. This is Captain Darac.'

The introductions were made and Granot got straight to the nitty gritty. 'Madame Triot has just been shown a photograph of Zena Bairault and she is 100% sure that she was the same young woman who left the store in a tearing hurry through the exit into Rue Gioffredo earlier – an exit not covered by CC which is why Zena chose it, presumably. She reports that there were no differences at all in the look and hairstyle of the fugitive from the photo, so we know that when she left the store, at least, Zena was neither in disguise nor had changed her appearance in any way from the image we're circulating. I've passed that on, and also a description of what she was wearing...' He consulted his notebook. '...A mid-grey knee-length skirt with a plain cream blouse with three-quarter sleeves. Quite independently, a junior assistant who passed Zena moments before she hurried into the shoe department supports Madame Triot's assessment of the photo and her description of the clothing.'

'Excellent.' Darac gave the woman an approving nod. 'And an excellent description, madame – thank you.'

'And there's more,' Granot said, finally ceding the floor.

'As your colleague said, Captain, I didn't know the young woman was this Zena who you're looking for or I would have come forward right away.'

'Don't worry, madame. Your contribution is already helping us to find her. And you have something else for us?'

'Oh, yes. She was in a *real* hurry this Zena girl, recklessly, you could say because she ran into a lady who had been shopping with her daughter, a little one of about seven, who were on their way out of the store. And I mean *ran into*, Captain. She knocked the lady off her feet on to one the displays and, fortunately, it broke her fall. If it hadn't been there – and as late as yesterday afternoon it wasn't! – she would have landed face down on the floor.' She cued in the gravity of her next point with an almost Flaco-like scowl. '*And* this lady was pregnant, Captain. Fairly well on, too, and so we were all concerned. Staff and other customers alike.'

'Did she require treatment?'

'No, no. We helped her up and she was fine. We made sure.'

'And Zena. What was her attitude to what she had done?'

'She fell over, too. Got up, turned and said something foreign which I think meant "sorry" and rushed away.'

'She turned to face you?'

'Not just me. Everyone.'

'And she was apologetic?'

'Yes, and she looked it, too. Also, she put her hand out as if she wanted to help get the lady up but thought better of it. When you think what she had just done, I suppose it's not surprising she didn't want to hang around.'

'Indeed.'

Darac ran a hand through his hair, an outward expression of a change in an inner process; a sign that his trajectory through the accumulating facts of the case was realigning. Unless Zena had still been acting out the part of a beguiling young woman, a scenario in which showing remorse and a desire to help the skittled mother would have fitted the persona, she had certainly not followed standard assassin tradecraft. In turning to face the crowd, all of whom could have identified her subsequently, she was exposing herself to further risk. But Zena was young, Darac knew, and this could have been her very first mission.

Another pivotal point might be established in Bonbon's questioning of Vivienne Urquelle. In terms of odds, her possible involvement in her husband's killing was a long shot but longer ones had been known to pay out.

'Thank you once again, Madame Triot.' Darac signalled to a uniform. 'This officer will escort you back to the mix zone. For the time being, if you would just wait with the others who've given statements. Section B, Granot?'

'B, yes.'

'Right.' Madame Triot turned to leave but she hesitated and then gave her forehead an admonishing tap. 'Sorry, I knew there was something else, gentlemen.'

Time was tight but Madame had delivered thus far.

'Not at all,' Darac said. 'Please, go on.'

'It's about the mother's little girl. Emma, she was called.'

'Emma? It seems every other little girl is called by that name at the moment.'

'It goes in cycles, Captain. Her mother also called her Rapunzel.' She gave a knowing smile. 'For fun, you know. That didn't go down too well with the little one.'

'Rapun...?' A shock ran through Darac like a high voltage current through water. The pregnant mother had to be Noëmi, surely? 'Madame, look at this, will you?' He scrolled through the photo folders on his mobile. Where is it? It's got to be... Ah! 'This is a video clip of a children's party.' He shared a look with Granot. 'Is this..?'

'Uh... yes. That's her! *And* the mother. How do you..?'

'It doesn't matter. You said, "It's about the mother's little girl." *What* about her?'

12.02 PM

'Our next station stop will be Fontan-Saorge. First recorded as a settlement in the 10th century, Saorge is home to the miraculous 17th century Franciscan monastery of Notre-Dame-des-Miracles, and set as it is among the lofty peaks, gorgeous gorges and rushing waters of the upper Roya Valley, Saorge is considered one of the 40 most beautiful villages in all of France. *Mesdames et messieurs*, we are now but a few kilometres from the view that in my opinion is *the* most marvellous of all in our journey of marvels. And so when we emerge from the tunnel, I urge you to look up to the right in our direction of travel.'

Zena's direction of travel was quite the opposite. As calmly as her hammering heart would allow, she was making her way to the rearmost carriage.

'And now emerging from the darkness of the tunnel as if from hibernation into the light of summer. There... is... Saorge!'

The reaction of Zena's fellow passengers was even more enthusiastic than it had been to Peillon and she was glad of it. Connected by pairs of push button-operated doors, each carriage brought a whole new gallery of faces but not one pair of eyes turned to Zena as the door slid shut behind her. She glanced at her watch. Three minutes to go. Three minutes to reach the station before the *flics*, working their way slowly through the train from the front, reached her.

The feeling of nausea she had relieved back in the apartment was returning but as the seconds ticked down, she was heartened by the thought that the odds were with her now. The guide's rhapsody to Saorge continuing as Zena picked her way between the seats, she found herself imagining the commentary taking a sinister turn – the guide making glowing references to the daring young poisoner from Eastern Europe whom police were looking for all over the Alpes Maritimes but who might be aboard this very train. *And indeed there... is... the miraculous... Zena!*

Stop it, you idiot! she told herself. Concentrate!

Reaching the end of the carriage, she risked a glance behind. No sign of the *flics*. Or indeed of the village, as the train, rounding a shoulder of the *massif,* made the final turn towards the station. Almost there! She pressed the button.

The door didn't move. She pressed the button again and it was only then she realised she had reached the back of the train. No more space to put between her and the *flics*. No more faces to interest and possibly detain them. She spun around as the train entered another tunnel. It was just a short one, if she remembered correctly. A short one and then the station was right there.

Another glance at her watch. Two minutes to go. *Two*, only. But then her stomach turned over. Figures were looming through the double doors at the far end of the carriage. She told herself to calm down. It could just be passengers getting ready to... But no, it *was* the flics. The outer door slid open. The men paused, one sharing a few words with a passenger. Zena looked around. The toilet. The toilet was just a step away. She could hide in it. But dare she? Dare she go in and close but not lock the door so there would be no indication anyone was inside? If it showed engaged the *flics* were bound to knock, try the door, get the guard to open it. It would be all over. If it appeared vacant, though, they might just leave it alone. But if they did push it open, she was trapped. Caught. Done for.

The inner carriage door slid open. There they were. Less than 20 metres away. She had no choice. Hoping to God they hadn't spotted her, she stepped quickly into the toilet, closed the door and sat on the closed seat lid. Sunlight began to flood through the frosted glass clerestory as the train emerged from the tunnel. She stood and peered out at the blurred form of the builder's yard on the road below the tracks. The train slowed further. She was almost there. But she needed the train to stop. Stop and open its doors. She sat down, listening. Was that footsteps outside? It was. Shit, shit, shit! The door flew open, hitting her knee.

'Oh, pardon!'

A tourist. Embarrassed. Gone.

Zena closed the door but still didn't lock it. Voices outside. Raised voices. Shouting. The train jolted to a halt. She left the toilet and, keeping her back to the carriage, hovered over the step down to the exit door. The *flics* were arguing with a passenger. Arresting him, by the sound of it. What a break! She glanced over her shoulder. A Maghrebi-looking individual. He was resisting. Open the fucking doors! Threats. Blows. Handcuffs now. The man was bundled away down the train.

'With a population of just over 400 inhabitants...'

The doors opened and Zena stepped down into the bright, still heat of midday. Trailing a couple of passengers in her wake, she headed quickly out under an archway towards the Promised Land that was the small parking area beyond. She had made it. *Made it!* She considered using her prepaid. But it would still be better to wait.

'*Excusay mwa, mamwazel?*'

An elderly couple. Clueless. But pleasant. Good cover now she was out in the open.

'May I help you?' Zena said to the woman.

'Yes, and thank goodness you speak English! Considering how much we love France, our French is *tray mal!*'

'English is fine.'

'We were wondering, now we have lost sight of the village, how do we get there? Do you know?' With a sweep of a sunburned arm, she indicated the "lofty peaks" and, what was it? "gorgeous gorges and rushing water of the upper Roya Valley" that was all around them. 'We don't have to trek up and over that, do we?'

'No, no. You walk along to the right there and after a few minutes you come to a road tunnel...' The woman screwed up her face as she peered tremulously into the unknown.

'Come with me,' Zena said. 'I'll take you the first bit.'

'Oh *mare see!* She's going to show us, Harry. *Tray jorntee!*'

'No problem.'

'What on earth was that commotion on the train just now? Do you know?'

'Arresting an immigrant,' Harry said, definitively. 'Probably a refugee without papers. Asylum seeker.' He gave Zena a look. '*Say vray?*'

'You may be right,' she said. 'This way.'

They set off across the parking area.

'Pulverised stone, this surface,' Harry said. 'Compacted. Bit rough round the edges, I must say. Remarkable how weeds and grasses—'

'I must say your English is excellent, my dear. I keep saying to Harry, don't I, Harry? We really must do something about our appalling French.'

But then Zena couldn't understand English, or French or any language or sound. All she could hear was a loud thrumming in her ears. Don't faint, for God's sake! But she was going to, wasn't she? As the Englishwoman's mouth continued to open and close, the thrum turned into a rapid *womp-womping* noise that grew louder and then, hanging on to their hats, the couple screwed up their faces all the tighter as they gazed incredulously upwards. A shadow fell over them as words cut through the noise and ricocheted around the buildings.

'Mademoiselle Bairault! Down! Down on the ground. Down or you're dead!'

The helicopter was landing just metres away. Soldiers. Haz-Mat suits. Machine guns. Shouting. What to do now? Nothing. There was nothing she could do. Any thoughts of taking the English couple hostage evaporated on contact with Zena's reason. She had no weapon to make any threat stick. It was probably lying on the floor back in *Pal-Mas*. Rolled under a fitment after she had dropped it. Besides, taking a hostage prisoner...

Before she knew it, Zena was face-down in those weeds and grasses, the tang of dog faeces in her nostrils, a knee in her back and her rucksack, wig and glasses ripped off.

'Don't move!'

'Searching subject!'

She felt gloved hands exploring her. A stab of pain. And another.

'Clear!'

'Searching bag!'

Hands grabbed her wrists and bound them behind her. Not handcuffs. A pull strap.

'Bag clear!'

Now she was hauled on to her feet. Frogmarched to the helicopter. Thrown in. The bag thrown in after her. The scene went quickly away beneath her: the orange-pink station buildings; the clueless couple, miniatures now, appearing to revolve like figures on a musical box as the helicopter turned on its axis. And then it swung away, following the line of the gorge, the river, the road and the railway line back to where she had begun her journey.

Now what? Zena asked herself, and in a curiously delayed reaction, only then felt violated and lost and without hope.

A voice from behind. Female. Cultured.

'Mademoiselle, I am truly sorry for the painful indignity to which you have just been subjected.'

Zena turned.

'I am Commissaire Agnès Dantier of the Brigade Criminelle in Nice. Who, and what, are you?'

The girls had already played three rounds of *main-à-main*. No teachers were in sight. Nathan was performing his wrecking ball act in the far corner of the playground. Everything was set for Emma's big reveal. As Jamilla and Danielle closed the gap, she bent forward and, giggling with excitement, ripped back the flap that concealed the zip that opened the compartment that contained the pocket that held her treasure trove.

As if holding a butterfly, she cupped both hands carefully around it and stood.

'What is it?' Clara said. 'Come on. Show us!'

'Yes, Emma.' Danielle mugged her hurt face. 'You've got to!'

'I'm not *just* going to show you,' Emma said. 'We're *all* going to have a go!'

Jamilla jumped up and down. 'Yee-eees!!!'

Somewhere out on Avenue St. Jean Baptiste, a speeding police car whooped a warning.

Emma uncapped her hands. 'It's perfume! And there's loads!'

'Yay!!!'

'It sprays. You call it an anomat... anatom...'

'It's "atomiser," ' Clara said. She looked closer. '*Chanson de Minuit*. Way *cool*, Emma!'

Emma was so happy at that moment, she forgot what she was doing and clapped her hands. The atomiser jumped in the air. And landed safely on her backpack in the centre of the circle.

'I want to go first!' Sara said as Emma snatched up the

fallen hero.

Emma held firm. 'No, Sara. You have to wait your turn.'

The police car was closer now, its warning whoop getting louder and louder.

Emma took off the cap. She took Clara's hand....

Shouting. A blur of bodies running towards them. Mata in the lead. Security guard Albert hobbling behind. Madame in the rear. Shouting words that included 'Nooooo!!!!'

'Spray me!' Clara said. 'Now! Hurry up!'

Tyres squealing, the police car powered into the street and skidded extravagantly to a halt. Emma saw her *papa* jump out and clear the playground fence in one scrambling leap.

'Emma!' he screamed, sprinting towards them. 'Drop it! Throw it away! Now! It will hurt you all!'

Emma's six year-old brain was in turmoil. She knew she had been bad but she couldn't let Clara down. Turning her back to the onrush, she pressed down on the nozzle, and a cloud of scent misted Clara's wrists. Next, she turned the spray on Jamilla. Then Danielle. Then Sara. Finally, for she was a good, polite girl after all, she aimed it at herself.

12.16 PM

The senior staffroom was still off limits so it was the logical location to take crucial calls. At Darac's feet, a device that RAID Commander Novotny had had sent over within the past quarter of an hour was tuned to a transmitter relaying comms to and from the helicopter. At that moment, it didn't matter to Darac that the thing didn't appear to work. His jaw clenched, his gaze locked on to a bare patch on the wall opposite, it was the mobile he was holding half-way to his ear that commanded his entire attention.

Standing next to him, Granot's head was bowed, his massive frame still as a statue, a monument to monumentality itself. Added together, the pair had served over 40 years in the police. In all that time, they had never experienced the feeling they were sharing now.

They knew that staff at *Maternelle Niel* had reacted the moment they had picked up their call. They knew that Farid had got the message in time to roar past *Pal-Mas* and deliver Armani to the playground as fast as was humanly possible. They also knew that no one had been able to prevent Emma from spraying the killer scent directly on to the skin of her friends and herself.

'How long is it now?' Granot said, still staring at the floor.

Darac glanced at his watch. 'Three... minutes exactly.'

'That's a minute longer than it took Urquelle to collapse.'

That may have been true but neither of them knew what was happening since Farid had had to abandon his call from the scene. Darac didn't want to, but he kept picturing the likely scenario: a frantic Armani performing CPR; ambulances speeding round to St. Roch's intensive care unit; parents called in; the heavily pregnant Noëmi among them.

Darac closed his eyes. What kind of nightmare must this be for them? What excruciating torture? It was immature, Darac knew, but for the first time in his life, he was actually grateful for the knowledge that he would never have children of his own.

The phone throbbed in Darac's hand. Granot's head jerked up.

'It's Frankie. A text.'

Heard the Pal-Mas news. What the hell? Are you alright, Paul?'

'She's just checking everything's OK.'

'What are you going to tell her?'

'That it is. They won't release the *Mat* story for some time yet.'

'Right,' Granot said, his voice returning to the floor along with his gaze. 'Of course.'

Lightning-fingered on a guitar fretboard, Darac was a painful plodder on a mobile keypad screen so he dictated a quick, positive response instead, concluding it with the assurance he'd call Frankie later for an update on her father's operation, now less than three hours away.

'*Four* minutes gone, now,' he said, glancing at his watch. 'Come on, Farid – ring for God's sake!'

Granot raised his head once more but this time, the look in his eyes chilled Darac to the bone.

'We all know what state a man like Armani will be in if little Emma has been killed,' he said. 'Have you thought what his breaking the news to Noëmi will do to them both? With a couple of months still to go on her pregnancy? Apart from all else, she could go into premature labour and lose the baby.' Granot seemed to descend into a still lower place. 'My Odile knows what that's like and so do I.'

Darac's emotions were already running high. He couldn't allow them to overtop. Not now.

'I had no idea. Well, you know I didn't. I'm... so sorry, man.'

'Sorry, of course. But this Mademoiselle Bairault? Let me tell you something. If the murder weapon she dropped and little Emma picked up *does* result in her death, and the other kiddies, I swear to you that members of Armani's team won't be the only ones wanting to see to it that Mademoiselle will never make it to court.'

'No, no, no. Granot. We cannot...'

The RAID device finally crackled into life.

'Dara.. ? Agnès. Can you... me? Over.'

Holding a look with Granot, he pushed in the transmit button on the control panel.

'Just barely, the signal's terrible. But go ahead. Over.'

'We have appreh   the fugi.... She swears she has .. ..ea how poison got ....iser. We're landing at the Cas.... in about eight... Come soonest. Over.'

'Listen, Agnès, we've got a hell of a situation here.'

Darac's mobile rang. His eyes went to the caller ID field. Farid.

12.22 PM

As she opened the office door, Astrid was concerned at what she might find. She found Elie calmly working at her desk.

'Hi, Tridi.'

'We've... just got in from the Cascade.'

Elie signed a cheque, matched it to an envelope, and ticked a box on an accompanying sheet. 'Good class?'

'Yes, yes.'

'Excellent. Lunch should be particularly lovely today. Jean-Claude has—'

'Elie! Drop the ostrich routine, will you? There's no time for it.' Astrid locked the door behind her. 'For any number of reasons, members of my group will be turning on their mobiles about now and at least one of them will discover what happened at *Pal-Mas*.'

Elie consulted the sheet and began making out another cheque. 'They've announced only that the victim was a 45 year-old man. Besides, I told everyone but you that Urquelle had been called away.'

'You *still* haven't told Zoë and Mathieu?'

'No.'

'You should, Elie.'

'My plan is to hang up a notice in Reception after your final classes.' Another envelope. Another tick in the box. 'Remember?'

'Are you sure the only reason you wanted to do that was so no one would clock just how delighted you are Urquelle is dead?'

'What other reason could I have?'

'I don't know but I didn't think much of your plan when the news was death from natural causes. Now we know it's murder, it requires more than an impersonal notice, Elie. You should tell Zoë and Mathieu before lunch. *At* lunch, you should give the news to everyone else.'

'Tridi, you work with the police on murder cases all the time, right? It's nothing to you. *And* you know the whole sorry story of have-a-go hero Gérard Urquelle. Naturally, it might cross *your* mind that he could have been the *Pal-Mas* victim.' She signed the cheque. 'But the others?'

'Well, the fact there's police cordon tape wrapped around Urquelle's Jaguar – which my lot saw on our way in – might tip the wink to some of them.'

'Not necessarily.' Elie annotated the sheet and reached for an envelope. 'No, I don't think so.'

Keeping up this calm, methodical rhythm was not indifference on Elie's part, Astrid suspected. But what exactly was it?

'Elie, stop what you're doing and look at me. You need to tell them. Now.'

Finding it difficult to hold Astrid's gaze, Elie slowly set down her pen. Closing her eyes, her fingertips went to her temples and she began massaging them with slow circular strokes.

'Elie, I know you don't want to spoil everyone's final day fun but...' Another interpretation presented itself. Astrid's cool blue eyes filled with shards of ice. 'That's *not* the reason, is it?'

'Don't be hard on me. I've already had the owner of this place, Georgina Meier, on the phone laying down the law: "It's your job to *ensure* the Villa comes out of this with its reputation intact!" Elie opened her eyes. 'But not you Tridi, as well. I can't bear it.'

Astrid's head was a battleground of conflicting imperatives, but her heart knew only one truth and, at least for the moment, it held sway. Nevertheless, she resolved that if she couldn't convince Elie to make the necessary announcements, she herself, would.

'Babe,' she said. 'Stand up. And put your arms out.'

The women embraced and it was some moments before they released each other. It was only then that Astrid's gaze fell on the corner table behind Elie's desk, home to a modest collection of Villa ephemera. Since their post-breakfast chat, something had been added: a beautiful, though empty, white porcelain bud vase. Next to it, a folded gift card lay half-open. It read: "With love, V".

A horrible new possibility occurred to Astrid.

'*That's* new.' She indicated the vase. 'And lovely. Vivienne make it?'

'Uh, yes. She came in to... But the police wouldn't let her take any of his things away. Well – you would know.'

Astrid nodded. And she also knew what she needed to do next. She glanced at her watch. There was just time.

'Elie, I'm going to ask you a question that others will shortly be asking you – people who are far more skilled than I am at such things. Are you with me?'

'Yes?'

'I wouldn't necessarily blame her if she did, but do you think Vivienne hired the woman who appears to have murdered her husband?'

'No,' Elie said, with a curiously precise emphasis.

Astrid took a breath. And another. 'Did you and Vivienne hire her, together?'

'No!'

The office door rattled in its frame. And then, knocks. Three of them. Light but urgent.

'I'm answering that.'

As Astrid went to the door, Elie quickly removed Vivienne's card to her desk drawer, sat down once more and, smoothing her jacket lapels, prepared to face whatever came next.

What came next was Zoë Hamada and Mathieu Croix. They did not look happy.

'Glad you're here,' Astrid said, admitting them. 'Elie's got something to tell you.'

12.22 PM

Assisted all the way by Djibril Mpensa, Deanna was on the verge of a breakthrough and everyone knew it. But if ever there were a double-edged moment in the life of a crime pathology lab, this was it. The poisoner's first victim had collapsed in a state of extreme physical and mental dysfunction slightly less than three hours ago and Deanna was now one single result away from identifying the poison responsible. With the shattering news from *Maternelle Niel*, the stakes were higher than ever. Positively identifying the poison would also determine which, if any, antidote could be administered to the stricken children. The flipside of the coin was that if Deanna's guess proved wrong, the process would have to be started from the beginning and it might take hours to reach the same point.

With the now fully excavated corpse of Monsieur Gérard Urquelle at their backs, Deanna and Mpensa's eyes were trained on a computer christened, for reasons no one could remember, "Monsieur Go-Go," favoured for its ability to render the spectrometer's clustered linear dispersal patterns in the sharpest resolution.

The Monsieur usually made a curious sheep-like *baa!* sound before displaying its findings.

Sometimes, it flashed them up without warning.

12.23 PM

No other parents had arrived as yet. Too soon after the incident.

Armani didn't know it was possible to feel such pain. He wondered how long he could go on feeling it and live. Perhaps it wouldn't be possible. But he had to be strong. Had to.

Emma's "numbers" were "good," though, it seemed. Indeed, they were *"really* encouraging." "Practically normal." Urquelle, Armani knew, had looked and behaved *entirely* normally moments before he died.

Emma was in a coma, as were the other girls, but it had been induced. To protect her. To save her life. Just as six years ago, having carried Emma for 42 weeks, Noëmi had been induced to *give* her life. Now, Noëmi was in labour once more. Six weeks early because of the shock. Her numbers were good, too, it seemed. And baby Fabien's. There was "nothing to worry about." Nothing to worry about!

Going off shift, Darac's nurse friend Suzanne had looked in and said something about babies far more premature than Fabien growing happily healthy, or healthily happy or something like that, thereafter. She didn't say there was nothing to worry about but that was nothing to worry about, was it?

Noëmi had insisted he sit with Emma. *She* needed him most. She had insisted it. Insisted in words and tears and kisses and hugs. And so he left Noëmi there. Left her in good hands. The best. And Suzanne was going to stay with her. And keep her mobile on. In touch. Just ring me. I'll be there. Promise? Promise.

Noëmi...

Emma...

Fabien...

Armani looked at the traces of Emma's really encouraging numbers, and the practically normal tubes, lines and wires feeding and monitoring the breathing of his so, so, little *grand*. And he wept once more.

He had to pull himself together. He needed to call Suzanne. Use of mobiles by visitors was strictly forbidden in the hospital's intensive care unit but since he was a police officer deemed to be working on the case, Armani had been given special dispensation. As he slipped the phone from his pocket, it rang. No need to call Suzanne, after all.

'Suzanne?'

Darac and Granot were hurrying towards the shoe department exit into Rue Gioffredo.

'Armani?' Darac said, shouting into his mobile. 'Listen, this is very important. Deanna has narrowed down the categories of poisons that could have killed Urquelle in the way it did, and she is certain that Emma has *not* been poisoned. Repeat, *not*. Emma is completely OK and so are the others. Do you hear me? Deanna says the fatal dose was administered between six hours and thirty hours ago. Do you see? It means that the scent Emma picked up in the store was just *that*. Scent! Deanna is talking to the ICU now. They'll soon be bringing Emma back to you both, man. Completely unharmed!' Darac gave Granot a look but he had turned his head. 'Emma's OK! Can you hear me, Armani?' He held the phone away from his mouth. 'He's weeping.' And so, he suspected, was Granot.

Darac's Peugeot was waiting a little further down the street, a magnetic beacon attached to its roof, a uniform from Foch behind the wheel. Clocking the advancing pair, he got out.

'Listen, Armani, we're shooting off to the Villa des Pinales now but I'm not ending this call until I'm sure you've heard and understood what I'm saying. OK? *Have* you?'

Thanking the uniform, Darac took back his keys and as he and Granot climbed into the front seats, he heard the words, 'Deanna, you beauty' emerge through Armani's tears and the nightmare he and Noëmi had endured, Darac supposed, was over. The exchange that followed had to be brief, but as Darac ended the call, it was with a definite flourish that he flicked on the roof beacon, zigzagged through the crawling one-way traffic and accelerated into the almost empty bus lane running alongside. In the far distance, a couple of single deckers were pulling into a stop. He'd worry about them when he got there.

'Alright, Granot?'

'Never better,' the big man said. 'Now let's go and find the *actual* poisoner.'

'Absolutely. Deanna reckons they'll come up with exactly what was administered and when sometime in the next hour. Could come any second.'

'It'll take twenty minutes to get up to the Villa. Fifteen, though, if you head for Gorbella.'

'Avenue Saint-Lambert's probably quicker.'

'Not if you trespass on the tramway. How are your slaloming skills?'

'We'll find out. Gorbella, it is.'

The traffic to their left was still slow and solid as they closed in on the two stationary buses. Both were signalling to pull away from the stop.

'You can get in some practice now,' Granot said. 'Gorbella will be easier than this. All you have to dodge on the tramway is trams. Haul it over!' he shouted at the traffic. 'Steady, now, Darac.'

With the beacon's thrashing beam acting like a snowplough, vehicles keeping pace with the buses nosed aside and although Darac approached the widening gap at less than half the speed the Caserne's ace driver Wanda Korneliuk would have managed, he got through it unscathed.

As the potentially appalling consequences of Emma's travails appeared to be no longer an issue, the exchanges between Darac and Granot began to loosen up.

'Can I open my eyes, now?' Granot said, as they regained

the bus lane.

'You as well, huh?' Darac began to picture the operation ahead. 'Logistics, Granot. We're going to have a lot of people on the ground up at the Villa. Two-way radios would have been useful but there'll be too many ears around. Agreed?'

'Agreed.'

Darac glanced at the dash clock as they approached the turn into Boulevard Carabacel. 'The rest of the squad shouldn't be too far behind us.'

'Bearing that in mind, how do you want to kick things off up at the Villa?'

'Astrid has a lot of stuff for us on Urquelle, she said, and she was going to fill me in later. Considering what we now know, I'd better grab her as soon as we get there, I think.'

'Interrupt Astrid's lunch?' Granot gave a snort. 'You'll be in for an earful. As it were.'

'You're right.' Darac grinned. 'She'll just have to bite the bullet. As it were.'

'While you're with Astrid, I'll obtain a list of all students, on-site staff and anything else that could be relevant from the administrative director, Madame... Tiron?'

'Elie Tiron, yes. Be at your most diplomatic, Granot. According to Astrid, Madame is a very *sympa* soul but it seems she would have preferred to have swept this particular problem under the carpet. And that was when she believed the poisoning had happened elsewhere.'

'What director *isn't* like that?'

'To be fair to her, protecting the students' final day frolics was her motive, Astrid believes.'

'As long as she doesn't seek to protect the murderer, we'll get along fine.'

'Absolutely. Right, I need to make a couple of quick calls.' He tapped in a number and waited. 'Did Bonbon and

Flak get anything from Vivienne Urquelle, do you know?'

'The cold shoulder,' Granot said. 'That was about it.'

'That's going to have to change.' Darac's call was picked up. 'Agnès?'

'I'm observing Zena through the two-way at the moment, Paul,' Agnès said, smiling redundantly at her. 'It's all of three minutes since she learned the serious heat is off.'

'One very relieved young woman, I imagine.'

Sitting slumped on the interview room chair, Zena was grinning, laughing and crying all at once.

'You could say that. I agree with your Madame Beaumont, by the way. Zena has quite a presence. And she's remarkably sanguine, considering what's happened. I still have to hold her to account on some issues, of course.'

'Of course. Give her my best regards, nevertheless, will you? She's had a rough time.'

'I will, indeed. Later on, I'll give Frènes the low-down. If I tell him now, he'll be on a screen near you before you can say "And action!"'

'Absolutely, and the later the good folk up at the Villa learn about Zena's innocence, the better. Whoever *did* poison Urquelle must be feeling pretty smug about things. I'm going to make that point to Astrid in a moment. All students are due to check out at 9.30 tomorrow morning, by the way.'

'I'm familiar with the place, actually. Did a two-day flower-arranging course there some years ago. Your dear *papa* was still teaching there occasionally so that's how long ago it was.'

'So you didn't come across the current director, Elie Tiron?'

'No, it was before her time. I checked *in* at about 5, as I remember. I take it there no new groups of students turning up at that time today?'

'No, fortunately. The weekend is given over to day-schools and they're not due until 11 o'clock in the morning. And they won't be checking into bedrooms, of course.'

'That's useful. Unless the layout has changed, there are several well-equipped classrooms and when I was there, a couple of them were not in use. If that's still the case, requisition one as an ops room. I doubt you'll need Crowd Control as such, but I can transfer them *en bloc* from *Pal-Mas* and they'll keep everyone in place on the site. Also, I'll see if I can keep on at least some of the extra uniforms we drafted in earlier. Serge Paulin's group is free now and I'll deploy them, too.'

'Perfect. We'll need 24-hour gatekeeping on the ops room, if we get it.'

'How was the take-down operation in *Pal-Mas* going when you left?'

'Almost completed – you know how fast R.O. can move things on when he's in the mood. And that's good because Deanna's more precise findings could come in at any minute and we'll need him and his team up at the Villa. I think it would be useful to have Erica on site, too, by the way.'

'I'll let R.O. know as soon we end this. He can call Erica in. Right, Paul – depending on how things go here, I've a meeting to squeeze in with Frènes, who will be *so* disappointed we're no longer dealing with a case that merits issuing half-hourly bulletins to the media and granting, or rather begging to take part in, interviews.'

'Annie Provin will feel the same.'

'Indeed. Then I have other fish to fry at the Palais de Justice, and on the housekeeping front, I ought to issue a formal thank-you to Albert Cassani.'

'He really came through for us at the store. Agnès. Give him my regards, too, as and when. And tell him that Madame Nadine Beaumont and Mademoiselle Jade Moreau were especially helpful to us. Credits to the organisation – all that.'

'Just jot those names down... Right, I'll make the calls and then I'll continue with Mademoiselle Zena Bairault. It seems Zena *is* her forename, by the way. Any thoughts on what her story is?'

'Some.'

'Me too.'

12.42 PM

By the time Darac and Granot pulled into the Villa's car park, Suzanne was calling with news that the Tardelli family's travails were not over yet. Her tone, though, was upbeat.

'Six weeks preterm is not *ideal,* Paul, but it's routine stuff for our Obs and Gynae teams. I've just had a word with Dr. Lauresc and she assures me that Noëmi is very healthy; that the pregnancy up until now has been problem-free; that there were no complications with her first birth, and so on. Added to that, the unborn baby is doing absolutely fine. There were cheers in the delivery suite when news came that Emma and the other little girls were none the worse for their adventure. To say that that cheered Noëmi is the understatement of the century.'

Darac pulled on the handbrake. He and Granot stayed put.

'And what about the future for the little one?'

'Emma? She's bouncing around. She could go home actually, but they'll keep her in for a day or two.'

Darac could picture it. 'That's great but I meant the even littler one – Franck? No, Fabien.'

'Fabien Alexander Vincenzo Tardelli, as Armani insisted on telling me.'

A frisson ran up and down Darac's spine. And did so again.

'Alexander, you say? Not Alexandre or Alessandro?'

'No, no – Alexander. Unusual name for them to have chosen, isn't it? With their heritage.'

Something was nagging... And then Darac saw it. Saw it in all its Armanian glory. For the moment, he felt too overcome to speak.

'Paul, are you there?' Silence. 'Granot, are you?'

'Yes, yes.' Granot said, welling up for a second time in the hour. 'It's the name. Triggered a memory of another little one. Threw us a bit, that's all.'

'Sorry, I do realise how rough this must have been. I know how close you all are.'

'We're fine.' Darac wiped his eyes with the heel of his hand, then exhaled a couple of sharp, clearing breaths. 'Absolutely fine. Uh... Had you met Armani before today, Suzanne?'

'No, but I've heard a lot about him over the years. Something of a rogue, I'd gathered, but he's a lovable one, I can see.'

'Yes, he is.' Darac shared a look with Granot. 'He's lovable, alright.'

'Look, Paul, I have to go but the message from here is that there's nothing to worry about. Nothing to worry about at all.'

Commissaire Agnès Dantier had no idea how much time she had spent questioning suspects and witnesses over the years, but in a slack moment just three days before, Granot had estimated that 20,000 hours would have been about right. That vast experience coupled with unerring instincts made her a formidable interrogator. She knew when to bully, when to probe and prod, to encourage and reward. And, often the most effective technique of all, she knew when to remain silent.

'So you see, Madame Commissaire,' Zena said, dabbing her eyes with a tissue, 'I *had* to get out of Ukraine. Politically, the situation is... It's very difficult and it's going to get worse. Much worse.' Her mouth hardened into a sneer. '*Russia*,' she said, more a sound than a word, urgent and sibilant as a chill gust of wind. 'Russia, madame, is going to ravage my country.' The blood drained from her cheeks. 'I worked in the Academy of Arts Library in Lviv. Not a qualified librarian, I spent most of my time stacking shelves like in a supermarket. But I enjoyed it there and I grew as a person. I had to go to work, you see.' She looked both ashamed and protective, suddenly. 'My family...'

'Take your time,' Agnès said.

'Well, university was out of the question – put it that way. I could have risen in the library, taken courses and qualified. But it was the bigger picture that stopped me. I felt uneasy. I knew what was going to come. I felt I had to do something. And then a friend in the city got me involved with... let's just call it a group. Hard line but not, on the surface, violent.' Pressing her lips together, she shook her head. 'No. Not the *surface*.'

'I understand, Zena. Oh, for the recording, I suppose we should note your full name?'

'Of course. It's Zena Mariana Kovalen.' She spelled the surname. 'I was born Kovalenko but I came to hate the patriarchal implications of that final syllable so I had it lopped off.'

Agnès smiled. 'Good for you.'

'So, all this must sound... classic, I imagine. You're wondering what precise incident led to my escaping my native country? I blew something up. I put someone in hospital. Perhaps I killed them? No, I didn't do any of those things because I abhor violence. But if you're in such a group as I was, you *cannot* abhor violence.' Her complexion began to take on more colour. 'I really do not know what would have happened eventually. Perhaps I *would* have killed someone. Killed one of the Russians hell bent on raping my country.' She seemed far away, suddenly. 'Instead, *I* was raped, madame. By one of my own group. Its leader, in fact, and I was meant to be grateful like the others for his attentions, for his instruction and his "protection." I was not. That man violated me and robbed me of all that was personal and valuable. My passport – everything. So I had to leave. You see? Don't you?'

'Yes. I do.' Although Agnès was not fully *au fait* with the minutiae of the asylum system, she felt sure that those concerned would look favourably on Zena's case. 'It's absolutely clear that you had to leave.'

'But I couldn't.'

'Because the rapist held your passport.'

Zena smiled bitterly, her eyes filling with tears. 'I had dropped the suffix of my surname, madame. Cut it off as a message to my family and to girls in other families. But that man? That great liberator? He took *all* of it. He took my entire identity.'

Agnès had a lump in her throat as she continued. 'If one has to leave but cannot, escape is the only option, isn't it?'

Zena nodded.

'How did you manage it?'

'My bank account was no longer my own but I had never trusted banks anyway. I had cash. My own and from my grandmother. With it, I bought contacts. And with the services provided by those contacts, I made it *all* this way.' She looked around the interview room and laughed. 'Big success, huh?'

Agnès could only imagine what it had taken to have made it this far. 'Your command of what to you is a foreign language is remarkable, Zena.'

'Thank you.'

'Clearly, that's one reason you opted for France. Are there others?'

'Would you believe me if I said that I have always believed in the civilising value of French culture? Not all of it, of course. But French literature, art, cinema and especially music have made the world a better place, I think. Do you believe that, too?'

Agnès's features were at their most feline when she smiled. 'I am French so of course I believe it.'

Zena shrugged. 'It *is* true. For me, I mean.'

'When you arrived, why did you opt to live as an illegal immigrant, rather than apply for asylum?'

'I thought about it long and hard – what was best. If I had believed asylum would definitely have been granted, of course I would have applied for it. But I didn't believe. So I didn't apply.'

Agnès made a note to slip in a call to Examining Magistrate Reboux immediately after the interview. As erudite and dedicated as his colleague Frènes was small-minded and self-serving, Reboux would be sage counsel.

'But why did you make your way here? Why Nice?'

'I cannot and will not betray my contacts.'

'Zena, I'm afraid that down the line, other officers may ask you to do just that. I, however, am not asking it.'

'I will say only that there are people living in this region who made it easier for me to come here than elsewhere. And not all of those people are money-grabbing bastards, either. Some are altruists.' She frowned, lending her mien a quality that seemed particularly Eastern European to Agnès. 'Altruist - that word exists as a noun?'

'Indeed it does. Zena, I believe I know the answer to this question but I have to ask it. Why did you run away the moment your customer collapsed? You knew you were innocent of any wrongdoing.'

'Yes, but I didn't know for certain that the scent in my vial hadn't been poisoned, for some reason. Spiked, if you like. You must know that such things are not unheard of where I come from. But I *did* know for certain that whatever had caused that man's death, I would be questioned, my forged papers checked, and my identity blown. Flight was my only option.'

Agnès could hardly credit how desperately unlucky Zena had been in all this. 'Vis-à-vis your story, you were clearly not going to retrace your steps all the way back to the Ukraine. Where *were* you heading?'

'Somewhere in Italy. For many reasons, it would have been very, *very* much a second choice for me but I probably would have survived OK there. Survived long enough to be able to have made – no mounted – *mounted* another bid to come here, at some point.'

Italy... Agnès decided not to tell Zena that the RAID

helicopter dispatched to monitor passengers leaving the *Train des Merveilles*, had caught up with it only after it had left Breil-sur-Roya. Had Zena alighted there, she would have been on her way to Italy now.

Under the circumstances, it may have been of small comfort to Zena but Agnès had a happier story for her. 'You might like to know that Madame Nadine Beaumont spoke up for you during questioning.'

Zena's eyebrows rose. 'Really?'

'Despite how things looked, she wouldn't have it that you were guilty of anything. Further, she told anyone who would listen just how bright and wonderful she thought you were.'

Zena's head dropped. 'That's very sweet. I thought all the bonhomie was just, you know, professional. I would have been quite happy working in the store. At least for a time.' She looked up. 'The other officers you referred to. The immigration people. When will they come?'

'Probably tomorrow.'

Agnès formally ended the interview and turned off the recorder. 'Because of your status as an illegal immigrant, you will be remanded for the time being.'

'In a detention centre?'

'Yes but don't despair, Zena. I strongly advise you to apply for asylum. I will personally see to it that your petition is properly made and considered.'

The look of gratitude in Zena's face touched Agnès deeply.

'You will?'

'I will.'

'Thank you, Commissaire Dantier. Thank you. You have been very kind to me. Even in the helicopter. What do you think my chances are?'

'Off the record, I anticipate the authorities will look with compassion at your reasons for escaping your native country. And even further off the record, your chances are markedly better than they would have been if you weren't white, educated, and a fluent French speaker fully engaged with French culture.'

'Ah.' Zena brightened a little, but Agnès could see she was perplexed, too. 'Doesn't the first article of the French constitution proclaim that the State shall ensure the equality of all citizens before the law, without distinction of origin, race, or religion?'

'It does, yes.' Agnès's deadpan expression spoke volumes.

'Double standards? Hypocrisy? Well I never thought France was *Utopia*, madame.'

'That's wise.'

'Nevertheless, being granted asylum here would still be a dream come true. However, I will keep my hopes...' She clasped her hands tightly together. '... Like this.'

'That's wise, also.'

'Would you answer a question for me?

'If I can.'

'Why does the city of Nice need a "green lung?"'

'I'm sorry, I don't know what you mean.'

'It was something I noticed among the promotional material at the Promenade du Paillon building site: "A green lung for the city".'

'Oh, of course – the new gardens, *miroir d'eau,* et cetera. I don't suppose there's a *need*, as such, but I do think it will be a beautiful development. And few will mourn the loss of what it's replacing – things like the fumey old *gare routière*, for example.'

'Ah.'

Agnès was about to offer her hand when she remembered she had another crumb of comfort to offer. 'The officer who was leading the investigation on the ground asked me to pass on his regards to you, incidentally.'

The concept appeared to aggravate Zena and the shrug she produced failed to hide it. 'Gloating? Triumphalism? I am used to such police officers.'

'No, no. Captain Paul Darac is not such a one, I assure you. His concern for you was quite genuine.'

Zena seemed puzzled, intrigued and then amused at the idea. 'Captain *Paul Darac*, huh? Not the musician, I imagine. Or do you have jazz-playing police captains here? Another reason to love your country.'

Agnès would have loved to reply: 'We do, actually. Commentators have dubbed such officers "poètes-policiers." But she couldn't. Indeed, she realised she shouldn't have named Darac in the first place. 'There's a jazz musician with the same name?' she asked, innocently. 'A good one?'

'A guitarist, yes. To my ears, very good. I've heard only one CD but I loved it. What was the name of his band?' Zena searched the library shelf that was mid-air for the answer. 'The Denis... or David... no, *Didier* Masso Quintet, I think. *At The Blue Devil Club Again* was the title of the CD. To my ears, excellent.'

Agnès couldn't wait to pass this on to Darac, starved as he was of feedback from those at the Caserne.

'Do you like jazz, madame?'

Agnès stood. 'We'll leave things there. Jazz? Not really. Not at all, in fact.'

'Pity.'

Agnès offered her hand and, taking it, Zena looked into her eyes.

'Thank you again, madame.' She held the gaze. 'Despite what you implied about the State just now, you are very lucky to live in such a city as this.'

In the context of a police interview, no one had ever made a comment like this to Agnès before. 'Perhaps, Zena,' she said. 'I should remind myself of that more often.'

12.51 PM

As things panned out, Darac had indeed committed the crime of interrupting Astrid's lunch but for once, she hadn't felt particularly hungry. Chicken satay skewers with a peanut dipping sauce followed by a Thai green curry was all she had been able to manage. The pair had then decamped to her room where she had gone over all the material she had on the have-a-go-hero case, the priapic approach to life of Monsieur Gérard Urquelle, and Elie Tiron's relationship with the needy and, Astrid was wont to believe, needlessly slain Karen Bicoud. Finally, Astrid had provided notes, each accompanied by a lightning sketch, on anyone who appeared to have had a connection with Urquelle, or had expressed any sort of opinion on him, or had so much as brushed elbows with him over the past three days.

Her loyalties torn, she had decided to stick just to the bare facts in outlining Elie's initial rejection and subsequent acceptance of Urquelle's account of the jewellery store shootings. Besides, Astrid had an ace up her sleeve to play on her friend's behalf if needed.

'When is your final class due to start, Astrid?'

'At 1.30. Same is true for Zoë and Mathieu Croix. Understandably, some of the students were in two minds about it at first, but the vote was unanimous in the end. Are you OK with that?'

'Granot and I are very much in favour of it.' Thoughts of Darac's paternal ancestors flashed through his mind. 'It's a lot easier pulling individuals out of a corralled space than chasing them all over the landscape. For questioning, I mean.'

Astrid gave him a look. 'You shouldn't pull any student out of a class without first obtaining the permission of the tutor concerned.'

Darac smiled. 'Do you give it?'

'Well.... yes, I suppose so. And I'm confident the others will, too.'

Darac's smile faded a little. 'I'm sure you realise that whether a student lives just down the hill in Cimiez, like Monique Dufour, or in St Petersburg like Thea Petrova, *no one* will be allowed to leave here tomorrow morning if they haven't at least made a statement and confirmed their contact details for the next days. We've got a small army of people here to take them so it shouldn't delay things too much. Granot will be breaking that news to everyone in the dining room at this very moment. I'm afraid the instruction goes for you too, Astrid.'

She shrugged. 'Seems someone here is a poisoner – it has to be that way, doesn't it?' She looked anxious, suddenly. 'Hope it doesn't turn out to be Chef Jean-Claude. He's keeping a dessert back for me – panna cotta with seared apricots and fig sauce.' She shook her head. 'No, he wouldn't tamper with a beautiful thing like that.'

Darac laughed.

'Listen,' Astrid went on. 'We'll have to go down in a minute but from everything I've dug up, do you believe Urquelle *intended* to kill both poor, sad Karen and the robber Eddy Lopes? Because if he did and, although I just paint pictures and you guys are the detectives, it surely narrows down the list of suspects to anyone connected with those two victims, doesn't it?'

'I thought you were set on protecting your friend Elie? She's the most likely perp of all those you mentioned.'

Astrid shook her head. 'Ah, but she's not.'

'Because she eventually changed her mind about Urquelle's story? That doesn't really work, Astrid.'

'No, no. Because she has no idea about something I discovered and which I haven't mentioned to you yet.'

'And are you going to?'

'Darac! Of course I am. But talk me through your take on the robbery that went wrong – or didn't.'

'Let's look at the so-called gunman Eddy Lopes, first. He was a down-and-out with a sore need of money, right? If Urquelle *had* lured him into the scheme with a promise of splitting the proceeds of the robbery afterwards, such a man might well be hungry enough to fall for it. You could picture the persuasive Urquelle coaching him, couldn't you?' Darac produced his all-purpose con-man's voice. "You push your way in while I'm standing by the door, Eddy, OK? I'll pretend to be scared stiff. Karen, my assistant *will* be, believe me. You smash the CCTV camera with your gun, right? You toss a holdall onto the floor. You order her to fill it or you'll kill her and me. I beg you not to, and tell her to do as she's told. You leave with the stuff. Afterwards we meet and split it. I do the rest." Except, Urquelle didn't.'

Astrid nodded. 'That's just how I see it.'

'Instead, he grabs the gun, finesses shooting Lopes and Karen, taking one in the big toe for his pains but boy, was it worth it. In one fell swoop, Urquelle got rid of a lover threatening to spill on their affair to his well-heeled wife Vivienne, thereby providing her with the grounds for divorcing him. With his meal ticket intact, the have-a-go hero was then catapulted up the ranks at his jewellery firm.

Killing Karen and Lopes in the way he did was win-win. For him.'

'Exactly, Darac. Exactly!'

'There's only one problem with this scenario and although I'm not particularly impressed with how the Monegasque police appear to have handled the case, they did at least unearth that one problem. And it's a highly significant one.'

If Darac had just played a card that Astrid was waiting to trump, he was given no indication of it. Having worked for a time as a living statue – indeed, it was in that role that she had first encountered Darac – Astrid's poker face was a thing of complete inscrutability.

'By any chance,' she said. 'Would that problem be an individual named Denis Marut? The eyewitness to the shootings? A man Urquelle was supposed to have no connection with whatsoever and whose account of what he saw was the sole reason the local police believed Urquelle's bollocks story?'

Darac may not have been able to read Astrid's expression but her words were clear enough. A revelation was clearly coming and the prospect made him smile. 'Come on, Astrid, what is it you discovered and haven't mentioned to Elie?'

'Nothing much. Just that Marut died in a road accident eight months after the hearing. The circumstances were suspicious. I believe Urquelle was responsible.'

'After eight *months*? Astrid, Urquelle collapsed two *minutes* after his circumstantially suspicious encounter with Zena Bairault and there had been no wrongdoing there at all.'

'Marut plummeted to his death off the D 2564 above Ricard. Brakes had failed.'

'It happens – as citizens of Monaco know only too well.'

'Marut had been driving a classic sports car. An English Triumph TR4 built in 1963. As you no doubt saw when you and Granot arrived, Urquelle was into classic cars, as well. That carmine red beauty all wrapped up in ribbon was his 1957 Jaguar. His pride and joy, he called it. He told me he had rebuilt the car from the ground up. He knew every nut and bolt. What does that suggest?'

'That *theoretically,* he would have been well capable of tampering with the brakes of Marut's vehicle. But the two men were strangers. Apart from a penchant for vintage sports cars, there's nothing substantive connecting them.'

'Urquelle very proudly told me his Jaguar had twice won the *Concours d'Élégance* at an important retro car event.' She brought up another screen on her laptop. 'He wasn't lying – that's him on the top step of the podium in question. This is 2004, look.'

'OK.'

She scrolled images until she found shots of Urquelle and a second man working on their vehicles at an event from the year before. Wearing overalls covered in oil stains, the men were shown in one photo feigning bafflement at having to assemble a simple two-piece jack, and in another, draining champagne flutes with their forearms comically entwined.

'As you often ask others, Darac – anything strike you?'

'The guy Urquelle is larking around with is the one who was standing on the bottom step of the podium in the earlier shot.'

Astrid scrolled on.

'Indeed he was,' she said, finding another image and for the moment, withholding it. 'Have a stab at his name.'

1.15 PM

Occupying a central position on the first floor at the rear of the building, the Salle Milhaud was one of the Villa's larger classrooms. Used mainly for music appreciation courses, the room was unoccupied at the moment and as no classes were booked in for the next three weeks, Granot had had little difficulty in persuading Elie Tiron to make it available to the Brigade.

On the floor below, the three concluding classes of the week were underway with a full complement of students and tutors, and with a close eye being kept on the Villa's permanent house staff, every potential suspect for the murder of Gérard Urquelle was effectively in lock-down. By 9.30 tomorrow morning, that advantage would be lost.

Under its pink stuccoed ceiling, the Salle was a thing of faux-rococo touches and thickly piled carpeting, but the wall at the head of the room was faced entirely in whiteboard. Darac was transcribing Astrid's notes on to it as the remaining members of his team and officers from other units made their entrances behind him. News of the Tardellis' escape from hell had spread and the buzz of voices was so buoyantly upbeat, it put a smile on Darac's face even as he scribbled hurriedly on.

The sumptuousness of their temporary home further lifted everyone's mood and, drawing inevitable comparisons with the rough-hewn charms of the squad room at the Caserne, several wags advocated a permanent move. A stoppered stone flask of water and a glass placed at every chair? Unheard of. Earlier, Elie Tiron had readily agreed to Granot's suggestion that he witness the flask-filling process and had drunk a glassful in front of him. Granot was able to report back that however Urquelle had encountered the poison that killed him, it wasn't in the tap water.

Even more unusual for a squad room was the provision of a baby grand piano. Where was Didier Musso when you needed him? Not that this particular gathering would have appreciated his talent – unlike, Darac had been astonished to hear, confirmed DMQ fan Zena Kovalen a.k.a. Bairault. Agnès had already updated him on her story, adding that she intended formally to back Zena's application for asylum; an application Examining Magistrate Reboux was confident would ultimately prove successful. It would probably be well down the line but Darac was already looking forward to welcoming Zena at the Blue Devil.

At the moment, he was looking forward to locating the pin magnets necessary to attach Astrid's thumbnail sketches to the whiteboard. The drawings were of such quality that they identified their subjects as clearly as their photo IDs, and gave more of an insight into their characters. As Astrid herself saw them, of course.

Behind Darac, Bonbon was working the room with a striped paper bag.

'Caramel, Serge?'

'Better not, Bonbon.'

'The modern rugby player's lot?'

'That, and if I had *one*, I'd want to demolish the whole packet.'

Sitting in front of Serge, girlfriend Erica had no such qualms. 'What kind of caramels, Bonbon? *Au beurre salé*?'

'Of course. *And* they're from Cours Saleya.'

'You sweet man,' she said, taking one, and Bonbon continued happily on his rounds.

Moments later, the final member of the complement

arrived, a uniform closed the door, and the buzz in the room rose another notch. Among the voices, Darac heard the sound of someone prodding F above middle C on the piano, a Bechstein no less, and upon whose perfectly polished lid, a notice read: PLEASE DO NOT TOUCH.

'Leave it alone, Perand,' Darac said, without looking.

Laughter rippled around the room.

'Lucky guess, chief,' the young man said, as he took a seat next to Flaco. 'Lucky guess.'

'And yet,' Darac said, as he at last found the magnets. 'And yet.'

'How many keys are there to the Salle?' Perand asked, as always, seeking immediately to regain a perceived loss of cred.

'On the piano or for the door?' Granot said, earning a further ripple from the throng and a moue from Perand. 'Two sets of keys. Elie Tiron gave me both.'

'Both? How do you know there wasn't a third set nestling in Madame's pocket?'

Perand's point-scoring ways usually set Granot's teeth on edge but in the past hour, the big man had lived through such huge emotional turmoil that it hardly seemed to matter. The boy was small-minded? Yes, he was. So what? 'Perhaps she does have a third set,' Granot said, serenely. 'But if she tries to use them, our burly Officer Bielle outside might have something to say about that, no?'

Bonbon's foxy eyes twinkled naughtily. 'You'll be saying you're worried about people glancing in and reading all our secret stuff on the whiteboards next, Perand.'

'Someone could! You've never heard of ladders?'

Crime scene co-ordinator Jean-Jacques 'Lartou' Lartigue was a large, bald black man with a curiously delicate voice. 'I don't think Officer Bielle's colleagues down below would allow anyone to tiptoe up to the windows carrying a five-metre ladder, position it and then climb up.'

More laughter but Perand wasn't beaten yet. 'What about the new thing – drones?'

Still above the fight, Granot had heard enough, nevertheless. 'Drones? I'll tell the lads to shoot them on sight when we're in here; when we go out, we'll close the curtains. Chief, you ready?'

'One second.' Darac belatedly headed the notes persons of interest and finally turned to face what was a sizeable group, his immediate team augmented by senior forensic officer Raul Ormans's unit, and a coterie of uniforms from Commissariat Foch whom Agnès had managed to retain from Palais Masséna. Each was taking shots of the whiteboards on their mobiles.

Voices quietened.

'OK, let's get to it everyone,' Darac said, his words punctuated by the rattle and gasp of flasks being un-stoppered all around the room. 'First, I need to remind you that Astrid may be a glorious human being and a fabulous artist but she is not a trained detective. I also need you to consider the fact that she and administrative director Elie Tiron are good friends; that the same goes for perfume course tutor Zoë Hamada; further that, to use her phrase, she's "down with" – and this won't surprise you – head chef Jean-Claude Costeaux and everyone in his catering staff...'

Another ripple of laughter.

'... also that she has a cordial relationship with head gardener Barthélémy Issako; odd-job man Lionel Fournier – and so it goes on. A conflict of interest hardly covers it. So what value should we place on what our Astrid has come up with here?' He indicated the whiteboard. 'I think we should place a *huge* amount of value on it. Hoping that we get interrupted by Deanna at any minute, let's start with Elie Tiron and her relationship with the murdered jewellery salesman Gérard Urquelle.'

Darac went on to recount everything Astrid had passed on to him. At the end of it, Granot was first in with a comment.

'We've never had a steer like this at the start of any investigation in my time with the Brigade.' He blew a kiss in the general direction of La Salle Fernand Léger where Astrid was teaching. 'God bless the girl.'

'This isn't meant to sound facetious,' Bonbon said. 'But so *many* steers.'

Raul Ormans's actor-ish tones boomed out into the stuccoed space. 'Indeed. I'm reminded of one of those English country house murder mystery stories. Almost everyone here appears to have had a motive for killing Urquelle.'

'Except the English teacher,' Erica said, out of habit shaping to anchor any stray strands of her blonde hair behind an ear and forgetting that she was experimenting with a barrette. 'One Alan Davies.'

Ormans gave her a look. 'Which probably means *he* did it.'

'Let's not run a sweep on it,' Darac said, 'but sadly, and quite understandably, I think Elie Tiron is the likeliest killer.'

'My money is on that shady half-Russian woman,' Lartigue said. 'Thea Petrova.'

Perand shook his head. 'It's the paper magnate Bassette. Oldest motive in the world. Bassette all the way.'

'Sorry to be Captain Killjoy, people, but we need to move on and I think it makes sense to start with the so-called have-a-go-hero case. I think we look first at Denis Marut, the man deemed an eyewitness to the shootings and without whose testimony, Urquelle's story would surely not have been so readily believed. The shootings began, remember, with shop assistant Karen Bicoud taking a bullet in the centre of her forehead. In fact, so *exactly* in the centre, it seems that the weapon firing that bullet must have been deliberately aimed.' He eyeballed Raul Ormans. 'R.O? You're our ballistics expert. Am I wrong?'

'No, I agree with you absolutely. The chances of an accidentally discharged round finding that spot are infinitesimally small.'

'Thank you. I've already given you my thoughts on how Urquelle may have tempted Eddy Lopes into the robbery shtick. We know Urquelle and Marut were friends – something the Monegasque police had no idea about – and so here's another scenario to consider. Urquelle to Marut: "All you have to do, Denis old boy, is say you saw what I tell you, and this briefcase full of cash will be yours. OK?" Marut accepts, lies to the police as arranged but a few months later, perhaps feeling he's been short-changed by his oily old pal, he asks him for more. "No way," says Urquelle. "Pay or I'll spill," replies Marut. Yes, it's speculative, but given all Astrid unearthed, you can see that the final act of this scenario could well play out in a fireball of twisted metal somewhere below the D 2564.'

'It could *very* well do that,' Granot said.

'Indeed.' Bonbon picked up his flask and, with some difficulty, flipped over the metal catch to release the stopper. 'Chief, now would be a good moment to tell us that Marut's still-grieving girlfriend is Madame Thea Petrova, or Marcia Calon or Barbara on Reception.'

'Quite, Bonbon. Astrid didn't have time to dig any deeper on Marut but establishing a connection between him and anyone here may be key to this whole thing. Flak, Perand?

You've got student and staff lists there plus more info on the whiteboards. That should be enough to start you off. Work it out between you. Anything really significant, shout it out immediately.'

'OK, Captain.' Flaco said, and the pair put their heads together.

Darac turned to the rest of the group. 'Elie Tiron, now. We know that she initially believed, as we ourselves now *strongly* believe, that Urquelle had murdered her needy friend Karen Bicoud. We know she initially wanted to exact revenge on him. But we only *believe* it was Marut's eyewitness account that changed her mind. Astrid is sure that Elie knew nothing of his friendship with Urquelle, or his subsequent death, and so had no reason to conjecture what may have gone on behind the scenes between them as we just have. Astrid sets a lot of store by that but whether Elie knew more about Marut than Astrid believes or not, we know there is a strong malign connection between Elie and Urquelle.

'He, incidentally, made it clear to Elie that he recognised her as Karen's friend. Whatever she believed about Urquelle's guilt, Elie has made no secret of the fact that she hated him for other reasons. When I asked Astrid how Elie had reacted to news of Urquelle's poisoning, she didn't want to comment but I don't think we should read *too* much into that. I doubt many here would shed tears if we heard Monsieur Jules Frènes had gone under a bus but none of us would actually push the man, would we? Or pay someone else to.'

'I'd do both,' Bonbon said, raising a laugh. 'Wouldn't cost anyone a cent.'

Darac's mobile rang. He checked the caller ID. His heart began to beat out of time.

'This is it, everyone' he called out. 'It's on speaker.'

The room fell utterly silent. As if it were a choreographed move, everyone leaned forward together.

'Darac?' The familiar tobacco-rasped voice was coming through loud and clear. 'Ready?'

'Go ahead, Deanna.'

'Gérard Urquelle was poisoned with acrylamide, an odourless organic neurotoxin that's soluble in liquids, and used in a number of industrial settings and contexts.'

As a jazz player, Darac was attuned to responding to complex statements at high speed, and he was already putting things together in his head. An odourless, soluble poison could easily be used to lace a glass of wine on Mathieu Croix's course; and those first two syllables – acryl – brought to mind Astrid's use of acrylic paints, a medium she favoured in her own work and in teaching. So that was two of the Villa's courses in play. Bonbon, Darac noticed, was already scrolling screens.

Deanna went on. 'The poison appears to have been inhaled...'

'So there really *was* a killer scent?' Darac said, picturing his father quizzing former pupil Zoë Hamada about it. Assuming, that was, that no one objected to what was another conflict of interest in the case.

'A killer certainly,' Deanna replied. 'But I doubt it was in the form of a scent – *and* I hadn't finished, Darac. The poison appears to have been inhaled, but also absorbed through the labial fissure of the mouth. From that, we conclude that by far the likeliest – and I stress that word – the *likeliest* carrier of the poison was a humble, non-filtered cigarette. And sure enough, Urquelle was indeed one of those terrible smokers one reads about.'

'Shame on them,' Darac said, sharing the joke. He gave Raul Ormans a look that said: "You know what to do, R.O."

Ormans nodded in response, took out his mobile and began tapping out a text. 'That's brilliant, Deanna,' Darac went on. 'You've laid out our next move for us. Do you have any more on this?'

'Although chronic obstructive pulmonary disease was yet to put in an appearance, and might well have been many years, even decades, away, Urquelle's respiratory and cardiovascular systems nevertheless do exhibit classic signs of damage caused by the sort of high-tar, high-nicotine, non-filtered cigarettes I myself favoured before I went on to the kiddies' fags I puff now. There's a cigarette case in Urquelle's effects, incidentally. No accompanying packet. The case has a capacity of 20 and it contains eighteen *Gitanes*. Two missing from a full load, as it were. I'm not expecting Map to find anything amiss with the remaining eighteen but he's running tests on them as we speak.'

Ormans made the note and Darac took this in as the whys, wherefores and what-ifs began trading fours in his head.

'Deanna, is it possible to estimate roughly how many cigarettes Urquelle smoked in a day?'

'Roughly is the keyword here but combining everything I see before me and taking my own personal experience into account, I would doubt there were any days in which he didn't smoke at all; and few in which he exceeded 20. There's a pattern to the times people like to smoke. A cigarette after each meal and a couple in the evening is a very common one. This wouldn't stand up in court but I wouldn't be surprised if Urquelle's habit ran along those lines.'

'Interesting... And because of that habit, he winds up both inhaling and absorbing acrylamide through the skin. Have you been able to narrow the timeframe in which this happened? Initially, you gave us between 6 o'clock Thursday evening and 6 o'clock this morning.'

'We're now looking at between 8 o'clock and 11 on Thursday evening. Another detail. Urquelle had had sex sometime on Thursday evening or the small hours of Friday morning. Or at least achieved orgasm. Possibly more than once.'

'Par for the course, as it were, for what we know of his habits. We'll look into that, obviously, but back to that three-hour window.'

'I realise it's a wide open window and I hope we'll be able to narrow it further. Naturally, we'll bring you more precision on anything else we've discussed when we have it. And I would like to have more of that myself, believe me. On a different note, I would also like to have Urquelle's cigarette case which is art deco-ish, solid silver and rather beautiful. Much nicer than the one I used to have. Thinking of pinching it. Once the engraving is removed, who would know?'

Grins all round.

'No one here heard a thing,' Darac said. 'Is the engraving itself of interest?'

'No, just his initials – G.R.U.'

From the maelstrom of ideas and connections competing for attention in Darac's head, a stray broke clear away. 'G.R.U?' he said. 'That's what the KGB is known as these days.'

'I doubt they issue silver cigarette cases to their agents advertising the fact.'

If the laughter that broke around the room was at Darac's expense, his own was part of it. 'Fair point, Deanna. You mentioned the industrial applications the poison has. Is there a non-industrial context, as well?'

'Not really. Acrylamide *is* produced when starchy foodstuffs are burnt and there's some evidence that lab rodents ingesting large quantities of cremated chips over a long period may eventually develop cancer. But in the form and the potency we're talking about, acrylamide is not a poison one would encounter in everyday life. It cannot be harvested like privet berries or castor beans, for example, and unlike some other deadly poisons, it cannot be purchased for domestic use as a rodenticide, herbicide et cetera.'

'This is all really useful, Deanna.'

'We'll release Urquelle's smoking paraphernalia et cetera to you as soon as we can. We've already cleared his wallet, his pocket diary and his phone. Nothing of interest to us there. Should be with you soon.'

'Excellent.' Another idea formed, bounced off a couple of others, attached itself to an earlier thought and kept building. 'A question, Deanna – was it your habit to refill your case when the last cigarette had been smoked or might you refill it when there were still a few left?'

'No, no – the former. Smoke the lot, then refill the lot in one go. Otherwise, you end up with half empty packets all over the place. It's not written in stone, of course, but I don't know anyone who doesn't use a cigarette case that way.'

'Interesting. OK, we're up and running now, Deanna. Brilliant and very quick work as always. *Chapeau* to Map, too.'

As the call ended, Ormans was already getting to his feet to address his team.

'Just a second, R.O. Need a couple of words with Elie Tiron. I'll be quick.' Darac checked the whiteboard for her internal number and tapped it in. 'Listen in, everyone.'

'Hello, Elie speaking.'

'It's Captain Paul Darac, madame. A belated hello.'

'Oh, yes, hello, indeed. Though I feel we have met already. I've heard a lot about you from Tridi.'

Smiles. Moues of surprise. *Sotto-voce* repetitions – "Tridi" was entertaining all those in the Salle who had worked with Astrid.

'Ditto about you from... Tridi,' Darac replied, trying not to emphasise the pet name he had never heard anyone use before, and unconsciously storing it away to tease her with later. 'Listen, I need to come and talk to you in person. Will you be in your office in say, half-an-hour?'

'Yes, I'll be in here until at least 7 o'clock. After then – well, that may be up to you.'

'Thanks for understanding.'

They ended the call on a cordial note and Darac ceded the floor to Ormans.

'Alright, my lot,' he said, getting to his feet. 'Urquelle's use of a cigarette case notwithstanding, wherever there are smokers, there are both new and discarded packets to consider and, even if the fags in question have no filters, there will obviously be spent butts somewhere. You will have observed that smoking is not permitted anywhere within the building which is replete with smoke alarms. Our most fruitful hunting ground therefore will probably prove to be a designated exterior smoking area and any attendant refuse bins. We've still got Patricia on loan from Path so I've just texted her to red-zone that area and tape it off. She had already done this with Urquelle's room and his car and those are the stages upon which we shall initially strut our stuff. Although we'll keep our eyes open for anything else of significance, neither of those two initial searches should take too long. Depending on what we find and other developments, we'll then head off to the smoking area. Marie-France?'

A fresh-faced young woman wearing a thoughtful expression raised her hand.

'You and I will headline in Urquelle's room. Franck, take a couple of our finest supporting players and work through the car. I am more hopeful than confident that they will yield anything of real interest but we have to start somewhere.'

' "Every journey," ' Darac said, leaving out the conclusion. 'But before you go, let's set out the next half-hour or so. I've yet to meet Elie Tiron in person so I'm going to check in with her shortly. En route, I'll have a quick word with Astrid who will be able to give me chapter and verse on the smoking area – who frequents it, et cetera. I'll update you straight away on that, R.O. Then I'll introduce myself to the two other course tutors. According to no less an authority than my *papa*, Zoë Hamada is one of the sweetest souls around. Such people have of course been known to commit murder.'

Momentarily taking his eyes off his laptop screen, Bonbon grinned at Darac. 'What's his take on the wine man, Mathieu Croix?'

'Only that anyone who doesn't love Bandol Rosé probably needs psychiatric help.'

'I agree with your esteemed father,' Ormans said. 'What's your best case scenario on this smoking development, Darac?'

'Best? That sometime between 8 and 11 o'clock yesterday evening, someone, preferably Astrid, saw a fellow tutor, student or staff member insist that Urquelle try one of his or her own cigarettes; that that person proves to have regular access to stocks of acrylamide; and finally, that corroborating evidence is subsequently recovered from the culprit's room and/or car, by you and/or your team.'

'One can dream. And worst case?'

'As at *Pal-Mas* – that a psychopath working in a factory somewhere contaminated a product which found its way to a random victim entirely by chance.'

'Let's hope the truth turns out to be very much closer to the dream than the nightmare.'

'Indeed. All set, R.O?'

'All set.'

'Good hunting.'

As the forensics team filed smartly out of the room, Darac turned to Perand. 'How are you getting on with Denis Marut?'

The young man scratched his chin which despite the earliness of the hour was so black with stubble, it appeared to have been rubbed with charcoal. 'Marut was a bachelor, an only child of now elderly parents. He had a few cousins but I can't see a link to any of the students. Still have a few more to check out, though.'

'Right. Flak?'

'I'm working on connections to members of staff. Ditto on the result so far.'

'OK.'

Sitting in the row behind, Bonbon eyebrows suddenly flew up.

'Bonbon?' Darac said, spotting this. 'You've got something?'

'I'm reading about those industrial uses of acrylamide that Deanna mentioned. It turns out one of them is as an additive in producing china clay.'

Flaco's ears pricked up.

'And?' Darac said. 'I'm none the wiser.'

'Flak and I learned that Vivienne Urquelle is a potter. Workshop at home, kiln – the lot. Sells quite a few pieces.'

'But she doesn't *produce* the clay she uses, surely? She just buys it, presumably.'

Erica raised a long, slender finger. 'And,' she said, 'It wouldn't be possible to extract a chemical additive such as acrylamide from finished clay. Certainly not in a domestic environment.'

Bonbon nodded. 'You're both right, of course, but you'll see where I'm going with this in a minute. I've just discovered the source of the long-suffering Vivienne's money – the money that thanks to Astrid's conversations with Elie Tiron, we know dear old Gérard Urquelle, a man of few fixed principles and even fewer fixed trousers, was so anxious to keep his mitts on. Vivienne was born Vivienne Lacourt. In 1901, Vivienne's grandfather Albert founded *Lacourt et Fils Argile à Porcelaine* in Contes. In short, producing clay is the family business.'

'Are they *still* producing it?' Darac said.

'One of my antiques dealer mates lives up near there. The Lacourt place is probably the smallest operation like it around that area but it's always clattering and slurping away whenever I drive past.'

'*Is* it now?' Darac stared at the floor.

' If Vivienne wanted to acquire a jarful of acrylamide, she wouldn't have far to go, would she?'

Intrigued by what seemed a significant jump forward in the investigation, Perand and Flaco had temporarily abandoned their searches, but then Perand appeared to go to another thought and began tapping away on his laptop.

'Granot,' Darac said, looking up. 'Where are you on this?'

'We know Vivienne had a *motive* for wanting to get rid of Monsieur Unfaithfully Yours. With at least potential access to acrylamide, it seems she had *means,* too. *Opportunity*? Well, they were married, weren't they? I don't know how easy it would be to doctor a cigarette with the stuff but Vivienne *was* in Position A to do it.' He gave Erica an almost apologetic look. 'We know chemistry is not your area but you're always savvy on anything scientific, right?'

'It's been known. Fire away.'

'*Could* a cigarette be doctored and it not be immediately obvious to the smoker, do you think?'

Erica smiled. 'You mean that it might give the game away if in a packet of lovely tight little white tubes, there was one horribly lumpy old effort that looked as if the dog had been at it?'

Another ripple of laughter

'Something like that.'

'That's why it would be easier to doctor a roll-up than a commercially manufactured cigarette.'

Darac realised he wouldn't be the only one who knew Astrid smoked only roll-ups. He said nothing.

'However,' Erica went on, 'Deanna referred to acrylamide's soluble properties so that would make life much easier for the poisoner. If I were seeking to kill someone in this way – say Serge when he comes in late from training...' She felt a gentle tug on her barrette from behind. 'You all saw that. Anyway, I would create a suspension and inject it via a fine needle through one end of the cigarette. With a little practice to arrive at a quantity that wouldn't wet the paper around the area to the extent that on drying, it would crinkle and be obvious, the end result would be a lethal cigarette that would look and feel in the hand indistinguishable from its neighbours. However, during smoking, I suspect that the heated-up poison solution might well have seeped a little, and that would account for why some of it was absorbed through the skin of his lips, as well as inhaled.'

Once again, Darac felt the synergistic lift of working in a team that was so rich in individual talent, and although time was short, he couldn't help expressing it.

'Erica, if what you just came up with on the spur of the moment had been one of the DMQ's solos at the Blue Devil, there would have been shouts of "Yeah" about now, and waves of applause breaking around the room.'

'Don't spoil it,' she said, feigning disappointment.

'Well, I think that just about answers the "how?" question,' Granot said, smiling as several took Darac's hint and applauded Erica's performance. 'So we've got a good hand against Vivienne here, haven't we? Certainly enough to merit interrogating her again; and probably for extracting a search warrant from Frènes. You're off to see Astrid and co in a minute, chief, so shall I call Agnès to arrange it?'

'Just hold it a second,' Darac said. 'Motive, means, opportunity – all that is good, and we mustn't forget the simplest point of all about Vivienne: she knew Urquelle was a smoker, and that wouldn't be true for everyone here. So she laces a cigarette, places it in his case and starts playing the waiting game. And that's what worries me. She couldn't be sure *he* would smoke the cigarette in question, could she? He might unwittingly have offered it to someone else – to Astrid, for example, whom Vivienne had been taught by here and whom she liked. Despite all that precision injecting, the poison might have completely missed its mark, killing an innocent party into the bargain.'

Granot thought about it. 'That's persuasive,' he said, nodding. 'Yes, you'd think that to be sure, Vivienne *would* want to hand the lethal cigarette to Urquelle. Or at least be on hand to monitor the situation. She's not the psycho wanting to kill *someone*, is she? She wanted to kill *him*, specifically. *If* she did, that is.'

Flaco raised her hand.

'Yes, Flak?'

'She would have been surer of killing him if she had poisoned more than one cigarette in the case; and *definitely* sure if she had poisoned all of them.'

'Yes it would ensure he died but, notwithstanding the issue of the indiscriminate killing of others, it's a risky strategy for Vivienne to have adopted.'

Flaco's concentration face was in full scowl. 'Why, Captain?'

'Say she poisoned all of the cigarettes. Urquelle smokes the first one in the case, inhales the—'

'*And* absorbs,' Perand added, editing him.

'Quite right. Urquelle inhales *and* absorbs the poison but he doesn't die immediately. It happened 11 to 14 hours later. If Vivienne was capable of identifying a poison I've never heard of, learning its properties, precisely injecting it and so on, she would have known roughly how long it would take to act. So she would have to be absolutely sure, wouldn't she, that Urquelle would smoke all the remaining nineteen cigarettes in that time. Because if he didn't, somebody like Map would find a juicy poison-laced piece of evidence sitting right there in her husband's effects. That's why Deanna didn't expect Map to find anything untoward in the remaining eighteen cigarettes Urquelle actually left. Whoever poisoned Urquelle in this way, I'm pretty sure only one cigarette was involved.'

'Yes, I see that.'

'And on the question of *Vivienne's* possible guilt, I have another cavil. There's no way she, or anyone else, could replace one cigarette with another in an unopened packet, even if the packet weren't wrapped in cellophane, right? Refolding the inner foil so it looks untouched would be just one of the problems. I think a smoker would see straight-away that a packet had been tampered with. *But*, the fatal fag could easily replace a pukka one in an opened packet. Urquelle used a cigarette case, as we know – a case with a capacity of twenty and there were eighteen left in it. By the look of things, it seems that smokers have only limited opportunities to indulge their habit here – and Vivienne will have known that – but put this sequence together and see what you think.'

If a pin had been dropped softly into the carpeting at that moment, it would have been heard by everyone in the room.

'It would have been simplicity itself for Vivienne to have replaced a genuine cigarette in her husband's case with a poisoned alternative. Let's say she did just that. We know Urquelle left home at about 2 o'clock on Wednesday afternoon and wasn't in Vivienne's company... well, again, in fact. So even if the case were fully loaded when he left home, and bearing in mind that the poisoning itself happened between 8 and 11 yesterday evening, Urquelle had at least 30 hours in which to smoke only two cigarettes, one of which was poisoned. Based on Deanna's pattern of one cigarette after meals and two in the evenings – and that's pretty conservative, I think – Urquelle would typically have got through many more than two in that time. In fact, I suspect he smoked at least two driving his Jaguar to the Villa from Menton, and might well have been on his *second* loading of his cigarette case when he collapsed in *Pal-Mas*. You see what this strongly suggests?'

As mentor to the youngsters in the team, Darac was in the habit of turning such questions into something of a quiz but he needed to push things on. 'It suggests Vivienne could not be *directly* responsible for his murder. Yes, she could have *colluded* with an accomplice to do it – as we wondered when it looked for all the world that Zena Bairault had done the deed itself in *Pal-Mas* – but she could not have slipped the lethal cigarette into his case, herself. But we're nowhere near establishing such collusion.'

Granot ploughed a few extra furrows into his brow. 'Monsieur Darac, we'll make a decent detective of you yet.'

Having made the Lacourt discovery, Bonbon was happy that Vivienne was still just about in the frame, albeit as one of a pair. 'We're obviously going to question Vivienne again and far more formally this time. But I agree – let's leave the search warrant alone. You have to pick your battles with Frènes. OK on that?'

Darac nodded. 'Absolutely. Granot?'

'Fine.'

'Right, I'm heading off,' Darac said, getting to his feet. 'While we're yet to get our teeth fully into things, this would be a good time to run the usual checks on every name on these whiteboards and on the staff roster. Could save a lot of time later.' He gave Granot a look, all it took to establish that it would be his role to allocate suitable forces to the task. 'Back as soon as I can.' He scanned the room. 'Any questions, anyone? Any answers?'

With no full-width desk to sprawl over, Perand had opted to sit horizontally on his chair – no mean feat when consulting a laptop. In the manner of a swimmer performing backstroke, he raised a straight arm. 'I've got something, chief.'

'For God's sake,' Granot barked, all serenity gone. 'Sit up straight, man!'

Perand wriggled and shuffled into a roughly upright position.

'*What* have you got, Perand?' Darac said.

'There's someone here with much better access to large quantities of acrylamide than rich old Vivienne. And according to the notes on the boards, he has just as good a motive.'

'Go on.'

'It's my own tip for the top – Ralf Bassette. Every sheet of paper the man's factories turn out has been strengthened with your favourite poison and mine.'

1.47 PM

'We won't be overheard out here,' Astrid said, closing the door of the Salle Fernand Léger behind her. 'And I won't be needed for a while, Darac. They're going to start nominating their choices for the painting prize I mentioned, shortly. I sense it won't be quite as knockabout as usual.'

Darac's brows rose. 'Not exactly in mourning, though, are they?'

'Alan is. Alan Davies. Well, not *mourning* – just saddened and shocked. Anyway, what's the latest?'

'The very latest is that I recognised every face in that room from your thumbnail sketches more easily than from their photos. A truly remarkable talent, you have.'

'Thanks – and so do you. Ever hear *me* play guitar, by the way?'

'What?' The half-smile that invariably played around Darac's lips turned into something fuller as visions of wildly explorative duets flashed across his mind; he and Astrid trading four-bar phrases on themes inspired by the visual arts and beyond. 'I had no idea you played.'

'Really?' she seemed surprised. 'Yes, I've got three chords completely down. C, F and... D, I think. No, G.'

'Ah. Excellent.' His visions simplifying somewhat, Darac updated her, and the pair went on to discuss the smoking area in detail, a spot she referred to as the drag strip. 'Now let's go to last night, specifically,' he said. 'When did people go into dinner?'

'From about 7.15. Forks up was 7.30 on the dot, as it always is.'

'Elie had already gone home by this point, hadn't she?'

'She had, yeah.'

'Is she a smoker, by the way?'

'No, no.'

'And dinner went on until?'

'About 9.45. Most people repaired to the terrace for a chat and to take the air. It was a warm and softly fragrant evening, I didn't blame them.'

'Did Urquelle and Lydia join them?'

Astrid shook her head. 'She went off either to the lounge or her room or possibly his; he headed for the back yard where the air is slightly less fragrant. After a quick exchange with Zoë to make a date for a nightcap with her and Mathieu later, I joined Urquelle and several other sinners out there for a smoke.'

'How long did you stay?'

'I left a couple of minutes after 11. *He* was still there.'

'Alone?'

'By that time yes, but he'd had company.'

It was Darac's turn to shake his head but this time in wonderment. 'Astrid, this is getting better and better. We could hardly believe our luck that you, of all people, were here for us in the first place. *Now*, we're approaching the fanciful best–case scenario situation I've just put to R.O.'

A cheer went up in the Salle.

'That's the end of the first artist's pitch,' Astrid said, distractedly. 'Best case?'

'Deanna's given us a timeframe between 8 and 11. That means you were present during the entire period in which Urquelle unwittingly took the poison. He couldn't have

306

smoked in the dining room so talk me through the scene in what you call the drag strip.'

'I need my sketchbook. Won't be a sec.'

Opening a closed door is apt to draw glances from those inside. As the acclaim for what looked a routine depiction of the Baie des Anges subsided, just two students continued looking through the crack as Astrid slipped back into the room. One was the nominated artist, a woman Darac recognised as Claudine Bonnet. It was an intrigued look, fascinated, even a little excited. The other was Ralf Bassette, a man who had seemingly forgiven his wife over her affair with Urquelle; a man who had unlimited supplies of acrylamide at his disposal; and a man who Max Perand was not alone in suspecting as guilty of murder. Bassette's gaze was altogether different.

The door closed once more.

'Here we are.' Astrid opened her sketchbook, and with Darac looking over her shoulder, got to work. 'There were six of us out there to begin with.' Her pen moved quickly and decisively over the paper. 'Urquelle, first. He was sitting alone on this bench facing Barthélémy's shed – the gardener. We'll mark it bench A.' She annotated the map accordingly. 'He lit up straight away, taking a cigarette from his case.'

'Could you see well enough to tell what kind of cigarette it was?'

'There are lights of various types by each bench, and it's quite well lit out there in general but no – I was too far away to tell the brand. *However,* I'd had the dubious pleasure of sharing a cig with him the night before – the Wednesday. He smoked *Gitanes,* unfiltered.'

'How many did he smoke when you were together?'

'Just one. I didn't stay long.'

'Did you happen to notice how many cigarettes there

were in the case?'

'Not last night but on the Wednesday it was almost empty.'

'Ah, yes? That makes it virtually certain that Vivienne did not *directly* poison him.'

'Does it?' Astrid said, her illustrated sketch map beginning to take shape. 'I know you always say you can never tell but I can't picture her doing such a thing, anyway. However shitty her relationship with that arsehole was.'

'You may well be right.' He glanced at his watch. 'Better press on. So we've got Urquelle on bench a alone. Where are you?'

'Over by this greenhouse with... Ralf Bassette.' Six rapidly executed lines and the man was right there. 'We'll mark that bench B.

'Did he stay with you until you left – Bassette?'

'We left together.'

'In that case, Bassette has just joined Vivienne in the not-*directly*-guilty camp.'

Astrid's pen stopped moving. 'Ralf? Are you kidding? He's...' She searched for an appropriate adjective but let it go. 'I wish I'd never told you about his wife's affair with Urquelle, now.'

Darac decided not to mention Bassette's ready access to the killer poison, acrylamide. 'If he's innocent, he's got nothing to fear, and it's looking more likely he is.'

'He's as gentle as a gentle thing, honestly.' The pen resumed its work. 'OK, the henpecked Jérôme Calon was sitting by himself roughly half-way between us and Urquelle. The other two were the women from Zoë's class I told you about – Monique Dufour, who wasn't smoking and Alicia Roy, who was. Both of them were a bit pissed. And they seemed to have their eyes on Urquelle but when about five minutes after I got there, Alan Davies turned up and went to sit next to him, they tottered off.'

'Had their eyes on him in what way?'

'Like a couple of overgrown schoolgirls. Giggling, little asides. Get the picture?'

'Got it.'

Astrid went on to describe what she saw as a congenial conversation between Urquelle and Davies.

'How long did it go on for?'

'About half-an-hour. Before you ask, they had one cigarette each. Alan smokes unfiltered *Camels* and he...' She made a note on the map. 'He offered one to Urquelle.'

Recognising that this could be the breakthrough they had all been waiting for, Darac absently ran a hand into his hair and kept it there. 'And?'

'Urquelle declined and had another *Gitane* from his case, his second of the evening up to that point. He was still smoking it when a put-out Laurent Salins arrived on the scene.'

'Put-out – why?'

'I don't know whether it's an old Finnish proverb or just my mother's family's take on things but growing up, I always told that if you expect nothing from life, nothing is what you're likely to get. That's Salins for you – a walking self-fulfilling prophecy that life is out to get you. In this case, I think he just wanted a word with Urquelle and was miffed to find him occupied with someone else. He had only to wait a minute or two, though. Alan left, shared a few words with Salins in passing...' Converging arrows traced the move. '...Then Salins joined Urquelle at the bench.'

'Anything of interest there?'

Astrid bit the end of her pen while she thought about it. 'A couple of things, maybe. While Salins was still talking to Alan, Urquelle took out a diary and made an entry in it. Noting down Alan's contact details, probably. You remember Alan admired Urquelle the have-a-go-hero, and although he believes it was an accident, he was grateful to him for icing the awful Eddy Lopes. Admiration, gratitude – you can see why Urquelle might have wanted to stay in touch with someone like that. Might have been of use to him later, mightn't he?'

'It seems he was an arch manipulator of people but I doubt he was noting Alan's contact details. He was more likely to have done that during their conversation than after it.'

'Yes, that's true, I suppose.'

'We should be able to check that entry shortly. Urquelle's wallet, diary and phone are en route from Path. How did Urquelle's conversation with Salins go? Could you tell?'

'*Not* so congenial. At first, anyway. Something was said that made Salins move as if to leave but Urquelle said something else and he stayed. From where I was sitting, the conversation that followed looked interesting. Apart from being a moaner, Salins often has this wary look...' A few strokes of the pen and the image was achieved, enthralling Darac all over again and giving him an idea for another time. 'But after this rapprochement moment, he seemed to relax and the two of them gradually became almost... *conspiratorial* is far too strong a word but they seemed to find some common ground. *But*, although I didn't think anything of it at the time, now we know what we're dealing with, it's key. Urquelle must have run out of supplies from his case because Salins offered him one of his own cigarettes.' She drew the packet. '*Gauloise*. Unfiltered. And well within Deanna's timeframe, Urquelle smoked it.'

Darac looked into Astrid's pale blue eyes and smiled. 'You know I said we were approaching my best case scenario for this investigation?'

'Yes?'

'We've practically arrived. Did you see what he did with the butt?'

'Until last year, people used to just drop their butts and do a quick Charleston job on them to stub them out. Thanks to Elie, there are now lidded ashtrays by each seat.'

'And there's one by bench A? Say yes.'

'I'd have to say no.'

'Ah.'

'There are two. One either side.' The ashtrays duly materialised on the sketch. 'Salins either didn't notice his or felt his rights as a French citizen were being violated or whatever because he ignored his; Urquelle didn't. He used it. Each time. I'd swear to it.'

'And are the ashtrays—?'

'Emptied every day?' Astrid said, sufficiently au fait with Darac's thought processes to anticipate the question. 'This may be the Villa des Pinales and not the Café Cacapipi, but happily, they are emptied only every few days. I wouldn't bet my original Ed Ruscha print on it, but if within the next hour or two, forensics examine the butt pile in the ashtray Urquelle used last night, somewhere near the top they'd find—'

'One *Gauloise* among several *Gitanes? A Gauloise* superficially matching others swivel-heeled into the paving on the other side of bench A?'

'Exactly. And they didn't smoke after that.'

This was a breakthrough and as the pair shared a look, as if to celebrate with them, another cheer went up in the Salle. Darac took out his mobile.

'R.O? Got an update for you that needs acting on immediately.'

'Marvellous news – the pickings in his room are looking

very slim.'

'And keep your eyes on your inbox – I'm sending you a shot of a sketch map Astrid's just drawn of the smoking area. You'll be paying particular attention to bench A. Copy everyone else in on this, too, OK?'

Astrid laid her sketchbook on the floor and Darac did the needful, then continued with the call. At the end of it, she picked up the book and riffled pages.

'Let me bring something else to the party.' She arrived at the image she was looking for: a hastily retreating back, male, soft around the middle, a large head sunk into bulky shoulders. '*Voilà*. It's Salins.'

'What's the story here?'

'He was snooping around in the corridor along from my room. Last thing on Wednesday night, it was. When he heard my door open, he scuttled off. If scuttled is the word. Plodded quicker says it better.'

'What was he looking for? Or whom?'

'I don't know.'

'There are no public rooms on the top floor, are there?'

'None.'

'And Urquelle was on the floor below north-facing... Let's put a body in every bedroom, as it were.' Darac scrolled screens on his phone. 'Salins is on the first floor, too, I see.'

'Ah, yes?'

'And on your corridor... Next door is Mathieu Croix, then Zoë. Around the corner in the east-facing rooms, we have... Babette Bonnet, then her sister Claudine, Lydia Félix...' A number of possible explanations for Salins's behaviour occurred to Darac but he needed more to go on. 'Could be significant but we'll have to leave that one just now.'

'Sure.'

'Salins will be in the Salle de Bacchus with Mathieu

Croix now, won't he?'

'Should be.'

'Need to talk to Granot. You OK for the moment?'

'For the moment.'

'Good.' He tapped a key and waited. 'Astrid, do your students have any idea you're one of us, by the way?'

'No. In fact, the only person here who *does* know is Elie and I'd like to keep it that way if possible.'

'Well, it won't be easy to...' Granot came on, cutting short the reflection.

'Before you ask, chief, nothing significant has come through on the background checks so far; and Flak and Perand have completed the Denis Marut search. There was no clear connection to anyone here except Urquelle himself.'

'OK. Bigger fish, now. You're all au fait with the smoking area development?'

'All of us, yes – interesting.'

'I have more.'

'And we have Urquelle's wallet, pocket diary and mobile, by the way. They've just arrived from Path. Erica's taken possession of the latter.'

'Excellent. Obviously, when time permits, you're the man to go through the diary entries and the wallet contents in detail. Just for the moment though, it's the diary alone I'm interested in – it may figure in part of the reason I called in the first place. Astrid witnessed Urquelle writing something in that diary on Thursday night. Anything on yesterday's page?'

'A second... Thursday, the 13th is... blank.'

'OK. Is there a part for addresses in the diary?'

'Uh... No. But there is a notes section at the back... And it has a few entries.'

'Dated, by any chance?'

'No but you can easily tell the individual notes apart. Whether the last one is the one Astrid saw Urquelle make, I've no way of knowing. It's a column of figures. A calculation, possibly. And judging by the bottom line, it looks like a subtraction. Hang on.' Darac heard mumbling. 'Yes, it is. No idea what the figures refer to, of course. May be best if I email you a photo. It's all the rage today.'

'Isn't it? After I've updated you more fully on Laurent Salins, revise the whiteboards, then detail Bonbon and Flak to hoick the man out of Mathieu Croix's class and grill him.'

'You said you had more. Let's hear it.'

The update duly delivered, Darac ended the call and opened Granot's email. The calculation read:

6238
2344
1000
1500
1394

'It is a subtraction if you add it up,' Astrid said. 'Up from the bottom. What do you make if it?'

'Two different kinds of numbers here, aren't there? Nice round ones like 1,000 and 1,500 and three very sharp ones. The bottom one explains itself. The others? Don't know. But one thing I *do* know is that when Granot gets stuck into this problem, he'll find the answer. And no one in any force would find it quicker.'

In the Salle, a cheer went up for another work under consideration. An also-ran, by the sound of it.

'I wonder whose that was?' Astrid said, fine frown lines appearing on her forehead. 'Probably Alan's. His work's not figurative enough to be popular.' She shook her head. 'Sorry, switched off there for a moment. Yes, Granot always seems to come up with those sorts of answers quickly.'

'When do you normally break for coffee?'

'Around 3.30.'

'We might take statements from those who appear to have no connection with Urquelle then. Suspects, as we've already discussed, might be pulled at any time.'

'By suspects you mean Salins?'

'Salins and any others who emerge. As things stand, the cigarette he gave Urquelle does appear to have been the direct instrument of his death. But there's a qualification. You may not be aware of this but on his registration form, Salins cited himself as a call centre manager. It's not clear how such a person could have got hold of an industrial poison. It suggests someone else may have been involved. Someone who does have access to these substances.'

An extra couple of lines appeared to form on Astrid's forehead. 'That rules out Elie, surely. And Vivienne. And I shouldn't think Alan Davies sprays industrial poisons on his eight lemon trees.'

'Yes, I doubt that,' Darac said, noting she hadn't exempted her other favourite, Ralf Bassette. But there again, how could she? The man was an industrialist, after all. Erring on the side of caution was an approach Darac rarely adopted but he decided not to enlighten Astrid about Vivienne's family business connection, or go any further down this particular line. 'I'm off to the Salle des Rêves next, by the way. Just for a few minutes. Zoë mentions that if I enter quietly through the kitchen at the back, probably no one would notice. No one except Zoë, of course.'

'You won't be present for the presentation of the perfumes?'

'No, no. I'll have slipped away before then.'

'Good, because as soon as the first student returns to her seat, they would see you.'

'Quite.'

'Why are you doing this anyway?'

'I'd like to gauge what state Lydia Félix is in before we talk to her more formally. And just to gain a general impression. Have you spoken to her?'

'Once. Briefly. Difficult to warm to someone who was so obviously flattered by the attentions of a creep like Urquelle. But she seems pleasant enough. Intelligent. Rather pretty, as I hope my sketch catches. Zoë says she's top of the class, by the way. She and a rather dignified older lady named Cinzia Veri are her pets this time. Very engaged students, both.'

'Whereas Urquelle was totally the opposite. Hmm.' Darac went to another thought. 'In case you're worried, by the way, Zoë is very much off the hook for the murder.'

Eyes wide, Astrid exhaled sharply. 'She had better be or you'll have your *papa* to answer to, for one.'

He grinned. 'You're right, there.'

'And Darac...' She hesitated, an unfamiliar look for her. 'In fact, *Paul*, may I?'

'Ah, the using my forename shtick, huh? It's been tried, Astrid. Many times.'

'And?'

'Works like a charm. What do you want to say?'

'Actually, I *shouldn't* say this, I know, but... when you get to her, please go easy on Elie.'

'As I said about one of the others, if she is innocent, she has nothing whatever to fear. If she turns out to be guilty, I promise you that I, and everyone else in the team, will treat her with compassion and with sympathy.'

'Thank you.' Tucking her sketchbook under an arm,

Astrid reached for the door handle. 'So – back to it.'

'One second. I've got something to say, too. A moment ago, I stressed just how invaluable Granot is to the Brigade. I hope you realise that you are, too, Astrid. In fact, more than that – you're irreplaceable.'

Astrid may have been invaluable and irreplaceable but for the moment, she was also incapable – incapable of speech. But then she rallied. 'I bet you say that to all the geniuses,' she said, throwing the line away like a pro but then her expression changed. 'Thanks. Paul.'

Darac smiled and by way of a valediction, gave her shoulder a squeeze, a signature sign-off for his inner circle.

As she opened the door, one pair of eyes locked immediately on his.

They were the eyes of Ralf Bassette.

1.59 PM

Like her mentor before her, Zoë Hamada usually enjoyed every minute of the last class of the course. Inevitably, things were different this time. She wondered how Martin Darac would have played it if one of *his* students had been murdered, possibly by one of the others? Appreciating how useful his father's expertise and experience might prove to the investigation, Captain Paul Darac, Zoë had heard, had summoned Martin to the Villa.

Fond of her former boss, she had been heartened by the news. And, having sourced, secured and maintained all the materials used on the course with her customary meticulousness, she was sure Martin would confirm that she had done everything by the book.

It hadn't been *her* fault that the deeply unpleasant Urquelle had ignored her instructions pertaining to their outdoor lesson on aldehydes, a class she had entitled *Cyanide and Salad*. She had made it crystal clear that she alone would open the double-jarred examples she had selected for the experiment which would take place in the centre of the terrace garden, well clear of the building. So of course, having asked "Which is the smelliest?" Urquelle had thought it funny to open the one labelled sol: trans, cis-2, 6-nonandiel en route. It was Zoë's practice to open such jars wearing a respirator mask and then invite her students to witness the remarkable smells released at a distance of some three metres. Urquelle's exposed nostrils were less than half a metre away when he opened the nonadienal jars, releasing a smell so bland in its familiar form – cucumber – but of such surreal intensity in its chemical concentration even in solution, that he promptly dropped both jars, spilling some of the contents harmlessly on his hand. Too bad.

Yes, Zoë had very much looked forward to having Martin on board so she was dismayed to hear that he wouldn't be able to make it until around 6.30 – by which time the murderer could have poisoned several more victims and been long gone. But then she received a text. Learning that the poison that killed Urquelle had in fact been administered in the form of a cigarette came as a huge relief and she took particular pleasure in the fact that it was Martin's son Paul who had sent it.

And there he was now, unmistakably his father's son, slipping unnoticed by her students into the back corner of the room. Taking stock. Taking stock and waiting to pounce? Zoë couldn't let such speculations get in the way. She was about to deliver her pre-presentation address.

'First, I must issue a word of caution about something I

referred to briefly in our introductory class on Wednesday.' At this point, she usually made a jokey reference to health and safety regulations but wisely ditched it. 'It concerns the use of my word "unique" in relation to the scent you have now each successfully created on the course. I want you to picture this scene. Having returned home, you are sitting at your dressing table, perhaps preparing for a night out and you proudly turn to your own, lovingly crafted scent. As it mists the pulse points on your neck and wrists and you're enveloped in its gorgeousness, a worrying little bell rings in your head. "I've smelled something like this before," you say to yourself. "It's like *L'été de L'Amour* or *Au-delà de Minuit*, perhaps. What I've made *isn't* unique at all, it's a replica of another scent." The point I should have made more explicitly on Wednesday evening is that *all* scents are replicas...'

As Zoë's speech continued, Darac's gaze remained fixed on Lydia Félix and from his corner position, he could follow every shift in her expression – as it was reflected in her right profile, at least. It was clear that the class was proving a struggle for her. But in what respect? At some moments, she turned to her elderly neighbour, Cinzia Veri, wearing an entertained, unambiguously happy expression. At others, her head dropped, and Darac assumed at first that the weight of her grief was the cause. But then he realised he had misinterpreted her body language. He craned his neck to the side. She was texting or emailing someone.

Before Darac ghosted back through the kitchen, he estimated Lydia had sent and read at least three messages. An easy job for Erica later.

He was en route to the Salle de Bacchus when he received an email of his own. He called the sender immediately.

'Serge? Darac. What have you got?'

'I've discovered Laurent Salins is not who he says he

is. His real name is Léo Banda and he's not a call centre manager either.'

'Tell me he's an acrylamide importer and there could be a promotion in it for you.'

'In that case chief,' Serge said. 'I'll be hanging on to my rank for a bit longer.'

2.10 PM

Mathieu Croix was arguing the case for decanting any red wine of "suitable age and heft" when he looked up to find all eyes sliding to the door behind him. Unconsciously performing a comic double-take, he followed them. Having missed Granot's lunchtime briefing, he was unaware that the three remaining classes were subject to possible interruption and, having left his mobile resolutely switched off, he had not received a call advising him that two officers were en route to do just that. Consequently, he was surprised at the appearance of the pair: a twinkle-eyed wiry fellow sporting a gravity-defying shock of reddish hair; and a short, strapping young black woman wearing an expression of such deliciously smouldering menace, Croix felt a frisson he hadn't experienced since the days of Madame de Douleur's *Maison des Fouets*.

'May I help you?' he said, a remark hardly likely to provoke the young woman into a frenzied assault but he lived in hope. The wiry one gestured him to join them in the doorway.

'Monsieur Croix? Lieutenant Busquet and Officer Flaco.'

'Flaco?' Croix said, relishing the sound of her name. '*Flac-o*! Splendid.'

As a bemused Bonbon continued sotto voce, voices in the room rose, adding a further layer of insulation. 'You seem surprised to see us, monsieur.'

'No, no, I understand in general, of course. Has there been a development, then?'

'You could call it that,' Bonbon said, playing down what was a fully fledged breakthrough. 'I'll explain briefly why we're here.'

While Bonbon spelled things out, Flaco ran an eye around the room and, like Darac earlier, recognised every face from Astrid's notes: the obsequious yet haughty Marcia Calon, her eyes burning, darting around the scene as if hoping an arrest would happen here and now, right in front of her. However sanctimoniously triumphant Marcia may have appeared, Flaco sensed she wouldn't have wanted the suspect – whoever he was – to go quietly. She would have preferred to witness a violent struggle, the captive dragged out writhing, spitting, kicking. That Marcia herself had initially appeared on the list of suspects would have astonished and mortified her, Flaco knew.

Embarrassed by the blatant zealotry of his wife, Marcia's husband Jérôme looked fearful of the unpleasantness that might be about to materialise. When Flaco had embarked on her career with the Brigade, she wouldn't have believed a little mouse like Jérôme capable of committing or planning a murder. Now she knew differently. She also knew that if he ever did do such a thing, Marcia was certain to be the victim.

Astrid had made it clear in her notes that there was almost certainly more to Thea Petrova's relationship with Urquelle than the series of unplanned encounters at trade shows Thea herself had claimed. Initiating, conducting and ending casual affairs appeared to have been a way of life for Urquelle; an ending that proved all too final for Karen Bicoud. From Astrid's account, the imperious Thea wasn't the type to accept being discarded by anyone. And why should she? Flaco's first look at the living person accorded both with Astrid's pen and ink sketch and her comments. If Urquelle had sought to ditch Thea, Flaco could imagine just how violently, how vengefully, the woman might have responded. But since the breakthrough, Flaco and Bonbon had little need to *imagine* anything about the life and loves of the fake fur saleswoman Madame Thea Petrova. A 100% genuine suspect had emerged form the crowd: the ruddy-complexioned man they now knew as Léo Banda.

Bonbon stepped forward and smiled. 'Monsieur Salins?' he said, maintaining the deception for the benefit of the others. 'We'd like to borrow you, if we may.'

Chuntering disgruntledly to himself, Banda had no option but to comply. Of course, his fellow class members didn't know why the police wanted to speak with him but as Flaco watched the watchers, she could almost read the think bubbles hovering above them: "He looks like a killer." "He must be a person of interest, at least." "Perhaps he just saw something – he's always creeping around." "He did it. I'd put my wine cellar on it."

Marcia Calon's particular reaction was exactly as Flaco would have expected and that went for Jérôme's, too. Thea Petrova seemed not to care one way or another. In itself, showing a lack of interest in the fate of a character like Banda might have seemed unsurprising. But if Astrid was right, and Thea and Urquelle had shared beds all over Europe and beyond, the degree of the woman's impassivity Flaco found harder to fathom. She looked closer. Was there just a hint of a reaction visible behind Thea's façade? If there were, Flaco felt, it was a curious one. It was puzzlement.

Except that it was taped-off and featured a team of white-clad figures, the designated smoking area was exactly as Astrid's drawings had led Darac to picture it. Before he could check in with Raul Ormans, he needed to sign in and suit up with red zone gatekeeper, Patricia Lebrun.

'Captain. Thought you were avoiding me.'

'No, no, no,' Darac said, exchanging kisses of greeting with the woman he had met on his first day with the Brigade and with whom he had worked virtually every day since.

She proffered her clipboard. 'Your autograph, please. I know you're all disappointed if I don't say that.'

'Well, we wouldn't know what to do, otherwise.'

Darac signed, filled in the time and began slipping on a pair of crime scene overalls that were slightly too small. 'How's R.O. doing?'

Her eyes swivelled to Astrid's bench A. 'I think he may have turned up trumps already.'

Darac's mobile rang but, balancing on one leg, he was unable to take the call immediately.

'Just while you sort yourself out,' Patricia said. 'Thank God that little Emma Tardelli and the others are alright, huh? We were all devastated when we heard what had happened.'

From extreme pain to extreme joy within the space of about fifteen minutes? Darac had been scarcely able to imagine what Armani and Noëmi had gone through for real earlier and the feeling hit him with renewed force. That, in an entirely positive sense, it was a scenario being played out again in the maternity suite at St. Roch only added to its effect. 'I know,' he said, finally able to reach for his phone

'Unimaginable. Ah, it's Erica. I'd better take this, Patricia.'

'Of course.'

The pair air dapped their latexed knuckles and Darac headed slowly towards the action.

'Erica, what have you got?'

What she had was a breakdown of Gérard Urquelle's mobile traffic since Wednesday evening. Of brief duration, all four incoming calls were from the head office of Urquelle's jewellery firm, and five of the six outgoing were to the same number. The sixth was to the city cab company, made that morning. Late on Wednesday afternoon, a text from Vivienne had been received. It read:

> *Don't get too drunk tasting all that wine, Géri.*
> *And don't forget to give my best regards to Astrid Pireque*
> *and Elie Tiron. See you Friday evening, V*

The reply, sent almost three hours later:

> *My darling V, I'll try not to. Get drunk, that is.*
> *And I'll try to sell a few more pots for you. Not that you need*
> *my skills in that department. Very dull crowd here though the*
> *place is spectacular as you say, and I'm sure the course itself*
> *will be stimulating. E.T. duly regarded and sends her best*
> *back to you. A.P. yet to be got. I count the hours, Géri*

'Surprisingly warm exchange,' Erica said. 'His and Vivienne's, I mean.'

'Didn't sound as if they were at each others' throats, did it? But if I were going to kill *my* cheating husband, and I knew someone like you was going to report what I wrote to someone like me, jaunty togetherness is precisely the tone I would adopt.'

'I got lost in all those pronouns, Darac, and the concept of you having a husband didn't help. But I take the point. What about Urquelle's reply?'

'That's more surprising, in a way. If he wasn't used to being addressed so warmly, it didn't show. And of course, he couldn't know that anyone *but* Vivienne would be likely to read the text.'

'Interestingly, earlier exchanges between them read more matter of factly. The main topic of conversation appears to have been what time the man was likely to arrive home following his latest work trip.'

'Which is what you would expect, I suppose. Other numbers? Have you had time to look back at those?'

'I've gone back a couple of months. As far as I can see, no call has been made or received from any of our principals here.'

'Too much to hope for.'

'I'm going to look further back, though. You never know.'

'Excellent, Erica. Share what you've learned with the team, will you?'

'I will but once the passcode had been decrypted, scrolling back through emails and texts is something any 8 year-old kid could do, you realise?'

'I'll send out for one but in the meantime, could you stick at it? If anything more technical comes in, I'll let you have it immediately.'

'Sure, and that, by the way, was a particularly apt segue. A piece of long-promised kit has just turned up here in the ops room – the live feed camera set-up.'

'Really? You know, until Agnès mentioned it the other morning, I'd forgotten all about it.'

'So had Bonbon. And despite my best efforts in the demo, how to use it. Fortunately, Flak's *au fait* so she's handling the transmission end of the Banda interview.'

'Wise. And at the reception end?'

'Granot. He's surprisingly good with tech – even though he's got hands like hams.'

'Very true. Good work, Erica, I'll check in later.'

'I count the hours.'

Darac rang off just as Raul Ormans called him over to Urquelle's bench. In his latex-gloved hand was a small cardboard evidence canister containing a crushed cigarette butt.

'We've just removed this insignificant-looking atrocity from the ashtray on Urquelle's side of the bench. It *has* to be what remains of the *Gauloise* gasper Urquelle accepted from Salins-stroke-Banda – it's the only candidate. In other words, my good friend, what you see before you is the murder weapon.'

'Great work, R.O.'

'It's Astrid's eagle eyes we have to thank for this. If we only knew in advance when a crime was going to take place, dispatching her to the scene would save us a great deal of head-scratching.'

Darac grinned. 'Agreed.'

Ormans handed the specimen to an assistant. 'Our man's waiting by the front entrance. Tell him to secure it in his pannier and on no account just slip it into his pocket. Hurry.'

'Right, boss.'

'Motorcyclists, Darac. Insane, the lot of them. But he'll be able to slice through the traffic even more speedily-stroke-recklessly than the remarkable Wanda Korneliuk could in her car. I've already told Deanna the sample is on its way. Now they know exactly what to look for, the result will be practically instantaneous, she says. Add in the journey time, we should have an answer...' He glanced at his watch.

'Just shy of 3 o'clock.'

'Excellent. Bonbon and Flak are about to interview Banda, R.O. They need to be apprised of your find, too.'

Ormans nodded his large, aristocratic head in the direction of a young woman tapping away on a laptop. 'Marie-France is doing so as we speak.'

When a murder investigation began to gather momentum, Darac often felt a surge of energy that wasn't quite like any other. He felt it now. He also felt a sense of unease. Things were going too well, weren't they? But then he remembered the live feed camera.

'Think it will work, R.O.?' he said, deeming it unnecessary to specify the *it* in question.

'Erica trained everyone up. Flak's there to hold Bonbon's hand. Of course it will.'

'And if it had been Bonbon and say, me, instead?'

Ormans thought about it. 'Just remembered a prior engagement,' he said, and went to join Marie-France.

2.27 PM

Léo Banda unhooked a card reading PLEASE DO NOT MAKE UP MY ROOM from the doorknob and ushered Bonbon and Flaco into his room.

'And leave you door side?' Bonbon said. 'After you, mate.'

The man shrugged and they followed him in. Bonbon's expectation that such an unkempt individual was likely to keep his room in a concomitant state of disarray proved not to be the case as he gestured him into a wingback chair sitting in the far corner. The room was immaculately tidy.

'Nice and big, isn't it?' Bonbon said, leaning back against

327

the door. 'By the look of things, the maid has been in.'

'On the contrary.'

'Alright if I sit here, monsieur?' Flaco indicated the dressing table next to her. Without waiting for a reply, she pulled out the chair and turned it to face him. 'With the new regulations coming in soon, we'll be trial videoing the interview.' She set the camera on the table and angled the viewing screen. 'You alright with that?'

With his arms folded and his outstretched legs crossed at the ankles, Banda appeared not just alright but strangely in control of the situation.

'Sure,' he said, shrugging.

'Just check you're in vision and everything is working.' On the back of the camera was a button labelled live link. She pressed it and the light above it turned from solid red to flashing white and then, after only a few moments, to solid green – just as Erica had told Flaco it would. 'Ye-es... that's fine. I'll let you know when we start recording.'

'Start recording, eh?' Banda grinned. 'Recording *and* transmitting. You've got a live camera there. Where are the pictures going back to? Commissariat Foch? Joinel? The dear old Caserne Auvare?'

The locations with which Banda seemed so casually conversant were well out of range. The link was with the ops room which was no more than 30 metres away.

'Somewhere like that,' Flaco replied.

'Water?' Bonbon said.

'Never touch the stuff. Could do with a fag but it'll have to wait.'

'OK, ready?'

Banda shrugged.

'Formalise things, will you, Officer?'

It was done and Bonbon got down to the nitty-gritty.

'Monsieur, on Wednesday of this week, a call centre manager by the name of Laurent Maurice Salins of the Riviera Apartments in Saint-Philippe checked in here at the Villa des Pinales. By today, Friday, that gentleman has morphed into one Léo Patrice Banda of the Boulevard Pierre Sola in Riquier. And he's a private detective. Quite a rare one, as it turns out because as far as we can determine, Léo has never served as any sort of police officer in France or anywhere else, or as a member of the armed forces. Right so far?'

'You're not wrong.'

'How long have you been a P.I.?'

'Twelve years.'

'And before?'

'Guess.'

'So you'd be able to answer any questions on the subject if it came up in conversation, I'd go for call centre manager. Right again?'

Pressing his lips together, Banda gave a little nod. 'Absolutely right. I'm going to have to watch it with you, I can see.'

'Well, that's enough fun for one day. What are you doing here, monsieur?'

' "Monsieur" and the polite *vous* form, is it? I didn't mind the "mate" approach, to be honest, but now you're broadcasting, it's fair enough, I suppose. Why am I here? I'm on a case. As you are. Tell me what you want to know and I'll give it to you. But I'd appreciate it if you were quick about it, Lieutenant. I think I'm in the running to win a bottle of Krug back in the Salle.' He re-crossed his legs. 'Not that there's much in the way of competition. My fellow wine buffs don't know port from starboard, practically.'

Studying the man, Bonbon reflected that physically, Léo

Banda looked exactly as Astrid had depicted the creepy, irritating moaner she had encountered as Laurent Salins. Banda's own character, it was clear, was very different. Bonbon had interviewed hundreds of murder suspects in his time. Many had proved to be guilty and many of them had loudly protested their innocence throughout. A smaller number had quietly feigned it. A smaller number still had feigned both innocence and ignorance of the charges about to be brought against them. Of those, about one in ten had succeeded, at least for a time, in persuading Bonbon that they had no idea they were being questioned *as* a murder suspect. Banda was one of those. Or at least, it was another prize for which he was in the running.

'OK,' Bonbon said. 'What case are you working on? Who's your client?'

'I wouldn't normally divulge such confidential details but since we're dealing with murder here, and I'm anxious you won't arrive at the erroneous conclusion I had something to do with it, I'm going to make an exception.'

Bonbon shared the briefest of looks with Flaco. 'Go on, Monsieur.'

'Client – Madame Vivienne Urquelle. Case – how can I put this?' He pinched the end of his bulbous nose three times in quick succession. 'Trying to get the goods on good old hubby Géri so she could divorce him without penalty.'

'By what means?'

'The usual. Logging the comings and goings in his room. Concentrating on the comings, if you catch me.'

'And that is all Madame Urquelle wanted from you?'

Banda's brow lowered, flattening the crazy paving-like creases on his forehead. 'Yes? What else would she...' The penny dropped. 'Ah.'

Bonbon decided to let him think about it for a moment.

'Been on my feet quite a bit today.' He eased his weight off the door. 'Sit on the end of your bed if I may.' He did so. 'Not in shot, am I, Officer Flaco?'

'No, Lieutenant.'

'Excellent.' When he looked back at Banda, the man's rolled neck was glistening with sweat. Promising, Bonbon thought to himself. 'Let me take you back to last night, monsieur. The smoking area.'

'Listen, before that, I want to show you something on my mobile. It's important.'

Feeling his Sig Sauer automatic nestling snugly against his chest, Bonbon smiled. 'OK.'

Banda stood, and with some difficulty, extracted the device from the hip pocket of his too-tight trousers. 'Make a note of the passcode, if you like.' He gave it and Flaco duly took it down. 'This contains all my personal and work stuff. I'll find my contract with Vivienne.' He rolled his eyes. 'Madame Urquelle, I mean. I took a photo of it.' He found it and handed Bonbon the phone. 'See?'

The contract, for "services rendered," was signed by both parties and contained a number of disclaimers and other clauses. One that caught Bonbon's eye was that should the Banda agency have been unable to supply the evidence necessary to prove adultery on the part of husband Gérard Urquelle, the agreed fee was to be considered unearned and repaid to the client.

'Yes, I see she hired you as you stated,' Bonbon said, relaxing Banda a little. 'But this in no way implies that she didn't also hire you to kill him, does it? It could be a smoke-screen.' Bonbon's eyes twinkled. 'Odd that "taking out a contract" on someone has come to mean what it has, isn't it? It's the one agreement for which there never is a written contract.'

'I assure you, I was hired to catch the shit with his pants down. That's all.'

'I know the guy had form in that respect but how did you know you would get what you wanted?'

Banda pursed his lips, nodded a few times, then took a deep breath before answering. 'I... took along a little insurance. Go to my email inbox. Top left on the lock screen.'

'I've got the same phone. Hang on.'

'You'll see several messages from a Yana Vanier, including some sent in the last hour.'

'Yana Vanier...' Bonbon found them. 'And she is?'

'Better known to you as Lydia Félix. See the one sent at about a quarter past one, this morning?'

'I see it.'

'Read it and play the attachment. Just a minute or two, maybe, because it's 63 minutes long, unedited, and sparing your blushes, it's sound only. Forward it to yourself, to HQ, your boss – wherever you like.'

Although neither Bonbon nor Flaco had heard the voices of the have-a-go hero and his supposed conquest for the night, there were sufficient name checks and other clues in the five-minute sample Bonbon played to leave little doubt. Astrid, for one, would be able to ID the voices with certainty later. Then Bonbon read Yana/Lydia's accompanying email. It strengthened Banda's story.

'We will have to question Yana formally now, you realise? Not just take a statement from her.'

'Of course. She won't object, I'm sure.' He sat forward intently. 'If you look in my photo folder, the last two shots are Yana entering Urquelle's bedroom, time tagged at 11.53 Wednesday night. Note that her blouse buttons at the back and that all of them are fastened. The next one shows her coming out tagged at 0.55 and the top two buttons are undone. Just having snaps of her going in and out of the room at that time of night with the buttons shtick would be enough to get Madame U her way in the divorce court, believe me. Let alone all the grunt action she recorded.'

Bonbon checked the images. 'If you say so.'

'Note the clever way she looks both ways along the corridor without giving the game away that I was standing right there each time.'

Bonbon's elastic band of a mouth formed an upside-down U. 'Impressive. In its way.'

'Isn't it? If challenged in the divorce court later about why she hadn't seen me, I'd say I was standing in the cleaner's supply room with the light off, shooting through a crack in the door. Actually, I was standing in front of it in plain sight.'

'Considering it could be proved Yana works for you, might entrapment not be an issue here? From a legal standpoint?'

'It might if I'd ever used Yana before. I hadn't. She's a nurse, by the way. A nurse in need of extra cash at the moment. A nurse with a brother I know who owes me one. A nurse with a healthy appetite for sex. A perfect combination, no?'

'I think you've established you were hired to snoop, and snoop you did.' Bonbon gave Flaco a questioning look. She responded with a disdainful nod. 'To both our satisfactions. You've also freely admitted to being perfectly happy to mislead officers of the court.'

'Lieutenant Busquet...' He made an effort to gather himself before continuing. 'Urquelle was a complete low-life. Madame had a couple of other P.I.'s following him before. He got away with it both times. You want to know how?'

'Go on.'

'By buying them off. I know because one of them is a mate of mine. Urquelle offered him more to look the other way than Madame had to catch him at it and he accepted the offer. So when the time came, he reported back to her that hubby hadn't strayed on this particular weekend when he'd actually spent practically all of it in bed with some woman. My mate refunded her and told her not to hesitate if she wanted to use him again. She declined, eventually, coming to me. Because I knew what had had happened to her before, I felt sorry for her and took the job.'

'You're all heart, monsieur.'

'Yeah, yeah. So we turned up here and got going. Yana hooked him immediately and things looked good but somehow, he saw through my front and wound up offering me the same sort of deal he did to my mate. Last night, this was. I accepted, by the way. It was one of the reasons he went into the city this morning – to get the cash.'

Bonbon scrolled his own mobile to refresh his memory about the calculation Urquelle had made in his diary. The bottom figure was 1394. 'How much did you agree on?'

'Twelve hundred euros. Madame's fee was a thousand. But what he didn't know was that I was still going to shop the bastard to her so she could divorce him.'

'And giving you two pay days for the price of one.'

'Why not? He was a bastard, I'm telling you and I'll tell you something else. I very much doubt she will shed a tear for him. But if you honestly believe that she may have hired me or someone else to kill him, you're way off-beam. She's not that person.' He set the features of his gravel bucket of a face into an unfamiliar configuration. 'I would stake my reputation on it.'

Trying not to laugh, Bonbon shared a look with the study in scowling seriousness that was Yvonne Flaco and lost the urge immediately. 'Nevertheless, monsieur,' he said. 'Let's take a close look at the first of those possibilities, shall we? From about 10.20 to 10.50 last night, you were in conversation with Urquelle in the Villa's romantically named designated smoking area.'

'I told you I was.'

'No, you said only that your conversation had taken place last night, not where or when. Have you smoked today?'

'Yes. One before breakfast. One after.'

'Got the packet there?'

He indicated the inside breast pocket of his jacket.

'If you please?' Bonbon said, casually, holding out his hand.

'The sprinkler will go off.'

'Just hand it over, monsieur.'

Banda shrugged. 'Sure.'

Bonbon slipped on a glove. 'Just to be on the safe side. You know how it is.' The packet contained 15 pristine *Gauloise* cigarettes. 'And this is the one you had with you last night in the smoking area?'

'Ye-es?'

Bonbon showed it to Flaco and the camera. 'I'll hang on to this.' And then it was bound for the lab but Bonbon needed to build things a little before mentioning it. 'Give you a receipt later if necessary.'

'If necessary?' Banda laughed, sourly. 'Jesus. And what's this interest in my smoking habits all of a sudden?'

'Urquelle left for the city immediately after breakfast. Did you see him beforehand?'

'No.'

'Uh-huh. Now, last night, at about 10.25, you offered Urquelle one of your cigarettes.' He brandished the packet. 'From this.'

The roll of fat around Banda's neck began to flush red. 'Because he had run out.' And he began to sweat. Profusely. 'Simple.'

In interrogation, the twinkling merriment of Bonbon's mien was never so effective as when it suddenly disappeared. 'The cigarette you gave him, monsieur.' He clapped his hands loudly together '*That* very one, yes!? Are you with me!?' He continued calmly. 'That very one monsieur, we believe, contained the lethal neurotoxin that killed Gérard Robert Urquelle. Do you have anything to say about that?'

All the colour draining from his neck and his cheeks, Banda's eyes turned glassy and for a second, Bonbon wondered if the man might faint.

'Monsieur?'

Banda shook his head as if coming to after a punch. 'What do I have to say, Lieutenant? Only this.' He took a few steadying breaths. 'If Urquelle hadn't run out of fags, *I* would have smoked the one that killed him.'

Banda's reply gave Bonbon pause and he conveyed this to Flaco in a look. She too, he could see, was entertaining the thought that with all the concentration on Urquelle, perhaps everyone had overlooked another possibility. One worth pursuing? For the moment, Bonbon decided to go with it.

'Monsieur,' he said. 'I imagine the Alpes Maritimes is littered with irate husbands, wives and lovers to whom your many names are mud. But do you think any of these people might hate you enough to want to kill you?'

Stating the proposition so baldly made Banda wince but he appeared even more anxious than Bonbon to come up with an answer. 'I don't know. Who have I..?' In lieu of a magic lamp, he opted to rub his chin but after a good few moments, no genie had emerged. 'No, Lieutenant. Of all my cases, Urquelle was the one who had by far the most to lose, and it clearly wasn't him, was it? I've no idea. Honestly.'

'On the cigarette you gave him – who else had access to the packet? Yana Vanier, perhaps? A bedside table... Middle of the night... You snoring away...'

Banda shrugged. 'Sadly, I'm not her type. Even for cash.'

It was Flaco's turn to wince but she said nothing.

Banda closed his eyes. 'Let me just recap this. I opened the packet after lunch yesterday. Smoked one then. When I went into the yard last night, I had a second one, gave Urquelle the third, then didn't have another until the two this morning.' He opened his eyes. 'Yes, that accounts for all of them. Now the key interval here, and I'm sure you'll agree with me—'

'Monsieur Banda, you're still well in the frame for this murder but I'll humour you. The key interval is from the moment you put the packet back into your pocket at lunch-time yesterday until you took it out again at about 10.25 in the evening. Now, did anyone have access to it during that time? Think.'

The magic lamp came in for another buffing. And after another good few moments, this time, a genie of sorts did emerge.

'Well, before dinner, I did go to the bar. A little table in the corner. It was hot so I took my jacket off and draped it round the back of my chair. I didn't leave it unattended as such – to go to the toilet or anything – but I did get up briefly to exchange a few words with Yana.'

'And so you *did* leave your jacket unattended.'

'It was out of my line of sight for less than a minute.'

That's all it would have taken, Bonbon reflected. 'This corner table. Were you sitting with anyone?'

'Yes,' he said, his brow lowering. 'I was sitting with Ralf Bassette.'

Darac noticed Elie Tiron's office door was half-open as he strode into Reception and although he couldn't see Elie herself, he heard her handling what sounded like an involved enquiry on the phone. With time to squeeze in a couple of calls of his own, he continued towards the rear entrance, a portal which framed the view of the gardens beyond so perfectly, he wondered at the provision of the sign bearing a pointing finger and the words TO THE GARDENS set up alongside. Would visitors have been left in a fug of incomprehension without it? The young crowd control officer on duty at the door didn't appear to have taken offence, anyway.

En route to sharing a quick word with him, Darac glanced across at the reception desk but he had to look closely to spot Barbara herself. Bent over piles of paperwork, all that could be seen of her was the top of her pinned-back auburn hair.

'You could do with need a sign reading TO THE RECEPTIONIST,' he said pleasantly. 'Should I be needed, I'll be just outside. Back in a moment.'

'Should I be needed, Captain, I'll be right here,' Barbara replied without looking up. 'Until midnight, probably. Damned computers.'

'And that's being kind to them.'

At the door, the crowd control officer stood to attention and saluted. 'Captain.'

'Officer?'

'Balaise, monsieur. Emil.'

'Is your boss around, Emil?'

'No, monsieur. He's stationed at the front entrance to

the site.'

'No need for all the parade ground stuff, then. Anything to report?'

'Only that Madame at the desk there makes me feel tired just watching her work.'

'Quite. You were with us at *Pal-Mas*?'

'Yes, Captain. Upper Avenue Jean Médecin entrance.'

'So you'll know what to do if Annie Provin's TV lot get wind of all this and turn up?'

'Yes, but they won't get this far. In fact, they won't get on site at all – there's more of us here than you might think. We've got people at the south terrace gate, for instance, so no one could sneak up that way.'

'Excellent. If however a gentleman by the name of Martin Darac appears at the front entrance, I would be grateful if he could be admitted.'

'Is Monsieur with the force, too?'

'Only the force of nature. He's my father. But we do need him.'

Balaise grinned. 'I'll pass the word.'

'Thanks. I just need to make a quick couple of calls. Back in a minute.'

'Captain.'

Darac had arrived at the Villa in too much of a hurry to check out the view but stepping outside splendidly made up for it. Bounded by a carved polychrome balustrade, the parvis was an elegant platform from which to take in the landscape but as he walked forward, it was the view below that drew him first. The staircase itself was a thing of beauty, falling away like a pair of dropped fans to the upper parterre before plunging in a series of narrower steps across the lower terraces to the Villa's pine-hemmed perimeter. Beyond, the landscape opened up and out into a panorama of such spectacular beauty, it almost overwhelmed him. But as Darac parked his backside on the invitingly rounded rail of the balustrade, his gaze settled on an altogether more down-to-earth subject: gardener Barthélémy Assako pushing a wheelbarrow along the lower parterre. Darac kept his eyes idly upon him as he made the first of the calls.

Although she was now officially off-duty, his friend Suzanne was still holding station at L'Hôpital St Roch. From her, he learned that Armani, having taken it upon himself to apply and reapply cold compresses to every square centimetre of Noëmi's exposed skin, was getting in everyone's way. There was no news yet on the birth itself, but everything, Suzanne reaffirmed, was sure to be fine. Finally, Noëmi's mother was happily ministering to a fully awakened Emma in the children's ward.

Darac's second call was to Frankie.

'Benjamin's surgery may take *six* hours?'

'Possibly longer. My mother insists that whatever happens, she'll be fine, so I'll be back tomorrow, Paul. Probably in time for your second set at the club – assuming you can get a couple of hours away from the case. What an amazing turn of events in that one, by the way.'

'Wait until I tell you about Zena Kovalen a.k.a Bairault. But listen, even if the case doesn't need me for a few hours tomorrow evening, I could still just drop out, you know. It's a DMQ gig, not the Lincoln Centre Jazz Orchestra on tour.'

'No, no, no. It's a Saturday. It's special. I won't hear of it.'

'You're sweet, do you know that?'

'I can't wait to see you, darling.'

At that moment, Darac *could* see Frankie; see her almost as clearly as if she were standing in front of him. 'Me, too, sweetie. Me, too. Oh, something else to tell you. Because of the terrible experience the Tardellis went through earlier,

Noëmi went into labour with the shock. Six weeks prematurely.'

Darac heard a gasp on the line but nothing further. 'I know, Frankie. It's a shock to everyone. But the medics are as sure as they can be that there won't be any problems – and that includes my friend, Suzanne, too.' He was just about to voice the thoughts he'd been having about the joys and pains of parenthood but something stopped him.

'I really can't wait to see you, darling,' Frankie said, again. 'We'll talk in the morning.'

They ended the call and Darac got to his feet feeling a sense of foreboding that went beyond the unease he had experienced earlier. He was walking back into Reception when his mobile rang with a possible cause. He turned on his heel and went back outside.

'Darac? Deanna. First, we have now tested R.O's cigarette butt for traces of acrylamide.'

'And you've got a result?'

'A definitive one.'

'Excellent.'

'Not so excellent, I'm afraid. It's negative.'

'Ah.' Darac's heart sank. 'That… is a pity.'

'That's putting it mildly. A word on the evidential provenance of said cigarette butt. A combination of R.O. and Astrid is about as ironclad as one could wish for, so I'm confident Urquelle *did* smoke it. However, to provide the incontrovertible confirmation the reports require, the sample has gone for DNA sequencing. We won't have that result for a day or two. I'm sorry about this development. Truly.'

'Don't be.' Darac was too experienced a detective to conclude that all the Brigade's efforts of the past hour would prove to have been in vain, but the finding was a setback nevertheless, and a big one. 'You did stress in your initial report that you were dealing in likelihoods, not certainties.'

'That's generous, Darac. Thank you. But we do have something of which we are *totally* certain.'

In an interview with Agnès some years before, Annie Provin had stated her conviction that life for a homicide detective appeared to be one rollercoaster ride after another. "Oh, no,' Agnès had countered. "It's much more up and down that that." Her words came back to Darac now.

'Go on, Deanna.'

'We first thought that the poison had been inhaled by the victim and only secondarily absorbed through the skin. We're now sure it was the other way around.'

Darac went to run a hand through his hair but it got snagged half-way. 'I don't quite follow you.'

'In other words, it was while Urquelle was smoking an innocent cigarette, possibly the *Gauloise,* the remains of which we have just examined, or a different one entirely, that he somehow encountered the acrylamide in a form he absorbed through the lips.'

As always, Darac's mind was alive with possibilities but none spoke to him. '*Somehow* is the word, alright. Not even Bonbon would suck one of his beloved sweets in between puffs on a fag, for instance, would he?'

'No, no.'

'And I take it there was no lip salve in his personal effects?'

'Don't you think we would have thought of that? I'm sorry! We're rather fraught here.'

'No apology necessary. So how do you think he may have encountered the poison?'

'Again, we're dealing with likelihoods, but the *most* likely involves drinks, especially alcohol or coffee. There were traces of both alcohol and caffeine in Urquelle's blood but we're not looking at the liquids themselves. It's the vessels that contained them we're interested in. The rims, to be exact, for obvious reasons.'

'They could have been smeared with the stuff? The acrylamide?'

'Yes.'

'An important question, Deanna. Are we still working with that three-hour timeframe?'

'That's my second reason for calling. We have been able to narrow it to one hour only. The poison found its way through Urquelle's lower lip into his bloodstream between 10 o'clock and 11. No further narrowing will be possible.'

'Don't worry, that works out perfectly – this is the period in which Astrid had her eyes trained on Urquelle. She hasn't mentioned drinks in our earlier conversations but if Urquelle did have one, she will have noted it. I'll call her in a moment.' Bonbon and Flaco's interview with Banda flashed across his mind. 'But first I'll brief Granot on the cigarette development. He's running our ops room here and he can relay it to the others.'

'Let me know Astrid's response soonest, would you?'

'I will.'

Darac wasted no time in updating Granot and vice-versa.

'You did think things were going too well,' the big man said, in conclusion. 'I'll let Bonbon know right away, and ask him to put the drinks question to Banda.'

'Good.'

'We were getting pretty excited about Ralf Bassette in here but we can forget that now, it seems.'

'Vis-à-vis the cigarette angle, certainly.' Darac went to a different aspect. 'Sponsored by the long-suffering Vivienne, the glorified badger game Banda was operating with Lydia

Félix as was – is there any more to come from that, do you think?'

'Not material to the poisoning, I shouldn't think.'

'No?' Darac gave it a further moment's thought, then binned it. 'No. Just finally, the live camera link from Banda's room. Working well?'

'The sound and pictures froze momentarily a few times but as Erica pointed out, the in-camera recording will be 100% so those moments are not ultimately lost. Consensus here is that it's going to prove very handy in some situations, especially as the gizmo itself is only slightly bulkier than a mobile phone.'

They ended the call and as Darac tapped in Astrid's number, Elie Tiron emerged from Reception, announced that she was sorry she had been tied up earlier but was ready for him now.

'A couple of minutes, madame?'

'Of course.'

She went back inside as Astrid picked up.

'I've gone out into the corridor, Paul. Go ahead.'

Darac explained what he needed and why.

'Shit! I thought we'd nailed it.'

'My sentiments exactly.'

'But anyway... Drinks out on the drag strip? Sometimes, yes. Coffee, and especially spirits. On Thursday evening? Let me think...'

As his bandmate Dave Blackstock had delighted in pointing out, Darac was a devout atheist. While he waited for Astrid's verdict, he felt his faith slipping slightly.

'No, Paul. No drinks for Urquelle at any stage. No one else did, either. Not even water. I'm the only one of the smokers who carries a bottle around.'

Darac loved Astrid's certainty but he didn't love dead

ends and that is exactly where they found themselves. He had always accepted that there would come a time in his career when he led an investigation up a blind alley and couldn't find a way out. It was still early days, but perhaps that time had come.

'OK, we're back to square one and by now I was hoping to have reduced the number of suspects to just two or three. Until we know exactly how Urquelle met his death, it makes almost everyone here a suspect, in a sense. If that remains the case, 9.30 tomorrow morning may be pushing it for an easy check-out.'

'Understood. Reluctantly so, but understood. Have you seen Elie yet?'

'Seeing her in a minute. I'll let her know how selected things are looking. And of course, I'll have to question her on any part she may have played in Urquelle's murder.'

'Go easy, remember. No third degree stuff.'

'Astrid, do you know what the third degree is?'

'No, but it sounds bad.'

'I'll go easy. And naturally, if anything else occurs to you about Urquelle, call me immediately.'

'Listen, we'll be breaking for coffee in quarter of an hour or so. Shall I come and find you?'

He thought about it. 'Why not?'

'In the meantime, I'll play back that whole episode again in my mind.'

Reflecting that a live feed from the camera in Astrid's head would be far more useful to the Brigade than its new all-singing, all-dancing gizmo, Darac ended the call and headed back to the building. He made all of two steps before his mobile rang once more.

'Erica. Got something?'

'From Urquelle's mobile. Our friend the deleted email

has come through for us again. 53 of them to and from the same person, to be exact. Astrid's feeling was spot-on.'

Darac began to brighten. 'Thea Petrova?'

'Thea "I want you again and again and again" Petrova. Or at least, that's what she felt at one time.'

'Her feelings cooled eventually?'

'Seems so.'

'Erica, I know you've had only a few minutes on this but do you have enough there to piece together a rough timeline for their relationship?'

'Just creating a slide of it, coming to a screen near you, very soon – or the ops room to be exact.'

'You know if you and Astrid ever tired of the Brigade, you'd make a hell of a private detective team. But *don't* tire of it. That's an order.'

'As you put it so nicely. Urquelle and Petrova met for the first time four years ago at a trade show in Vienna. From that first night, it was full-on and increasingly frequent sex all the way until 18 months ago when things started to get more casual.'

'How does that show itself?'

'Things like Urquelle suggesting they stay at a particular hotel in Lausanne as they had before and she replying that she'll have to be on a tight leash because her boss will be around. Next time, perhaps. But when it comes to the next time, she may not make the show at all. Whenever they do get together again – and it happens, just less frequently – it inevitably turns into the same steamy sex-fest as before. *But* with a difference.'

'That being?'

'If the later emails are anything to go by, the steam seems to have been generated mainly by him. And very mechani-cally, too. He starts using words like "screw" and "shaft" and while the man had a limp, it seems he wasn't limp in other departments. Very proud of his "tool," he was. She, on the other had, no longer refers to it or to the act itself at all. And when she *had* done so earlier on, incidentally, her language was intensely passionate rather than crude – referring to how much she craved his body and how he was the only one et cetera. Naturally, he fired similar things back to her, once or twice referring to how dead his marriage was since he'd met Thea.'

'Interesting.'

'I tell you the sense I have about these two. I think her passion for him waned when she realised she was not the sole object of his, which was something he claimed in several emails early on.'

'More and more interesting. Before this few days, when was the last time they got together?'

'Uh... February. In Dubai.'

'And?'

'Not much was said, or rather written. "Your room at 7?" "Make it 8." Things like that.

'Since then, any references to meeting up this week?'

'Yes and no. In early May, Urquelle wrote: "See you in summer?" Thea replied: "September, perhaps." No mention of the Villa so maybe it wasn't planned. Maybe it came as a surprise to them both.'

'Thea had taken courses at the Villa before so her presence here isn't that surprising. Gérard Urquelle had never set foot in the place. Vivienne had, of course. Taught by Astrid, herself. Hmm. We need to talk to Thea, obviously.'

'I recommend fire retardant overalls.'

'Point taken.' Another question emerged from the maelstrom. 'She kept calling someone, didn't she? From here, I mean. Astrid saw her a few times, speaking animatedly but at a discreet volume in Russian.'

'We can't access her mobile, though. Not without a warrant and that will take time. Although...'

'Yes?'

'I do of course know her number from Urquelle's phone.'

'Of course you do and this *is* a murder case for God's sake. I'll ring Frènes later to authorise it. In the meantime, go for it. I'll take responsibility if shit and fan come together at some point. I'll plead a breakdown in comms and general confusion. Usually works.'

'Good, I'll get right down to Thea's calls. It will just yield numbers and names, of course.'

'It could still prove very useful. And Erica, I loved your analysis of her email exchanges with Urquelle. Top work.'

'I'm underpaid. You know that, don't you?'

'I know.'

They ended the call and Darac finally made it back into the lobby. If anything, he felt the stacks of papers and cards on the receptionist's desk were higher than before.

'You still there, Barbara? Or shall we send in a search party?'

'Still here, Captain. Computer still down. Damned things.'

Partly because he was a soft-hearted soul; partly because he had told Astrid that he would; and partly because he sensed it would be more effective, Darac took it very easily with Elie Tiron from the start. His first impressions supported Astrid's assessment of her friend. Elie did indeed appear to be a *sympa* soul and one glance was enough to suggest something else: "Tridi's" nonconformist personality was something to which Elie was clearly attracted but had only latterly sought to emulate. Coloured shocking pink, and cut super short, her radical hairdo was a copy of a style Astrid had sported some months back, and Darac also detected a family resemblance to some of her mannerisms of speech and body language. Of course, Elie may have always expressed herself in this way but there was no doubting who was following whom in the rad-chic stakes. The room was replete with photos of staff, tutor and student groups, snaps from holidays and the like, and in every shot in which Elie appeared, her hair was brown, shoulder length, and cut in a far more conservative style.

'I know we have work to do,' he said. 'But the postcards...' He indicated the cork board behind Elie's desk. 'It's impossible not to look at them.'

'You can see the ones Tridi has sent, can't you?'

'The kitsch ones with the hand-written captions, at a guess.'

She smiled. 'Yeah.'

He recognised a couple of images from a recent DMQ tour of Scandinavia.

'Who's been to Copenhagen?'

'Me. This May. Just for a few days.'

One card in particular rang a bell: a depiction of a wooden panel bearing intricately carved letters in Arabic script. He examined it more closely. 'This is from the Islamic art museum, isn't it?'

'Yes! The Davids Samling Collection – although Tridi says that's tautology because "samling" means "collection" in Danish.' She swivelled in her chair. 'Beautiful, isn't it? The panel is from a pulpit, they think – a minbar.' She swivelled back. 'You know it, obviously.'

'My band played the jazz festival there last year. Some of us went along to the museum. Luc, our bass player loved this particular thing and checking out the catalogue description, he said: "You'll never guess where they found this. It's from a minibar." He wasn't joking, sadly.'

Elie laughed. 'That's priceless.'

'Yes, Luc will never live that one down.' It was time to get serious but unless he was angry, Darac's habitual expression wasn't one to strike fear. 'I mentioned work. Shall we?'

'Yes, of course.'

'Let me go over what I know of your involvement with the so-called "have-a go-hero" Gérard Urquelle, and if I leave out anything significant, perhaps you would fill me in.'

Elie immediately looked under siege but Darac felt that there was nothing obstructive, evasive or even defensive in how she responded to what followed.

'Do you have anything to add?'

'No. I was obsessed, Captain, and I admit it. I hated him and still do. But I believed ultimately that he hadn't killed Karen. Or the gunman.'

'*I* do.'

She looked astonished. 'What?'

'I believe your suspicions were entirely correct.'

'But the eyewitness – Marut. What about his testimony?'

'False. There's no need to go into it in detail but we all believe that not only did Urquelle pay Marut to lie in court, he subsequently killed him to keep him quiet.'

'Marut is..?'

'Dead? Yes. Murdered? Yes, we believe so.'

Unable to speak for the moment, Elie sat back in her chair.

'I would love to be able to give you a moment but we have some way to go.'

'I should have gone with my first instincts,' she said, shaking her head. 'I knew Urquelle was an out-and-out bastard.'

'Did you kill him, Elie?' he said, gently, and not having

the faintest idea how she could have done so.

'No, Captain, I didn't.' She took off her glasses, dabbed her eyes and didn't continue until she put them back on. 'But I salute whoever did.'

'Do you think that person may have been Vivienne Urquelle?'

Elie shook her head. 'Tridi asked the same question. No. Emphatically. Though, Lord, if anyone had more reason.'

A knock at the door.

'I know that knock. Is it alright?'

'Yes, yes.'

'Come in, Barbara.'

She hovered in the doorway. 'I'll need to trawl around in here for some stationery et cetera, shortly.'

Elie looked to Darac once more.

'We'll be about five minutes,' he said, glancing at his watch, and hoping that Astrid would have come up with something since they spoke.

'I'm not quite ready yet, anyway. I shall return in ten.'

Barbara took her leave as briskly as she had come.

Elie caught Darac's look.

'Don't be fooled, Captain. Behind that hard, no-non-sense exterior lies an even harder no-nonsense *in*terior. But I don't know what I'd do without her. Especially with not having Clarice here this week of all weeks.' Turning to the postcard board, Elie indicated a shot of an apartment house façade in which there was scarcely a straight line to be seen. 'She's on a Gaudi jag in Barcelona. Lucky thing.'

'Indeed.'

'But all this brings me to a question of my own.'

'Vis-à-vis your diminished resources, what will happen later?'

Darac spent the next few minutes outlining how things

might go. Although Elie had no choice but to accept the situation, he was pleased she did so with good grace.

'Would you mind if we left it there, Captain? I need to go and eat something. Missed breakfast.'

'Of course.' He got to his feet. 'But I must advise you against missing breakfast. Lieutenant Granot, with whom you liaised earlier, is something of an expert on nutrition and he reckons breakfast is the most important meal of the day. Alongside lunch and dinner, that is.'

Elie was smiling as she picked up her handbag and walked out into the lobby.

'Aren't you going to lock the door?'

'What is there to steal? Besides, Barbara needs to come in.'

'Oh, that's right.'

'Don't even close it, usually. People can see at a glance if I'm in rather than knocking and waiting.'

Across the lobby, some progress appeared to have been made in the transformation of paper mountains into smaller peaks.

'Hey, where are you going with my date?' Astrid said, emerging from the lift.

'Nowhere,' Elie said. 'Late lunch for me. See you later.'

'I suppose I'll just have to make do with him, then.'

Earning a quizzical glance first from Barbara, then from crowd control officer Emil Balaise at the door, Astrid linked arms with Darac and the pair headed out on to the parvis. Below, Barthélémy Assako had advanced his wheelbarrow to the upper parterre. Everything else remained as it had fifteen minutes before.

'Walk and talk?' Astrid said. 'Or bums on balustrade?'

'The latter. If there's a sudden emergency, we might be faced with an uphill not-much-fun run to get back.'

'Good point. Top of the steps?'

'It's where I called you from earlier.'

'Let's relive that madness.'

They unlinked arms and sat turned in to one another.

'Elie was smiling when you left the office just now,' Astrid said, slipping on her shades. 'Thank you.'

'That's alright. Tridi.'

'Aah... I was wondering how long it would take you to discover my pet name. And, considering what we've all been to each other – me and the Brigade – I bet you've wondered why I never shared it with you before.'

'Do you know? I did.'

'Some other time, I'll tell you. But use it, by all means.'

A voice from below.

'Mademoiselle Pireque?'

Astrid turned and looked down. 'Barthélémy – didn't hear you.' She indicated the barrow. 'You've oiled out the squeak.'

'Oh yes.' He smiled but it faded as he gave Darac a suspicious, even hostile, look.

'This is Captain Paul Darac of the Brigade Criminelle. But don't worry, he isn't giving me the third degree. He's a friend. Of a friend.'

All was well.

'Monsieur,' Barthélémy said, the smile returning.

'Beautiful gardens,' Darac said, realising it was a lame comment and resolving not to add "And how many assistant gardeners do you have?" to compound the felony.

'Thank you. There are four of us in the team.'

'Right.' At least he hadn't added "before you ask."

Barthélémy turned to Astrid. 'Tisa has done another painting for you, mademoiselle. It's in my bothy.'

'Bless her! Busy now, Barthélémy, but I'll come along later.'

'Alright, mademoiselle.' A nod to Darac. 'Monsieur.'

Darac smiled by way of a valediction and Barthélémy wheeled the barrow silently away.

'Sweet man, that,' she said, watching him for a moment. 'Tisa, his daughter, is eight.' She turned back to Darac and looked at him in a way he felt she never quite had before. 'Tisa has no hands, Paul. No hands and only one of her forearms reaches what would have been her wrist. Born that way. And she draws and paints beautifully. A lovely, amazing, kid.'

'Born that way,' Darac repeated, one of the themes of the day crashing back into his head. 'I just don't know how parents... Anyway, look – Tridi?'

'Now you've used it not just to tease me, does it work for you? The name?'

'Not sure.' He pursed his lips. 'It *suits* you. And you seemed to transition from Darac to Paul without any difficulty.'

'Uh-huh?'

'But I might just stick to Astrid for the time being. OK?'

One day, the two *poètes-policiers* might discuss how Darac, known for his daringly free approach to playing jazz, could be so stodgily resistant to change in other areas of his life.

Astrid smiled. 'Of course you can.'

'Good, but listen...'

'I know. We need to press on. Let me give you a speed-reading version of every move I remember happening in that one-hour period in the yard.'

'Excellent.' He ran a hand into his hair and kept it there. 'Go for it.'

Astrid's account had barely begun when Darac saw it. Saw at least what could have happened. He needed Astrid to see it, too. 'Would you just go over that that last part again?' he said, dragging his hand out of his hair. 'From where Alan

Davies took his leave.'

'Ri-ight... Alan got up from the bench and on his way out of the yard, ran into Salins/Banda and stopped to chat with him. While they talked about something that seemed to puzzle Banda and amuse Alan, Urquelle took what looked to me at the time – and turned out to be – a diary out of his pocket. Then he took out his pen, and while he finished smoking his fag, started jotting down the figures you showed me – so he could work out how much he would have left from his personal monthly outgoings to offer Banda. Shall I go on?'

'This is the sequence we need to articulate more precisely if we can, Astrid: 'Cigarette – diary – pen – jotting – calcu-lation. Run it again through that remarkable mind's eye of yours.'

'OK.' Her brow lowered. 'Urquelle was already smoking when he took out the diary. He kept the fag in his mouth while he riffled pages. He found the one he wanted. Still with the fag in his mouth, and with the end flaring red occasionally as he took a pull, he took out his pen and wrote down possibly just that first line.'

'Wrote it down without thinking?'

'Yes. He knew that amount off by heart – as you would, if it were, say, your regular monthly salary.'

Darac felt his pulse quicken. 'And the second line he wrote?'

'He had to really think about it.'

'When I work something out, I often stick my hand in my hair. It irritates the hell out of some people, I know. Or I stare at the floor. Describe what he did.'

'He glanced up from the diary, beetle-browed. He stubbed out the fag, and then...'

'Yes?'

Astrid saw it, too, and she laughed with the joy of it. 'He tapped the pen against his lip, Paul. Tapped it repeatedly and at one point – why didn't I think of this before? – he actually put it in his mouth. The cap, I mean, *and* he put it in the same corner he'd parked his fag.'

'Yes!' Reaching for his mobile with one hand, he clasped Astrid's with the other and as one conjoined entity, they punched the air in triumph. 'You've done it, Astrid. We're up and running again.'

'It's great but if I'd had my wits about me, it would have happened earlier. I saw what he did but I didn't register it, somehow.'

'Hey – we were steered along the cigarette and then the drinks paths. It's a context thing. Without you, we would be nowhere. And now I need my hand back.'

'Oh, yes.'

He tapped in a number. 'Path didn't send us the pen along with the diary – it seemed immaterial to the case – so unless they've sent it to the Caserne with the rest of Urquelle's effects... Deanna? Thanks entirely to Astrid, we know, or we think we know, how Urquelle was poisoned. The timeframe works and everything else fits. She's here. I'll put her on.'

'It was the bastard's pen,' she said. 'The one bearing the inscription celebrating his magnificence as a human being. The pen *cap*, to be exact. I saw him sucking it, in effect. Like a child sucks a thumb.'

Among a most un-professorial stream of mainly Italian expletives, came the assurance that Urquelle's effects were still in situ and that the pen would be tested without delay. The call ended with the promise that the test result would come quickly thereafter.

'I now need to update Granot and the others in the ops

room,' Darac said, getting to his feet. 'A fully fledged team meeting.' They headed briskly back across the parvis. 'Might there be time for one of your signature cameo appearances?'

'Depends how long it goes on. I've still got the class prize to award; the open discussion to chair – that will be like no other; my concluding summary and pep talk. I'll be free at 5 for a couple of hours, though.'

'Excellent.'

They walked through into Reception as a crockery-laden trolley disappeared with a clinking shudder into the service lift.

'More paperwork?' Darac said, indicating what appeared to be a whole new mountain range away to their left. 'Does she ever stop?'

At the desk, Barbara was continuing to work on fast-forward, a task made all the more difficult by the slow-motion call she was having to deal with on the phone.

'Why not ask the multi-tasker herself?' Astrid deadpanned. 'She's had her coffee. She won't bite your head off.'

'I wouldn't blame her if she did.'

'And she has other talents, you know. Such as being probably the watcher in the place.'

'Second best, surely.'

'I have eyes only in the front of my head.'

'Ah, one of those, eh?' He pressed for the lift. 'Useful.'

'Have you had coffee, by the way?'

'Not yet but we're lavishly equipped up in Salle Milhaud. Two four-spout Gaggias, to be exact. I may never leave this place.'

'Two four-spouters? Impressive. Right, I'm away around the corner.'

'Astrid,' he said, giving her shoulder a squeeze. 'There could still be a very long way to go with this thing but thanks to you, I'm sure we're on the right road.' The lift doors opened. 'Now all we have to do is nail the killer.' He smiled. 'See you later.'

Sealing what had been a highly significant meeting with a hopelessly bungled high five, the pair upped the bathos in a flurry of wildly flapping fingers and, chuckling like children, went their separate ways.

3.42 PM

With Deanna confirming that Urquelle's pen cap had indeed been the carrier of the poison that killed him, the mood in the Salle Milhaud was as high as it was hectic.

'So what's this big news, chief?' Jean-Jacques Lartigue said, returning from a trip to his van. 'The pen cap with the poison...'

' " Is in the chalice from the palace?" ' Darac said, unable to resist.

'What?'

Ormans was already grinning. 'Wonderful! And what's the next line? "The vessel with the... *something* holds the brew that is true." *The Court Jester.*' Picturing the movie, he gazed nostalgically into space. 'They don't make them like that anymore.'

'With all due deference, Messieurs,' Lartigue said. 'What on earth are you on about?'

'Sorry, Lartou – old movie talk. Yes, the pen cap bore the poison. Now let's get into the how and why of it.' Unable to have found a convenient balustrade from which to conduct operations, Darac had positioned the Bechstein's piano stool at one end of the whiteboards.

'OK, everyone,' he said, picking up a marker and an eraser. 'What does Deanna's news do to our suspects list?' He got to his feet. 'The most obvious thing is that whoever did this knew of Urquelle's oral habits with his pen. Let's annotate the list.'

Granot shifted his weight on to one elbow, the easier to indulge in a habit of his own: twisting the ends of his moustache. 'On the face of it,' he said. 'It puts Vivienne Urquelle squarely back in the frame. Who would know "good old" Géri's ways better than her? And who had easier access to his pen?'

Darac reinstated Vivienne's name on the list but put a large question mark against it. 'Who? Another candidate is Madame Thea Petrova. Thanks to Erica, we now know for certain that Astrid's suspicions about her relationship with Urquelle were spot-on. He and Thea *had* been up close and personal for years. Very close, in fact.'

Erica raised a hand. 'And I've dug up more besides. Nothing conclusive, but it's of interest.'

'Excellent, we'll come on to that.' Darac underlined Thea's name. 'According to Deanna, it might take weeks of testing to determine when poison and pen came together so we can park that line for the moment. But let's go back to Vivienne,' he said, and turned to Granot. 'I see why you said that *on the face of it* this new breakthrough puts her back in the frame. Yes, she would certainly have known all of her husband's habits intimately but even scant acquaintances might have noticed him absently putting the pen cap on or between his lips. And, theoretically at least, several people here had access to that pen, Yana Vanier a.k.a. Lydia Félix, the most obvious among them.'

'Gaining and granting access usually goes with shagging someone,' Perand said.

'Except that she didn't have sex with him until he had already absorbed the fatal dose.' He eyeballed the young man. 'Pay attention, will you? I was thinking more of the fact that the two of them paired up in every session of Zoë Hamada's perfume-making course, sat together at dinner, et cetera, and so the pen would have been easily to hand.'

In an attempt to claim co-ownership of the thought, Perand nodded, sagely. 'That, too, yes.'

'If we look at how Yana/Lydia might have obtained the poison used to kill Urquelle...' Darac turned to the board. Under the general heading means was the sub-heading potential sources of acrylamide. It bore just two names: Vivienne Urquelle and Ralf Bassette. 'What do we see?' He gave Flaco a look. 'Flak?'

'That Yana would most likely get it from Vivienne via Banda, or directly from Vivienne herself if she was in on the badger game part of it from the start.'

'Exactly, and that leads us back to the whole problem with Vivienne as a suspect. Bonbon? You're the only one here to have questioned Vivienne, Banda *and* had a private word with Yana – talk us through it.' Remembering that the man's Catalan accent had been known to flummox those unaccustomed to hearing it, he grinned: 'In French, ideally. For the sake of our newer friends.'

By way of a response, Bonbon uttered a few words in an even more exotic tongue. 'That was Occitan for "I'll give it my best shot *and* spare you the *sardana* that goes with it." '

'Thank God.' Granot huffed. 'Whatever the sardana is.'

'A folk dance, you heathen.'

'The prosecution rests.'

'So – Vivienne,' Bonbon said, pressing on. 'I've checked out Banda's story and was able to verify the salient parts of it. Badly wanting to divorce Urquelle, Vivienne *had* previously hired several other P.I.'s to get the goods on him but they didn't come through for her. Banda, though, did succeed and so it seems she would have at last been able to divorce the prick on legs that was Gérard Urquelle – a divorce, remember, that would have proved financially painful for him, an easing of all sorts of pain for her. Now, unless hiring Banda was a smokescreen, it just doesn't make sense to have had her husband killed into the bargain, does it? For a number of reasons, Flak and I didn't buy that possibility even before I sneaked in a word with Yana Vanier. Afterwards, I still don't buy it. '

'Neither do I,' Darac said, rubbing out the question mark he had set against Vivienne's name. 'So barring a significant development on this strand, and there could be one down the line, I propose we remove Vivienne from our list of suspects. Any counter arguments?' He scanned the room. 'No? Right.'

He did the needful and then set a question mark against another entry.

'In many ways, Elie Tiron has a stronger claim to suspect status than Vivienne. On the question of access to Urquelle's pen, bear in mind that Elie has access to keys that open every door in this place, including Urquelle's bedroom. As to motive, we have chapter and verse on why Elie loathed Urquelle, and she freely admits to still doing so, incidentally.'

Erica's wispy eyebrows rose in sympathy. 'She's not alone there.'

'Indeed. As it happens, Astrid isn't the only one who believes Elie had no knowledge of the true story of the so-called eyewitness to the jewellery store shootings, Denis Marut. I believe it also. But anyway, what we may believe about *Elie* becomes somewhat academic once we've removed *Vivienne* from the list of suspects, doesn't it?' He indicated the two names listed under the means heading. 'Her potential supplier of the poison no longer a suspect, that only leaves the genial paper magnate from Strasbourg Ralf Bassette, with whom, like Banda and Yana, Elie apparently had no prior connection.'

'That we know of,' Granot said. 'I know time is really tight but we must be... Well, you get my point.'

'Yes and all this might change but for the time being, I propose we discount Elie Tiron as a suspect. Any counters?' He scanned the room. 'None? Fine.'

He pressed the eraser into service once more. 'Now we come on to the only suspect who also features on each of the motive, opportunity and means lists – Ralf Bassette, himself. Now...'

Darac's ringing mobile slowed his flow but it wasn't until he checked the caller's ID that it stemmed it altogether.

'Astrid?'

'I'm in Elie's office,' she said, her voice scarcely more than a breath. 'You'd better come.'

She rang off before he could reply.

'OK, something has happened down in Elie Tiron's office.' He gave Erica a look. 'Will our new live camera work back to here from there?'

'It should.'

'Bring it. The rest of you stay here. And stay tuned.'

3.53 PM

Having called for backup before abandoning his station at the rear entrance, young Officer Emil Balaise had taken charge of the situation in Elie's office.

'No one has been in here since Barbara called you over?'

'No, Captain.'

'Has anyone *tried* to come in?'

'No. It's been quiet as the... It's been quiet.'

'Thank you. Stay here for the moment. Erica – you OK over there in the corner?'

'Yes, the link's established with the ops room and I'm filming.'

'Excellent.'

Sending out a signal of her own – one that said she didn't want to advance any further – Astrid was standing with her back against the door. Darac caught her eye and smiled.

'You all right?' he said, well aware that she wasn't.

'I'm fine, Paul,' she said, her voice flat as if all the life had been hammered out of it.

'The door behind you locked?'

'Uh-huh. Let's just get on with it.'

Turning to Barbara, Darac reflected that she looked out of place sitting down; especially as she was sitting behind Elie's desk. In all other respects, it seemed it was business as usual for her.

'Barbara, talk me through what happened.'

'Certainly. You recall when you were here earlier that I mentioned needing to come in at some point to forage for some items of stationery?'

'Yes.'

'I got delayed by one thing and another and... Well, anyway, I was finally free so in I came and started gathering things up.' On the desk in front of her was a tray containing a varied collection of sundries. 'Happily, Clarice had left things in good order so it only took a minute or two but then thanks to the damned computers, I realised I also needed to check some paper records from one of the filing cabinets over where your colleague is standing. It was locked, Captain. All the keys live in here.' She indicated a drawer bridging the knee space between the desk's twin pedestals. 'So I sat down and opened it. Shall I?'

'Just wait a second, please.' Darac gave Erica a look and she moved in closer. 'Go ahead.'

Barbara opened the drawer and for a moment, Darac couldn't understand what he was seeing. And not just because of the untidy mess it presented.

'Did you touch it?'

'Of course not.'

'What *did* you do?'

'I closed the drawer, went to the door and called out to the officer here who came running. Then, while he was organising someone to fill in for him, I called Mademoiselle Pireque about my discovery.'

'That all correlates, Emil?'

'Yes, Captain. The timings, everything.'

'Astrid?'

'Yes.'

'When will Elie be back from her late lunch, do you think?'

'I don't know. Ten minutes, maybe? I don't know.'

'OK, Emil,' Darac said, scrolling screens on his mobile. 'You may leave but I've got a tricky brief for you.'

The young man looked as if he relished the prospect. 'Yes?'

'We're going to close the door after you but leave it unlocked so that when Madame Tiron returns from lunch, she will just walk in. By then, Barbara will be back in Reception so everything will appear as normal. With the exception of one particular person, if anyone else comes to this door in the meantime, dissuade them from entering but without raising a warning flag. Are you with me?'

'We usually stay stone-faced – what the boss calls "saying nothing as loudly as you can." If we're in a good mood, "keep back" and "move along" is about as chummy as we get. But I'll think of something. Who is the exception, Captain?'

'This man.' Darac showed him his phone. 'His name is Raul Ormans and he's our chief forensic examiner.'

'Check.'

'Now this is most important. Share nothing you have seen or heard in this room with your boss or colleagues. Right?'

'I don't know what all this fuss is about anyway, but I won't, Captain.'

Intending to issue a similar instruction to Barbara, Darac got no further than opening his mouth.

'I know,' she said. 'The same goes for me. Don't worry.'

'I don't. Emil? Off you go.'

Astrid stood aside and the young man took his leave.

'A quick question, Barbara. Is the filing cabinet drawer you opened usually locked?'

Her pencilled-on eyebrows rose. 'Uh... No, as a matter of fact, it isn't.'

'Thank you. I think that will do for the moment. Take what you came for, by all means.'

'May I get the forms from the cabinet I need, also? I didn't get as far as opening it.'

He thought about it. 'I don't see why not. Put the key back in the drawer exactly where it was, please.' He watched her perform the task with her customary efficiency.

'Thank you, Barbara.' Darac shepherded her to the door. 'It need hardly be said that your contribution is inestimable.'

'I'm used to it, Captain. Three previous directors need hardly have said it, either. And so they never did. Madame

Tiron is the only one who has.'

Sharing a look with Astrid so nuanced that it was difficult for Darac to read, Barbara took her leave.

The object of fascination was still lying undisturbed in the drawer. Darac fired off a few shots on his mobile, rang Granot and then asked Erica to zoom right in.

'Granot? Are you all seeing this upstairs?'

'We bloody well are. What the..?'

'Exactly. Send R.O. down here with his fingerprint kit, will you? We've got a lookout posted but he knows who he's looking out for.'

'Will do.'

'We'll pick up the filming again when he gets here.'

He ended the call and turned to Astrid. 'If you feel you should be back with your class?' He let a raised eyebrow complete the thought.

'You two can take it from here? Is that it?' Astrid took a couple of deep, settling breaths. 'Look, I know my divided loyalties have been an issue from the start and this development apparently pushes things way over to one side but my opinion is still worth *something* isn't it?'

'Of course it is. What are you talking about?'

She shook her head. 'I'm sorry, Paul, Erica. It's just... This doesn't look good for Elie, does it?'

'We've got shots *and* film of the thing lying in situ so let's take a closer look.' Darac took a pair of forensic gloves out of his pocket, stretched them a couple of times and put them on. It was just as he lifted the focus of all their attention out of the drawer that Elie walked in. She appeared more relaxed than before.

'A party? Thanks for inviting me to...'

Elie's face froze. Darac was holding a fountain pen. A *Lepic*. And it bore an inscription. She looked at each face in turn. 'How have you got that?'

Astrid looked her in the eyes. 'Babe, I think what... we would like to know is, how have *you* got it?'

With Erica looking into the provenance of the mystery pen – now en route to Deanna – and Astrid having returned to her class, Darac had drafted in Flaco to assist him in interrogating Elie Tiron. If she was finding at least some comfort in the familiar surroundings of her office, the presence of a female officer and, by mutual agreement, Darac's continuing use of her forename, it wasn't apparent to Granot and the others viewing the live camera feed in in the ops room.

'Elie, you realise what this development looks like?'

'I don't care what it looks like. I have never seen that pen before and I have no idea how it found its way into my desk.'

Elie's desk phone rang and out of habit, her hand went towards it before she remembered the agreed protocol. The answerphone kicked silently in and after a beat, Darac continued.

'Well, I'll *tell* you what it looks like, Elie – that at some time in the recent past, you purchased a luxury *Lepic* pen identical to the one Urquelle was presented with by his firm five years ago. In conversations, you have freely admitted that thanks to your obsessional digging into the have-a-go-hero case, you knew every detail about this pen, including the inscription engraved on the barrel.'

'Yes, I knew all about the pen. So what? I *didn't* buy another. I couldn't afford it, for one thing, nor know where to buy such an item and then have it engraved? No, Captain. I did not buy that second pen. Why would I?'

Darac hadn't pegged Elie as a particularly gifted actor but if she was lying, she was turning in quite a performance. 'Why *would* you? How does this sound? Familiar with Urquelle's habit, you doctored the cap of his own pen, not knowing exactly when the poison would take effect, but knowing enough to be sure it would happen while he was here at the Villa. What you couldn't have known was that he was going to dash off into the city before class this morning. Dash off never to return.'

'But I *didn't* poison his pen,' she said, more a plea than a rebuttal. 'I wouldn't have the faintest idea how to.' Her defiance may have given way to distress but, like a boxer on the ropes who sees an opening for a counterpunch, she suddenly found the energy to throw it. 'Yes, yes – that forensics person,' she said, sitting forward in her seat. 'Monsieur Ormans, he didn't find a single fingerprint of mine on the second pen, did he? *Did* he, Captain.'

'Elie, he didn't find a fingerprint, full stop. The pen had been wiped.'

'Ah.' She slumped back but, perhaps because she had at least thrown a punch of her own, appeared to take the blow well. 'Tell me something,' she said, a little more settled than before. 'What was I supposed to have done with this second pen?'

Although it was still early days, changing the angle of attack was a tried and trusted ploy in any interrogation and Darac had additional reasons to go for it now. Flaco's interrogation face was a thing of such Jesuitical severity, it had been known to unnerve hardened criminals into making mistakes. Whether it would unnerve a fundamentally good and valuable member of society like Elie Tiron remained to be seen but Flaco had recently added a new string to her bow. The coaxing, conversational technique she had learned from her mentor Darac was just one of many approaches he had picked up from his own mentor, Agnès Dantier. He judged this a good moment to put it to the test.

'I'll bring Officer Flaco in here.'

'What are you supposed to have done with the second pen?' she began. 'You knew that wherever and whenever the poisoned Urquelle eventually collapsed here on site, you, as director, *you* would be called immediately to the scene. At which point, you intended to remove the murder weapon itself from, say... Urquelle's jacket pocket, and replace it with your harmless exact copy. Even if they thought of doing so, our forensic teams could examine the copy forever, couldn't they, and never find anything amiss. Unfortunately for you and for lovers of natural justice, you never got the opportunity to execute that substitution.' Flaco's scowl explored an even deeper level of scrutiny. 'Why? Because Urquelle and his pen were in the morgue, weren't they? Where they belonged, if you ask me.'

Darac watched Elie carefully as she returned Flaco's gaze. Frank and with no suspicious tells, it would have convinced many a young detective of her innocence.

'Officer, I told Captain Darac earlier that I'm glad Urquelle is dead. I can't deny it. It would be a lie and five minutes checking on your part would prove that. *But* I didn't kill him and this business with the pen changes nothing. I have no knowledge of it at all.'

Flaco gave Darac a look and a little eyebrow semaphore between them established that she should carry on. Employing a variation on a skill honed by years of playing in a high-quality jazz group, Darac was able to listen attentively to one conversation while constructing a second one in his head. The presence of a replica pen in the desk drawer of self-confessed Urquelle hater Elie Tiron was hugely incriminating. But incriminating to whom? If she had acquired the second pen as a substitute, why didn't she ditch it once she had learned that Urquelle had died off-site? She had certainly had enough time to have secreted it somewhere far more secure than a desk drawer. She could have transferred it to the glove compartment of her car, hidden it somewhere in the grounds, any number of things.

And if she had known that the second pen was sitting in her desk drawer, albeit jumbled in with a lot of other items, would she have left her office door unlocked for Barbara, someone she knew would be rummaging around for things in her absence? And it had then been Barbara who had found that a normally accessible filing cabinet drawer had been locked, a circumstance that led her directly to the drawer containing the pen.

And from whom could Elie have acquired the poison, acrylamide? The team had ruled out Vivienne Urquelle as a possible source. There *could* have been a connection between Elie and Ralf Bassette, but a number of officers were working expressly on finding one and coming up empty.

Darac was leaning heavily towards the theory that someone else had planted the pen to incriminate Elie when his mobile groaned against his chest. Two texts had come in, the first of which he had missed in the rush to set up the interview. Checking the ID, he felt his spirits lift. It was from Suzanne at Hôpital St. Roch.

Paul, in case you were thinking of it, it would be better if you didn't contact Armani at the moment. There are complications with Noëmi and the baby.

I'm sure everything will be fine in the end but I'll let you know later.

Kisses, S

Complications? A chill ran down Darac's spine. Hadn't the Tardellis suffered enough for one day? For a lifetime? *Two* lifetimes? But Suzanne was still confident, it seemed. Or were her reassurances... Not now. He looked at the second text, just in. It was from Erica.

Call me immediately.

4.39 PM

'You alone, Paul?'

'Yes, I'm outside the rear entrance. You've got something on the pen already?'

'Plenty. Part of the ego-massage of a luxury item such as a *Lepic* pen is its exclusivity, right? But that makes their provenance easy to trace and not only because just a few outlets sell them. The pen we found was numbered, Paul, and not a batch number, either; a number that identifies it individually. It was purchased at 2.27 in the afternoon of May 18th this year at a store by the name of, hang on... *Pedersen og Reiter*, a jewellers on a street called Strøget, in Copenhagen, Denmark. The pen cost 6,700 Danish krone – about 900 euros – and was not engraved at that point, incidentally. It must have been done later.'

Copenhagen? And May? Annie Provin's analogy of the rollercoaster ride was up and running once more. 'And the purchaser's name?'

'A Madame Jeanne Dubois, apartment 3, Rue Racine, 2bis, Paris 75006. You know what's coming next.'

'There's no such person at said address?'

'Or said address, either.'

'Erica, not more than two minutes ago, I'd made up my mind that someone had planted that pen in Elie Tiron's desk to incriminate her.'

'And now?'

'Put it this way. I know for a fact that Elie spent a few days in Copenhagen this last May.

'Ah.'

'*Ah*, indeed. I take it the fictitious Madame Dubois didn't write a cheque or use a traceable card to pay?'

'No, she paid in cash.'

'Didn't the store people think that unusual?'

'Unusual, yes, but not unprecedented – especially for us card-phobic French, apparently. Paying in cash wasn't the only way in which she made an impression. I spoke to the under-manager of the store, one Laura Madsen, who although her accent was execrable, has serviceable French. When she overheard the somewhat hit-and-miss conversation in Danish going on between Madame Dubois and the assistant serving her, Masden stepped forward to take it on in French. Declaring that she was keen to practise her Danish, Madame D rebuffed her in a way that was less than polite.'

'Impolite? A Parisienne? Sounds as if Elie had got into character pretty well.' If it indeed was her. 'Do you have more, Erica?'

'Oh, yes. CCTV covers the front door, the till et cetera, and so everyone entering and exiting the store is filmed. The security firm they use is going to send us the file from that afternoon and we should have it any time. I know you're not its biggest fan, but that's the wonder of digital technology, Paul.'

'You're right, it is. Let me know the second you get it, will you?'

'Of course.'

'Great work, Erica.'

He ended the call and rang Agnès with the update.

'You had entirely reasonable grounds for doubting Madame Tiron's guilt, Paul, but this Copenhagen development does appear to remove them. If the CC evidence backs it up, cautioning her and bringing her in is really your only option.'

'Agreed.'

Lost in thought, he barely acknowledged Officer Emil Balaise at the door, or Barbara at her desk as he walked back into the building. Despite everything pointing to it, he was still harbouring a nagging doubt about Elie. Partly, it was the postcards from her Copenhagen trip which had sparked an open and free conversation about it. There were three possibilities here. One: Elie had been negligent in leaving such a clear connection to the purchase of the substitute pen in plain sight. Two: she had left the postcards on display deliberately, reasoning that it would have been more suspicious to have not done so. Three: she was innocent of the crime and it was the person who had ultimately planted the pen in her desk who, somehow knowing when Elie was due to be in Copenhagen, had travelled to the city at the same time and purchased the pen as one "Madame Dubois," thus initiating the sequence of incrimination.

He hovered outside the office door for a moment. At his back, Barbara worked tirelessly on.

On re-entering the office, the first thing he noticed was that the Brigade's new camera gizmo was still broadcasting sound and vision back to the ops room from Clarice's desk. The second was something he hadn't noticed before: the leave calendar attached to a pin board on the wall behind it. The working week of May 16th to 21st contained two entries. Elie had been off from the 17th to the 20th; providing further damaging evidence against her. Barbara had been off for the whole week. The two of them off at the same time? How did that work?

'Sorry I've been so long,' he said, and whispered "It's looking bad for her – more in a moment" in Flaco's ear as he resumed his seat. 'We might have to draw things to a close very shortly but I have a quick question.'

'Yes?' Elie said, apparently none the worse for her solo encounter with Flaco.

'I've just spotted that back in May when you were in Copenhagen, Barbara was also on leave. Unusual, surely, for you both to be off simultaneously? How did Clarice cope by herself?'

The question appeared to wrong-foot Elie. 'Oh, uh... no, I don't think it has ever happened before – but she wasn't. Clarice wasn't by herself, I mean. Our night man Bruno stepped in. Not a patch on Barbara, of course, but he's fine and he gets on with the students brilliantly.' The wary look persisted. 'Why is this of interest, Captain?'

'It isn't, really. We both manage teams, don't we, and staffing issues interest me, I suppose.'

'I see.'

Actually, as Flaco herself knew, few things interested Darac less but he didn't want to show his hand just yet. 'Please continue for the moment, Flak.'

'Of course, Captain. So, madame...'

Darac stared at the floor. Yes, things were looking bad for Elie but perhaps that was exactly what the true culprit had intended the Brigade to conclude. His thoughts turned to Barbara, who certainly knew when Elie was taking her Spring break, and almost certainly knew her destination. Barbara who had *also* been absent from work on the day the substitute pen had been purchased. Barbara, the true and trusted factotum, addressed by all by her forename only, like a child. Barbara, whose mixed messages on Elie couldn't hide the bitterness she so obviously felt at being overworked, overlooked and undervalued. Barbara, the woman with eyes in the back of her head. Barbara, the finder, when all alone in Elie's office, of the incriminating pen.

He felt a throb against his chest. Erica:

That CCTV file is in. We're holding.

He replied:

Flak and I will be right with you.

'Flak, the officer on point at the rear entrance – will you bring him in, please?'

'Immediately,' she said, taking her leave.

'Elie, classes are going to break shortly, aren't they?'

She consulted her watch. 'Any minute now, yes.'

Good. I need Astrid. 'We're going to leave you in the care of Officer Balaise. Not for too long, I hope. You'll find him quite *sympa*.'

'I'm sure.' She gave a tired smile. 'But I don't really need a babysitter. Or do you think I might make a run for it without one, Captain?'

'No, I don't think that but this way, I would know *you* wouldn't think of it, either.'

She nodded, exhaled deeply and sat back in her chair. The door opened and Flaco entered with Balaise. For a moment, Darac wondered about removing the live camera but then realised how useful it could prove.

'Look after Madame Tiron, would you Emil?'

'Certainly, Captain.'

'Feel free to chat but I would remind you that the camera set up on the desk over there is sending a live feed back to the ops room. Continuing a protocol we've already established, Madame cannot send or read emails, texts or answer the phone. Alright? '

'Check.'

'Just quickly, Elie,' Darac said, setting the tone for Balaise, 'When will Barbara be going home this evening?'

'Not possible to say. She has to work the hours necessary to fulfil her role. On a Friday, it can't be before 8 o'clock because that's when Bruno comes on. But without Clarice and with me *hors de combat* for at least some of the time, it might be as late as 10, tonight.'

'Does she ever attend the celebration dinner?'

'Attend as in partake?'

'Yes.'

'No, no. I hardly ever do, myself. The urge at the end of the week is to get home as early as one can, you know.'

'I know only too well. Flak? Let's go.'

Wondering when Elie, or Barbara, come to that, might be seeing their homes again, he followed Flaco out of the office. Once out of Barbara's earshot, he called Granot. 'We're en route. Listen, we need to know which of our suspects apart from Elie were out of the country on May 18th this year. In Denmark, specifically.'

'Suspects plural? I thought we had only one left?'

'Humour me. We need checks on the following: the

receptionist Barbara...'

'Surname?'

'That's her issue right there – or part of it. It's Artaud. Barbara Florence Artaud. Also, check on Thea Petrova, Yana Vanier, and although so many things suggest otherwise, it wouldn't hurt to include Vivienne Urquelle.'

'OK, but I'm not sure how easy it will be determining Thea Petrova's whereabouts. She lives in St. Petersburg, doesn't she? Europol has an agreement with the Russian Federation but it doesn't stretch to exchanging personal data.'

'You're forgetting she has dual nationality.'

'But don't tell me – the other nationality is North Korean.'

'No, no. La Petrova is half-Swedish.'

'I'm on it.'

5.03 PM

With seats in the front stalls, Darac's team had a clear view of the widescreen TV that had been brought in for the occasion. Raul Ormans, his people and the remaining uniforms from Foch were sitting in pairs around their laptops in the cheaper seats at the back of the room. Surrounded by an array of keyboards of which any prog-rocker would have been proud, Erica was conducting affairs from stage right.

'Just a quick update for those of you who don't know,' she began, 'Pathology have now examined the *Lepic* fountain pen discovered in Elie Tiron's desk earlier and found it to be a perfectly standard specimen free of any contamination.' She picked out the large, round face of crime scene coordination officer Jean-Jacques Lartigue. 'Lartou, it's on its way back to us here so it can be logged.'

'OK, Erica.'

She resumed to the whole group. 'The pen was purchased in the store of *Pedersen og Reiter* – I love "og" by the way – at 2.27 on the afternoon of the 18th of May this year. The CCTV file we're going to look at is time-tagged from 1 o'clock and I've run it forward an hour because in that time, no one remotely resembling Elie Tiron entered the store. In fact, only five people entered in total: two males, three elderly females. Granot have you finished playing travel agencies yet?'

'Just completing the last request...' A final check of his screen and a thick finger delivered a blunt force injury to the send key. 'Now we wait. No reason why it should take long, really, although it sometimes does.'

'I'll hook you back up.' Slender fingers pitter-pattered at the keys. 'Are you with us?'

'Something's happening...Yes, I am.'

'Good. I'm going to press play and as if by magic, all of you at the back should find yourselves in the wonderful Land of Og.'

Paired with Darac, Astrid showed not a flicker of amusement.

'If you don't,' Erica went on. 'Sing out and I'll sort it.'

In synch with one another, laptop screens and the TV blinked a couple of times and then the same image formed up: an interior shot focussed on the jewellery store's front door. On the pavement outside, vague figures ghosted to and fro and in the bottom right-hand corner, an inset showed a section of a counter containing tills.

'Pretty sharp for CC,' Erica said. 'Anyone *not* seeing it? No? Good.'

'We shouldn't have long to wait, Astrid,' Darac said, softly.

She didn't respond immediately but then her eyes darted sideways and she nodded. A minute went by. Three. Five. Eight. And then a blurred shape looming toward the door racked into focus as it opened.

'Here she is,' Darac said. 'And it *is* Elie Tiron. I'm so sorry, Astrid.'

'Elie Tiron? What are you talking about?' Perand said, earning a stare from Flaco. 'Yes, apologies, chief, but this woman looks nothing like her. Look at her hair – long, dark, curly.'

'*That*, Perand,' Darac said, his eyes remaining on the woman until she walked out of frame. 'That is how Elie has worn her hair for most of her life. Check out the photos in her office.' He turned to Astrid and for the second time that day, he couldn't understand what he was seeing. Her head back, her eyes closed and both arms raised, she was beaming.

'Yeees!' she cried out, punching the air. 'For once, Perand, I'm happy, delighted, *ecstatic* to side with you!' She turned to Darac. 'Whoever that person is, Paul, it is emphatically not Elie. It's someone who hadn't realised that she had abandoned the mop of chestnut-brown curls that had been her signature look for years, and replaced it with the radical cut and dye job she has now. That woman on the screen is wearing a wig. And I must say, it's a very accurate replica of what Elie's hair was like. Done from photos, I guess.'

Darac's mind was alive with questions. Before he had the opportunity to ask the most obvious one, Astrid was back in.

'Elie first had her new cut done on her birthday which is April 30th. I've seen photos of the whole ceremony on her phone. They're date-tagged, of course. It was two weeks *before* she went to Copenhagen. Erica, can you run the sequence again?'

'Sure thing.' She grinned. 'Tridi.'

'Just a matter of time, wasn't it? But you can rib me all you like, sweeties, I don't care.'

The sequence played again. 'Another thing. I've studied posture, attitude and gait extensively over the years, right? Look at the way this woman moves. It's not as fluid as Elie. Not so light on her feet. I would say she's slightly older, too. And a tiny bit shorter.'

'I see that,' Flaco said. 'Maybe even more significant is that she's looking away from the camera. But there's nothing much to look at on that side wall, is there? She wants to be seen and identified as Elie Tiron, this woman, and she thinks the hair alone will do it for her.'

'Spot-on, Flak,' Bonbon said, watching the woman. 'Spot-on.'

With her work in support of Elie's innocence completed, Astrid sat back in her chair and as the moments ticked by, voice after voice only strengthened the case she had made on her friend's behalf from the beginning.

Granot caught Erica's eye. 'Can you release me from the CC file? I need to be checking other stuff.'

'Yes I can. In fact, might this be a good moment to put everyone back on?'

Nods all round. More rapid tip-tapping and it was done.

'I think we're all agreed,' Darac said, giving Astrid's shoulder a squeeze as he got to his feet. 'The woman in those sequences is an impostor, and whatever we may think of the no-good louse Gérard Urquelle, bear in mind that, laying the groundwork right back in May, said impostor has been trying her damnedest to make us believe that a good and totally innocent person is guilty of the murder she herself was going to commit.' Taking up his station at the whiteboard, Darac erased Elie's name from the list of suspects. 'I sense our collective dander is well and truly up about that.'

'Spot-on again,' Bonbon said.

Astrid brandished her mobile. 'Paul, may I tell Elie what you have just done?'

'Good idea but you won't be able to call her.'

Up-and-coming rugby player Serge Paulin raised a hand. 'I could nip down and tell her in person if you like? Might be quickest.'

Two long-standing members of Serge's ever-growing legion of fans, Granot and Bonbon made a comment which wryly questioned his assertion; girlfriend Erica made a comment which wryly questioned the true value of do-gooders in society.

'Just do it, Serge,' Darac said, smiling. 'Thanks, man.' He turned to the others. 'So now, the question is simply – who? Who *is* this imposter?'

Perand's grin was at its most lopsided. 'Well, it's clearly not my former fave, Ralf Bassette in drag.' Laughter from all quarters. A rarity. 'It's Barbara, I'll bet you.'

'Barbara, the embittered underling,' Darac said, reprising his thought from earlier. 'A person who feels she's better than all of them put together and has had it *so* up to here, she seeks to punish her boss? It's been known. Only one problem. People spot the smallest changes in the appearance of someone they work with every day, don't they? A glance through a half-open eye is all it would have taken Barbara to have clocked Elie's new hairstyle. She's hardly likely to have posed for the cameras in the pen shop three weeks later sporting the former style.'

As if realising he should have quit while he was ahead, Perand shrugged and said nothing.

'Correction, chief,' Granot said, peering at his laptop

screen. 'There's only *two* problems with Barbara as a suspect. The first of my border security requests is back. Barbara Artaud did not travel anywhere abroad on her week off.'

Darac erased Barbara's name from the list of suspects. 'So that leaves us with Yana Vanier, Vivienne Urquelle and Thea Petrova.' He underlined all three names and turned to face the group. 'Erica, before we shot off to wonderful, wonderful Copenhagen, you mentioned you had something on Thea. Not conclusive but interesting, you said.'

Astrid's ears pricked up.

'Oh, that's right, I forgot all about it.' She made a pistol of her hand and shot herself in the temple. 'Strange, considering it represents probably the only non-technical detective work I've done since I started at the Caserne. Bonbon showed me how to go about it.'

'It was nothing,' Bonbon said, theatrically wiping a slick of invisible sweat from his brow. 'A cheque will do, by the way.'

'It's on its way. Yes, I discovered that both her parents died in a fire when she was still a teenager – well, *just,* she was 19. And she was questioned for some days about it.'

Darac parked his backside on the piano stool. 'Do you have more?'

'Thea's mother was Swedish and the family had a second home there... Hang on.' She consulted her tablet. 'Near the town of Matfors. Well – "second home." ' She made a so-so gesture with her hand. 'It was more of a large wooden shack of a place called a..?'

'Stuga,' Astrid said.

'Yes, that's it. I suppose that's because it was...'

Out of the corner of his eye, Darac saw Granot studying his laptop screen once more. 'Just a second, Erica. Granot?'

'Vivienne's result is coming in. She... *was* abroad in the

middle of that week.'

'*Was* she now?'

'Yes... Let's see. Ah. But only a few kilometres down the coast. Bordighera.'

Darac rose. 'So who's going to say it?'

'And then there were two?' Bonbon offered.

'Give the man a prize.'

At the whiteboard, Vivienne Urquelle followed Elie and Barbara into the land of Erasure.

'I'll give *you* all a prize instead,' Bonbon said, producing a soggy-looking paper bag from his jacket pocket. 'Screaming Hab-Dab, anyone?' He smiled, enticingly. 'They're from Cours Saleya.'

Possibly because of the state of the bag, there were no takers except Astrid.

'*Là là!*' she said, as the sherbet and popping candy started to get to work in her mouth and Serge Paulin came back into the room. All eyes went to him.

'Elie Tiron both thanks and sends her best regards to everyone,' he announced, and on resuming his seat, turned to share a *sotto voce* word with Astrid. 'She asks that you check your email shortly, if you can?'

The inside of her mouth performing a reasonable impression of the Villa's water-jet fountain, Astrid confined her response to a thumbs up.

'So, back to the Petrova family fire in Sweden,' Darac said, for Serge's benefit. 'Erica?'

'Yes, a malfunctioning stove was identified as the cause of the blaze, which since the... stuga?'

Another thumbs-up from Astrid.

'The stuga was of all wooden construction, it burned to the ground. It happened overnight and both Thea's parents were asleep in it at the time. A local newspaper reported that it was only through a lack of evidence that no one was charged, and implied, only just this side of legality, that if charges had been brought, they would have brought against young Thea.'

Darac ran a hand through his hair. 'What was Thea doing when the fire was raging, Erica? Did you find that out?'

'Yes, I did...' She brought up another page on her tablet. 'She was out all night with a boyfriend, thus avoiding – and I'm quoting "the fiery fate of her parents" – and securing for herself a decent little inheritance some forty years or so before she otherwise would have done.'

For some moments nothing was said as trained police minds all around the room tried to work what they had just heard into something substantial and relevant to the case. Some sat stock still, thinking. Some made searches on their laptops. Darac stared at the floor.

It was Darac who spoke first.

'How's this? It's speculative but it doesn't wander *too* far from established facts. Let's say that lovers Thea and Gérard Urquelle *both* had guilty secrets. And somewhere down the line, they shared them. Quite a bond, that could be. And to some mentalities, a source of sexual arousal, perhaps. It was dangerous, of course, but as long as they stayed together, it was a mutually assured destruction situation, wasn't it? Neither could shop the other without their own murderous past being potentially brought to light. We know from Erica's examination of Urquelle's deleted emails that the heat had started to go out of their relationship, at least on her side, and that on *his*, sex had descended into something of a mechanical routine.

'Having painstakingly traced a timeline of their relationship from those emails, Erica believes that this cooling on Thea's part resulted from the growing realisation that she was no longer the sole object of Urquelle's passion – something he had claimed many times in their earlier days. If Erica's right about this, and I believe she is; and if Astrid's assessment of Thea's character is right, and I believe she is, too, I suspect the regal Thea's reaction had less to do with feelings of humiliation and betrayal *per se*, but what it might mean about her pact with Urquelle. Their destruction was no longer so mutually assured, was it? There may have been a third party to take into account – another lover with whom Urquelle may have shared his secret, A fourth party, a fifth – who knew how many? That was his business. No problem. *But* what if he also shared what he knew about *Thea's* murderous past with one of these women? A woman such as, say, Yana Vanier? To eradicate any prospect of a potentially ruinous outcome like that, Thea's thoughts may well have turned to murder. As it seems they may have done before.'

'Given the situation,' Granot said, twisting his moustache, 'I think Thea does have a compelling motive. But if it turns out that she was at home in St Petersburg, or Dubai or wherever, on the afternoon of Wednesday 18th of May, it will be a compelling motive that goes no further.'

Her eyes locked on her screen, Flaco's hand rose slowly into the air like a diver surfacing with a find. 'Captain?'

Darac felt a familiar frisson. 'Yes, Flak?'

'I've just discovered possible means to add to that motive. Thea Petrova has an uncle on her mother's side. One Sven Ludvigsson who lives near a place called… U-me-å in the north of Sweden. Umeå.'

Astrid had just speed read a very sweet message from a very relieved Elie and she now had a second reason for smiling: Flaco could have been referring to a body in outer space for all her familiarity with what Astrid knew was a sizeable and significant city.

'Pronunciation, Astrid?'

'Fine, Flak. Pretty good, in fact.'

'Uncle Sven works in waste water management, sewage and so on. He's the boss of quite a big operation.'

'A dirty job,' Perand said. 'But somebody... So?'

Flaco closed her laptop. 'I don't know what sort of relationship Thea has with her uncle. None, maybe. But I've just discovered that acrylamide is used extensively in the water management industry. More extensively even than in Ralf Bassette's paper-making business.'

'This is coming together now, isn't it?' Darac said, as the mood in the room continued to lift. 'Thea could have slipped the poisoned pen into Urquelle's jacket at any number of occasions over the last few days.'

Granot noticed only then that a new document was displaying on his screen. 'Hold up, everyone. Third week of May, third week of... Well look at that. Yana Vanier a.k.a Lydia Félix?'

'Yes?'

'She was at home right here in la belle France.'

With a buzz of voices rising behind him, Darac erased Yana Vanier's name from the list.

'One suspect,' he said, facing the group once more. 'One suspect left.'

Bonbon resumed his seated contortions. 'How do we play it from here?'

'We won't be playing anything if the remaining...' Granot stopped in mid-sentence. 'And here it is.' The room hushed as he peered at it. And peered again. 'It's in a different format.' Little seen in the past few hours, the frustrated walrus was back in town. Back with a vengeance. 'And it's in sodding Swedish. Astrid? Help us out here.'

She was already on her way.

'Not particularly good with complicated forms,' she said, looking over Granot's shoulder. 'Especially digital ones.'

'I'll scroll. You translate.'

'OK, Ah, yes, I see... On Tuesday, May 17th this year – that's the day *before* the pen purchase of course – Petrova flew into Stockholm from St. Petersburg.'

'And transferred to a flight for Copenhagen, presumably?' Perand said. 'Or took a separate flight the next day?'

'Uh... No. She stayed at the Hotel Aglund in Kungsgatan, Stockholm for three days and then flew back to St. Petersburg.'

'Are you sure, Astrid?' Darac said, his brain, if not his heart, sinking along with the collective mood.

She straightened. 'Absolutely sure.'

A varied collection of oaths rose into the air and fell flat. Expressing the extent of the setback in his own curious way, Bonbon sat up like a good little boy in his chair. '*Now* where do we go?'

'Where do we go? Astrid said, perplexed. 'What do you mean?'

Perand took it upon himself to explain. 'Thea couldn't be in two different countries at once, could she?'

'No, you can't be in two countries at the same *moment*, but on the same *day*? Yes, you can. Definitely.'

Perand got to his feet. 'Let *me* see that.' With the air of a teacher irritated at having to explain things yet again to a slow pupil, he moved in and took charge. 'Yes, look – the document trail shows just one border was crossed – Russia to Sweden on the 17th; Sweden back to Russia on the 20th.'

'If she had flown on to Copenhagen, you're right, Perand. It couldn't be done. The train, though, is a different story. I have relatives all over Scandinavia and I've caught the high-speed service from Stockholm to Copenhagen and vice-versa on several occasions. I've never done it there and back in one day but I'm sure it would be possible. Erica, could you check that?'

'Only too glad to.'

Perand still wasn't satisfied. 'But even if you could do that, you're still left with the border issue.'

'No, you're not. Do you know where Copenhagen is in relation to the Swedish mainland?'

'Well, not exactly. But that's not the point, is it?'

'Spanned by a road and rail bridge, a strait of water called the Øresund separates the two countries. Thousands of people commute back and forth across the bridge between Copenhagen and Malmö every day. Taking that route, no official has ever asked to see my passport. Either of them. As it happens, neither is Swedish or Danish but Thea *does* have a Swedish passport as well as a Russian one. If an official patrolling the train had been feeling picky and asked to see it, one glance at the cover and he or she would have walked right on down the train.'

'Oh.' Perand essayed his impression of a spoiled child and nailed it. 'Well how was I supposed to know local stuff like that?'

The hum of voices started up again and when Erica reported that several trains a day could indeed have whisked Thea to Copenhagen via Malmö in time to purchase the pen, *and* got her back into Stockholm by nightfall, the place was buzzing.

'It's Thea, alright,' Darac said. 'Thea Petrova. We've got means. We've got motive. That just leaves opportunity. Don't think answering *how* Thea got the pen into Elie's desk will detain us for too long, do you?'

Granot was the loudest of a chorus of voices expressing the same thought. 'Elie's open door policy?'

Darac nodded. 'Managers are fond of claiming that their doors are always open when they are patently not. Elie's nearly always *is* even when she's out. It would have been simplicity itself for Thea to have slipped in and done the deed.'

Flaco nodded but her brow was low. 'What about Barbara, Captain? Not many opportunities to slip into Elie's office unseen with her on the opposite side of the lobby.'

'Good point but would Thea have needed to slip in and out unseen? With so many coming and going, some just on a pretext to have a quick chat, it wouldn't really matter if she were seen, would it?'

'I see what you mean. No – maybe not.'

'I'm really not trying to hog the spotlight, people,' Astrid said, sheepishly. 'Bu-ut, I think I can give you that pretext. Thea's I mean.'

'Go for it! Erica's smile was as wide as it was warm. 'We *love* the Astrid Pireque Show.'

'Same here.' Bonbon reaching for his hab-dabs. 'Best watch of the week!'

'Hear, hear!' Granot said.

'Except for the Barça match,' Bonbon added, casting Granot a wicked grin.

As a stretch to his fellow lieutenant's bonhomie, Bonbon's reference to FC Barcelona may not have spanned the Øresund but it was still a bridge too far for Granot. 'Pah! *Le Gym* for ever!' he bellowed, and in his black eyes and red face surreally displaying his beloved OGC Nice's team colours. 'Don't listen to the Catalan fool, Astrid. Carry on.'

'I think I'd better. Yes, in a conversation I had with Thea yesterday, she expressed what I felt was genuine interest in taking my next painting course here. I knew it was in early April but I couldn't remember exactly when. She said

"No problem," she herself would check. Next year's teaching calendar is up in Elie's office so A: Thea had a perfectly legitimate reason for paying a visit. B: Yes, I take your point about the traffic in and out of the office, Paul, and yes, Barbara works hard and she can practically see around corners but she *does* abandon her desk from time to time. Elie abandons hers far *more* frequently. All Thea had to do was to wait until neither of them was in situ and she could have planted the pen totally unseen.' She made a moue. 'Sorry – not quite as exciting as before, that, was it? *And* a bit long-winded, but I bet it's what happened.'

'I wouldn't bet against you, Astrid.' Darac said, once again expressing the feeling of the meeting. 'Ever.'

Bonbon twisted himself into an unlikely contraposto in his chair. 'So, we've got means, motive and opportunity on Thea Petrova. The only thing we haven't got is Thea, herself. So, my dear friends and colleagues, I repeat what I said a few minutes ago: where do we go from here?'

In one of those insights some may have attributed to the fertility of Darac's imagination; some to his talents as an improviser; and others to a more prosaic source – being able to recognise an inescapable conclusion to a sequence of events when he sees one – Darac knew exactly where to go and how to get there. 'I think we can prove she's guilty.' Smiles, nods and asides bobbed up and down in the wave of positivity that broke around the room. 'It just needs a little preparation. Astrid, when it comes to taking statements from the students, who would you say is likely to be the most compliant from Mathieu Croix's course?'

'Compliant as in unlikely to make a fuss?'

'Yep.'

'There's a husband and wife combo – the Calons. The husband, Jérôme, is your man. Compliant as crème anglaise, he is.'

Darac grinned as he made the note.

'Perand? You're interviewing Jérôme. Choose one of our colleagues from Foch to assist you.'

Perand shared a look with the leader of his comedy fan club and with a combination of eyebrow semaphore and nodding, completed the deal. 'Done, chief.'

'And which two of Zoë's students fit the bill, Astrid?'

'Uh....' She pursed her lips. 'I wouldn't call her compliant in a submissive sense at all, but the rather beautiful older lady, Cinzia Veri comes to mind.' 'I don't *think* she would have a problem cooperating with the authorities. Especially if – don't kill me, Erica – it was Serge who was asking the questions.'

'Astrid!' Erica said, essaying exasperation rather than murderousness. 'Despite my best efforts, butter-wouldn't-melt Sergie here already believes he's God's gift to women.'

The young man was already blushing. 'I've *never* believed that!'

'Serge?' Darac said, stifling a grin. 'You'll be charming Cinzia. And to go to the ball with you, there are three Cinderellas from Foch still left to choose from.'

'He turned. 'Davide? I promise to have you back before midnight. OK?'

'I've heard that line before.'

A second pairing sorted, Darac asked Astrid for another nomination from Zoë's class.

'It might seem strange but the very up-for-it Monique Dufour might work well. She's the class clown and I think she'd think it was a bit of a hoot to be questioned.'

'Granot – think you can handle her?'

'Yes, but only if I have...' He turned to make his selection. 'Mojamé by my side. Alright with you, Mo?'

'Honoured, Lieutenant.'

'Now your students, Astrid.'

'May I ask what the *exact* purpose of these non-contentious interviews is?'

'Principally, to lull Thea into thinking that we're whisking through everyone quite quickly – hence the need for a nice, smooth start. And *that* will send her a message, won't it?'

'It will?'

'It will. More on that later.'

'That's good to know,' Erica said, her face a study in cluelessness.

'Astrid?'

'Oh, right. Uh... I'd steer clear of Claudine Bonnet. Her sister Babette would probably be a good choice. Alan Davies is an interesting one. He's excellent company and so on but he's very much an individualist. The type who likes to set his own course rather than go with the flow.'

'So steer clear of him, too?'

'Not sure. Although he was well aware of the media hype implications of terms like "have-a-go hero," he did believe Urquelle was worthy of respect for what he did that day. And while we know he was wrong to have assumed it was accidental, Alan *was* grateful to him for killing the scumbag that was Eddy Lopes. And he's the only one I've heard say that he hopes Urquelle's killer will be caught and soon. Except in a general way, no one else seems to care about that, particularly.'

'For our current purposes, do you think he cares a little too much?'

'Perhaps.' She pursed her lips. 'Yes, not Alan, I think. Although Ralf Bassette was a suspect, he didn't realise that, of course. I'd go for him, I think. Another charming, interesting guy. Especially if he commissions a portrait from me. '

'Ralf it is. Bonbon, you're in the frame. OK?'

'Appropriate, considering they're artists.' He turned to the remaining uniform from Foch. 'Marcel, watch and learn.'

'If you say so, Lieutenant.'

Darac then told Perand, Granot, and Bonbon how he wanted their interviews to go and when to start them. Then he turned to Flaco. 'Flak, you and I are going to interview Thea.'

'Right, Captain.' The slightest smile played on her lips. 'What will be *our* approach?'

'I'll tell you in a second. Erica?'

'Command me.'

'This is what I would like you to do in the meantime.'

6.11 PM

In Geneva, Benjamin Lejeune was now over three hours into his life-saving heart operation. At the Hôpital St. Roch in Nice, with her loved ones in attendance or nearby, Noëmi Tardelli was in the throes of bringing a new life into the world. That was the upbeat take on things. The more sobering was that Benjamin's operation was also a life-threatening procedure that was only about half-way through; and that "complications" were endangering Noëmi and her six-weeks premature baby.

Darac wasn't expecting to hear from Frankie until her father was recovering from his operation. There had been no word from Suzanne at St. Roch for the past two hours. Darac had considered texting her at several points in that time, and he tried to convince himself that it was only because he had to concentrate so completely on the case that he hadn't. Tried and failed.

Darac's admiration for Astrid's drawing technique only deepened as Thea opened the door to her room and he studied her face up close. The set of her cheekbones; the Slavic tilt of her eyes and their smoky stare; the full, sharply-lined mouth; and above all, that queenly mien. Astrid had captured it all perfectly.

'Madame Petrova, thanks so much for allowing us to squeeze you in to our schedule.'

'In my country, Captain, when the police ask to see one, one sees them. Please come in.'

Thea repaired to the desk and gestured Darac and Flaco to sit in the chairs she had drawn up facing her.

'If you have no objection, we'll be using this.' He took the Brigade's battered old sound recorder out of his bag and set it on the desk between them.

Thea signalled her assent with a slight sideways incline of her head, a slight fluttering of her eyelashes, and a slight shrug of the shoulders. If recording their "chat" was an imposition, she had succeeded in implying it was only a slight one.

'I'm sure you've noticed we're talking to everyone here. It just helps us keep track.'

'Track.' Another nod, frontal this time, and accompanied by a knowing look. 'Of course.'

He turned to Flaco but, her attention appeared to have been captured by the top-of-the-range cosmetics littering the dressing table away to their right. It was a nice touch, Darac thought.

'Officer,' Darac said. 'The list, when you're ready?'

'Oh, sorry, Captain.' Essaying a one-woman-to-another look, she smiled at Thea as she bent to retrieve her tablet. Thea gave not even the slightest of smiles in response.

'You can tick Madame Petrova off.'

'Right.' Flaco scrolled a list of names, reading out each one under her breath. Under her breath, but just loud enough to hear. The last name was Elie Tiron's.

'Better check this thing is still working,' Darac said, pressing a couple of buttons. 'Seems to be alright. Just do a little test.' He pressed record and sat back 'One, two, three. Talking with Madame Thea Petrova in a moment. Interview six. One, two, three.' Darac rewound and pressed play. In a loud and clear voice, the trio heard Elie Tiron say:

"This has been a complete waste of my time, Captain—"

And then Darac interrupting her:

"—As it turned out, yes it was, madame but..."

Darac shot forward in his seat, knocking the device to the floor in his panic. Flaco made a grab for it and hit stop, but not before the recorded Darac concluded his remark to Elie:

"... we didn't know that at the start, did we?"

'Uh, I... think we'll continue without the recorder, Madame Petrova – it's not behaving. If that's alright with you?'

A nod. Business-like or curt? And was that suppressed anger in Thea's eyes or resolve? Darac couldn't tell. But of one thing, he was sure. His plan had got off to a promising start.

'Officer,' he said, turning to Flaco. 'The time grid now, please.'

Throughout the building, students were stepping out of their showers and into their formal evening attire. The Villa's celebrated celebration dinner, an experience Astrid had described as the "best nosh bash this side of *Le Chantecler* " was due to begin in just half-an-hour.

With two exceptions – Darac and Serge Paulin – the contingent from the Caserne was gathered in the ops room. In the manner of fighter pilots waiting for the instruction to scramble, the banter was inconsequential, comedic, and never once referred to the challenge that lay ahead. If indeed it did: there was no guarantee that the instruction, coming via a held call on Granot's phone, would be delivered at all. But if it was, it would consist of just one word: "Now." Granot's role was to acknowledge and then, when the moment was exactly right, to give the counter instruction. The rest was down to Darac.

'Nice of the kitchen to let us have a copy of tonight's menu,' Bonbon said. 'No *Hab-Dabs Criant* in the dessert section, note. I must have a word with Chef.'

Granot performed his particular take on the Gallic shrug, a championship standard example. '*Steak au Poivre à la Jean-Claude*? Who would want a dish like that?' He checked his headset for slippage – there was none. 'Apart from every non-vegetarian on the planet. Still, I'm glad Monsieur Martin Darac will be able to enjoy it on our behalf. Richly deserved after his contribution to the case.'

'Was there one?' Perand said.

' "So, the poison wasn't in the scent, then?" I think it was. Well worth a free gourmet dinner.' The faux grin disappeared. 'There's *Loup-de-Mer en Papillote* on as well, you realise. *Loup! De-mer!*'

'I'd settle for a bowl of the *Soupe aux Truffes*,' Erica said, breaking a bread stick in half. 'Can you imagine?'

Raul Ormans was engaged in the neglected time-passing classic that was the twiddling of one's thumbs. First one way, and then the other, he was quite the virtuoso, it seemed. '*Soupe aux Truffes*? I had that dish once. Three-star Michelin place in Paris.'

'Verdict, R.O?' Lartigue said.

'It was... nice.'

Staring wistfully into the distance, Erica was moved to nod. 'What an inspiring story.'

'So what's the *worst* meal anyone's ever had?' Perand said, and the waiting game continued.

7.18 PM

The luggage room door was open only the merest crack but it provided a view of the comings and goings in Reception, nevertheless. As long as Darac kept quiet and made no extravagant moves – he had Barbara in tow to ensure he didn't – no comer or goer would have spotted him. Two further pairs of eyes were looking on from similarly hidden viewpoints.

He felt a throb against his chest. 'Take over a second, would you, Barbara?' he whispered, and took a step back. She nodded and slipped stealthily in front of him.

The text was headed "Addition to Tomorrow Night's Set List?" and it was from DMQ bandleader Didier Musso. With Barbara evidently relishing her watching brief, Darac had no qualms about reading further. The proposed addition was a cool, funky blues the band hadn't performed in a while: Billy Cobham's 'Red Baron,' a "personal request" from a mate of Didier's. Band members were asked to cast their entirely free vote by typing the single word "Yes" or "No, I have neither the time, talent, perspicacity, nor the inclination to make such a last minute..." And so on it went for a half a dozen more lines. Darac voted as he was supposed to and as Monday night's rehearsal felt like a very long time ago, he ran an eye over the rest of the list to refresh his memory.

Having gone brilliantly in rehearsal, the number Darac was looking forward to playing most was a mindbogglingly difficult new Thelonious Monk-inspired Didier composition he'd entitled 'Outro-spection.' Climaxing the second set with a version of The Impossible Gentlemen's 'You Won't Be Around To See It' was another delicious prospect.

Something Darac *didn't* want to be around to see was a text from Hôpital St. Roch saying that despite everyone's best efforts, all had gone disastrously wrong in the delivery suite. It was now three hours since Suzanne's last text. His finger hovered over the reply icon but as if in warning, he felt a tug on his sleeve.

'Captain?' Barbara said. 'I think it's happening.'

7.21 PM

'A pop-up van somewhere in Madrid, it was,' Lartigue said, looking as if he was about to vomit just thinking about it. 'Churros and chocolate. We wondered why there was no queue. A couple of hours later, I was popping it up all over my new shoes.'

In a gesture favoured by baffled people everywhere, Bonbon raised both hands palms uppermost. 'How many times have I told you to stay away from...You know what.'

'Churros?'

'No.'

'Chocolate?'

'Me? Hardly.' Bonbon couldn't bring himself to say "Madrid" out loud. 'I meant the so-called capital of Spain, you fool.'

Granot's earpiece buzzed.

'Quiet! It's the chief.'

'Now.'

'Check. Listen out for my counter instruction.'

As the pulses of every officer in the room began to beat faster, all eyes turned to the TV. The establishing image had been playing for some minutes and as movie sequences went, a medium close-up of Elie's desk was perhaps not the most riveting in history. With "Action!" called, the spectacle picked up considerably. Hurrying away from the camera, the actor was little more than a pixel-pocked blur until she turned into shot and stood on her mark; a mark she didn't realise was there. Her face racked into sharp focus. Anxious. Desperate. Frantic. It was the face of Thea Petrova. The team knew it couldn't be anyone else but they cheered anyway.

'Shhhhhh.'

With a gloved hand, Thea yanked the desk drawer open. Repeating a word in Russian, she began scrabbling frantically through it. And then her eyes flamed, the rummaging stopped, and she removed the thing she had come for.

Close the drawer! Granot said to himself.

And close the drawer is just what Thea did.

'Glad you found your pen, Madame Petrova,' Darac said, appearing in the doorway as Serge Paulin slipped in behind him.

Thea managed a smile. 'I don't know what you mean, Captain. What pen?'

'The one Officer Paulin and I know you've just stuffed into your pocket along with your gloves.'

'What... nonsense.'

'Then what are you doing in here?'

'I was looking for Elie Tiron but she seems to be elsewhere.' Thea shrugged, as casually as she could manage. 'I'll catch her later.' Another smile. 'Excuse me, officers.'

'Hold it there, madame,' Serge said, widening his stance.

'What is this? I told you I just needed word with Elie. Now let me pass, please. I shall be late for dinner.'

Wearing a bag slung across her shoulder, Elie herself appeared. 'Here I am. What do you want to see me about, Thea?'

'Oh. I was wondering about taking Astrid Pireque's course next April. But she didn't know date – know *the* date. She didn't know it. So I came in to check.'

'I thought you had already done that.'

'No.'

'But you checked just now?'

'I don't know how.'

'Strange. You seem *au fait* with how everything else works in here. And every*one*. Down to the last detail.' She indicated the wall space above Clarice's desk. 'It's there, look. Headed course calendar in large letters.'

'I didn't see,' she said, tossing her head dismissively.

'Madame Petrova,' Darac said. 'If I may just direct your attention to something else, we could save a lot of time. Take a look at the shelves behind you.'

She turned.

'Do you see *that*?'

'See what?'

'Officer? Show our new toy to the lady.'

Serge reached between a couple of files.

'Small, isn't it? Small but powerful.'

Thea's face fell.

'No need to look so glum,' Darac said. 'My team loved your performance earlier. They are watching you now. Why not give them a smile?'

To Darac's great surprise, Thea did smile for the camera, albeit sadly, and the look persisted as she turned back to him. 'Well, alright, Captain. I didn't want this to come out, but... you're right.' She produced the pen and deposited it in Serge's gloved hand. 'To be honest, I was going to drop it down drain or something.' A sideways glance. 'I'm sorry Elie, I was trying to help you but now as *I* seem to be in trouble, I think you had better explain how this replica *Lepic* has come into your possession. Can you?'

'Yes, and so can Captain Darac here. *You* secreted it in my top desk drawer, Thea. But first, you took the steps necessary to ensure that Barbara would find it there. Straight-as-a-dye Barbara who was sure to report it to the police.'

Essaying pity, Thea shook her head. 'Elie, I think your hatred of Gérard must have disturbed your brain. You are talking rubbish.' She turned to Darac. 'Captain, tell her that a simple check will verify where and when this pen was purchased.'

'Oh, it has already. It was 2.27 on the afternoon of May

19th this year.'

'Really? That's when I was in Sweden. Stockholm, in fact.'

'Yes, we've checked. You stayed at the Hotel Aglund. Records show you took breakfast that morning and you were back in your room in the evening.'

'That's right. But you haven't said *where* the pen was purchased.'

'Didn't I? Oh, it was Copenhagen. Pedersen and Reiter, the jewellers.'

Thea's eyes narrowed. 'Copenhagen? Weren't you on holiday there at that time, Elie?'

'And just how do you know that, madame?' Darac said.

'We discussed our holiday plans for the year when I was here last time. Like everyone does. Small talk.'

'I see. And you remembered both the place *and* the time?'

'Yes, besides, it's...' Thea glanced towards Clarice's corner but said no more.

Darac's brows rose. 'Besides, it's blocked in on the holiday planner right alongside the invisible course calendar?'

Thea shrugged. 'I see one thing; I don't see other. It's normal.'

Darac turned to Elie. 'But, yes, I'm afraid CCTV camera footage does confirm exactly where you were at 2.27 in the afternoon.'

Thea nodded in the manner of a chess player who knows that checkmate is now just a couple of moves away. 'And where was that, Captain?'

'The Davids Samling. New hairdo and all, Madame Tiron went in at 2.06; out at 4.23. Their security firm has just very kindly emailed a still of each.'

Elie reached into her bag. 'No wonder you were so shocked to see me when you checked in, Thea – and why you tried to get out of me just when I'd had my locks shorn. Good job I didn't level with you or you wouldn't have gone through with your plan, would you?' She displayed the prints. 'Yes, here I am, look. Useful thing, CCTV, eh?' She moved in close to her. 'I will always be grateful to you for ridding the world of that rat Urquelle. But I will never forgive you for trying to implicate me.'

'And when you came in here just now,' Darac said, 'you were about to do it for a second time, weren't you, madame? Putting the pen somewhere even a dull-witted bunch like us was bound to find it.'

Elie had one thing more. 'And do you know what I love, Thea? I love that you are in the position you are now because you ended up incriminating *yourself.*'

Thea stared into space but she found no answers to her predicament there. All she saw was that the writing was well and truly on the wall, and that her substitute pen had written it. Exhaling deeply, she tossed it away.

'Officer Paulin?' Darac said.

Serge stepped forward. 'Come with me, madame.'

10.11 PM

With the interrogation at the Caserne completed in less than two hours, the team headed across the compound to their cars in a most unfamiliar state – they were all wide awake. And, as someone once said, the celebrations didn't begin to end there. It was while they were en route from the Villa that Armani broke the news that he and Noëmi had become parents for the second time. After a dicey few hours, all danger was past and mother and baby were doing just fine. The sense of relief and joy this gave everyone was tempered by a sobering realisation: the baby head-wetting party to come was likely to prove a life-threatening experience of its own. In the meantime, anyone game for a quick one was welcome to join Armani at home. The only disappointment for the team was that Emma had not been allowed to join him. Not that she herself minded. Fussed over by the staff and with both sets of grandparents in situ, the little one had asked if she could stay in hospital for a whole extra week.

For the moment, all team talk was about the case.

'By how much will Petrova's confession reduce her sentence, do you think, Captain?'

'Not sure, Flak, but not by *that* much. She had no real alternative, did she?'

'And her new boyfriend – the one who did the engraving on the substitute pen. Do you believe he hadn't knowingly aided and abetted Thea in the perpetration of her crimes?'

'She says he didn't and that's probably enough for even a mediocre lawyer to convince a jury.'

'OK.'

Bonbon may have been all out of hab-dabs, but he was in an upbeat mood, nevertheless. 'You know the most impressive thing about your performance this time around, chief?'

'That at no point did Frènes threaten to throw me off the case?'

'No, though that was special. It was the accuracy of your speculation on Urquelle's relationship with Petrova, and how its breakdown might have led to what it did. Pretty near spot-on, that turned out. As did the plan to trap Petrova.'

Granot was in no mood to demur. 'Nifty – hoodwinking her into thinking we had missed finding the pen. I said we'd make a decent detective of you yet.'

'Cheers, guys. But it was Astrid – she was the real star of this case.'

'Hear, hear,' Granot said, his car doors adding an echoing chirrup as he remotely opened them. 'Hers was a brilliant performance from the start.'

'Ahem. Ahemm!'

'And you, Erica. You were very good, too.'

'Ah, there's nothing like an unsolicited testimonial.' Having finally had enough of her barrette, Erica unclipped it and shook out her hair. 'And that was certainly nothing like one.'

Granot glanced at his mobile. 'Good – Agnès is already there. See you shortly, people.' As the remaining four continued on their way, a cry of "Sforza i Tardelli!" rent the air as the big man pulled away.

'Seriously, Erica,' Darac said, picking up her point, comically made though it had been. 'The rest of us probably are guilty in that respect. We've got so used to your remarkable talents that perhaps we do take them for granted.'

Following Astrid's lead earlier, Erica linked her arm in his. 'Actually, Paul, you don't. Never have.'

Feigning outrage was not one of Darac's more convincing turns, but he took a stab at it. 'But has it ever occurred to you to show your gratitude by turning up at the Blue Devil occasionally?'

'Of course not,' she said, prettily. 'Silly, silly man.'

'Well here's something for you to contemplate. Remember a million years ago when it looked for all the world as if Urquelle's killer was a certain Mademoiselle Zena Kovalen?'

'Yes, and after all she went through to get here, too. What a *hugely* unlucky break.'

'Absolutely, though Agnès is pretty sure her story is set

for a happy ending.'

'Excellent news.' They had arrived at Erica's Smart car. 'But where are you going with this?'

'It transpires she's a jazz fan. Zena, I mean.'

'Really?' Erica's hair fell forward as she bobbed into her driver's seat. 'The shock of it all, probably,' she said, gathering up the strays and corralling them behind her ears. 'It's excellent news, nevertheless. See you chez Armani.'

'I'm parked more or less opposite,' Flaco said, pausing as Erica pulled away. 'Interesting day.'

'Wasn't it? Great work, Flak.'

'As always,' Bonbon added.

'Thank you, gentlemen. Goodnight.'

'Hey, aren't you joining us?

'Well...'

'Come on.' Darac smiled at her, warmly. 'I was going to say "let your hair down" but I guess cornrows don't lend themselves to that.'

She smiled. 'No but I'm on early tomorrow. And Sunday.'

'You don't drink, do you?'

'Alcohol, he means.'

As if the matter required thought, she pursed her lips before answering. 'No-o. I don't.'

'Well then?'

'Actually, I... have a date.'

Bonbon's twinkle-eyed curiosity was at its foxiest. 'At this hour? Anyone we know?'

Darac gave him a look. 'Bonbon!'

Flaco pursed her lips once more. 'No, I don't think you will.' As if her car were calling her, she cast a glance in its direction. 'I'd better go. See you probably Tuesday.'

Valedictory kisses were exchanged and Flaco took her leave.

'A date, eh? That's good.'

'Indeed but go no further, Bonbon.'

'I was just... you know. Wondering.'

The pair walked on in a pleasingly companionable silence and they reached Bonbon's car before either of them spoke again.

'You weren't wrong about the whole Zena business feeling as if it happened a million years ago,' Bonbon said. 'Time. Strange phenomenon.'

Darac's ears picked up. Bonbon had opened the door and he was going to have to put up with the consequences. 'You know what phenomenon the Zena business itself demonstrates, don't you, Bonbon?'

'I have a feeling I'm going to find out.'

'We've discussed it once today already: Leibniz's analogy of the two clocks. Zena sprays Urquelle. He collapses and dies. Ergo, she killed him.'

'Except she did no such thing.'

Darac spread his arms wide. 'That's the point of the analogy right there.'

'Well, I'm heading off to Place Wilson now and when I arrive, those two things will *not* be coincidental. See you in a few minutes.'

Darac's mobile rang.

'It's Frankie. Hang on a second, Bonbon – it'll be news of her father.'

'Darling? It's over and it went well.' He gave the thumbs up to Bonbon who gave a little fist pump in response and pulled quietly out of his space. 'The prognosis is good and mama is happy even though she'll now...' She mimicked her mother's voice... "have to buy him those new pyjamas after all." Honestly, Paul, my parents.'

'It's wonderful news,' he said, chuckling. 'And speaking of parents and wonderful news...'

SATURDAY, 17th SEPTEMBER

With the gig at the Blue Devil not even half over, it was clear that it was going to be one of those special nights. Configured as a sextet for the occasion, the DMQ had begun by tearing at breakneck speed into the aural amphetamine that was Sonny Rollins's 'G-Man' and the audience rode the high right there with them.

It felt all the more special that the concert was being recorded in its entirety, and in two different forms: sound – the results to be released as a double CD the band was thinking of entitling *Chase No Straighter*; and as a collection of drawings and paintings by an artist very definitely named Astrid Pireque. Darac had had no difficulty in convincing Ridge to grant her a roving commission for the evening and the only surprise of it was that he hadn't thought of setting up such a thing before. As the set progressed, Darac couldn't tell whether Astrid was enjoying or merely tolerating the music. But she was clearly loving the spectacle and the atmosphere of the club with its varied cast of characters. Her work, he knew, would be inspired and he couldn't wait to see it.

Darac was flying solo high above the outer reaches of John Scofield's 'Wabash III' when Frankie arrived. Their eyes met and for four bars or eight or more, it was as if his solo were continuing by itself, exploring without his control a dimension that was neither high nor low, fast nor slow. At some stage he must have closed his eyes and, as considerations of time and space returned, he was smiling as he came soaring out of the solo like a bird riding a current of warm summer air.

At the set break, involved conversations with the band, with Ridge, and with the sound man meant that it took Darac much longer than anticipated to catch up with Frankie. When he did, she was so lost in conversation with Astrid that for a moment, he considered melting back into the crowd but a stray glance put an end to the thought and, it seemed, to the conversation.

'Paul, you're playing wonderfully,' Astrid said. 'So they tell me. I'll leave you two to it.'

Darac reached for Frankie's hand but he had a parting word for Astrid. 'Happy with your work? Tridi?'

'No.' She smiled. 'Loving it. Thank you.' She planted a kiss on his cheek and slipped away.

Almost everything had felt right about Darac's evening before Frankie had arrived. Now she was here in his arms, and with the second set to come, and then the apartment, and tomorrow, and next week, and next year... Now, there was no *almost* about it. Everything was in place.

'So did Lisie buy those new pyjamas for Benjamin?' he said, in between kisses.

'Not yet... Probably hoping for a relapse.'

'Sorry to interrupt, people.'

They turned. Didier.

'Hey, Frankie. Listen man, Luc and I have just had a thought about the bridge.'

'Which one? The Golden Gate? The Øresund?'

'The one in 'Outro-spection.' When Charlie comes out of her first solo...'

Darac had long felt that, with its own particular sounds and scents, the Babazouk thrummed with life in a way that no other quarter of Nice could quite match. He felt it especially tonight, sitting out on his roof terrace with Charlie Mingus's 'Goodbye Pork Pie Hat' drifting across from the lounge, and with Frankie sitting alongside him.

He knew there was no sense in love. He knew that if ever there was a hostage to fortune, it was the concept of "the love of one's life." But he didn't care. If it were ridiculous to feel so happy and fulfilled – so be it.

He also knew that something had been amiss with Frankie before she had flown off to Geneva, and that the positive resolution to her father's health crisis had not fixed it.

'You know, I'm amazed you were able to play at all this evening. What time did you leave Armani's party?'

'Just after 4. The last one to go, thus upholding the proud tradition of jazzers and nocturnal species everywhere. And it wasn't even the party, Frankie. It was the pre-party party.'

'I don't blame him. After what they had all been through? Horrendous.'

'It was beyond horrendous,' Darac said, but then he smiled, or at least tried. 'They're giving little Fabien the middle name of Alexander. Alexander with an *e r* at the end.'

Darac looked far away suddenly and Frankie joined him there. 'Oh, Lord. I'll never forget that day.'

Nothing more was said until Mingus had drifted into the night and it was clear that no one was going to drift in after him.

'More music?' Darac said, coming back into the moment.

'Another drink? Or..?'

'Neither.'

Frankie took his hand, gripping it tightly as if fearing he might soon feel the need to relinquish it. It was only then that he noticed just how much tension there was in her shoulders, her arms – her whole body. This was the moment. Whatever had been on Frankie's mind, it was clear to him that she was about to reveal it.

'What is it, Frankie?'

She took a settling breath. 'Do you remember that first night, Paul? The first night we were here and we made love?'

'I don't know – it *was* all of three months ago.' He smiled, amused and astonished at the question in equal measure. 'Frankie, I'll remember it forever.'

'Do you remember that, as full of love and desire and excitement as I was, I pulled back at first and asked you just to hold me? You no doubt thought that I was nervous. Or a little ashamed, perhaps. I was still married, after all.'

He had actually thought how right it felt. 'But?'

'It was neither of those things.' Her head dropped. 'And for what it actually was, I am truly sorry.'

'Hey, hey.' He lifted her hand and kissed it. 'I can't imagine what you feel you have to tell me but whatever it is, know this: we love each other and that's all I need to know.'

They embraced and when they separated, Frankie's eyes were stained with tears. 'Reserve that judgement just for the moment, Paul.' She took a deep breath. 'Through a misunderstanding, or rather, a jumped conclusion, you had believed for some time that I was unable to have children. While we were no more than close friends, I saw no reason to disabuse you of that notion. But then we were no longer just close friends, were we? And as one by one, the obsta-cles all fell away, I knew with complete clarity what situation I would eventually find myself in.' She looked away. 'The truth is, Paul, that I am not infertile. I knew that if we were to make love I would likely fall pregnant unless I took measures to prevent it. Or asked you to. That first night, I did neither and it was the magnitude of my omission or commission, probably, that hit me, suddenly. *That's* why I pulled back.'

As if all the characteristic inventiveness, precision and speed of Darac's thought processes had been short-circuited, he couldn't think of a word to say in response.

'My intention was to wait until morning to talk about things. Talk openly and freely. That was my intention, Paul. I swear. But here's the reason why that didn't happen – why, just a little while later, I gave myself to you so completely and utterly.'

Still dumbfounded, Darac said nothing.

'For years, my maternal instincts have been strong, achingly so at times, and that's often presented a challenge to my thinking, to the more progressive values I also embrace.'

'I can understand that.' It was a start. 'Of course.'

'You're probably wondering now where *you* are in all this. What about your feelings, needs and wants? I'm sorry, Paul, that having denied myself for all of a couple of hours, I was overwhelmed by the feeling that, more than anything else in the world, I wanted to be with you and to have your children, my children, *our* children...' She looked into his eyes. '... That feeling was so powerful that it overrode any other consideration. Any. Since that night, I *have* taken measures and for some weeks I thought I had... got away with it, if you like.' She looked away. 'If at this moment you are picturing an open stable door in your mind's eye, I wouldn't blame you.'

'No, no, no.' He stroked her hair away from her eyes. 'But

you've waited until now to tell me this.' The reason seemed obvious. 'Why?'

'When I left for Geneva, my period was three days late and that never happens to me. Not even a day out, usually. So... after everything I've told you, Paul, what would you say if I...'

'Stop there, Frankie.'

Darac wasn't picturing a stable door. He was picturing a collage of images that came to him all at once: his great-grandfather striding along with a lamb cradled in his arms; the Tardellis suffering through the agonies of yesterday; the look of infinite happiness on Armani's face at the party; Darac's mother laughing; holding his father's hand at her graveside; standing alongside him on the top of her favourite viewpoint in the world.

'Frankie, at various times over the last few days, I've never been more painfully aware of just how impossibly onerous parenthood can be.'

'Ah.' She let go of his hand. 'You've answered my question.'

'No, I haven't. It's fear on my part, Frankie. The fear of how I would feel if I lost something so precious as a child. I suspect the cause of it is losing my mother at such an early age.' He took back Frankie's hand. 'Until a moment ago, I had forgotten something. When I was fourteen, my father and I walked up the baou at St. Jeannet – the first time we had done that since Mama's death. When we reached the top and looked over, I asked him an idiotic question: "If you had known before you married Mama that she would not live beyond the age of 32, would you still have wanted to marry her?" "Of course," he replied. "When she was alive, your mother enriched my life immeasurably and she still does, every day. There's no beginning to "immeasurable,"

Paul. And it has no end, either." *Papa* was right, wasn't he?'
He smiled, broadly, joyfully. 'Frankie, if you're telling me that
you are pregnant with our child? I would be immeasurably
happy.'

Darac felt all the tension draining from Frankie's body as
she subsided into his arms and it was some moments before
words came.

'Paul,' she said into his chest. 'I'm not pregnant.'

The words hit him as if he'd walked naked into an ice
shower. 'You're not?'

'No. It was the tablets, I suppose. Not used to them.
Threw everything out.'

'Frankie...'

She laid a finger across his lips, halting him. 'So no, I'm
not pregnant', she said softly 'But I do have a rough idea of
how it's done.'

END

ACKNOWLEDGEMENTS

Heartfelt thanks to my wife Liz and to Rob, Clare, Katey and Bryan without whose love, invaluable insights and all-round support, writing the Darac Mysteries would have been a very different call. Thanks also to David Gower, Susan Woodall, Lisa Hitch, Alex Carter, Boris Blouin, and Jacky Ananou. I needed you all. I owe particular debts of gratitude to Commandant Divisionnaire de Police, Jean-Baptiste Zuccarelli of Commissaire Foch, Nice, and to the doyen of booksellers, Richard Reynolds. For her many kindnesses and for her translation work both from texts and during live interviews with officers of the Police Nationale, special thanks to Katherine Roddwell. Finally, warm thanks to my publisher Robert Hyde.

TRACK PLAYLIST OF ARTISTS AND NUMBERS REFERENCED IN *ESSENCE OF MURDER*

John Coltrane: 'Syeeda's Song Flute' from the iconic *Giant Steps* album. This is Darac's favourite performance by the revered tenor man.

Weather Report: 'Black Market.' Luc Gabron, bassist in Darac's own band, the Didier Musso Quintet, admires the fretless bass playing of Jaco Pastorius. Especially Here.

Richard Galliano: 'A French Touch'. Nice's own superstar jazz accordionist features in character Zena Bairault's French music sampler in the novel.

Claude Debussy: 'Clair de Lune'. Ditto. Zena listens to Alexandre Tharaud's version.

MC Solaar: 'La Belle et La Bad Boy'. The rapper widens Zena's education.

Django Reinhardt: 'Nuages'. One of Darac's heroes, Django takes to the electric guitar for this version from 1953.

Wes Montgomery: 'Four on Six', in an easier swinging version from *The Incredible Jazz Guitar* than Darac himself plays.

Louis Armstrong: 'Willie The Weeper'. Unlike some DMQ band mates, Darac loves the life and energy of early Armstrong – as in this Hot Seven recording from 1927.

Sonny Rollins: 'G-Man'. This live version is one of Darac's go-to pick-me-ups.

Billie Holiday and Lester Young: 'All of Me'. Few would argue with Blue Devil owner Ridge Clay's contention that this is one of the greatest partnerships in jazz history.

Tony Kofi: 'Bishop's Move' from the album Silent Truth. The heart and finesse of the English tenor man's playing make him a favourite with audiences at the Blue Devil.

Clovis Nicolas: 'The 5.30 Dive Bar Rendezvous.' The DMQ loves the sound and musicality of the bassist, exemplified in this later track from *Freedom Suite Ensuite.*

Herbie Hancock: 'Dolphin Dance'. Luc Gabron's favourite bassist, Ron Carter, here playing with Tony Williams in the engine room of Hancock's stellar combo.

Kenny Barron: 'The Oracle.' Superb bassist Dave Holland duetting with Darac's all-time favourite pianist from the album *The Art of Conversation.*

Kenny Barron: 'Hush-A-Bye'. Trio recording anchored by drummer Ben Riley and another of Luc Gabron's favourite bassists, George Mraz.

Chet Baker: 'Long Ago and Far Away'. Characteristically silk-toned vocals and unassertive horn stylings.

Billy Cobham: 'Red Baron', a funky blues from the *Spectrum* album, and played by the DMQ at the Blue Devil towards the conclusion of the story. A Darac favourite.

Lincoln Center Jazz Orchestra: 'Take The A-Train,' from *They Came To Swing*. Darac enjoys Sir Roland Hanna's hugely inventive piano intro to this Ellington classic.

John Scofield: 'Wabash III', from the album *Time On My Hands*. The fleet-fingered guitarist here playing with top tenor man Joe Lovano. Another tune from the DMQ gig in the novel.

Thelonious Monk: 'Introspection' (Take 3) from *The Complete Columbia Solo Recordings*. This is the tune that inspired bandleader Didier Musso to write the fictitious 'Outro-spection' for the DMQ.

Domenico Modugno : 'Nel Blu Dipinto di Blu (Volare)'. Cheesy for many but an iconic song for Narcotics Squad Captain Jean-Pierre 'Armani' Tardelli in the novel.

Luciano Pavarotti: 'Torna a Surriento'. Further inspiration for Armani.

Andrea Bocelli: 'O Sole Mio'. Rounding out Armani's sojourn in song.